# PRAISE FOR *NINE LIVES*

'One of the most extraordinary, captivating and insightful accounts of involvement in the violent global jihad ever written. Aimen Dean has been through a remarkable journey and lived to tell the tale. This book shines a light on Islamist extremism in the UK and the charismatic extremist leaders who have been responsible for so much radicalization within British Muslim communities over the past two decades. It also provides an extensive insight into the ideologies that are used to justify terrorist attacks across the world and carefully maps out the main texts and interpretations that al-Qaeda and ISIS have relied upon over the last twenty years. The most extraordinary revelations relate to his involvement in al-Qaeda's efforts to create CBRN [chemical, biological, radiological or nuclear] capabilities. The final chapter sets out a manifesto for countering warped extremist narratives and winning over moderate hearts and minds. Above all else, the bravery of Aimen Dean comes across throughout the book. For many years, he risked his life, time and time again, penetrated the leadership of al-Qaeda and saved many lives. Britain owes him a debt of gratitude. A seminal book.'

**Richard Walton, Head of Counter Terrorism Command (SO15),
New Scotland Yard, 2011–2016**

'This captivating real-life spy-thriller is a must-read to understand the enduring threat of global terror. It provides a fascinating account of one of the most lethal terrorist groups, from the unique perspective of a courageous double agent – an excellent read all round.'

**Ali Soufan, former FBI Special Agent and author of
*Anatomy of Terror* and *The Black Banners***

'Like a Zelig of international jihadism, Aimen Dean has been on most of the major jihadist battlefields of the past three decades and met many of the most significant figures. The fact that for much of this time he was working to protect us all from the threats of such groups is a reflection of his own extraordinary personal bravery. This book is not only a gripping page-turner that reads like the real-life spy thriller it is, but also an extraordinary piece of contemporary history that provides fresh insights into some of the most well-known figures and battlefields of the global terror threat that continues to menace us to this day.'

**Raffaello Pantucci, Director of International Security Studies,
Royal United Services Institute, and author of *"We Love Death
As You Love Life": Britain's Suburban Terrorists***

'*Nine Lives* is as much an incisive history of the war on terrorism as it is a riveting true-life thriller. It tells the fascinating story of Aimen Dean's odyssey from al-Qaeda operative to key Western intelligence source. Together with Paul Cruickshank and Tim Lister, Dean has produced an important book that sheds new light on al-Qaeda's violent trajectory and its continued, stubborn resilience.'

**Professor Bruce Hoffman, Georgetown University,**
**author of *Inside Terrorism***

'A must-read for anyone interested in the inside story of the last two decades of the so-called War on Terror. This book defies easy classification. Is it an insightful book on intelligence tradecraft? Certainly so. Is it an important primer on the evolution of radical jihadism? Without question. Is it a key resource for our understanding of counter-terrorism policy and practice in the twenty-first century? Absolutely.'

**Dr Vince Houghton, Historian and Curator,**
**International Spy Museum, Washington, DC**

'*Nine Lives* provides a stunning inside account of the making of a senior al-Qaeda operative, who trained with the organization's master bomb-maker and WMD-specialist, who turned into an MI6 spy, foiling terrorist plots and uncovering al-Qaeda networks. The story of Aimen Dean is as close as you'll ever get to the real thing. The book provides unique intelligence insights into the inner workings of al-Qaeda before and after 9/11. It also reveals how MI6 used him as one of its most valuable intelligence weapons in the global war on terrorism.'

**Dr Magnus Ranstorp, Research Director, Centre for**
**Asymmetric Threat Studies, Swedish Defence University**

'This is the most fascinating book about al-Qaeda I've read in a long time. It is a realistic and down-to earth account of al-Qaeda's chemical weapons programme, told by one of its insiders. It's a must-read for everyone who wants to understand al-Qaeda and the evolution of international terrorism.'

**Anne Stenersen, author of *Al-Qaida in Afghanistan* and**
***Al-Qaida's Quest for Weapons of Mass Destruction***

# NINE LIVES

## My Time As MI6's
## Top Spy Inside al-Qaeda

## AIMEN DEAN,
## PAUL CRUICKSHANK
## AND TIM LISTER

ONEWORLD

A Oneworld Book

Published by Oneworld Publications Ltd, 2018

This paperback edition published 2019

ISBN 978-1-78607-540-6
eISBN 978-1-78607-329-7

This is a work of non-fiction. Some names and
identifying details have been changed.

Typeset by Hewer Text UK Ltd, Edinburgh
Printed and bound in Great Britain by Clays Ltd, Elcograf S.p.A.

Oneworld Publications Ltd
10 Bloomsbury Street
London WC1B 3SR
England

Stay up to date with the latest books,
special offers, and exclusive content from
Oneworld with our newsletter

Sign up on our website
**oneworld-publications.com**

# CONTENTS

# Jihadi training camps in Afghanistan before 9/11

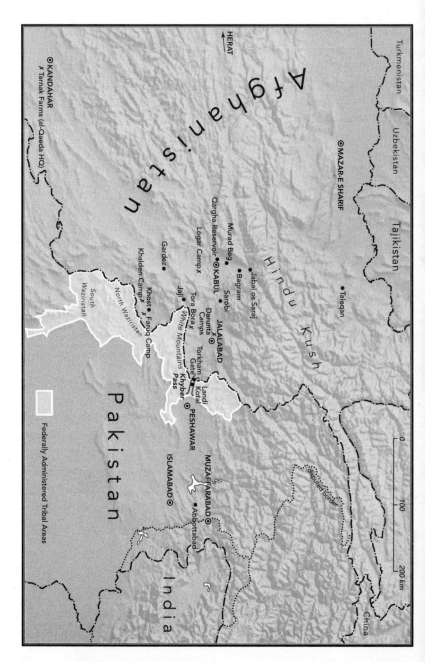

*Loyalty to the treacherous is treachery in the eyes of God.*
*The betrayal of the treacherous is loyalty in the eyes of God.*

Imam Ali

# NOTE FROM THE CO-AUTHORS

When any spy emerges from the secret world to tell their story, questions are naturally asked about the veracity of their account. Britain's intelligence services never comment publicly on such matters; nor is there generally a paper trail.

In the course of reporting on the threat from jihadi terrorism for the best part of two decades we have developed many trusted sources in and out of government on both sides of the Atlantic. This has allowed us to corroborate key details relating to Aimen Dean's work for British intelligence. This and our own research has allowed us not only to confirm critical associations and events but establish beyond doubt that there simply wasn't another informant inside al-Qaeda like him. In the years immediately leading up to and following 9/11, Aimen Dean was by far the most important spy the West had inside al-Qaeda, with his identity among the closest guarded secrets in the history of British espionage.

Aimen would probably never have contemplated writing a book had his cover not been blown by an intelligence leak in the United States. But he believes now is the right time to tell his story. His experiences and insights shed great light on the evolution of jihadi terrorism and what it will take to confront one of the great challenges of our times. Nobody can recall every last detail of their life perfectly, nor the exact order and date of every encounter. The chronology presented in this book is the result of many hours of research on the events he witnessed and the individuals he met. In describing technical aspects related to al-Qaeda's efforts to develop explosives, chemicals and poisons we took great care not to go beyond chemistry and details already in the public domain in the news media, academic studies, court documents, government reports and the like. As an extra precaution we consulted with leading experts on these types of weapons.

This book includes extensive notes. Those which may be of interest to the general reader are marked by stars in the text and included as footnotes. Substantive notes which may be of more interest to the specialist reader – as well as citations – are marked by numbers and are situated at the back of the book in the chapter-by-chapter endnotes. We also include a cast of characters, as well as a map of Afghanistan and Pakistan showing the location of jihadi training camps before 9/11. The exact position of the Khalden camp in relation to the town of Khost has never been definitively established by academic researchers. Our placement is based on Aimen's best recollection.

In several cases we have used pseudonyms to conceal the identity of individuals for a variety of reasons and this is made clear each time in the text. We refer to British intelligence officials by pseudonyms. This book includes quotations from the Koran and the *hadith* (the collected sayings of the Prophet Mohammed). These have been translated by Aimen. *Hadith* are cited by collection and their order number in the collection. Alternative English translations of the major collections are available on websites such as sunnah.com. The *hadith* citations in this book refer to the Arabic collections. The English numbering can be different because of the way translators have split up *hadith*. After the first reference the authors have omitted the prefix 'al-' for some recurring names.

Paul Cruickshank and Tim Lister, April 2018

# PROLOGUE:
# A WANTED MAN
## 2016–2018

I looked out at the broiling haze enveloping Dubai. It was an August afternoon in 2016 and I comforted myself with the thought that the month after next the sapping humidity would begin to ease.

I was packing for a family wedding in Bahrain, not one I was looking forward to in the mid-summer torpor. But it was the marriage of the oldest son of my eldest brother, Moheddin. I could hardly say no.

It was to be an all-male affair, in accordance with the conservative customs of my family. My wife wasn't coming to Bahrain but she was uneasy about my trip.

My five brothers and I had grown up in Saudi Arabia up the coast and across the causeway from Bahrain, but the tiny pearl-shaped kingdom was our homeland. We carried Bahraini passports and – for different reasons – we had enemies there. Moheddin was a veteran of the Afghan jihad and had held a government job in Saudi Arabia until forced to leave the Kingdom because of an unlucky and unwitting connection to an al-Qaeda suicide bomber.

Once I had sworn an oath of allegiance in person to Osama bin Laden and worked on al-Qaeda explosives and poisons experiments. But al-Qaeda's callous indifference to civilian casualties and the madness of a global campaign of terrorism were too much for me to stomach. It had corrupted the cause in which I believed: defending Muslims wherever they might be.

And so, in the parlance of espionage, I had been 'turned' by British intelligence. I was not an unwilling partner. In fact, I welcomed the chance to expiate any misdeeds during my four years as a jihadi. For the better part of a decade I had been one of the very few Western spies inside al-Qaeda until 'outed', by description if not by name, thanks to a clumsy leak that the British suspected emanated from the White House.

Eventually, someone in al-Qaeda joined the dots and worked out that the leaks pointed towards me as the informant. One of the group's most senior figures denounced me as a spy, and the dreaded fatwah followed. It was a religious command ordering my liquidation.

But here I was – eight years later – still in one piece. Some days, I even forgot that there were people out there who wanted to slit my throat. Surely by now it was a little late for the fatwah to be carried out? Many of those who wanted me dead had themselves been killed – in Afghanistan, Pakistan and Saudi Arabia – or were staring at the walls of a jail cell somewhere between Guantánamo Bay and Kabul.

'My nephew came to our wedding; I have to go to his,' I told my wife. 'There's really nothing to worry about.'

She looked pale. Three months pregnant, she was more than normally prone to anxiety.

'And look,' I continued, taking her hand, 'I'll be there less than twenty-four hours. The bad guys won't even know I'm in Bahrain.'

Tears gathered in her eyes.

'I just don't want you to go.'

Then, on the morning of 29 August, three days before the wedding, the groom-to-be called. 'Uncle,' he said, sounding less than effusive. 'Dad says hi, but he's had a message. The security services called. They said they understood you were planning to come to Bahrain. There's a threat against your life; they recommend you stay away. They say that in any case they are sending police officers to the wedding.'

It is rare that I am speechless, but for a few moments I said nothing. The combination of the news and my wife's intuition had knocked the wind out of me. It's often at such moments that one notices something trivial and irrelevant. I remember looking out of the window of our apartment towards the Arabian Gulf, and tracing the graceful loops of a hang glider drifting towards the beach.

I turned abruptly to see if my wife was listening. Thankfully, she had gone to lie down.

'It's unbelievable,' I said to my nephew. 'Does your father have any idea who it is?'

'He's been asking questions. He thinks it's Yasser Kamal and his brother Omar. They've been planning it for six weeks.'

Yasser Kamal: part-time fishmonger, full-time jihadi. He had enlisted me in an ambitious al-Qaeda plot back in 2004 to attack US Navy personnel based in Bahrain, the home of the US Fifth Fleet. Omar was going to be one of the suicide bombers.

I had fed all the details to MI6. When Kamal discovered, years later, that I had been working for British intelligence he had requested the fatwah against me.

'But how does Moheddin know about the plan?' I asked my nephew, still wrestling with my disbelief.

'Well, we can't be sure,' my nephew continued, 'but Omar's wife has kept on asking about the guest list. Were all the uncles coming?'

I made enquiries. The Bahraini police had discovered the plot because they were eavesdropping on Yasser Kamal. He had been stupid enough to talk with his brother about my impending visit; they had discussed following me to the airport after the wedding. In essence I would be carjacked. I was led to understand that they planned to use knives or machetes to dispense with me. They had also discussed filming my last moments as a warning to others who betrayed the cause. The gruesome video would then be uploaded to the Internet to mark the fifteenth anniversary of the 9/11 attacks.

Despite considerable evidence the Bahraini authorities decided not to move against the brothers, a typically pragmatic decision like many others that had allowed militants to operate there with considerable latitude. Firstly, they wanted to continue surveillance on the Kamals in case they were planning something worse than killing me, which was not very comforting. And they didn't want any awkward questions about a former British agent on Bahraini soil.

I decided to tell my wife about the plot rather than just pretend I was giving in to her entreaties. To my surprise she took the news calmly – seeing it as vindication of her female intuition. Needless to say, I have heeded such intuition ever since.

The sudden re-emergence of Yasser Kamal, the discovery that he was at large rather than in jail, gave me pause. But it did not surprise me, nor did I blame him for wanting to kill me. I had betrayed his cause because I had come to see it as an adulteration of Islam and a betrayal of the Prophet's words.

We were on opposite sides of a civil war that has consumed and splintered our religion, a conflict with a long and bloodstained history that appears to have plenty of fuel yet.

In the summer of 2016, the self-declared 'Caliphate' of the Islamic State in Iraq and Syria had passed its high-water mark: its many opponents were gathering for final assaults on its last redoubts. But its ideology was less delible than its grip on territory. And al-Qaeda – almost forgotten during the subliminal explosion of ISIS – still brooded menacingly, playing the long game. One generation of jihad was passing on its expertise and belief to the next.

As I write this in the spring of 2018 there are still plenty of men like Yasser Kamal out there, tens of thousands across the globe. Their anger towards the West runs deep. They see Islam under threat. They embrace radical interpretations of their religion that justify violence against anyone they deem not to be a *true* Muslim. And that includes millions of other Muslims whose inter-pretation of the Koran or whose customs they denounce as heresy.

I have witnessed that anger and the longing for martyrdom on battlefields in Bosnia. I have heard the narrow definition of the 'righteous Muslim' in Afghan camps and safe houses in Pakistan. I have sat in shabby London flats and field hospitals in Syria listening to young men with glistening eyes talk about prophecies that promised battles marking the approach of the end-of-days and a victorious march on Jerusalem. I have seen the thirst for vengeance after US missile attacks in Afghanistan.

I know and understand that mindset because two decades earlier I had shared it. I longed for martyrdom in the service of God; I saw Muslims in an epochal struggle of self-defence. I grasped at the noble ideal of jihad, only to be disgusted at its manipulation and indiscriminate application.

Soon after I was recruited by British intelligence, one of my colleagues joked that I should be called the 'cat' – as I appeared to have nine lives. I have used up every one of those lives fighting on both sides of this generational struggle, neither of which can claim a monopoly on decency or righteousness.

I am thankful for this opportunity to recount those lives and where they have led me, knowing that I may not get another in this world.

# MY FIRST LIFE: THE UNLIT CANDLE

## 1978–1995

I don't remember much of my father's funeral, but I was very nearly buried with him.

It was February 1983; I was four years old. He was going to take me out for a treat somewhere and to collect some groceries, perhaps to give me (and himself) some relief from the noise of my five older brothers. But I stepped on some broken glass in the kitchen. I was always running barefoot.

As my mother fussed over me and cleaned the smeared blood from the kitchen floor, my father picked up the car keys. He was killed minutes later at a junction when a truck ignored a stop sign. A mundane errand and a random accident left six boys without a father and a widow with a lifetime of struggle ahead of her.

In the days and weeks after my father was killed, I vaguely recall the anxiety of seeing and failing to comprehend my mother's tear-stained, ashen face. My brothers suffered more than I did; they understood our father was gone forever.

We were the Durrani family, of Arab, Afghan and Turkish heritage. We were Bahraini citizens but residents of Saudi Arabia. It was enough to confuse anyone's loyalties. We lived in the ordered suburbia of Khobar, a straggling city on the Arabian Gulf which had one reason for its existence: oil. My father was a businessman, importing construction machinery from Europe and selling it to the Saudi–American oil giant Aramco, a little way up the coast. Aramco crude ran through the family's veins.

The Durranis knew no country as their own; we were a polyglottic clan for whom the adventure of new opportunities trumped the security of the familiar. Uncle Ajab had left Peshawar in Pakistan to settle in Saudi Arabia. And before moving to Khobar my father had worked in Beirut, the commercial nerve centre of the Middle East, where he had met my mother in the late 1950s. She was from the town of Chebaa in south Lebanon, a redoubt of Sunni Muslims surrounded by Shia villages. Her family are related to the Hashemites, a noble bloodline descended from the Prophet Mohammed. Being proud Sunnis was – and is – as much part of our heritage as being indefatigable travellers.

We were conservative Sunni Arabs in a very conservative Kingdom, where women went covered on the rare occasions they left home. But in the sanctuary of their homes, women like my mother exhibited extraordinary determination and resilience. Especially after my father's death she exercised great influence over her brood of loud sons.

I was the accidental runt of the family, to be blunt about it. My parents had their hands full with five sons spread across fifteen years; my mother had spent half her adult life pregnant. But I, Ali al-Durrani, was not to be denied, arriving on 17 September 1978. My brothers would affectionately tease me about being the 'accident' – the unexpected arrival. Whether it was because I was the cub of the family or I lived in the shadow of my mother, I was a studious child. I had a precocious interest in history and religion. I was slight, not interested in sport, and was rarely without a book in my hand. It should have been a recipe for persecution at school, but there are benefits to having older brothers: bullies soon found themselves dumped in garbage cans.

The days of my childhood had a rhythm whose measure was prayer: the five daily prayers of devout Muslims the world over. Each day, I was roused by my brothers before dawn for the *Fajr* (dawn prayers), which we said at home. Classes at school were arranged around the call to prayer.

7

As a child I found the holy month of Ramadan magical. I did not chafe at the daytime fasting; it seemed important and I felt grown-up observing it. And I relished the outpouring of good spirits as night fell. The streets were decorated with lights. In our hundreds, boys and young men dashed from the *Maghreb* prayer at the ornate Omar bin Abdelaziz mosque to the pastry stalls. It seemed like a month when as a religion we came together in unity and common purpose. But it was a cocoon in a world of gathering violence.

My earliest experiences nurtured a sense of sectarian identity. My mother was constantly scouring the local news channels for reports on the civil war that was tearing her homeland apart. Watching her furrowed brow and listening to her quietly beseeching salvation for her family made a deep impact on me. I absorbed her obsession with the news. My first memory of world events unfolding on TV was the assassination of Indira Gandhi, India's prime minister, in 1984. I was six.

I had endless questions for my mother as I sat next to her on the sofa, working my way through a bunch of grapes or savouring that most valuable of imports, Coca-Cola. Who were the Palestinians? Why did Israel invade? Why couldn't they stop the fighting? She had few answers; nor did anyone in the mid-1980s as Beirut was demolished.

There was conflict nearer to home, too, along the hazy, dripping coastline to the north. In the ghastly struggle between Iraq and Iran, my brothers dismissed the fact that Saddam Hussein had started the war. Nor did they much care about his use of chemical weapons on a battlefield that resembled an arid, stony Somme. We saw this as an existential battle between Sunni and Shia (even though many of Saddam's conscripts were Shia). To the Arabs on the western shores of the Gulf, the Iranian revolution and the Shia theocracy that had followed were deeply disturbing, as was the rise of Shia militancy through groups like Hezbollah in Lebanon.

My poor mother endured a barrage of interrogation. Who was the bearded man everyone was afraid of in Iran? Why were the

Persians bad? When she was exhausted I would turn my fire on my brothers, who would not hesitate to reinforce my budding Sunni identity. To grow up amid such upheaval was extraordinarily formative, an early and very real introduction to the political and religious rifts that would dominate my life.

Not that Khobar had yet been touched by this turbulence. It was comfortable and ordered in the 1980s; change did not come to Saudi Arabia quickly. Our Muslim identity may have been very conservative socially, but it was also utterly quiescent. Political agitation was unthinkable, which made the Durranis rather unusual.

Every week we would gather round the dining table after Friday prayers – six brothers and their mother. Invariably it was politics for the main course and theology for dessert. I was soon aware of the noble struggle in Afghanistan against the Russians, of the call to jihad* that had lured thousands of Arabs to the foothills of the Himalayas. There was much talk of a neighbour who had gone to fight.

In this age of video games, social media, countless TV channels, texting and apps, it may seem odd that just one generation ago a child could have become steeped in Islamic literature. But that was me: I was attending an Islamic study circle at the Omar bin Abdelaziz mosque by the age of nine, helping in a local Islamic bookshop by the age of eleven, and thanks to a photographic memory knew the Koran by heart at the age of twelve.** I found the mosque enthralling in the traditional sense of the word. Its minarets reached towards God; the latticed arches and acres of plush

* Jihad is a term that is often used very loosely, but it has distinct meanings in Islam. It originally stems from the root *juhd* meaning effort or struggle. In a religious context jihad covers two crucial aspects of Islam. One concerns the inner struggle against worldly temptations such as alcohol, theft, extra-marital affairs and so on – the struggle to be a better Muslim. The second aspect covers military struggle. Whenever jihad is mentioned in the Koran outside the spiritual context it usually means participation in conflict.
** I think about five of my twenty-five classmates had memorized the Koran by this age. While not an exceptional achievement, it brought respect.

blue-gold carpet instilled in me a sense of awe. Besides the Koran, I was particularly enchanted by large leather-bound collections of *hadith** and fascinated by the mysterious prophecies these collections contained.**

On 2 August 1990, just a month before my twelfth birthday, Saddam Hussein's army invaded Kuwait. The man who had won support in the Arab world for going to war with the Shia theocracy in Iran had turned his vast army on his fellow Sunnis. Khobar was just down the coast from Kuwait; for a few fevered days we expected Iraqi tanks to roll south into the rich oilfields of the Eastern Province. People stocked up on supplies, made sure their vehicles were fuelled, even bought gas masks – just in case.

Kuwaiti refugees – perhaps the most affluent exodus in history – arrived in their limousines and 4x4s, laden down with whatever valuables they had been able to grab before fleeing. And then US forces arrived – the infidel come to guard the Custodians of the Two Holy Mosques from a secular dictator who had just declared himself the true adherent of Islam. The world was upside down. But to me the American presence offered reassurance, a sense that Saddam (whom we had vocally supported against Iran) would be stopped and turned back. We had heard much – some of it no doubt apocryphal – of the looting and atrocities visited upon Kuwait by his troops.

The American soldiers in their desert fatigues went to fast-food restaurants around Khobar and manned their discreetly placed anti-missile batteries to deter the Iraqis' dreaded Scuds. I saw several of Saddam's missiles arcing towards Saudi territory before they were

* *Hadith* are sayings and deeds attributed to the Prophet Mohammed which began to be written down just over a century after his death, after being passed down orally by his disciples and their successors. There were hundreds of thousands of *hadith* originally written down but only approximately 40,000 unique *hadith* have been taken seriously by Muslim scholars over the centuries. Since then Islamic scholars have questioned the authenticity of at least three quarters of these.
** Among the books of *hadith*, the Persian scholar Muhammad al-Bukhari's collection (*circa* AD 846) and the *Book of Muslim* are considered the most authoritative by Sunni Muslims.[1]

taken out in mid-air. The Americans all seemed so much bigger and more muscular than the average Saudi, with a swashbuckling confidence and faith in technology that was so alien to our culture.

The government went to great lengths to persuade Saudis of the 'blessings of safety and security' – but others more worldly than me knew it was a charade. Without the Americans, we would have been hard put to resist Saddam's huge army, even if it was still recovering from a decade of conflict with Iran. The invasion of Kuwait brought war, politics and religion into everyday conversation. For a twelve-year-old already steeped in the region's turmoil, it was like attending finishing school.

Then, in the summer of 1991, just before I turned thirteen, my mother died of a brain aneurism. I was inconsolable. I had become the centre of her world as my brothers had grown into teenagers and young men. She was a spiritual person and wanted me to be pious, perhaps to become an imam. She was very proud of my mastery of the Koran and had encouraged my religious studies, getting my brothers to introduce me to prominent religious figures in Khobar.

When I lost my mother I lost a teacher, mentor and companion. I eventually found companionship and solace in an unlikely place: the six volumes and 4,000 pages of Sayyid Qutb's *In the Shade of the Koran*.

Qutb, the founding father of modern jihad and of a radical and profound interpretation of Islam, had written the book in times of pain and hardship, when he had been tortured in Egyptian jails in the 1950s and 1960s. I related to the suffering as much as the scholarship and the beauty of his writing. It took me two years to finish his masterwork. But it made a deep impression on me.

I was drawn to his explanations of God's sovereignty over creation, and his argument that most Muslims, corrupted by Western modernity and secularism, had lost sight of the divine. We had been plunged back into an age of *jahiliyah* (pre-Islamic ignorance). He made a defiant call, over the heads of the grand clerics and scholars of Islam, for the restoration of God's Kingdom on

Earth. His words about the state of the Muslim world and why change should come, even by violent means, were persuasive to me. God's law was supreme over man-made laws.

Qutb's central and revolutionary premise was that you cannot preach your way into power, for those who possess power possess the means of violence. If you shy away from wresting power from them by violence then you are doomed to failure.

His arguments were purgative to a teenager brought up in the sluggish complacency of Saudi Arabia. Even as I read Qutb's works, the real world was validating his philosophy. In December 1991, the Islamist party in Algeria – the FIS – won the first round of parliamentary elections. The Algerian army immediately staged a coup and put FIS party leaders in prison or sent them into exile.

Despite his radical challenge to the Islamic establishment, Qutb's writing was inexplicably tolerated by the Saudi establishment in the early 1990s. We frequently discussed it in a study group – the Islamic Awareness Circle – that I attended at the Omar bin Abdelaziz mosque. I was admitted to the group when I was nine after passing a general knowledge test designed for thirteen-year-olds. Those Friday lunches had been a good education.

The Circle was like a Scout troop but with religious underpinnings. We were as interested in camping trips and barbecues as we were in theological debate and current affairs. The 'rock children' of the Palestinian territories were our heroes. In those days the Palestinian cause was still dear to the hearts of young Arabs all over the Middle East, before it was overshadowed and then submerged by the greater struggle for the soul of our religion.

The Circle included individuals who would shape both my future and the emergence of Islamist militancy in Saudi Arabia. One instructor who visited from time to time was a lanky university student called Yusuf al-Ayeri. He had sunken eyes and a strong jaw that made him slightly forbidding, as did his intense and humourless demeanour. I cannot recall seeing him smile, let alone laugh.

Born into an upper-middle-class family in Dammam,* al-Ayeri told us that he had fought in Afghanistan against the Communists before coming back home to pursue Shariah studies. He had taken the writings of Sayyid Qutb very much to heart, constantly nagging the Circle about how Western culture was corrupting Muslim societies. He alleged, for example, that the patties at the Saudi franchise of the American burger chain Hardee's were made from pork. With a straight face, he told us that Pepsi stood for 'Pay Every Penny to Save Israel'. And when you held a bottle of Coca-Cola to the mirror, the reflected logo in Arabic read 'No Mohammed No Mecca'.

It was a shame as I loved Coke.

One afternoon, al-Ayeri ventured into still more absurd territory. The Circle was sitting on the carpet of the mosque's library.

'I have learned,' he said gravely, 'that some of you watch *The Smurfs* on television.'

*The Smurfs* – a cartoon series featuring blue and white anthropomorphous creatures living in a forest – were a global phenomenon. I looked down; it was one of my favourite shows.

'This is *haram* [forbidden],' al-Ayeri continued. 'The Smurfs are a Western plot to destroy the fabric of our society, to destroy morality in our children and respect for their parents. If you watch this you're going to start carrying out pranks and mixing magic potions. This is not normal; Islam forbids it.'

But he wasn't finished.

'There is also a lot of sexuality with the female Smurf. She dresses and behaves in a disgusting way.'

Despite al-Ayeri's proscription, I continued to watch *The Smurfs*. In a way, it was my guilty secret. On the other hand, I could think of nothing in the Koran or *hadith* that might be applicable to

---

* His family originally came from the town of Buraydah in the al-Qassim region of Saudi Arabia. The area was a key recruiting ground for al-Qaeda, including during its campaign of attacks after 9/11.

*The Smurfs*. If it was a Western plot, I told myself, it would only seduce the most gullible.

Among my fellow students in the group was Khalid al-Hajj, who was three years my senior. Khalid had been born into a Yemeni family in Jeddah and had moved to Khobar when he was very young. Olive-skinned, tall and athletic, he had large, deep-set brown eyes that had a strangely soothing effect. His level-headed disposition was the perfect foil for my hyperactive energy and tendency to be an insufferable know-it-all. Where I saw complexity, he saw black and white. At the same time, he had a restless soul.

We would have a long, close and turbulent relationship.

While in many ways we were yin and yang, we shared a deep religious fervour and a competitive streak. Khalid led a team which competed in Islamic poetry competitions against other Islamic Circles. I was the team's secret weapon, thanks to my memory and deep immersion in all things Islamic. I had memorized so much Arabic poetry that our team became champions of the Eastern Province. Khalid beamed when Prince Saud bin Nayef, then deputy governor of the province, presented us with the trophy.

Only once in competition was I bested. My nemesis was a young Syrian who left me lost for words after a two-hour poetry duel.

'I want a rematch, I know I'm better than him,' I had declared to Khalid, unfamiliar with the taste of defeat.

'Everybody knows you are very smart, Ali,' Khalid replied. 'One day you are going to be a fine imam or a famous professor of Islamic history, *Insha'allah*. But you need to relax a little. Sometimes you remind me of our cat at home; you always need your ego stroked.'

After my mother passed away, my brothers were my guardians, while Chitrah, an endlessly patient woman from Sri Lanka who was our maid, ensured I was fed and clothed. My brothers were very different from me – into sports and martial arts – but protective of their little sibling. And I was not the most difficult of charges: diligent and quiet, more likely to be buried in a book than climbing fences or hanging out with a bad crowd.

If there was an authority figure in my life it was my eldest brother, Moheddin, eighteen years my senior, a natural athlete who was powerfully built and held a judo black belt. After graduating in chemical engineering from King Fahd University in Dhahran, Moheddin had studied in Florida and California in the early 1980s. He dreamed of dropping out and becoming a hippy, travelling around the US in a multicoloured van. But he was nearly twenty years too late. The flowers and the music had given way to the Reagan Doctrine, and the United States was confronting its enemies aggressively, whether in tiny Grenada or Gadhafi's Libya. Moheddin was angered by what he saw as the United States' overbearing use of military power. In a fit of frustration he had smashed his guitar, come home to Saudi Arabia and turned increasingly to religion.

By 1989, Moheddin had grown a long auburn beard and felt it his duty to respond to the call of jihad. Even though he was by then married with a son, he went to Afghanistan for three months to participate in the tail end of the war against the Communists. He had flown out with a friend who would much later become a renowned leader of jihad in Chechnya.* For a quiet town on the Gulf, Khobar was turning out more than its fair share of militants.

On his return, Moheddin told us stories about the fighting around Khost and lectured us on the duty of every able-bodied Muslim to fight in defence of Islam. But by then his priority was to look after his growing family, and he substituted the romance of jihad with a more mundane existence at the regional chamber of commerce.

Moheddin was the brother I most respected but I was closest to Omar. Relaxed and free-spirited, he wore his religion lightly. He would light up any gathering with his wisecracks. His cheerful demeanour and good looks (he might have been named Omar for Sharif) made him very popular with women, and his job at Dhahran airport meant that, unusually for a young Saudi male, he had the

---

* This was the Saudi Ibn al-Khattab who knew both my brother and Yusuf al-Ayeri.

chance to mix with the opposite sex. There were even rumours of a clandestine romance among the check-in desks, which he denied with a cheeky smile.

At this time, my whole universe was male. Even during the famous Friday lunches, sisters-in-law and female cousins dined separately. Not once during my youth in Saudi Arabia did I see a female over the age of ten, besides my mother, who was not fully veiled. Even Moheddin's wife wore a veil in my presence.

In the spring of 1992 the Bosnian civil war broke out. Yugoslavia was falling apart. Slovenia and Croatia had already seceded from the federation that Josip Tito had so adroitly held together for decades. Bosnia was a patchwork of Muslims, Croats and Serbs, and the conflict had kicked off when the Muslims and Croats voted for independence. It quickly consumed the evening news broadcasts in Saudi Arabia, which depicted it as a Christian crusade against defenceless Muslims, with images and descriptions of Croatian and Serb atrocities against Bosnia's Muslims.

At that same time, my friend Khalid made a two-month trip to Afghanistan to train and fight with the mujahideen against the Communist government. He was just sixteen. Osama bin Laden had made the cause popular among young radicals; at any one time there were probably about 4,000 'Afghan Arabs',[2] as they came to be known, fighting or training in Afghanistan.* Many more became aid workers, teachers and medics, serving the tide of Afghan refugees that had arrived in northern Pakistan.

Khalid told me stories of battles around Jalalabad and camps in the mountains. There was no bombast in his accounts; he spoke in matter-of-fact tones about the duty of jihad.

'All Muslims should be trained because there always might come a day when we need to pick up arms to defend the faith,' he declared.

---

* The Saudi state was financing the Afghan resistance lavishly – to the tune of about $1.8 billion in the period 1987–9.[3]

My study group frequently talked about the Bosnian war and those who had gone to fight – including my school maths teacher, who was killed after just a couple of months in the Balkans.* From a prominent family, his father was a brigadier in the Interior Ministry, but in those days there was pride rather than shame in having a family member leave home to wage jihad.

At a book fair I bought an audiotape about Bosnia called *Drops of Tears and Blood*, in which students from religious seminaries there talked about the 'ethnic cleansing' of Muslims, their horror stories skilfully interspersed with religious hymns sung in Turkish and Arabic. At school we were shown a documentary, *The Cross Is Throwing Down a Challenge*, whose message was searing and simple. There was a new Christian crusade against Islam.

We were beginning to understand that we lived in turbulent times, especially for our religion and its most puritanical strand: Salafism.**

The term is often loosely and inaccurately used but essentially there are three strands of Salafism. In the study group we scoffed at the traditional quiescent variant, which our teachers mocked as 'royalist' because it posed no challenge to the Saudi royal family. This was a stagnant interpretation of Islam, cloaked in robes of tribalism and heavily ritualistic, inadequate for the challenges of our times.

My friends and mentors were gravitating towards a more politically active interpretation, best exemplified by the Muslim Brotherhood's involvement in social work and discreet political activism. This interpretation was obliquely critical of the

---

* His name was Osama Mansouri and he came from a distinguished family: his uncle was a government minister.
** Salafis believe that the Koran and the *hadith* as well as the consensus of Muslim scholars are in themselves sufficient guidance for a believer in Islam. They therefore insist on the literal truth of Islamic scripture, and practise a 'pure' and 'unadulterated' Islam that is as close as possible to that practised by the first three generations of Muslims after the Prophet Mohammed.

government, but not enough to get us into any trouble. We wanted Islam to be defiant – to free Muslims from the idols of capitalism and socialism – but we also wanted it to be spared human revisionism. As Qutb had put it: '[Islam] is a revolt against any human situation where sovereignty, or indeed Godhead, is given to human beings . . . As a declaration of human liberation, Islam means returning God's authority to Him, rejecting the usurpers who rule over human communities according to man-made laws.'[4]

The third strand was jihadi Salafism, a more radical call to take up arms in defence of Islam, one that was gaining support as Muslims perceived a growing offensive against their faith. In time, this movement became increasingly hostile to the Western powers and the sclerotic Arab governments they protected.

In Islam, holy war is fought to defend Muslim territories and communities against a military assault, either by a non-Muslim army or by Muslim aggressors. Such defensive jihad is considered to be *Fard al-Ayn*, a 'mandatory obligation', meaning that every able-bodied man and woman should participate in the defence of their territory and community.*

A few months before my fifteenth birthday, I gathered my earnings from my part-time job in the Islamic bookshop and set off for my first trip alone to Mecca. I was still immersed in the works of Qutb and his brother Mohammed; I read them like other young idealists had read Marx and Lenin. I took Qutb's seminal 1964 volume *Milestones* into the Great Mosque. Standing against one of the pillars facing the Kaabah, which hundreds of thousands of Muslims circle every year at the climax of the Hajj, I was absorbed in the book for three days.

---

* It is not the same as offensive jihad: 'Permission to fight is given to those upon whom war is made because they are oppressed, and most surely God is well able to assist them' (Koran 22:39). 'Fight for God's sake against those who fight against you, but begin no hostilities for God loves not the aggressors' (Koran 2:190).

It portrayed Islam as persecuted by the modern world, under threat from the West and secularism at a time when it was more necessary than ever for the salvation of all mankind. Only a revival of the 'true' religion among a Vanguard could create an Islamic movement capable of rising above and confronting those standing in the way of the spread of 'true' Islam. For Qutb this entailed all the existing systems of governments in the Arab world and all the secular ideologies of the twentieth century including communism. So deep and rich was the language that I read every chapter twice. I was transfixed by the message; the setting where I read the book no doubt illuminated its perspective.

Qutb had been rearrested in Egypt after writing *Milestones*. One phrase of his particularly resonated – that our words remained unlit candles during our lifetime, but at the moment we die for our beliefs they are lit. It spoke of the ultimate sacrifice.

A few weeks before he was executed in Egypt in 1966, Qutb had written from prison to a friend: 'I have been able to discover God in a wonderful new way. I understand His path and way more clearly and perfectly than before.'[5] He was looking forward to martyrdom.

By ordering him to be hanged, Egyptian President Gamal Abdel Nasser sealed Qutb's legend. His writings would have a huge influence on men like Osama bin Laden who were drawn towards jihad because, like Qutb, they believed Muslims had abandoned the basic principles of Islam and had become consumed with their existence in this world and not the next. They had been seduced by Western materialism and secularism.*

I was gravitating towards this viewpoint, mindful of a *hadith* attributed to the Prophet:

---

* Ayman al-Zawahiri, who later became leader of al-Qaeda, wrote that Qutb's philosophy was the 'spark that ignited the Islamic revolution against the enemies of Islam at home and abroad'. Qutb's brother, Mohammed Qutb, who helped to popularize his ideas, gave university lectures in Saudi Arabia which bin Laden attended.[6]

19

*'Whenever you start dealing in usury and you are content merely
with your livestock and agriculture and you abandon jihad then
God will subject you to humiliation at the hands of other
nations until you return back to the principles of your faith.'[7]*

In 1994 I was still some way from being a revolutionary. Restless
and rebellious perhaps and certainly sympathetic to the militant
cause against secular dictatorships in Egypt and Algeria, but the
idea of settling religious scores nearer to home in Saudi Arabia or
Bahrain by shedding blood was unthinkable. Indeed, the notion of
global jihad had yet to surface, but even as a fifteen-year-old I felt
humiliation as a Muslim. I despaired that civil war in Afghanistan
had ruined an opportunity to build an Islamic State (though the
Taliban would soon change that). At the time I was also reading
accounts of the serial defeats of the Arabs in their twentieth-century
wars against the Jews in 1948, 1956 and 1967.

Qutb's works had even greater resonance after the first Gulf War,
which had seen a Western-led coalition descend upon Arab lands. Two
radical clerics in Saudi Arabia were railing against the presence of the
infidel and warning they would only leave after 'reorganizing' the
region to serve their interests.[8] The sermons of Safar al-Hawali and
Salman al-Ouda hinted at the end-of-days: an apocalyptic battle was
on the horizon. I began to wonder if they were right: at the end of
1992, the US began its ill-fated intervention in Somalia and the following summer there was another cruise missile attack on Baghdad.

Both clerics were arrested by the Saudi authorities in September
1994 and imprisoned, a move that angered me and thousands of
other Salafis, including bin Laden. But their defiance reminded us
of the Islamic scholar Ibn Taymiyyah,* who had said seven centuries

---

* Ibn Taymiyyah (1263–1328) was based in Damascus at the time of the Mongol
invasions. He argued that Islam had become distorted by different sects and
schools over the centuries and needed to return to the Koran and the Sunnah (the
customs and practices established by and inherited from the Prophet Mohammed).
Long after his death his teachings deeply influenced the Wahhabi movement in
Saudi Arabia, other Salafi currents and the jihadi movement.

earlier: 'What are my enemies going to do to me? If they imprison me, my prison will become my retreat. If they kill me, I become a martyr. If they deport me, my exile will be my tourism. What are they going to do to me? My happiness is in my heart. My heart is in God's hands.'[9]

Within days of the clerics' arrest, and fulminating against the status quo, I decided I was one of Qutb's unlit candles.*

While I worked at the Islamic bookshop I would often have dinner with Khalid al-Hajj's older brother, Mohammed, who worked nearby. One evening soon after the Sheikhs' arrest, Mohammed told me that Khalid was going to Bosnia and I should say goodbye to him. Only the family knew, Mohammed said, 'but you are his friend and I thought you should too.'

I was stunned. I thought I knew Khalid well, but he had never mentioned his plans to me. At the time, the Saudi newspapers were full of stories about the Arab 'foreign legion' that had gone to fight alongside the Muslims in Bosnia against the bloodthirsty Serbs. The martyrdom of two Saudis in Sarajevo the previous year had been big news.

At that moment, sitting at dinner with Mohammed, I was struck by a lightning bolt of purpose – an epiphany. This was the path I needed to take, the answer that had been eluding me for months. Could I really stay at home and train to be an imam – toeing the government line and abetting injustice instead of answering Qutb's call to defiance?

I was not hungry anymore.

'I need to talk to Khalid,' I said. 'Immediately.'

I had an impulsive streak (and still do) but this was no rash euphoria. In a way the Gulf War, the Americans hanging around in

---

* Only in the mid-1990s did the Saudi establishment wake up to the challenge posed by Qutb's message, with the publication by Salafi scholars of a book that identified Qutbism as a threat.

Khobar, my readings of Qutb, the Islamic Awareness Circle, had all brought me to this moment. Certainly I was imbued with an ideology, but I was also a powder keg yearning for a spark. I did not want history passing me by.

Khalid was surprised to see me, and more surprised that I knew of his plans.

'How many of you are going?' I asked.

'Three.'

'Now it's four.'

'But you're fifteen. You can't just take off anywhere. War is not a poetry competition.'

'Correction: I just turned sixteen,' I interrupted.

Khalid was becoming desperate. He did not want to offend me, but nor did he want what he expected to be the burden of looking after me.

'Do you really think jihad needs you there?' he asked, almost pleading.

Without knowing where the words came from, I answered: 'I know jihad doesn't need me, but I need jihad.'

It might sound like a glib response, but I felt a moral and religious duty to take up arms.

Years later Khalid told me my reply had persuaded him that I should join the expedition. It had meant that I wanted to travel not as an adventurer in search of thrills and heroism but to better myself, to be part of a project that would make a difference.

I told my brothers that I was going on a camping trip with Khalid and some others for two days.

'Off with the Circle again, little brother?' asked Moheddin with a smirk.

He embraced me as I left – for longer than a camping trip warranted. He had a sense that I was off to do more than camping. He had known Khalid's group was leaving for Bosnia and expected me to join them, but he didn't want our brothers to know. He knew that Omar in particular would try to dissuade me. Moheddin told

22

me many years later that he had felt exceptionally proud that his little brother had taken it upon himself to wage jihad in defence of our faith.

I collected winter clothing, a radio, flashlights and a Swiss army knife, as well as about $3,000, the earnings from the bookshop that I had carefully saved for a higher education that would be on indefinite hold. I also bought a return ticket – as did the others – so as not to arouse suspicion among European immigration officials. I felt it unlikely I would ever make that return journey. I was going to be a Holy Warrior and seek martyrdom – and that outweighed the sadness that I would probably never see my family again.

The quartet comprised Khalid, myself, a young businessman from Khobar and a student from Riyadh. The businessman was the scion of a Saudi construction dynasty and was carrying the equivalent of $800,000 to donate to the cause. We split up the cash between us, in case one of us was stopped and searched. It was my first encounter with the way cash for jihad was moved.

We flew out of Dhahran for Vienna in early October 1994 and were asked just one question by the Saudi border security official as we were leaving: 'How are you boys going to manage in Vienna if you can't speak German?'

When we arrived at Vienna airport, our problem was not so much our inadequate German as the overwhelming abundance of young women. There were dozens of them in every direction. The miniskirts and jeans, lipstick and cleavage affronted my Saudi sense of modesty. At home, girls typically donned the veil from the age of eleven; here they seemed to wear less the older they grew.

Like a demented robot I kept moving my head in different directions so as to avoid setting eyes on this onslaught of the female form. I felt my virtue and dignity threatened and remembered the warning of the Prophet Mohammed: 'The first glance is for you but the second glance will be against you.'[10]

Before leaving the airport, the four of us went to a coffee

shop. I could not help glancing at a girl who was about my age, sitting with her parents at the next table. I remember her exactly, such was the impact on my delicate sensibilities. She had deep blue eyes and auburn hair that cascaded onto her slim, pale shoulders. A sleeveless lilac dress hung delicately on an already alluring figure. She smiled and I blushed scarlet, quickly averting my gaze.

'Khalid, can you switch places with me?' I asked my friend.

'Why?' he replied.

'I feel a bit uncomfortable.'

'Fine,' he said, making the swap.

'You rascal. Why didn't you tell me?' he hissed a few seconds later.

'Because you're older than me and more pious,' I replied. Temptation was the work of the devil.

The passage to Croatia and into Bosnia had been well trodden by the first wave of the mujahideen. Obtain a visa for Croatia in Vienna, touch base with worshippers at the al-Sahaba mosque, drop into the adjacent McDonald's for a fish burger. It was there that we began to discuss martyrdom, four young men from the desert in the city of Mozart and Strauss.

'How do you want to die?' Khalid asked, as he reached for the French fries.

The discussion energized rather than depressed us. That's why we had made the journey: to offer our lives for the cause. My friends decided they preferred being vaporized in an explosion so no remains would be left on earth. I, too, was gripped by the sense that this foreign battlefield would be my bridge to paradise. As the Prophet had said, with the first drop of blood all the sins of a martyr are forgiven. With the second they see their place in heaven. There would be no purgatory and no anxiety on the Day of Judgment. Not only would seventy-two virgins await, but as a martyr I could ask the Lord to grant eternal life to seventy of my relatives and friends.[11] I would be reunited with the mother I so missed and the father I had never got to know.

That evening Khalid and I made a pledge to each other: 'Brothers in God. Brothers in Faith. Brothers in Arms!'

The Croatian embassy in Vienna was not as helpful as we had hoped,* so we flew to recently independent Slovenia, the first of the Yugoslav republics to break away. Arriving on a balmy autumn afternoon at Ljubljana airport, we were lucky enough to find a Lebanese taxi driver to translate for us and the following day had freshly stamped Croatian visas at a cost of 100 Deutschmarks each.

We were asked few questions when we flew into Split. To avoid looking like a group we joined different queues at the immigration check. We had come up with the rather feeble ruse that we were on vacation and planned to go swimming. I made swimming motions with my hands to the border agent, just as out of the corner of my eye I caught one of my friends doing exactly the same. So much for subterfuge.

The Arab fighters gathered at the Pension Tommy, a villa overlooking the Adriatic just outside Split on the coastal road to Dubrovnik. By the time we reached the pension (one of the few hotels in war-torn Croatia doing a roaring trade) there was already a group preparing to cross into Bosnia, including two fresh-faced Palestinians from Milan called Marwan and Hazam.

Over dinner that night as the moonlight shimmered on the Adriatic, an Egyptian jihadi veteran told us about the war in Bosnia. The Muslims had been unprepared both militarily and psychologically and had anticipated neither the ferocity nor the brutality of Serb tactics. Only now were they coming to terms with the reality that the Serbs were hell-bent on a war of annihilation. Massacres had sent shock waves throughout the Bosnian civilian population; more than a million people had been displaced. The capital of Sarajevo was besieged and bombarded from all sides by heavy

---

* From the autumn of 1992 Croatia began restricting the flow of mujahideen through its territory. The following year there were clashes between Bosnian Croat and Muslim forces inside Bosnia. Tensions were reduced after the Washington Agreement in March 1994 ended hostilities between Croats and Muslims.

weaponry. The hillsides around the city were occupied by Serb snipers who showed no mercy to civilians, killing anyone who moved, regardless of age or gender.

The Egyptian explained why Bosnia was attracting a growing foreign legion of jihadis. The Bosnian civil war had erupted just as the Afghan jihad was winding down. The mujahideen had finally entered Kabul after twelve long years of struggle for the city, only to start fighting among themselves. Despairing of the internecine warfare, many Arabs had left and some had gravitated to Bosnia. So would eventually a few hundred Muslims of North African descent who lived in Europe.

Many of the 'Afghan Arabs' had received training in camps run by Pakistani intelligence: they were accomplished fighters but also well versed in everything from forging passports to laundering cash. Impressed with their prowess on the battlefield, the beleaguered Bosnian government had allowed them to set up a unit within the 3rd Corps of the Bosnian Army called the Mujahideen Brigade, and a growing number of Bosnian Muslims were now choosing to fight with the group. Their headquarters in Zenica, forty miles north-west of Sarajevo, was our destination.

Despite the danger, a daily bus service still shuttled between Split and Zenica. On a cool October morning we set out from the coast. The mountains of the interior loomed and the landscape of the barren coastline gave way to thickly forested hillsides. As our bus lumbered through small towns, churches were less in evidence and the minarets of mosques more frequent. Many were badly damaged. In one picturesque mountain village carpeted by red and orange leaves we saw a mosque whose dome had been split in half when its minaret had come crashing down. I had seen such images on videos back in Saudi Arabia, but seeing the destruction in person profoundly shocked me. For as long as I could remember my life had revolved around the mosque. Sadness, anger and indignation swirled within me.

Hazam, one of the Milanese Palestinians, said softly: 'Remember, this is exactly why we came.'

Zenica was a grim steel town in a broad valley. A Moroccan

was waiting for us at the bus depot. He came every day in a mini-van to pick up new volunteers. We were taken to our new lodgings: a dreary tenement on the edge of town that had once served as a dormitory for metal workers.

A wizened Egyptian stared up at us from a battered desk.

'Welcome to the Mujahideen Brigade. How long do you expect to stay?' he asked.

'Open-ended,' I replied without a trace of irony.

I was assigned number 324; I was the Brigade's 324th volunteer. Mohammed al-Madani,* a Saudi fighter, then took me to the store room to pick up a uniform. It was the first of our many encounters.

He certainly knew how to be condescending.

'We'll need to find you a baby-sized uniform. It may be difficult; Mothercare stopped manufacturing uniforms in your size!'

'I'm almost as tall as you!' I scowled, pulling myself up to my full height.

The store room was plentifully supplied: the shelves were packed with AK-47s, machine guns, RPG-7s, grenades and more. Al-Madani handed me boots and a green camouflage uniform issued by the Bosnia-Herzegovina army. It had a patch with crossing swords and the blue and gold Bosnian crest, the insignia of the 3rd Corps.

'How do you feel?' he asked.

'Like I've found my purpose – as if I was born for this.'

Within days I had met white American converts to Islam, Britons of Pakistani origin and plenty of Egyptians. Many of the Egyptians belonged to Gama al-Islamiya, a jihadi group attempting to overthrow the Mubarak government. They had fought in Afghanistan and were the commanders and trainers of the brigade and frequently paid the price for leading from the front.

Muslims from forty nations had come together in defence of other Muslims. It was the Islamic version of the International Brigade that had fought in the Spanish Civil War and I was immensely proud to belong to it. The overall commander was Anwar Shaaban,

* Not his real name.

a senior member of Gama al-Islamiya and a veteran of the Afghan jihad. More recently he had gained prominence as the firebrand imam of the Islamic Cultural Institute in Milan, and his associations with known terrorists had made him a wanted man in Italy.*

When I was ushered into his office, I was greeted by an avuncular figure in his fifties with thick glasses and a long beard flecked with grey. He was impressed I had memorized the Koran and had come to fight at such a young age.

I told Shaaban I had named myself 'Haydara al-Bahraini', the lion's cub of Bahrain, a title whose pretension still fills me with embarrassment.

'I hope from time to time you can help our Bosnian brothers in the brigade. They have, alas, lived for many decades under atheism and communism, so they don't always have the correct religious understanding,' Shaaban said.

It was true that many Bosnian Muslims wore their religion lightly, smoking and drinking and praying only occasionally. But the conflict had regenerated religious belief in Bosnia and an interest in jihad. While the vast majority of the approximately 100,000 Bosnians under arms in the civil war joined other units in the Bosnian army, some two thousand fought with the Mujahideen Brigade at any one time, outnumbering foreign fighters four to one.

One young Bosnian fighter who spoke a little Arabic was called Abdin. He told me that while he had been at the University of Sarajevo the Serbs had come to his village and killed almost every member of his family. They had raped one of his sisters before killing her.

* Under Shaaban, the Islamic Cultural Institute in Milan, a former garage turned into a mosque, became a key logistical hub for the Bosnian jihad. My two Palestinian travel companions on the bus had attended the mosque. Shortly after 9/11, the United States Treasury Department labelled it 'the main al-Qaeda station house in Europe [used] to facilitate the movement of weapons, men and money across the world'. Shaaban had links to Omar Abdel Rahman, known as the Blind Sheikh, who was convicted for a part in the first attack on the World Trade Center in 1993. US intelligence agencies also linked Shaaban to the casing that year of the US embassy in Tirana, Albania, for a potential terrorist attack.[12]

'My other sister, we don't know what happened to her,' he said with sad resignation. For Abdin, jihad offered consolation and vengeance.

The conflict would sow bitter fruit. Two decades later, more than 300 Bosnians would travel to Syria and Iraq to support ISIS, one of the highest number per capita from anywhere in Europe.[13] Bosnia was a crucible for modern jihad.

A few weeks after arriving in Bosnia, I was sent for training at al-Siddiq camp north of Zenica. I was reunited with Hazam and Marwan, the two Palestinians who had travelled with me into Bosnia, and we became fast friends. Khalid, as a 'veteran' of Afghanistan, had been dispatched straight to the front lines.

The sloping encampment an hour's drive north of Zenica high up above the hamlet of Orašac consisted of a stone villa housing our sleeping and eating quarters. It was surrounded by outhouses, an exercise yard and firing ranges.[14] For a boy from the Arabian Desert, the green mountains and the first snows of winter added to the sense of wonderment. It was a time of blissful fulfilment, even if boot camp and parade drill had to be endured. The prospect that I might not leave Bosnia alive sometimes gave me pause, but I accepted and even embraced the prospect of martyrdom should God so decide.

I was excited to handle a weapon and they were in plentiful supply thanks to gunrunners from Hungary and Croatia. A good quality AK-47 would cost some $250. Within days I was able to take apart and reassemble an AK-47 blindfolded. We did target practice with rifles, machine guns and then heavy calibre weapons, including the 20mm Yugo gun. My ability with maths and map reading soon made me competent in firing mortars.

I knew most of my brothers were worried about me and I tried to reassure them with regular letters that I was engaged in humanitarian work and was in no danger. I ignored their pleas to return home; home had become something of an abstract notion since my mother's death. And for the first few months I wasn't in any danger. We were either training or snowed in; there was little fighting in the Balkan winter.

There was, however, plenty of schooling. A Saudi cleric called Sheikh Abu Ayoub al-Shamrani spent hours expounding in lectures on the virtues of jihad. We were here to protect Muslims' lives and lands. Shamrani also talked about jihad to remove obstacles to the spread of true Islam around the world.

'There are powerful forces conspiring to stop the message of God from reaching people's hearts and they need to be confronted by force,' he said.

I recognized the words. He was paraphrasing the manifesto of Sayyid Qutb.[15]

In past centuries, offensive jihad had been the prerogative of the Supreme Leader of the Muslim community, the Caliph. However, Qutb had argued that in the absence of a Caliph today a Vanguard of mujahideen could lead jihad. The reason, Shamrani explained, was that this jihad was in essence a battle to defend our religion, creating the same obligation for Muslims to act with or without a Caliph's blessing as in 'defensive' jihad.

He turned to a passage by Qutb: 'If we insist on calling Jihad a defensive movement then we must change the meaning of the word "defence" and mean by it "the defence of man" against all those elements which limit his freedom. These elements take the form of beliefs and concepts, as well as of political systems, based on economic, racial or class distinctions.'[16]

He paused to survey his congregation.

'Ever since the European powers abolished the Caliphate,* the Muslim nation was left without a figurehead. Brave Muslim scholars like Sayyid Qutb realised there was this third kind of jihad which, although practised during the time of the Prophet,

---

* Early Muslim rulers were known as Caliphs and were expected to lead and defend the worldwide Muslim community. Sunni Muslims have a particular reverence for the 'four rightly guided Caliphs' after the Prophet Mohammed's death. In more modern times Ottoman Sultans, despite reigning over many non-Muslims, referred to themselves as Caliphs until Turkish nationalists abolished the title in the early 1920s. The Caliphate al-Qaeda seeks to restore – and ISIS claimed to have restored – is the one that jihadis imagine ruled over early Islam.[17]

subsequently went unrecognized. We refer to it as jihad *al-Tamkeen* [empowerment]. It is a jihad to restore Muslim sovereignty. Look around you. Is it not we who are the Vanguard?'

His words made me uncomfortable. Qutb had depicted secular rulers in the Arab world as part of a global plot to marginalize and dilute Islam.[18] While many of the Egyptian jihadis in Bosnia hoped one day to overthrow Hosni Mubarak, I could not countenance shedding blood back home. I approached the Sheikh when his lecture was over.

'One thing worries me,' I said. 'Against whom should we wage this new form of jihad? Are you suggesting we fight our own governments and armies?'

'I'm not saying that,' said the Saudi cleric, much to my relief. 'But one day our governments may take sides *with* the West in the face of the jihad to restore the Caliphate If that happens, fighting our own governments would not be a matter of choice, but of the survival of our faith.' He fixed me with a serious gaze. 'You may be sceptical that such a day might come, but some of us will survive Bosnia and fight in new battles, so mark my words.'

Some of my comrades were already *takfiris*: to them secular Arab leaders were apostates who needed to be excommunicated. I had not reached that point – not by a long way – but the perspective was clearly gaining ground.*

For now our hands were full enough fighting the Serbs, but some of what he had said stayed with me. There was something about being in Bosnia that made Qutb's writing take on new meaning.

In the spring of 1995, after the snows melted we decamped to a new base a dozen kilometres south of Zavidovići which was nearer the front lines. In the shadow of a mountain ridge near a village called Kamenica, the Mujahideen Brigade set up camp in a

---

* *Takfiris* believe Muslims who do not subscribe to their extreme interpretation of Islam are apostates and potentially worthy of death.

clearing alongside a fast-flowing stream. The jihadis called it *Masada* (the Lion's Den) after Osama bin Laden's famous forward-operating base in Jaji, Afghanistan, close to Soviet positions in the 1980s. At any one time 500 Bosnian and foreign mujahideen were stationed there. In an irony typical of Bosnia, our white all-weather tents had been 'borrowed' from United Nations supplies. Such was its contempt for the UN, the Brigade had painted out the logos.

I had the sense that a big engagement was imminent. We were being trained on mortars and grenade launchers, and one night a feast was laid on. Slaughtered lambs were thrown in pits and covered in charcoal. Then we were told to gather around the camp-fire. Pointing to a large map, our commanders announced we would be joining a Bosnian army offensive to drive back Serb forces north-east of Zenica and open the road to Tuzla. There was real optimism among the mujahideen. With Muslim and Croat factions no longer at loggerheads, the tide of war was turning against the Serbs.

The offensive had the backing of Bosnian President Alija Izetbegović, whose commanders saw the jihadis as shock troops ready to run towards the bullets. I hoped our tactics would be somewhat more sophisticated but like my comrades eagerly antici-pated the opportunity to worship God through jihad.

On the first day, skirmishes quickly escalated into exchanges of mortar fire. My fear was tempered by real exhilaration, adrena-lin pumping as I ran from trench to trench carrying orders. I could see the flashes of enemy mortars firing at us some 400 metres away and quickly learned to gauge the distance of an incoming impact.

We lost two men that day; it was a rapid education in battlefield survival. But all my fears and doubts evaporated as I fired the opening salvo of my jihad. The privations no longer mattered. The lack of sleep and wearing full combat gear even when we did sleep, being soaked through by torrential rain, the diet of cold tuna: all were sacrifices to be embraced.

My love of maps made me a natural choice to be part of the

reconnaissance unit, probing enemy positions. But my short-sightedness meant I couldn't go close to enemy lines – which was perhaps just as well, because some reconnaissance teams would get within ten metres of enemy positions on what seemed like suicide missions.

I found my calling operating mortars. Day after day we would fire 82mm or 120mm shells towards Serb positions which our spotters had located behind forested hills a mile or two away. That most of the mortars we used were Yugoslav or Russian added a sense of poetic justice. One after another, we loaded the heavy shells into the firing tubes before crouching with our palms clasped to our ears. The sound was unforgettable – a deafening detonation more felt than heard as the mortar roared towards the unseen enemy. After each muffled impact in the distance, I felt a sense of satisfaction at the possibility that a few more among the butchers and rapists of our fellow Muslims had been liquidated.

To this day, I have no idea how many of the enemy I may have killed through mortar fire. But our indirect fire – at times intense – must have taken a toll on the Bosnian Serbs.[*]

Through the summer of 1995, the Bosnian Serbs resorted to ever more atrocious massacres as their military position weakened. The nadir was reached in July when they murdered more than 7,000 Muslim men and boys after overrunning what was risibly described as the safe enclave of Srebrenica. It was one of the worst crimes against humanity of the twentieth century. Shocked into a response, NATO finally carried out air strikes on Serb positions around Sarajevo, which we viewed as far too little far too late.

---

[*] Between May and September 1995, the Mujahideen Brigade fought three major battles alongside Bosnian army forces as part of this strategic plan. The operations were codenamed 'Black Lion', 'Dignity' and 'Badr' and involved a mixture of artillery strikes and suicidal uphill offensives to storm Serbian bunkers. I fired mortars in the first two battles. Later accounts described the Mujahideen Brigade directing 'devastating pinpoint artillery strikes on the heart of Serb defences'.[19]

We wanted revenge; there was a visceral impatience at the Masada camp. In August we were told that we would soon advance on Serb positions in the Ozren Mountains. I was given a crash course in battlefield first aid. We were short on medics and the fighting was expected to be intense. Far from being disappointed, I welcomed the assignment. I would be in the middle of the action rather than behind the front lines. After midnight on 10 September we set off, moving stealthily towards the Serb bunkers dug into a steep wooded hill. We were just one element of an offensive to liberate the strategic village of Vozuća.*

Our battalion advanced up the hill just after dawn. An intense barrage of fire from the Serbs in their bunkers above created a killing zone. Within minutes, dozens of our fighters were cut down. Again and again I crawled up the hill to tend to the injured and dying, dragging their mangled bodies away. I must have made thirty trips. Those whose lives could be saved were loaded onto a Bosnian military helicopter. But too often a comrade who was alive and whimpering at the top of the hill was silent and inert before we reached the bottom.

At one point a Yemeni fighter beckoned to me for help. He was writhing on the ground in agony, having been shot several times in the lower abdomen. Parts of his intestines were hanging out. I very nearly vomited.

'Quieten down or you'll draw Serb fire towards us,' I whispered to him.

I injected him with a shot of morphine, but he carried on screaming.

'Are you a drug user?' I asked him. In my paramedic training I had been told that this could reduce the effect of the morphine.

'No, brother. But I chew qat,' he gasped, referring to the narcotic popular in Yemen.

I administered two more shots of morphine. That stopped the screaming. I reached through the blood with my hands and pushed

---

* The battle would later become known as the Battle of Vozuća and was known as 'al-Badr al-Bosna' among the mujahideen.[20]

his intestines back into his stomach and tied my scarf tight around the wound. As bullets and mortars exploded around us, we managed to get him onto a stretcher.

Eventually our forces broke through Serb lines. As I looked for fighters who might be wounded but still alive, I heard someone wailing for help in Arabic from inside one of the abandoned Serb bunkers. As I went to investigate, I felt something catch and wrap around my legs.

'Stop! Stop!' yelled the fighters behind me.

My legs were entangled in wire. I had dragged up no fewer than four landmines. Things seemed to move in slow motion: I saw the Arab fighters throwing themselves to the ground, bracing for the explosion.

I stood motionless, expecting to be cut down by a sniper's bullet at any second but knowing that one step in any direction would bring the certainty of death.

One of the fighters crawled towards me very slowly. I held my breath. He began to pick away at the wires curling around my legs. His fingers moved carefully but with extraordinary calmness. As he disentangled me, he spoke softly.

'God be praised. For one of these not to explode I would call you lucky. Two would be extremely fortunate; three a miracle. And four, well, God must be watching over you,' he said.

'Maybe God doesn't want me,' I told him.

As I clambered back down the hill, I was jolted from shock to disappointment. After a year in Bosnia, I was still very much alive. I had been sure this would be my bridge to paradise, a place the Prophet had described as beyond imagination. Of the five medics assigned that day, only two of us had survived. My brothers in arms were now in paradise but I had been left behind. I could not hold back the tears. I felt like a loser among winners. I made a silent prayer asking God to reunite me with my friends soon and vowed to embrace jihad as never before. Maybe God would then find me worthy.

There was too much work that afternoon saving the lives of others to allow me to dwell on mine. A British Pakistani fighter named Babar Ahmad* was stumbling through the woods holding his bloodied skull. He had been hit with shrapnel. He leaned against me and we staggered down the hill.

The battle was over; my day was not. I had to attend a make-shift hospital and morgue in an underground car park in Zavidovići to help identify the fallen and collect their wills, final letters and personal effects. It was a grotesque scene. I slipped on sticky streaks of blood that lay fresh on the floor. In the morgue there were rows of corpses on the floor covered with blankets. I saw the bloodied bodies of forty-four of our fighters, many of them friends. The student from Riyadh with whom I had travelled to Bosnia was among them. So were Hazam and Marwan, the young Palestinians from Milan, who had also been working as paramedics that day. The wounds of many of the dead were horrific, but I was struck by the serene expressions on their faces. Truly they were in paradise.

When I got to the last corpse, I thought I had begun hallucinat-ing. A soft whimpering came from under the blanket. It was the Yemeni whose intestines had been blown out. The doctors had declared him dead; they had been spectacularly wrong. He had regained consciousness and was still clinging to life. I arranged for his rapid evacuation to hospital. He would recover and fight on several other jihadi battlegrounds, including against US troops in Iraq. In a 2005 interview with *Rolling Stone* magazine, he recounted how a Bahraini medic had saved his life twice in one day in Bosnia.[21]

I met Khalid al-Hajj that night. He had been fighting on a different section of the front with Anwar Shaaban and told me excitedly how the people of Maglaj had cheered the arriving muja-hideen after they broke the Serb siege of the town. Across a broad front line, 2,000 Bosnian soldiers and our 500-strong Arab contin-gent had decisively pushed back a force of some 4,000 Serbs.

---

* In the following years, Babar Ahmad would pioneer placing jihadi content on the Internet. After 9/11, he famously fought and lost an eight-year battle against extradition to the United States, where he was convicted of terror offences. He returned to the UK in 2015 after a US judge decided he should serve only a short additional period of time in prison.

'How was the day for you?' he asked.

'Tomorrow' was all I could muster. I was too exhausted to talk.

It was in Bosnia that I first saw – just days after my seventeenth birthday – how quickly war and religious hatred can demean mankind. The collapse in Serb lines had resulted in our battalion taking some 250 Serb prisoners. Most were Chetniks, members of Serb militia who had terrorized Bosnian Muslims through a systematic campaign of rape and killings.

Many were brought to the Masada camp in the week that followed the battle and held in abandoned buildings. There were disagreements in the junior ranks about what to do with them. For one faction, inflicting torture was just retribution, especially after Srebrenica. The suffering of prisoners was to be relished. Others said that summary execution with a bullet to the back of the head was enough, citing the Prophet's dictum that if you kill you should be merciful about it. Yet another group said prisoners should be handed to the Bosnians as we were on their territory.

I believed we should use the Serbs as bargaining chips to win the release of prisoners, but not out of any sympathy for them. In the preceding months I had seen too many mass graves outside Muslim villages, some holding the skeletons of infants, to countenance any mercy towards the Chetniks. To me at that time they looked subhuman, grotesque and filthy. I was haunted by their wild, staring eyes.

When I suggested to Khalid that we could bargain our prisoners in exchange for Muslim civilians, he cut me off with a disbelieving stare.

'We need to dispatch them all to hell,' he said. Many of the Bosnian fighters, whose families had suffered so acutely at the hands of the Serbs, felt the same. Word spread that Shaaban had made a decision.*

---

* After the victory, Shaaban was among the commanders greeted by Bosnian president Alija Izetbegović. The moment was filmed and later featured in a jihadi video posted online. While the international community was putting pressure on the Bosnians to rein in jihadi fighters, the Bosnians saw them as useful.

'There will be a killing party soon,' one of our commanders said in a menacing tone.*

I was asked to participate in what happened next but could not bring myself to do so. As the first prisoners were brought in front of us in a clearing alongside the camp and crudely beheaded, I approached a young Saudi fighter from the town of Taif that I had befriended.

'Abu Dujana,' I said, 'do you think if the Prophet was here he would agree with this form of execution?' I asked him.

'He beheaded people in Medina,' he said.

'But Islamic law dictated executions should be done with a swift strike to the back of the neck. Call it a merciful dispatch. Not like this. We are becoming like them.'

He shrugged and turned away amid the primal screams of the victims.

Some of the condemned men were wearing jeans and casual clothing rather than military uniforms. One of our commanders said they were Chetnik spies and collaborators. But looking back now, it is possible some were civilians.

Khalid wanted to see them all tortured and beheaded. And that's what happened. During the course of several days, our brigade put to death more than one hundred prisoners.** They were paraded, told to admit to crimes and executed in batches, while several of our fighters recorded the scene with camcorders.[23] There was nothing surgical about the executions: axes, knives and even chainsaws were used. Some prisoners were crudely beheaded, their heads kicked across the dust. Many looked terrified as they were

---

* I later learned Shabaan's rationale was that a large number of Serbs could pose a strategic danger if they were let go.
** I was told the dead were buried in mass graves a few miles from the camp. In 2015, at a press conference held with a Serb association working for the families of war victims, Zoran Blagojević, a local Serbian politician, said: 'Twenty years ago a horrific crime was committed in Vozuća that a human mind cannot grasp – ritual murders including beheadings committed by the Mujahideen.' He said that more than 400 Serb soldiers were killed during Battle for Vozuća and the days that followed and more than 130 were still missing.[22]

forced to witness the killings. Others were defiant to the last, saying they would rape Muslim women again if given the chance. One was foolish enough to claim he was a magician and could not be killed. His head was placed on a concrete block, and another block was dropped on it.

Several dozen had been executed by the time it was Khalid's turn. His eyes had a glazed, demented expression that I found deeply disturbing. He dragged a prisoner onto the bloodied earth, forced him to the ground and, crouching over him, began sawing at his neck with a serrated hunting knife.

Khalid had always viewed the world in a binary way. If he was going to fight the enemies of Islam, he was not going to be inhibited about it. In his view the Prophet had prescribed such forms of execution; there was no debate. After decapitating the man, Khalid kicked away his head in contempt. I turned around and left.

For hours I sat unsettled in my tent as the muffled screams resounded across the valley. Even if they couldn't be traded and our leaders believed they had to be executed, I was sickened by the spectacle I had just witnessed. It was perhaps the first step of jihad's descent into altogether darker territory.

The massacre of Serb fighters after the Battle of Vozuća was later featured in trials at the International Criminal Tribunal in The Hague, where Bosnian commanders asserted they had no control over the Mujahideen Brigade.* Of the 250 Serbs taken prisoner by the brigade, I am aware of only twenty being spared.** Weeks later, I felt my views vindicated when we exchanged them for some 200 civilians.

* The International Tribunal documented the killing at the camp near Kamenica of around 50 Serb soldiers who had been taken prisoner after the Battle of Vozuća. According to court documents, most of them were killed by the Mujahideen Brigade at the camp between 11 and 17 September 1995.[24]
** My understanding at the time was that more than 100 of the 251 prisoners condemned to death were killed at the camp near Kamenica, a higher number than so far documented by the UN. I do not know what happened to the others, but it is possible they were executed elsewhere.

We travelled to Sarajevo for the prisoner swap. I was tasked with helping to escort the prisoners and was appalled by the scenes of devastation as our convoy descended from the hills above the airport, speeding past the pockmarked apartment towers of the Dobrinja district where so many civilians had been cut down by mortars and sniper fire. Even though the Serbs had abandoned most of their positions around the city after NATO's belated intervention from the air, row upon row of headstones in the city's beautiful public parks spoke of their deadly legacy.

The exchange took place on a bridge over the River Bosna in the Otoka district. We were well armed just in case the Serb contingent at the other end of the bridge tried their luck. Once the Spanish UN peacekeepers on the bridge gave us the signal, we released the prisoners.

I will never forget the scene that followed. Scores of women and children, gaunt and pale, began to stream towards us from the other side. They were like ghosts leaving a concentration camp. Their clothes were tattered and many were shivering with cold. Tellingly, there were no boys over the age of ten. By now a growing number of Sarajevo residents, including refugees from other parts of the country, had gathered nearby, desperate to be reunited with relatives. Tears of joy turned to anger and despair as they found out how many of their family and friends had been killed.

I noticed an elegant, elderly lady anxiously looking on. Finally, she moved towards a beautiful young girl who could not have been more than thirteen years old. Perhaps she was her granddaughter. She looked malnourished. The sadness and weariness in her eyes will always haunt me. What unspeakable crimes had been committed against the girl and her other family members? Where were her parents, her siblings?

As the two hugged and wept, I couldn't hold back tears. The pain these people had suffered was beyond endurance.

What I saw that day on the bridge over the River Bosna provoked a conflict inside me which would resurface time and again in years to come. It made me so angry that I wanted to fight those responsible for such horrors until my dying breath. But at the same time it also made me so distressed that I felt I would never want to fight again.

There was a sense among the mujahideen late in 1995 – as talk of a truce gained momentum – that Bosnia was the beginning of a larger struggle. It seemed to many of us that the West had come to save the Serbs from further territorial losses. The Americans and the Europeans appeared wary of Muslims asserting themselves in Europe. The odd alliance between Washington and the Afghan mujahideen as part of a bigger struggle against Soviet expansionism was long gone. Now we – the agents of resurgent, fundamentalist Islam – were the enemy.

Among my fellow jihadis in Bosnia were three Moroccan Canadians. They were ordinary young men; two had worked at a gas station. I asked them what had inspired them to travel all the way from Montreal to this mountainous corner of Europe. Besides defending Bosnian Muslims, came the answer, being in the Balkans put them closer to the inevitable conquest of Rome by Muslim armies near the end-of-days, as had been prophesied in several *hadith*.[25] Over the next two decades I would frequently be struck by just how powerful the prophecies of the Koran and *hadith* would prove in dictating the behaviour of both men and movements.

Someone else who believed in the coming showdown between Islam and the Christian West was our Smurf-hating instructor from Khobar, who came to Bosnia after completing his Shariah studies.

Al-Ayeri revealed to me he had spent time with bin Laden in Afghanistan and Sudan in the early 1990s, and had even travelled on a mission to Somalia to scout out its potential for jihad.*

* Al-Ayeri told me that, in Sudan, bin Laden had kept in touch with jihadis on other fronts including Afghanistan, Chechnya and Bosnia through radio transmissions using coded references. A biography later posted on an al-Qaeda website stated al-Ayeri became a bodyguard to bin Laden before travelling with him to Sudan. He never mentioned his role as a bodyguard to me. He

'There was much I could not tell you at the Islamic Awareness Circle. I was more operational during those years than I led people to believe.'

Influential jihadis such as Khalid Sheikh Mohammed, who would just a few years later mastermind the 9/11 attacks, were encouraging the belief that a war of civilizations was inevitable.

'KSM' had arrived in Bosnia after being involved with his nephew Ramzi Yousef (three years his junior) in a conspiracy known as the Bojinka plot to blow up a dozen US airliners over the Pacific. He had slipped out of the Philippines before he could be arrested. He was a freelance terrorist, associated with but not yet belonging to al-Qaeda.*

I met him at a wedding for one of the Arab fighters in Zenica. He was neatly dressed, with a trimmed beard, the very opposite of the figure who would be captured in Pakistan eight years later, dishevelled and overweight. He immediately warmed to me because he had lived in Bahrain for a time; we soon discovered that one of his mentors was married to a cousin of mine. KSM made no mention of his recently aborted plans in Manila, but had plenty to say about the future.

---

told me he travelled to Somalia to assess the potential for jihad there but did not fight there.[26]

* The Bojinka plot unravelled in January 1995 when Yusuf's bomb-making operation was discovered in the Philippines. KSM had previously spent time fighting in Bosnia in 1992 according to the 9/11 Commission Report. He did not tell me about this earlier trip when I met him. Born into a family from the Baluchistan region in Pakistan near Iran, KSM had grown up in Kuwait, attended university in the US and participated in the Afghan jihad against the Soviets. Between 1992 and late 1995 he held a government job in Qatar while moonlighting as an international terrorist. His animus towards the United States stemmed from his anger over US support for Israel. His earliest contribution to international terrorism was contributing funds for his nephew Ramzi Yousef's attack against the World Trade Center in New York in 1993. When I met him in 1995, KSM was travelling to various countries from his base in Qatar on behalf of the jihadi cause. No mention of his autumn 1995 trip to Bosnia is made in the 9/11 Commission Report.[27]

'Bosnia is a sideshow,' he said with more than a whiff of condescension. 'America is the true enemy. The Arabs here should move to Afghanistan. There's a camp called Khalden in Khost province, where a new force is being built.'*

'So why did you come here?' I asked somewhat impertinently.

'To find the brightest and the best among jihadis. You know the end is in sight here, but what will happen after the war?' he asked me as the wedding party got into full swing. 'The question is: are we going to roam the globe from one hopeless battle to another trying to save Muslims, and then see someone else come in and reap the reward?' Soon he had a table of six hanging on his every shrewd word, including Khalid al-Hajj and Yusuf al-Ayeri.** 'How long do we have to go from one front line to the next defending minorities at the edges of the Islamic world, only for secular governments to take over, to allow alcohol, nightclubs? Why do we expend the blood of the best and brightest on fringe conflicts for which we get no credit? Not a single brothel will be closed.'

To end this cycle, he said, we had to resurrect the spirit of jihad within the Muslim world.

His little speech was among the earliest signs that jihad was morphing from an instrument to defend Muslims to one aimed at bringing down America and its allies. At the time, I listened respectfully but somewhat sceptically. KSM insisted America would

* When I first met him in Afghanistan in 1996, Osama bin Laden also said he viewed jihadi efforts in Bosnia as a 'sideshow'. Bin Laden felt that the primary role of jihad was not to protect Muslim lives but to protect their souls. If at the end of jihad no Islamic State could be created then precious resources would be wasted.

** Also listening were Mohammed al-Madani, the Saudi jihadi who had teased me about my uniform size, and Abu Zubayr al-Hayali, a senior Saudi figure in the Bosnian jihad I would later be reunited with in London. The Bosnian jihad was an incubator of the global jihadi movement. Around 900 foreign jihadi fighters fought there in the course of the war. Around 300 died, while 600 went home or moved on to other fronts. The atrocities of Christian Serbs against Bosnian Muslims, and the perception of Western indifference, increased hostility against the United States and the West.[28]

impose its 'New World Order'[29] on Islam, a homogenized offering of Disney, fast food, malls and secular government. We had managed to get visas to come here, he claimed, because the Americans wanted us to come to Bosnia to get killed. There was nothing less than a global war being waged against Islam to suppress our religion. How much the US would come to wish that this operational genius had been among the Arab contingent to find martyrdom in Bosnia.

Before we parted, he gave me contact details for a man called Abu Zubaydah in Peshawar, Pakistan, an independent operator close to al-Qaeda's leadership who was the metaphorical gate-keeper of the Khalden camp. KSM's recruitment drive was not wasted: the first four leaders of the Saudi branch of al-Qaeda would all be Bosnia veterans, as would many other influential figures within the group.*

The radicalization of those who remained in Bosnia may well have been hardened by the ambush that killed our leader, Anwar Shaaban, one of his deputies, Abu al-Harith al-Libi, and close associates just outside the town of Žepče. They were on the way to a meeting in Zavidovići on the very day the Dayton Accords which had been brokered in Ohio were signed in Paris – 14 December 1995.[30]

I was in the Zenica headquarters at the time. Someone ran into the dormitory shouting an order: everyone into full combat gear and to the mosque downstairs. As soon as we were assembled, the military commander of the group, an Algerian called Abu Ayyoub al-Maghrabi, told us the brigade would raze Žepče in revenge for the ambush, which was allegedly carried out by Croatian

---

* In Sarajevo, shortly after the prisoner handover, I met Qasim al-Raymi, who later become the leader of al-Qaeda's affiliate in Yemen, as well as Naser al-Ansi, another future senior figure in the group. Al-Raymi told me he had spent time in Afghanistan, where he met bin Laden and had fought against the forces of South Yemen in the 1994 war. Other graduates of the Bosnian jihad were Ramzi Binalshibh, the link between Bosnia veteran KSM and the 9/11 hijackers, the 9/11 hijackers Khalid al-Mihdhar and Nawaf al-Hazmi, and the Finsbury Park cleric Abu Hamza al-Masri.

troops.* We were busy preparing anti-aircraft weapons and other gear when a Bosnian general arrived to tell us that Dayton had finally been signed, and all foreign fighters must disband. The news was met with disbelief.

'The assassination of our leaders and this wretched treaty are no coincidence,' shouted a fighter next to me. 'Someone somewhere planned this! We will not allow this betrayal of our martyrs. We will fight the Americans if they land here. And we will start by burning Žepče to the ground.'

The Bosnian general stood his ground: 'If you go through there, you will have to go through your Bosnian brothers. We have two divisions in the area.'

To my relief, our Algerian commander did an immediate volte-face, announcing that this was the last day of the brigade, which would now disband and hand over its weapons. There were howls of protest, acute anger against the United States and other powers that had brokered Dayton. But I had no appetite for witnessing another massacre.**

I was already thinking of my next step. I felt uneasy about hanging around waiting to be demobilized. We had too many enemies. With a few friends from Saudi, including Khalid al-Hajj, I left Zenica. Our reflex was correct; most of the remainder were evacuated to the Croatian capital Zagreb, where they were photographed and fingerprinted, marked as jihadis. Only twenty or so slipped away unrecorded.

---

\* Croat forces denied Shaaban was deliberately targeted. It is possible he was killed because of his role in orchestrating a suicide bombing against Croatian police two months previously.[31]

** Years later, after I started working for British intelligence, I learned from the Saudi jihadi Abu Zubayr al-Hayali that Shaaban had begun planning a campaign of attacks against a NATO-led implementation force which was expected to be deployed once the Dayton Accords were signed. Shaaban and other jihadis felt these forces were being sent by the West to weaken the mujahideen and stop Bosnia from becoming a safe haven for the Gama al-Islamiya.[32]

I called my brother Omar from Split. His delight at hearing my voice and knowing I was still alive was tempered by anxiety.

'We want to see you as soon as possible but things have changed here.'

'How so?' I asked.

'There's a different attitude. Jihadis are looked on with some suspicion. You might be detained if you come back.'

A month earlier, a suicide bomb attack against a US-operated National Guard Training Center in Riyadh had killed five Americans and injured more.[33] The Saudi royal family was beginning to realize that it could neither contain nor direct the fury of jihad, a fury it had encouraged and exported.

But where should I go next? Even after fourteen months in Bosnia I did not feel the lure of home comforts; indeed, the very notion of 'home' seemed alien. The thought of college courses, listening to some ageing, blinkered teacher droning on about how Saudi Arabia had won its independence was beyond depressing. I would be like a falcon being returned to its cage. I knew others felt the same way, unable to contemplate 'settling down'. Some had families they wanted to return to and jobs to reclaim, but those of us who had spent a year or more in Bosnia had lost our moorings. Many were regarded as stateless outlaws.

I for one was blasé about the prospect. I was a citizen of the world now – before my eighteenth birthday.

KSM's arguments had also made an impact on me. I didn't regard my time in Bosnia as wasted. I had come to defend Muslims who would otherwise have been slaughtered and I had been inspired by fraternity with hundreds of others who had turned Qutb's words into action. But because of the betrayal at Dayton I had begun to see that Bosnia was merely an episode in a much larger struggle that pitted the defence of our faith against power-ful enemies.

The Prophet had foretold that the Vanguard of jihad would 'hurry from one front to another, never harmed by betrayals, until God's commands descend'.[34] There had to be a larger purpose, I felt, than our being the fire brigade of jihadism. KSM had a point in stressing that we had to build a truly Islamic way of life, rather than expend our effort in a place where Muslims slowly drowned amid a tide of corrupting Western influences.

As Qutb had written: 'It would be naive to assume that a call [to Islam] is raised to free the whole of humankind throughout the earth, and it is confined to preaching and exposition. [ . . . ] When . . . obstacles and practical difficulties are put in its way, it has no recourse but to remove them by force so that when it is addressed to people's hearts and minds they are free to accept it or reject it with an open mind.'[35]

After the 'betrayal' at Dayton I, too, started to believe in a wider plot by powerful forces to stifle Islam and target Muslims around the world. At my core nothing angered me more than the oppression of my religion. I needed to be part of the Vanguard fighting back on behalf of vulnerable Muslims.

And I was after all just seventeen. Anger and indignation were as much part of me as ideology. I was horrified by the suffering of Muslim populations around the world. As the Bosnian war wound down, we turned our attention to the Caucasus, where Muslims were suffering at the hands of an indiscriminate Russian military campaign aimed at snuffing out the region's aspirations for independence. Among young jihadis, the videos emerging from Chechnya were a hideous confirmation of the brutality Russia had inflicted on Afghanistan.

From their mountain camps, in what to me was another clear-cut example of defensive jihad, some Muslims were fighting back.

If I could only reach Chechnya, surely the martyrdom I had been denied in Bosnia would be close at hand.

# MY SECOND LIFE: JALALABAD AND THE JUNGLE

## 1996–1997

The quickest way to the Caucasus, it seemed, was through the former Soviet republic of Azerbaijan, now an oil-rich dictatorship. I wanted to go with Khalid, who seemed to have recovered some equilibrium after his descent into psychosis in Bosnia, but his best efforts to get a visa came to nought. By contrast, I quickly found part-time work with a Saudi charity, the Haramain Foundation. And so, early in 1996, I arrived alone in the windswept Azeri capital, Baku, on the shores of the Caspian Sea.

I had what can only be described as a memorable welcome to Azerbaijan. There were three taxis waiting when I finally exited the dingy arrivals terminal in the early hours of the morning. Three heavily mustachioed cab drivers with bulging waistlines sprang out to secure the fare. Two of them started wrestling for my bag. Fisticuffs followed and soon they were on the ground mauling each other.

The third driver saw his chance and bundled me and my luggage into his taxi.

Unfortunately, this was not the end of the drama. We had barely driven ten minutes when a taxi pulled up alongside us at a stop light. The evident winner of the heavyweight wrestling bout at the airport sprang out and marched towards us. He did not look happy. Within moments another fight was underway.

Unsure how long it would be before a winner was declared, I hailed a passing car.

'Can you take me into town?' I asked in a mixture of Arabic and sign language, brandishing the Azeri currency I had collected at the airport. The unshaven, bleary-eyed driver motioned me to the back seat. My relief was short-lived; the stench of cheap alcohol infused the car. After swerving through the streets of Baku, he screeched to a halt and looked at me unsteadily.

'Hotel' was the only word.

The Haramain Foundation had an office and three staff in Baku, in a pleasant if somewhat shabby villa with a garden. It was more than a charity.* Its staff – a Tunisian dentistry student called Fathi and two Palestinian students from Lebanon – had a direct link to the leadership of the Chechen resistance and were organizing supply convoys through Dagestan to a commander called Ibn al-Khattab.** The Azeri authorities seemed well aware that the Baku branch of Haramain was doing more than caring for refugees, but a senior intelligence officer and a prominent politician were also on the payroll, to the tune of $70,000 a month. We were not harassed.

The snows of the Caucasus Mountains made travel to Chechnya impossible for several months, but the staff needed my help in the office – to cook the books. I spent my first few days there inventing the names of volunteers so we could get more funding. There were plenty of other book-keeping tricks, and they worked well until we heard that someone was coming from Haramain head office to check on the operation. We had claimed to be looking after 11,000 refugees; in fact it was closer to 5,000. So once the delegation had visited one camp, we moved thousands of bewildered refugees to another to 'make up the numbers'.***

* I had been put in touch with the Baku branch by a Saudi go-between, Abdullah al-Wabil. He was a family friend and had fought with the Arab fighters in Afghanistan. By 1997 he was one of the biggest fundraisers for Khattab.
** Khattab, the Saudi jihadi leader with whom my brother Moheddin had flown to Afghanistan a decade earlier, was the only Arab of any note fighting in the Caucasus at that time.
*** Because of its failure to monitor what its regional offices were doing in various places around the world, the Haramain Foundation was later designated for terrorism ties by the US government.[1]

We also made the most of Baku's reputation as the windy city by pulling down tents and making children cry, then videoing the fabricated calamity and sending it to Haramain's headquarters with a plea for more money for shelters. A pliable local doctor falsified certificates for various fictional procedures, with invoices attached. We were raking in six figures every month, enough to pay off our Azeri patrons and buy supplies for the Chechen resistance.

As soon as the snows began to melt, a truck made the trek twice a week through Dagestan to Chechnya laden with food and medical supplies. Among the inventory were bags of American rice and stacks of mayonnaise. Al-Khattab insisted it was the perfect fuel, when mixed with rice, to power jihad against the Russians.

There were very few Arab mujahideen making their way to Chechnya at this stage; al-Khattab said he preferred local fighters. But he made exceptions for those with useful skills, and once the winter eased we managed to smuggle in two Saudis who knew how to handle anti-aircraft guns. I was disappointed not to join them, but hoped I would be allowed to follow in their footsteps.

As the weather turned more spring-like we had an unannounced visitor. He was Egyptian and clean-shaven but for a pencil-thin moustache, with beady eyes that peered through thick-rimmed spectacles. His name was Ayman al-Zawahiri and he was then leader of Egyptian Islamic Jihad, a terror group seeking to topple the Mubarak regime in Egypt.*

After a failed attempt to assassinate President Mubarak in Ethiopia the previous year, Zawahiri's group had been ejected from their perch in the Sudanese capital, Khartoum, where they had found shelter alongside Osama bin Laden.** To have gone home

---

* Zawahiri was a doctor from a well-heeled Egyptian family who became involved in jihad in Egypt in the 1970s. After being imprisoned for three years and tortured by the Mubarak regime after the assassination of President Anwar Sadat in 1981, Zawahiri joined the anti-Soviet jihad in Afghanistan where he befriended bin Laden. In Peshawar he built up the operations of Egyptian Islamic Jihad before decamping to Sudan in the early 1990s.

** Zawahiri's group was expelled after Sudanese authorities learned that two boys accused of a plot to kill him were executed by the group on his orders.[2]

would have invited immediate arrest and probably a death sentence. Zawahiri and his lieutenants had been on the run ever since (hence the loss of the beard), looking for a place to pitch their tents.

'Dr Ayman', as we called him, was not an easy guest, constantly carping about our lack of security (he was unaware of our arrangement with local officials), given to pomposity and insisting, despite the Russian checkpoints, that he must get to Chechnya immediately.* I found it difficult to believe Zawahiri led an organization with such credentials as EIJ, not least when he let loose his high-pitched laugh. He also had a curious dress sense, wearing a high-buttoned grey tunic and matching trousers that made him look like a member of the Egyptian Communist Party or Dr Evil in the Austin Powers films.

It was difficult to know whether he had travelling companions; we never saw any. He took a room at the villa and nagged us daily. At his insistence, we sent a message to al-Khattab, who asked us to try to dissuade him. If that didn't work, he said, Zawahiri could only come if the driver (a trusted aide) was willing to carry him.

The driver was Mohammed Omar, who had good relations with some of the police in Dagestan, no doubt oiled by some hard cash. The problem was the mobile checkpoints set up by the Russians, particularly for a prominent Arab jihadi travelling on a Sudanese passport without a visa. There was also the growing presence of Russian regular forces in the republic. To try to deter him, we provided Zawahiri with a greatly inflated estimate of the troop presence.

None of it worked. Omar eventually relented and the Egyptian VIP clambered into his truck for the long and difficult journey into Dagestan and across the mountains. We chuckled at the thought of him wedged between cartons of mayonnaise.

---

* At this point in the Chechen conflict, the Russians were not monitoring traffic entering the Caucasus from former Soviet republics as intensively as they later would.[3]

Three days later Omar returned with a batch of fresh orders from al-Khattab.

'Oh,' he added casually. 'The Egyptian – he was arrested.'

Zawahiri had barely made it into Dagestan before being detained at a mobile checkpoint twenty miles from Derbent. We let him stew for a while to teach him a lesson, but we eventually asked Omar to open negotiations with the local police to secure his release. After thirteen days he was a free man thanks to $10,000 that we raised, most of which probably did not make its way to the Justice Ministry. Such a sum demanded some imaginative accounting. Had I not been able to scrape the money together, the man who would become bin Laden's deputy and then his successor as leader of al-Qaeda might have had a very different career path.

Zawahiri appears to have been persistent; when he returned to Baku he set up shop in the office of a charity linked to his group. Months later, he tried to get into Chechnya again, this time with two other veterans of Egyptian Islamic Jihad.[4] All were travelling as businessmen on false passports – but not very convincingly. This time Zawahiri and his associates were transferred to the custody of the Russian Federal Security Service (FSB) and spent several months in detention in the Dagestani capital, Makhachkala, before being freed for 'time served'.

'God blinded them to our identities,' Zawahiri poetically wrote later.[5]

Zawahiri's tenacity appears to have stemmed from his belief at the time that the Caucasus could become the foundation of an Islamic state, a belief encouraged by the ceasefire in 1996 that included a partial withdrawal of Russian troops from the region. From there, jihad could spread throughout Central Asia.[6] But his second abortive journey would be the last instalment of Zawahiri's obsession with Chechnya.[7] Shortly thereafter he abandoned efforts to establish his own brand of jihad and headed for Afghanistan to deepen his fateful alliance with bin Laden.

Like Khalid Sheikh Mohammed, who had decamped to Afghanistan a few months after I had met him in Bosnia,[8] and

Osama bin Laden, who arrived there in the late spring of 1996, Zawahiri saw Afghanistan as jihad's safe haven.

I shared the Egyptian doctor's frustration. After the sense of purpose and exhilaration that I had in Bosnia, months of book-keeping and tedious administration in Baku had left me stale and impatient. There were no heavenly rewards for good accountancy. And, as a callow teenager, I had misunderstood the Chechen struggle. It was more a nationalist uprising than a front for jihad. There were a few foreigners there, including a Jordanian cleric who had reportedly won over a destitute village with a free feast every week. But the Chechen separatists were wary of funds and recruits from Arab countries; their presence would help Moscow paint the rebellion as Islamist extremism.

I began to despair of ever getting to Chechnya.*

'What can I do?' I asked Fathi on a breezy afternoon as we weeded the villa's neglected flower beds.

'Afghanistan,' he replied simply.

KSM had said the same. Afghanistan would become the base for a much larger project. No longer would jihad nibble at the edges of conflicts in remote mountains. It would become the guiding light towards the eventual establishment of a new Islamic order, a place of purity that Qutb would recognize.

'KSM said I should go to Khalden,' I said. Khalden was the main camp near the city of Khost.

'No,' said Fathi, drawing out the word in warning. 'Darunta.'

I had never heard of the place.

'Near Jalalabad. The brothers there are more intelligent and educated.'

He gave me a number to call in Pakistan.

The city of Peshawar is capital of the then aptly named North-West Frontier Province in Pakistan. Like Casablanca in the Second World

---

* In August 1996, Chechen rebels would launch a successful offensive to retake the capital Grozny. So successful was the offensive and so profound the demoralization of Russian forces that at the end of the month a ceasefire was agreed under which Russian troops would leave Chechnya. By then I was gone.

War, it was full of spies, smugglers, refugees and schemers. Its crowded streets reverberated to the screeching of two-stroke mopeds and the monotonous calls of street traders. The ordered suburbia of Khobar, the wooded mountainsides of Bosnia, the howling winds of Baku – none prepared me for the teeming chaos of Peshawar.

Peshawar had become a gateway for jihadis seeking to enter Afghanistan in the 1980s, and Islamist militants had brought a new dimension to the city. Despite my efforts to blend in, dressed in the flowing *salwar kameez*, I felt as if I was wearing a sign that read 'visiting jihadi'.

Fathi's contact number belonged to a guest house used by the Hezb-e-Islami, a fearsome militia led by Afghan warlord Gulbuddin Hekmatyar which operated several training camps for Arab fighters in Darunta. Hekmatyar was a legendary figure whose fighters had been lavishly funded by Pakistan's military intelligence – the formidable ISI – during the Soviet occupation. Most of the money had come from the CIA but was distributed by the Pakistanis. Hekmatyar had provided support to Arab foreign fighters like Osama bin Laden in the belief they would reinforce his power base. For Hekmatyar it was all about power.*

The talk in Peshawar in the spring of 1996 was all about a fundamentalist movement in Afghanistan led by a mysterious cleric called Mullah Omar. The Taliban had emerged from the madrassas of Afghanistan and Pakistan in the early 1990s before seizing most of southern Afghanistan. They now had their eyes on taking the capital, Kabul.

The rise of the Taliban had divided Arab opinion in Peshawar. At the Hezb-e-Islami guest house I met a fair-haired Iraqi Kurd sympathetic to the Taliban cause. His name was Abu Said al-Kurdi.

* After the defeat of the Communists in the early 1990s, Hekmatyar was a major player in the fighting between Afghan political factions, and had laid siege to Kabul. Osama bin Laden had tried to intervene but had been rebuffed by Hekmatyar. Dispirited, he abandoned the country for Sudan.[9]

'Just be careful,' he told me one evening. 'Hekmatyar wants us to fight against the Taliban.'

'I have no intention of picking sides. I just want to get the best training I can,' I said. I wanted the specialist skills that would guarantee a place on the front lines of jihad, not in its back office.

He looked at me intently, his dark green eyes trying to work me out.

'I want you to meet somebody,' he said.

He led me across town to a villa with high walls. Once we entered the courtyard a tall metal gate clanged shut behind us.

An unsmiling man came towards us; he wore round spectacles that magnified small, sharp eyes and had a neatly groomed beard. He might have passed for a university professor, but he was one of the most influential figures in the world of jihad. His name was Abu Zubaydah.* Abu Said al-Kurdi, it turned out, was his deputy.

Abu Zubaydah was an 'operator'; he managed travel flows between Peshawar and the camps, including the Khalden camp KSM had recommended. He also helped Kashmiri militant groups, which afforded him some protection from the ISI. Abu Zubaydah would soon become the bank manager and quartermaster for al-Qaeda without formally joining the group. The arrangement suited al-Qaeda, which felt that having its own office in Peshawar would invite trouble.

Worried about spies sent by Arab regimes, Abu Zubaydah made it his business to know about every would-be jihadi arriving in town. He was intrigued by the arrival of a seventeen-year-old 'veteran' of the Bosnian war. Over the course of an uncomfortable hour he grilled me about my upbringing in Saudi Arabia, fighting in Bosnia and my intentions in Afghanistan.

---

* Abu Zubaydah would gain notoriety when he was captured after 9/11. The CIA 'waterboarded' him eighty-three times, before he was transferred to the detention centre at Guantánamo Bay.[10]

'I want to give myself to jihad,' I told him. It was the unvarnished truth. On the threshold of adulthood, I was demanding to be taken seriously. 'I know mortars, I've been in battle. I've carried the bodies of martyrs. I am ready,' I said.

'But why Darunta? Why not Khalden?' he replied.

'I was told it was the best.'

For a few moments, Abu Zubaydah's default severity slipped from his face. There was a hint of empathy, even.

'Then I can hardly stop you,' he said with a grimace.

My escort into Afghanistan was Mohammed Hanif, an Afghan doctor working with Hezb-e-Islami. He was amiable enough, though the swaying of the bus sent him to sleep. Even when the bus lurched through the hairpin bends of the Khyber Pass like some demented fair ride, Hanif was undisturbed.

At the border we had to get off and walk into Afghanistan through the Torkham Gate crossing. There was nothing resembling passport control; I was told identity papers were seldom checked on either side. The colonial 'Durand Line' that had in 1893 arbitrarily divided Afghanistan from the part of British India that became Pakistan had little relevance to the Pashtuns on either side of the border.

It was an almost medieval scene. The potholed road was crowded with vehicles piled with basic goods heading into Afghanistan and porters buckled by years of back-breaking work. In a few hundred yards, I felt I had stepped back a few hundred years. No more the teeming bazaars on the Pakistani side, the pickup trucks and intricately painted lorries kicking up trails of dust as they ferried goods along the crowded roads. Instead, a vista of donkeys and carts, and people whose dress was made of the same dull, rough fabric as that of their ancestors. On the side of the road, an old bus sat abandoned, falling apart. I was told to wait next to it. Hours later, I was surprised to see the bus splutter into life, expelling thick grey-blue smoke. Dozens of people clambered on board; Dr Hanif and I squeezed among them.

I was shocked by the absence of vehicles on the road or almost any form of life beyond it as we made our way to Jalalabad, the capital of Nangarhar province and the largest city in eastern Afghanistan. Jalalabad clung to a few vestiges of a better past – such as the grounds of a once-royal residence. But its chief characteristics were grinding poverty and the damage caused by a decade of war – sprinkled with a few villas built on the proceeds of heroin trafficking. Compared to Mostar and Sarajevo, it was a dun-coloured medieval heap. Dr Hanif proved to be a handy companion because I came down with a bout of diarrhoea after my very first meal in Jalalabad. The locals, I discovered too late, included an obscene amount of animal fat in all their cooking, though the dirty water may also have been the culprit.

It was a relief to leave Jalalabad and head to the clean breezes of Darunta. No more than a collection of mud-brick dwellings perched on the hillside, it did enjoy a breathtaking setting – with the majestic White Mountains straddling the border with Pakistan in the distance. Beneath, a man-made lake stretched northwestwards, looking like a well-fed silver serpent. Darunta was the site of one of Afghanistan's most important hydro-electric dams, built by the Soviets in the 1960s.

Darunta was drawing a growing stream of jihadis from across the world. Its remoteness made it seem beyond the reach of most adversaries. There were already four camps there. Two of them were by the placid lake, run by Algerians loyal to Hekmatyar. Another camp belonged to Jamaat-e-Islami, an Islamist Pakistani political movement.

An Egyptian who went by the name Abu Khabab al-Masri was just setting up another camp.* It would soon become one of al-Qaeda's most important resources – a place for training in making explosives and for experiments with chemicals and toxins. At that time, Western intelligence knew nothing of its existence or purpose beyond satellite images that showed 'someone' had decided to occupy a hillside a few hundred metres from a former Soviet compound.

My initial destination was a Hekmatyar-affiliated camp. When I arrived I was taken aback to see a familiar face.

---

* He would later be killed in a 2008 airstrike in South Waziristan.

'Farouq,' I shouted.

He ran towards me and we embraced.

Farouq al-Kuwaiti was from a Bedouin tribe that inhabited barren scrub and salt marshes between the Iraqi port of Basra and Kuwait, an area that had seen more than its fair share of combat and oppression in recent decades. He had dark features and his muscular frame was accentuated by his modest height. He had joined the Mujahideen Brigade in Bosnia months after me, and although he was eight years my elder he had taken a mischievous pleasure in obeying 'orders' from his teenage companion. He was a good listener; I was the incessant talker.

Within a few weeks Abu Said al-Kurdi also turned up, bringing a dozen Arab fighters with him from the Khalden camp. While he was suspicious of Hekmatyar, he acknowledged al-Qaeda needed his firepower. We got on well, the Kurd, the Bedouin and the Bahraini. It was an adventure, a time of camaraderie and shared purpose. But my connections to them would have deep and utterly unexpected consequences.

It was in Darunta that I became imbued with the routines and rhythms of being a jihadi, routines that stressed religious preparation and knowledge as much as physical fitness and expertise with a weapon. If Bosnia had been the school of jihad, Afghanistan was its university. As part of my matriculation, I decided to take on a new *kunya* (jihadi alias), Abu al-Abbas al-Bahraini. Changing names was common practice in order to confuse security services.

Every day would begin with the call to the *Fajr* when what seemed like millions of stars pricked the sky's impenetrable blackness. The mountain air was astonishingly clear and invariably bitter. As we prayed the darkness gave way first to indigo and then orange, and we welcomed the gradual warming of the sun as it finally climbed clear of the mountain peaks.

There was a feeling of unity at the camp; we were brought together by a potent combination of devotion and purpose, an immutable belief in the duty of jihad. But the Afghan camps were not just about contemplation. We were preparing for action. And that frequently meant that *Fajr* would be followed by a long mountain run. To some of the fit young men in the camp, like Farouq, this was a pleasure. To me, never the athletic type, it was torture – especially before breakfast. I would arrive back at the camp gasping for breath and bent double, slumping down at our long communal table, much to Farouq's amusement. It was hardly a meal to anticipate: cracked wheat and sugar, and if we were lucky an egg and some mashed potato, accompanied by hot, sweet green tea.

Then came the part of the day I most enjoyed: the classes, often led by Egyptian veterans, on handling and maintaining weapons and battlefield tactics. The *Zuhr* prayers were followed by a basic lunch, of which lentils were invariably the main ingredient, and then religious studies were led by one of the more educated camp members. Many were illiterate and had only a basic – if tenacious – grasp of Islamic history and the Koran.

The average day had little in the way of recreation. We usually had just one hour in which to relax, and would play board games like Snakes and Ladders or draughts, innocent pastimes in those pre-ISIS days. Occasionally, a Mars bar bought in nearby Jalalabad would be divided among four or five of us, every last morsel savoured. To my delight there was one tradesman who always seemed to have Coca-Cola in stock. I'd bring bottles back to the camp and cool them in the lake. I needed my sugar fix.* As I walked around the camp I was invariably followed by a stray cat I had named 'Hindh'. Much to the mirth of the other jihadis, I had adopted her (or perhaps it was the other way round) soon after arriving at Darunta. I had always had a soft spot for cats. At night it often curled up next to me.

The late afternoon might involve shooting practice if there was enough ammunition available. A tin can would be placed on a hillside some 200 yards away and there were serious bragging rights for whoever was the first to send it dancing off the rock.

---

* When in subsequent years I attended al-Qaeda camps, I found out that bin Laden had banned all American snacks and drinks. Once, when I was caught drinking a Pepsi, I was forced to clean the primitive toilet facilities as a punishment.

Between the classes and physical training were the afternoon *Asr* prayers, and at sunset the *Maghreb*. And, finally, the last act of the day was the *Isha* night prayer.

There was little variety to the routine but its rhythm was reward in itself. There was never any danger of being bored and sleep came quickly every night – even on a thin mattress in the draughty dormitory.

There were many moments of levity. Once when it was my turn to organize the guard roster I found I was short of names because those training on mountain warfare claimed to be too tired. Farouq al-Kuwaiti suggested I enlist one of our Snakes and Ladders regulars, a young Saudi with an infectious sense of humour called Abu Abdullah al-Maki, who had just come down from the hills.

'You know perfectly well I don't negotiate with terrorists,' I replied, trying to keep a straight face.

Living like family, our friendships deepened. We felt privileged despite our spartan surroundings. We were chosen, the Vanguard of jihad. We were preparing for the march on Jerusalem, metaphori-cally if not literally. It might take generations, but of its inevitability we had no doubt.

In those early weeks we received courses on a variety of weap-ons and explosives. We learned counter-surveillance and counter-interrogation techniques and how to deceive Pakistani border guards. One ploy was to pretend to be attending a madrassa, one of the religious seminaries that had sprung up in both Pakistan and Afghanistan. We were taught how to detect spies, to watch out for people who asked a lot of questions or seemed insufficiently committed to prayer. We were also taught how to interrogate pris-oners. One technique involved forcing prisoners to drink copious amounts of water, tying their hands behind their back and then placing adhesive tape around their urethra to prevent them from urinating.

'It doesn't leave a mark and it certainly makes them talk!' an Algerian instructor told us.

Another course focused on hostage-taking and was led by an American of Moroccan descent from the Boston area, who went by the name Salahadin.* One of his fingers had been reattached after an explosion, but not very expertly. He ran through the various ways to take control of hostages, recommending that women and children should be separated from the men to create tension.

Immediately, images of the Muslim women and children freed from Serb captivity on the bridge over the River Bosna flashed before me.

'I'm sorry; this is not for me,' I said abruptly, getting up and leaving the room.

'What do you expect from someone who adopts cats?' a Kuwaiti jihadi quipped.

Later Salahadin came up to me.

'You'll obviously not be assigned to take hostages because you'll end up releasing them immediately and giving them taxi money,' he said with a smirk. He spoke Arabic with an American twang, which made me smile. 'Don't worry; there will be some other role for you.'

And there would be.

One afternoon there was a buzz at the camp that Abu Khabab, the Egyptian bomb-maker, had wandered over to pay a visit.

A distinguished looking man of upright bearing with chiselled features and a thick greying beard dyed with flecks of henna was standing in the exercise yard, talking to a fellow Egyptian, Abu Abdullah al-Muhajir, our camp's religious teacher. Al-Muhajir had left his PhD studies in Pakistan after being implicated in planning a suicide bombing against the Egyptian embassy in Islamabad, and would later become the head of al-Qaeda's Shariah college, its ideological motor.

Never wracked by shyness, I approached them.

---

* This was his *kunya* (fighting name). I never found out his real name. I heard that after the Taliban captured Kabul, he moved with Hekmatyar to Iran.

'Forgive me,' I said to Abu Khabab. 'Are you the one they describe as the master bomb-maker?'

His eyes creased with a grin and he threw his head back as he chuckled.

'All I do is mix salads, young man,' he exclaimed.

He noticed the crestfallen look on my face.

'That's because we're still equipping the camp,' he added with a wink.

Born in the Mediterranean port of Alexandria, Abu Khabab had studied chemistry at university before becoming a lieutenant in the Egyptian army's bomb-disposal. He was one of the early wave of Arab fighters to come to Afghanistan in 1986.[11] He had walked with a limp since more than a hundred shrapnel fragments lodged in his leg from a mortar round in the 1989 battle of Jalalabad.*

Now, in his mid-forties, he was emerging as the dean of bomb-makers in the Afghan camps.

Abu Khabab had not formally pledged loyalty to bin Laden, insisting on his independence, but he worked closely with al-Qaeda. He was kept financially afloat by a small group of fundraisers, including two jihadis who lived in the United Kingdom and who had spent time in his camp.** One of his earliest students (though in Pakistan, not at Darunta) had been a young Pakistani called Ramzi Yousef. Yousef had tried to blow up the World Trade Center in New York in February 1993, later telling the FBI he had wanted to build a device capable of toppling one tower onto the other.[12] The

* On his arrival in Afghanistan, Abu Khabab (real name: Midhat Mursi al-Sayid Umar) had teamed up with Abu Burhan al-Suri, a former colonel in Syrian intelligence specializing in sabotage. Their complementary skills provided al-Qaeda and other jihadi groups with a variety of increasingly powerful explosive devices.
** One was Abu Hamza al-Masri, the hook-handed Egyptian cleric at Finsbury Park, who is now serving a life sentence in the Supermax facility in Florence, Colorado (more on him later). Another I will call 'Abu Hudhaifa al-Britani', a British Pakistani who grew up in Birmingham. A third source of funds was the American Jordanian jihadi Khalil al-Deek. I first met Abu Hudhaifa and al-Deek in 1996 while they were attending Abu Khabab's camp. More on them later, as well.

blast created a 100-foot crater in the underground parking garage and killed six people, but the building stayed upright. (Eight years later, his uncle, Khalid Sheikh Mohammed, would accomplish what Yousef could not.)

Abu Khabab had a first-hand account of the plot because Yousef had, incredibly, managed to escape New York within hours of the explosion and fly to Pakistan. It would be months before he was caught and extradited back to the US.

'The trouble with Ramzi,' Abu Khabab would later tell me, 'was that he made two basic errors in preparing the device.'[13] He walked me through how the blunders had reduced the force of the blast. Abu Khabab never tired of teaching. Those two mistakes may have changed the course of history.

My arrival in Afghanistan coincided with that of someone rather better known: Osama bin Laden. He flew into Jalalabad on a chartered jet from Sudan, where he'd become persona non grata thanks to Saudi* (and probably Egyptian and American) pressure.[15]

There was excitement in the camps when news spread that bin Laden had arrived. The Saudi millionaire was a revered figure; he had placed his fortune in the service of jihad. He had founded al-Qaeda in 1988 as an autonomous Arab brigade to attack Soviet forces in Afghanistan and had invested in safe houses and camps to train arriving volunteers. After Soviet forces withdrew in 1989, bin Laden returned to Saudi Arabia and sought to internationalize his efforts, continuing to support training camps in Afghanistan but turning much of his attention to overthrowing Communist rule in southern Yemen.[16]

---

* Although bin Laden refrained from ordering a campaign of terrorism inside Saudi Arabia until after 9/11, his relationship with its rulers had broken down by the time he left Sudan. Saudi Arabia revoked bin Laden's citizenship and he accused the Saudis of waging 'a war against Islam' after they jailed clerics opposing the presence of US troops such as Safar al-Hawali.[14]

By some accounts, the arrival of US troops in Saudi Arabia after the Iraqi invasion of Kuwait was a pivotal moment for him. He had offered (rather implausibly) to protect the Saudi royal family from Saddam Hussein by deploying al-Qaeda fighters but was rebuffed. He had then spent a year back in Pakistan and Afghanistan but had grown increasingly frustrated by the infighting among Afghan warlords. With the Pakistani government making life increasingly difficult for Arab fighters, he had relocated the core of al-Qaeda to Sudan, which at the time was controlled by an Islamist-leaning government at loggerheads with Egypt.[17]

Bin Laden's hostility towards the United States had only grown in Khartoum. He had railed against the presence of US troops in Saudi Arabia and viewed the arrival of US peacekeepers in Somalia as a plot to dominate the region. Reluctant to spill Muslim blood in the Arab world, he had begun to see the merits of attacking the United States, not only as a unifying cause for jihadis, but also as way to delegitimize the House of Saud which he assumed would have to rally to America's defence. He had sent men such as Yusuf al-Ayeri to foment a jihad against US forces in Somalia* and dispatched operatives to Nairobi to case the US embassy.[19]

Bin Laden had been joined in Khartoum by Ayman al-Zawahiri before his ill-fated trips to the Caucasus. Zawahiri's experienced Egyptian fighters strengthened the Saudis' hand, while bin Laden's money helped the EIJ organize attacks against the Mubarak government.**

When he arrived in Jalalabad, bin Laden was housed in a compound belonging to Younes Khalis, a warlord in his late seventies and a veteran of the anti-Soviet jihad who was now seen as above the fray. Bin Laden knew little about the Taliban at that stage; negotiating al-Qaeda's place within the complex rivalries of different Afghan factions would occupy his early days in Jalalabad.

---

* It later emerged that al-Qaeda had a hand in the downing of a US helicopter in Somalia, an episode made famous by the film *Black Hawk Down*.[18]
** Bin Laden and Zawahiri had built up relations through Osama bin Laden's closest aides, the Egyptians Abu Ubaidah al-Banshiri and Abu Hafs al-Masri.[20]

Soon after he arrived, we received word that the Sheikh would like to meet with fighters from the Gulf States. After getting permission from our camp's leadership, a dozen of us crammed into a Toyota pickup truck and made our way into the valley. All the talk was about the recent bombing in my hometown of Khobar which had killed nineteen US airmen.\* There were rumours bin Laden was responsible.

Bin Laden had taken over a very basic dwelling of mud brick. I was immediately struck by his height (he was about 6 feet 4 inches), which probably contributed to his air of calm authority. The al-Qaeda members we met clearly revered him. There were several Egyptians in the room with him, including the group's chief operating officer, Abu Hafs al-Masri.\*\*

After embracing every one of us, he bade us sit in a semicircle around him on the carpeted floor. He asked each of us in turn to tell him about ourselves. Speaking *sotto voce*, his tone somehow added to his understated authority.

'Please forgive us for the chaos. We had to leave Sudan in a hurry and we are still trying to work out where we will be staying,' he said. Bin Laden had lost a sizeable part of his fortune in Sudan, where he had invested heavily in agriculture projects.

I asked him if he intended to choose between the Taliban and the Afghan warlords.

'By staying here with Younes Khalis I've made it clear that I have no intention of picking a side,' he replied.

Farouq al-Kuwaiti was sitting next to me.

'Sheikh, are you going to open up camps again here?' he asked.

'We are looking into it. A big campaign of jihad lies ahead of us. And Khurasan [Afghanistan] is where we must build up our strength,' he replied. 'What is your plan?' Farouq pressed.

---

\* A remotely detonated truck bomb exploded outside the American military base in Khobar on 25 June 1996, killing nineteen US Air Force personnel.[21]
\*\* They also included Mustafa Abu Yazid, al-Qaeda's chief commander in Afghanistan after 9/11, and Abu Khayr al-Masri, who rose to become al-Qaeda's number two and was killed in a US air strike in Syria in 2017.

A ripple of laughter could be heard from the Egyptians.

'If you want to know what we are planning then join us and we will tell you,' Abu Hafs said dismissively.

Bin Laden smiled. I remember what he said next, word for word.

'My brothers, while we are sitting here the land of the two holy mosques and the lands of Arabia are being desecrated by the presence of the Crusader Americans and their Jewish masters, at the invitation of the unworthy rulers of Arabia. The Jewish presence in Jerusalem means we have to liberate Jerusalem, just as the Crusader presence in the land of the two holy mosques makes it necessary that jihad liberates our lands.'

As he paused there was utter silence.

'It is not Jamaat al-Qaeda's wish to spill Muslim blood in Arabia or fight against our brothers in the security services, but if they stand in our way we will not have any choice. If we don't wage this campaign now to drive out the Crusaders, who will? We will be cursed by the next generations. They are stealing our oil wealth and are extorting the royal family for protection money. They are supporting Israel against the Palestinians. They are bombing Iraq and starving hundreds of thousands to death through sanctions. Look at Bosnia. They betrayed the Muslims and rewarded the Serbs with half the country. It is our duty to drive them out of Arabia.'

Afghanistan had been foretold by a *hadith* as the future crucible of the struggle. Bin Laden raised his index finger as he recited:

> '*Armies hoisting the black banners shall march from Khurasan; no power will be able to stop them until they finally reach Jerusalem and hoist their banners above it.*'[22]

'My dear brothers, this blessed land of Khurasan, irrigated by the blood of thousands of martyrs, will be the launching pad for the armies of the black banners.'

Khurasan was the ancient Islamic name for Afghanistan and

its use by bin Laden did not go unnoticed. Al-Qaeda would be the vanguard of those armies – delivering salvation for Islam in its hour of need.*

His words tapped into a deep vein of hostility towards the United States among the Saudi contingent sitting around him and many more pious Sunnis in the kingdom. They disapproved of the influence of US oil companies and of the oil-for-security understanding between the House of Saud and successive US administrations. This arrangement, of course, had culminated in the arrival of US forces after the invasion of Kuwait.

'It sounds like you will end up fighting the royal family,' one of our group said. For many jihadis, including myself, this was still unthinkable.

'This is not our intention. But jihad to liberate our lands must start somehow,' bin Laden replied.

'Like the Khobar bombings?' Farouq asked.

Bin Laden smiled.

'As Abu Hafs said, if you join us we will tell you. As for what happened in Khobar, that was an honour we missed.'**

With that, his Egyptian 'minders' signalled it was time for bin Laden to leave. He insisted we should stay to eat at the compound, where we were served a meal of lamb and daal, a rare treat.

As we drove back to Darunta at dusk, the last rays of the sun retreating from the mountainsides, I reflected on what bin Laden had said. Al-Qaeda was clearly here to stay and formulating ambitious plans. But I for one was not ready to contemplate war in my own homeland. His speech had left me with more questions than answers.

---

* The fact that the Prophet Mohammed even mentions Khurasan as part of the Muslim world is seen by many Muslims as a prophecy in itself. When Mohammed was telling his followers all these prophecies about Khurasan and its importance, it was then an impossibly distant place, 2,000 miles away.
** There was much speculation in the years after the Khobar attack that al-Qaeda may have had a role, but in 2006 a US court found that Iran, through a Saudi militant group affiliated with Hezbollah, had carried out the attack.[23]

On 23 August 1996, bin Laden took his message to the world – issuing a communiqué demanding that jihad be initiated against the 'Israelis and Americans' to expel the 'polytheists from the Arabian Peninsula'.[24]

'By the Grace of God, there became available a safe base in Khurasan, high in the peaks of the Hindu Kush ... And today, in the same peaks of Afghanistan, we work to do away with the injustice that has befallen our *Ummah* (global Muslim community) at the hands of the Judeo-Christian alliance, especially after its occupation of Jerusalem and its appropriation of Saudi Arabia,' the statement read.

Again he had used the word Khurasan. Al-Qaeda's adoption of the black banners of Khurasan – more than 1,200 years after they had been hoisted on the eve of the Abbasid rebellion against the Umayyad dynasty – was highly symbolic. Al-Qaeda was following in the footsteps of the early Muslim generations. The Muslim profession of faith superimposed on a black banner was appearing in the camps in Afghanistan. It would soon become the banner of disparate jihadi groups; a version of the flag was later adopted by the Islamic State in Iraq and Syria, better known as ISIS.

Implicit in such branding was a bold claim. According to various *hadith*,[25] the black banners in Khurasan would not only see the Mahdi – 'the guided one', a messianic figure – emerge from within their ranks, but pave the way for his rule on earth close to the end-of-days.

The Islamic prophecies foretell that the Mahdi will be recognized by the Muslim community as their political and military leader, free the Muslim world from tyranny, create a just and victorious new order and set the stage for the return of Jesus Christ.\*

Al-Qaeda (and later ISIS) would see themselves as instruments of God laying the ground for the return of the Mahdi. It was an intoxicating message.

---

\* Belief in the eventual arrival of a Mahdi is very common among Sunni Muslims, but some Sunni Muslim scholars reject the notion, arguing the Prophet Mohammed himself was the Mahdi.

During my time in Darunta I made several trips into the mountains of eastern Afghanistan, relishing the thickly forested slopes and crystal-clear streams. But this was a challenging place. I suffered severe stomach cramps from the obscene globules of fat which laced every bowl of tired grey stew. Then followed my first bout of malaria; I was also stung by one of the ubiquitous yellow and black scorpions that had made a home inside my *salwar kameez*.* I concluded that our commitment was being tested by God.

We occasionally went west to Sarobi dam, not only a beautiful man-made lake with a breathtaking view of surrounding mountains but also a vast natural fortress that was the headquarters of our patron, Gulbuddin Hekmatyar. There we were able to train on Russian-made T-55 and T-62 tanks and missile launchers that had been captured from the Communists.

On one occasion, Hekmatyar came to speak to the assembled fighters. His wispy beard, black turban and spectacles made him look more like a theologian than one of the country's most brutal warlords. He was mild-mannered and soft-spoken, with excellent Arabic.

He told us about a dream in which he was holding two swords.

'With one sword I was fighting the Russians, but with the other I was fighting the Americans,' he declared. This was not a man wracked by self-doubt.

Maybe he thought it was what we wanted to hear, but there was rich irony in the remark, given that his war machine (Stinger missiles included) had been largely sustained by the US taxpayer.[26]

He spoke of his battles with other Afghan factions. (It was sometimes said about Hekmatyar that he spent more time fighting other Afghans than he did the Russians.)

'Only I can bring Shariah rule to Afghanistan,' he claimed, in an effort to outflank the growing influence of the Taliban. His own brutal commanders were hardly symbols of Islamic virtue but

---

* The *salwar kameez* consists of a long flowing tunic and baggy trousers. It is worn by many in south Asia.

Hekmatyar continued to enjoy the patronage of some Arab governments and benefactors.

Hekmatyar told us he had asked God in prayer who to ally himself with out of the many Islamist factions. There was the Taliban, of course, and there was a respected warlord called Ahmed Shah Masoud, who had prevented the Russians from conquering his stronghold in northern Afghanistan. His soul and conscience, Hekmatyar claimed, had told him to side with Masoud and with President Burhanuddin Rabbani. It was a fragile alliance riddled with intrigue. Perhaps he was tempted by the possibility of becoming Afghan prime minister.

It turned out to be the wrong decision. The Taliban were at that time preparing for a second offensive against Kabul and were attracting increasing support from the Pakistani security services at Hekmatyar's expense.[27] What was not yet clear was how the Taliban regarded the hundreds of Arab fighters who had now come to Afghanistan. Hekmatyar's men insisted the Taliban would detain us and send us across the border. From there, the Pakistani authorities would send us all to Saudi Arabia, where we would rot in prison.

We would soon find out.

One morning in early September, Hanif, the snoozing doctor, arrived at Darunta with news from the border. He told us that Taliban fighters had seized the Torkham crossing – presumably with Pakistani help – and were racing towards Jalalabad in pickup trucks. On 11 September, we heard explosions in the distance as the Taliban attacked and took the city. It was time to move on. Hekmatyar's forces blew up one of their own T-62 tanks to prevent the Taliban capturing it. Dozens of Arab fighters, myself included, joined them in a hurried retreat to Sarobi, east of Kabul. But there was no escaping the Taliban's rapid advance. We retreated from one outpost to the next, but their remorseless progress continued.

By the end of September the remnants among the Darunta Arabs were holed up on the outskirts of Kabul, a city in chaos. Ministries were burning files, looting had begun and warlords were preparing to flee. I saw Ahmed Shah Masoud leave by helicopter.

His eyes were bloodshot and he looked bedraggled – hardly the 'Lion of the Panjshir' as he'd become known. I also saw Hekmatyar again, making a hurried departure from the prime minister's office in a fleet of land cruisers; his 'dream' had become a nightmare.*

Many Arabs fled to Mazar-e Sharif in the north-west of Afghanistan or even across the border into the unruly Pakistani province of Baluchistan. But about forty of us, including my friends Farouq al-Kuwaiti and Abu Abdullah al-Maki, decided to stay and took refuge in what remained of the famous Balla Hisar castle, which was already littered with the wreckage of armour. An ancient fortress on a ridge overlooking Kabul, some of its walls were twelve feet thick. For a last stand there were worse choices. The sound of explosions and heavy gunfire grew louder and we braced ourselves for an onslaught.

At sunset on an already freezing October evening, just before the *Maghreb* prayer, we heard shouting outside. One of the Taliban called in Arabic for us to open the gate.

'There's nothing to be afraid of,' he called. 'You are our brothers.'

He came through the gate unarmed and repeated the message.

'Just come outside. You are our guests.'

One of the Arab fighters replied that we had been warned the Taliban would deport us to Pakistan.

The Talib laughed.

'Whoever told you that was lying.'

Farouq, who had always questioned Hekmatyar's demonization of the Taliban, argued we should give ourselves up and trust to providence. He had got to know some of the Taliban fighters when at the Khalden camp, an area controlled by the Taliban.

As soon as we stepped through the gate we were met by a dozen Taliban brandishing AK-47s. We nervously laid our own

* Hekmatyar fled to Iran after being ousted from power by the Taliban. Always unpredictable, he occasionally offered support to the Taliban and al-Qaeda in the years that followed but signed a peace deal with the Afghan government in 2016, paving the way for his return to Afghanistan.

weapons on the ground – at which point they came forward, picked them up and immediately handed them back to us with welcoming smiles.[28]

They assured us that the Darunta camps were protected and guarded with all our effects in safekeeping, but for now we were their guests and would stay that night at the Intercontinental Hotel, a Kabul landmark. It had seen better days – there was no electricity – but at least it still had a roof and running water, and some candles to make sure we didn't walk into walls or fall down stairs.

'I guess we're not martyrs in paradise,' al-Maki quipped when we were woken up the following morning.

The Taliban arranged transport back to our camps and gave us money and food. They were clearly allying themselves with international jihad, with al-Qaeda and bin Laden.

When the handful of us arrived at Darunta, the camps were virtually deserted. It was like a school without teachers; all the commanders had gone. For a week we tried to busy ourselves amid the treeless slopes and abandoned camps. I began giving lessons about the Koran, which became quite popular – but admittedly there were few alternative pastimes.

In time, once the Taliban's tolerance for foreign fighters was established, people began drifting back to the camps. One man taking advantage of the Taliban takeover, despite having pledged not to pick sides, was Osama bin Laden, who showered Mullah Omar with deference, supplied his retinue with expensive cars, and bought off rival commanders.[29]

Under Taliban protection, and with fresh funds trickling in from sympathizers in the Gulf, bin Laden began to build al-Qaeda up in Afghanistan, reviving and expanding his old network of safe houses and training camps. But I was wanted on a mission to the jungle.

By late 1996, al-Qaeda was settling into its place in the Taliban's Islamic Emirate of Afghanistan, methodically expanding its camps.

The Taliban had pacified much of the country, but were still antici-pating fierce battles against Ahmed Shah Masoud in the Panjshir and in western Afghanistan. I was frustrated that Muslims were continuing to shed each other's blood rather than focus their fire on aggressors bent on crippling Islam.

On a winter's morning, when the earth was as frozen as rock and my feet were numb despite an extra pair of woollen socks, I came across an unusually gloomy Farouq.

'The thought of another two months of this, maybe three,' he said shuddering. The scorching marshes around Basra were no preparation for the Hindu Kush in the depths of winter. The novelty of snowball fights – and digging latrines – had long worn off.

Farouq had recently been in Pakistan, where he'd met a few members of the Moro Islamic Liberation Front (MILF) from the Philippines. Filipino Muslims had long been part of jihad in Afghanistan but now the MILF (an acronym that would generate much mirth at academic conferences) wanted support on the home front. They were battling the Philippines military with the optimis-tic aim of establishing an Islamic State on the island of Mindanao, the second largest of the Philippines archipelago.

Farouq had been moved by the Filipinos' plight, and the thought of a tropical climate combined with the lack of action at Darunta inspired him to help. In those days there was no formal process or paperwork – people moved in and out of the camps as free agents.

'We could use your help, too,' he said, stamping his feet.

'Really?' I had begun to feel irrelevant at Darunta.

'Good Muslims in Kuwait have raised a lot of money for the Moro, but we have to get it there. I was screened and stamped when I left Bosnia; I'm a known quantity. You slipped out; you're clean.'

A new front of jihad beckoned. I relished the chance to be back on the front lines. I might finally attain the martyrdom that had been denied me in Bosnia, and if not, Afghanistan would still be here in a few months.

'I'll do it,' I said. The entire conversation had lasted five minutes.

I booked my flight to stop over in Kuwait, where I could pick up the money. I had also been invited to a reunion dinner of veterans of the Bosnia campaign.

The tepid warmth of the Gulf winter was a welcome relief from the dry bitterness of the Hindu Kush. The futuristic orbs of the Kuwait Tower and the tasteless extravagancies of Kuwait City were less appealing to my ascetic soul.

When I arrived at the dinner, I was stunned and delighted to see a grinning Khalid al-Hajj among the guests.

'You see, I'm still a free man,' he said, hugging me tightly. There were tears in his eyes. Perhaps my family's anxieties about a crackdown in Saudi Arabia had been overdone.

His year back home had done him good. The light was shining again in his eyes. As the group recalled the highs and lows of the Bosnian campaign, he took me aside.

'I think so often about that night you came to see me, when you found out I was going to Bosnia,' he said.

'You said something that stayed with me. I asked whether jihad really needed a kid like you. And you shot back that it was you who needed jihad. You looked so determined, grown-up all of a sudden. No longer the precocious kid whose hand shot up on quiz nights.

'Now it's my turn. I've been drifting here, unable to find the right path. So I'm coming with you to the Philippines.'

I couldn't help myself. I put on an expression of mock solemnity as I recalled that fateful discussion about Bosnia.

'You know Khalid, war is not a picnic . . .'

Before I left I was handed a small leather case with the money bundled together in $100 bills. I was told it had been raised from wealthy local families.* There was $150,000 in a variety of curren-

---

* Then, as now, fundraisers for jihad in Kuwait went house to house to visit the *diwaniyyah* of wealthy Kuwaitis, an annex to large residences where

cies. I had been selected as the courier, I was told, because 'you're young and you have a harmless face.' It was a compliment of sorts.

Seats 23D and E on the Kuwaiti Airways flight to Manila were an island among a sea of chattering Filipino maids on their way home for brief vacations from their jobs working for wealthy Kuwaitis.

'I'm glad the guys at Darunta can't see this,' I told Khalid, my head buried in my hands at the prospect of the next ten hours.

About an hour into the flight, a burly Kuwaiti in jeans and a black leather jacket approached and asked us to get up.

'Where are you from?' he asked. Before we had a chance to answer, he asked us to come with him and strode towards the front of the 747, making no effort to hide the fact he carried a pistol.

*Are we being arrested? Did someone tip off the authorities?* I wondered.

We entered a virtually empty Business Class.

'Relax,' the air marshal said. 'I just hated to see fellow Gulf Arabs surrounded by all those noisy women. Make yourselves comfortable.'*

We looked at each other in disbelief.

'So what's your story?' he asked, as we settled into the plush seats. 'Two young men off to Manila . . .'

'We're going for *dawa*,' (Islamic preaching) I said.

He raised his eyebrows.

'Come on, guys.'

There was an awkward pause.

'Don't worry, I'm not going to turn you in. My cousin was a martyr in Bosnia.'

---

extended family, neighbours and clients are welcomed. The *diwaniyyah* is essential to any fundraising venture in Kuwait. It allows women to be involved; because they cannot fight jihad themselves they are often more generous than their husbands. In more recent years large sums have been raised in this way for jihadi groups in Syria.

* All Kuwaiti Airways flights had air marshals after a hijacking in the 1980s.

It turned out we had both met him. The air marshal was moved almost to tears by our recollections of his cousin in battle and said he had been immensely proud of him.[30] Kuwaitis were very sympathetic to the Bosnian Muslim cause. Even a captain in the Emir's personal guard had gone to Bosnia to provide sniper training.

Our prestige was now such that we were invited to sit in First Class, and were taken to the flight deck to meet the captain. Nowadays we would both have been on Interpol's Red Notice and US no-fly lists.

For Khalid our upgrade had been a religious experience.

'Don't you see? This is God blessing our journey. When you are a mujahid God will make people serve you,' he told me.

Amid the cacophony of the arrivals hall in Manila, I found a bathroom and split up the cash, hiding it in pouches and pockets. I didn't need to; the customs and immigration procedures were cursory and we soon emerged into the dripping heat. A slight and dapper man approached us.

'I am Abdul Nassir Nooh,' he said. 'I am going to look after you until you go to Mindanao. I'm going to take you somewhere quiet. The ladies here think Arab men are a ticket to instant wealth,' he grinned.

I was shocked. I might have travelled a lot, but I was still an innocent in many ways. For most jihadis, even discussing the opposite sex was a taboo, let alone contemplating anything more intimate.

After a couple of days in a safe house, we were back at the airport for the flight to Cotabato on the island of Mindanao, 500 miles south of Manila. Again, the lack of scrutiny of two Arabs flying into an area of Muslim rebellion would be unthinkable today, as would be the reception we received on arrival.

Waiting for us without a hint of disguise was a senior member of the Moro Islamic Liberation Front – a short, well-dressed Filipino.

'Welcome to Mindanao,' he said, sounding more like a tour

guide than a jihadi. We were stunned by his immaculate, Egyptian-accented Arabic.

'My name is Ahmed Doli* and I know what you're going to ask,' he said as we climbed into his open jeep. He was apparently oblivious to the soldiers on guard at the airport, one of whom – in a surreal moment – offered a polite salute. 'I spent eighteen years in Egypt, got a doctorate at al-Azhar, then I taught in Saudi Arabia. So, yes, I speak Arabic. But now it's the home front.'

It was a journey of many parts. After driving for an hour or so in Doli's jeep, we transferred to motorbikes and rode pillion at breathtaking speeds along the coastal road. Then our little convoy turned onto tracks through the suffocating jungle. When the terrain became too steep for the bikes, we had to trek for hours on foot in the sweltering humidity upwards into the mountains. I frequently lagged behind; physical fitness was not my forte. I began to regret stuffing Arabian coffee, dates and Yemeni honey into my backpack. Khalid, by contrast, had a spring in his step all the way up the mountainside. Deep down he was a romantic and jihad was his life's romance.

The journey through the rainforest seemed to go on forever but the terrain was unforgettable. Dense jungle, every shade of green imaginable, gave way to glimpses of volcanoes; immense waterfalls brought blessed but all too passing relief from the heat. At last we reached what was known as the 'Arab camp', cut into a clearing in a high valley next to a waterfall. The air was clearer and the scenery spectacular.

Farouq was waiting for us, delighted we had brought the coffee and honey, as well as the cash.

'Welcome to paradise,' he said, smiling.

If it hadn't been for the humidity, the deadly spiders and snakes and other venomous fauna, I might have agreed. Soon after I arrived I woke up one morning to a burning sensation in one of my eyes. A

---

* Doli was a very senior figure in the MILF, on its Shura Council, the supreme decision-making body of the group.

leech was having breakfast; it took hours for me to recover my eyesight.

The novelty of jungle warfare soon wore off. The natural hazards didn't help, nor the long and pointless foot patrols in the soaking heat. But it was the torpor that was most dispiriting; it was more like an episode of *Lost* than *Homeland*. The Arab fighters rotated to the front lines several hours away on foot, where the MILF were protecting a mountain pass. Although Filipino troops were 200 metres away at times, we could barely see them through the dense foliage. The only way to target them was using mortars, but shells were hard to come by.

When not in action, which was most of the time, we whiled away the days in well-hidden camps. In a moment of desperation, I ordered some of the junior fighters to clear an area of grass and erect two poles. Over the following months, some twenty bearded Arabs spent hours playing 'beach' volleyball in the middle of the jungle.

I sometimes looked at my Bahraini passport and thought of throwing it in the fire and making a last stand in this tropical back-water. But then I thought of the effort required to provoke the Filipino army. There were occasional atrocities in the conflict – by both sides – but in general a stalemate. One MILF commander told me that the group had 80,000 fighters (a wild exaggeration) but only 25,000 weapons (probably also exaggerated) and so would never be able to take over the island (no exaggeration at all).

My dream of waging a religious war in the jungle on behalf of the oppressed Muslims of Mindanao was not to be. In the course of seven months, I was at greater risk of dying from snakebite than in a kinetic encounter. And yet perversely I did get wounded in one of the rare spasms of combat. A carelessly lobbed mortar from the Philippine army sent a piece of shrapnel slicing into my leg. I will never forget the searing sensation of a fragment of hot metal embedded in my calf.

My comrades hastily and clumsily dumped me onto an impro-vised stretcher and began hauling me along jungle paths. As I stared upwards at the gently swaying green canopy and listened to the sporadic chatter of gunfire in the adjacent valley, I began to think that this might after all be the moment of my martyrdom. I had no idea how bad my leg wound was, whether I was losing blood by the pint or overreacting to a flesh wound. Nor did I have much confidence in the ability of the MILF medics to patch me up. The stultifying heat lulled me into semi-consciousness.

When I came to I was looking up at a rough thatch of palm. The sun was just rising and the jungle was coming alive with bird calls. *I'm still alive*, I thought, *unless this is what paradise looks like*. I quickly discounted that thought as a jabbing pain shot up from my knee. I hesitated to look down in case the lower half of my leg was no longer there. Instinctively, I tried to move my toes and was relieved to feel a response.

A semi-trained medic from among my guerrilla comrades arrived at my improvised bedside to tend to my wound. Whatever he applied sent shots of searing pain straight to my brain. Within a few hours I was running a fever which only intensified in the unforgiving heat of late afternoon.

The next day, another self-declared medic arrived to examine me. There was more prodding and the application of more hideously acidic potions to my wound. I glanced at the bloodied bandages being removed and predicted the worst. Infection, gangrene, amputation. It was not so much the prospect of intense physical pain that disturbed me, or even having my leg cut off; it was more about whether such an ignominious end would qualify me for martyrdom.

Finally, a proper doctor arrived.

'I'm sorry,' he said, 'we can't give you general anaesthetic. The only way to treat your wounds is to apply a red-hot rod to cauterize the wound. It will hurt but it will prevent infection.'

He was right on one count.

'I will have four strong mujahideen restrain you during the procedure, which I promise won't take more than a few seconds.'

He smiled in an effort to reassure me.

'Take this,' the doctor said, handing me a thick piece of leather, 'and bite down on it, otherwise you might bite your tongue or hurt your jaw.'

The reassuring smile was suddenly a distant memory.

A fighter suggested I wear a scarf over my eyes.

'It's better if you don't watch,' he said simply.

I felt strong arms hold down my shoulders, hands and feet and clenched the leather strap between my teeth.

I was afraid of the pain, but more afraid of screaming or writhing. One of the fighters clasped his knees against the sides of my head.

Two seconds later, every nerve in my body was on fire and every muscle contracted in pure agony. If I had not been so heavily restrained I would have leapt into the air.

Excruciating pain rushed through my nervous system like a fire trying to escape a tunnel.

'It's done,' I heard the good doctor say, before my brain took command and rendered me unconscious.

Had that splinter pierced another part of my body I might not have survived the well-intended but rudimentary medical care I received. I probably cashed in my second life slowly recovering from the infection that persisted for months, apparently immune to the various antibiotics that my carers tried.

By the time I was back on my feet, I had become unreasonably scornful of this rambling front of jihad. MILF was even talking to the government about a truce. I needed to be tested on a battlefield that mattered, like Bosnia, where the survival of our faith was in jeopardy and where I could commit myself to God's will.

Farouq* and Khalid decided to stay on for a while, but I made the trek back down the mountain. It was August 1997 and I felt

---

* Farouq al-Kuwaiti (also known as Omar al-Farouq) would later become al-Qaeda's senior representative in Southeast Asia and its key point person to the Indonesian terrorist group Jemma Islamiya. He was arrested in Indonesia in June 2002 and transferred to the US air base in Bagram, Afghanistan, where he reportedly confessed he had been tasked with planning coordinated truck bombings on US embassies in Southeast Asia on the first anniversary of 9/11. That was not the end of his story. Together with three other al-Qaeda prisoners, including the future Mufti of al-Qaeda, Sheikh Abu Yahya al-Libi, he escaped from the Bagram detention facility in 2005. He then went to Iraq where he was killed in Basra during a gun battle involving UK forces in September 2006.[31]

like a ridiculous Gulliver, criss-crossing the globe in search of the defining front in jihad.

For the next decade at least, the jungles of Mindanao would be a stuttering but never quite extinguished front in the global jihadi cause. Only the emergence of the 'Islamic State' thousands of miles away would eventually ignite a more bloody and serious insurgency.*

One consequence of not being martyred in the Philippines was that I had overstayed my visa by over six months. This was of little concern to Abdul Nassir Nooh, the unflappable fixer who had greeted us in Manila months earlier.

'Just give me $200 and turn up at the airport four hours early,' he said.

The next day, Nooh met me outside the departure hall with a policeman in tow.

'This gentleman will ensure you get your flight,' he said with mock solemnity.

The officer silently escorted me through a side entrance and a maze of corridors before pushing open an emergency exit and ushering me into the departures area. Just two years earlier Ramzi Yousef and Khalid Sheikh Mohammed had devised a plot to use this very airport to smuggle bombs on board as many as a dozen American airliners over the Pacific. If my experience was any guide, it might have been very easy.[33]

---

* Two decades later Mindanao again became an active front for jihad when in 2017 an ISIS-aligned group called Maute, led by two sons of a former MILF fighter, occupied parts of the town of Marawi for months. Parts of another group – Abu Sayyaf – also pledged allegiance to ISIS and raised millions of dollars from kidnapping in the southern Philippines. They beheaded several Western hostages.[32]

# MY THIRD LIFE: THE PLEDGE

## 1997–1998

I woke with a start as the ageing Pakistani Boeing 727 began its descent into Peshawar. To the west loomed the White Mountains, a forbidding silhouette with the approach of dusk, the peaks glittering with fresh snow. The vista gave me a thrill. I felt somehow that I was coming home after a ludicrous outing.

When I landed, the haggard immigration officer, a man with red-rimmed eyes and a girth barely contained by his thick black belt, leafed through my passport.

'Croatia, Azerbaijan, Pakistan, the Philippines,' he said. 'Now back here. Why is a young Bahraini doing so much travelling?'

'I travel to learn about exorcism,' I replied. I invented the name of a religious teacher.

The reply might seem outlandish, but exorcism fascinates many Pakistanis. The officer was suddenly alert – and impressed.

'Then you are a young Sheikh?' he asked deferentially and quickly stamped my passport.

Peshawar International Airport was the usual cacophony of excited families, clamorous porters and incomprehensible PA announcements. I struggled through the crowds and the suitcases strewn across the hall and outside into the cool mountain air, tinged with the smell of smoking garbage.

I knew the drill. First stop: Abu Zubaydah's gated safe house.

82

Check in, deposit passport,* answer any questions about travel and future plans.

As al-Qaeda spread its tentacles across Afghanistan, Abu Zubaydah's place had become the hub of onward travel while also providing services such as bank transfers and false identity documents.** The all-knowing Pakistani intelligence service turned a blind eye to his work and maybe even assisted it.

Abu Zubaydah was always on the lookout for spies. I found him as severe and intimidating as before. He was irritated that I had flown into Peshawar, imagining Western intelligence had the airport under scrutiny.

'You should always arrive in Islamabad and get the bus,' he said like a schoolteacher too often let down by irresponsible students. 'What's your plan?'

'I hope to train with the bomb-maker Abu Khabab.'

Abu Zubaydah stared at me impassively.

'I met him last year at Darunta,' I stammered. 'I've heard his camp is now fully up and running. I want to make myself useful.' More silence. He used it as a weapon. 'The Philippines taught me the importance of bomb-makers.'

I'd been thinking of what I might learn from Abu Khabab since seeing a young MILF bomb-maker demonstrate his art by setting off a number of spectacular explosions in a jungle clearing.

'We shall see,' Abu Zubaydah replied.

It was not what one might call a happy house. Whenever a group of us was engaged in a lively discussion, it would quickly come to a halt when Abu Zubaydah opened the door and peered in – his dark, menacing eyes fixed like a cobra's behind his spectacles.

* After the Taliban takeover, Hekmatyar had fled to Iran with much of his organization and Abu Zubaydah now enjoyed something of a monopoly when it came to processing foreign fighters entering Afghanistan. The drill was now to leave our passports with Abu Zubaydah, who kept them in a safe in his Peshawar villa.

** Abu Zubaydah provided these services to al-Qaeda in return for regular injections of cash. He continued to act as gatekeeper to the independent Khalden training camp in Khost.

I made my way through the mountains to Jalalabad and a guest house for Arab fighters. I was an object of some curiosity, the only jihadi there who had served on the Mindanao front. Also staying there was a Saudi veteran of the Afghan conflict and now the head of Osama bin Laden's bodyguard, Abu Hamza al-Ghamdi.

To younger jihadis, al-Ghamdi was already something of a legend. He'd fought heroically against the Communists around Jalalabad and more recently had led a small band into Tajikistan, a former Soviet republic, to try to ignite jihad there.

One evening, as we sat on a threadbare rug eating the usual grey meat and rice, I began telling stories about the Philippines. Al-Ghamdi wanted to know more and we were soon deep in conversation. He was a magnetic character with a sly sense of humour and he was perceptive and persuasive in his views about the 'struggle'.

He also had plenty of stories to tell about Hekmatyar, who had fled to Iran after the collapse of the coalition in Kabul. Al-Ghamdi regarded him as a blowhard and a scoundrel, inherently untrustworthy. Apparently, Hekmatyar had once lied about bringing down a Soviet helicopter gunship with an AK-47.

'Not even Rambo managed that,' al-Ghamdi laughed.

The following day, he gave me a tour of Jalalabad, recounting stories about the fighting around the city. It was an autumn day of stunning clarity; the sun was still warm and even the squalor of Jalalabad could not spoil my good humour. As we walked, al-Ghamdi asked me more about the Philippines: jungle combat, the type of weapons we used, the calibre of our local comrades and of the army. He also took me to meet the Taliban's governor in Jalalabad. I was flattered to receive so much attention from such an influential figure.

We ended up in one of the few places that served passable food, and sat down with two banana milkshakes and Afghan fries – the equivalent in Afghanistan of dining at a Michelin-starred restaurant. Al-Ghamdi was candid with me about the rift between Saudis and Egyptians inside al-Qaeda. He felt bin Laden listened too much to the Egyptians, who had persuaded him to establish a base in Sudan and then used it as a launch pad for attacks in neighbouring Egypt. In al-Ghamdi's view, they were responsible for the group's hideous financial losses in Sudan.

'The Sudanese government betrayed us,' he said. 'They stole the assets we had – investments, land and businesses – worth $165 million altogether. It's money we will never see again.'

While not bankrupt, al-Qaeda was no longer brimming with cash, he said. Osama bin Laden had been cut off by his family years earlier, and donations from wealthy individuals in Saudi Arabia were no longer as generous since he had fallen out with the Saudi royal family.

Then came the pitch: the 'Gulf' bench inside al-Qaeda needed strengthening.

'The Egyptians, especially Zawahiri, they're pedantic.' He paused as he spat out the words with contempt. 'They can't stop going on about a revolution to overthrow Mubarak' – the dullard who had become president after Anwar Sadat's assassination in 1981.

'We need fresh blood: young, well-read, intelligent men like you,' said al-Ghamdi, looking at me earnestly. If he was trying to flatter me, it was working. It was time, he told me, that I set aside the wandering of youth and devote myself to 'core' al-Qaeda here in Afghanistan.

He put his hand on my shoulder.

'Remember this *hadith*:

> *"A victorious band of warriors from my followers shall continue to fight for the truth. Despite being deserted and abandoned, they will be at the gates of Jerusalem and its surroundings, they will be at the gates of Damascus and its surroundings, they will be at the gates of Antioch and its surroundings, and they will be at the gates of Taleqan and its surroundings. Then God will bring forth his treasure from Taleqan to resurrect the faith after it was made dead."*[1]

Al-Ghamdi punched out the word 'gates' for impact, delivering his peroration with dramatic effect. Taleqan was an ancient city in Afghanistan just a few hundred miles north from where we were sitting.

'The prophecies have foretold the armies of jihad will be in Khurasan, the Maghreb, Yemen, Iraq and Syria. Don't you see Abu al-Abbas? We are the Vanguard, we are the black banners that will march from Khurasan and liberate Jerusalem and restore the Caliphate before the Day of Judgment!'[2]

I understood now that Sayyid Qutb had used the term Vanguard because the emergence of Holy Warriors protecting Islam at its time of need had been foretold by the Prophet. The prophecies he was referring to were popular refrains in the camps:

*'If you see the black banners approaching from Khurasan, then join them for the Mahdi will be among them.'*[3]

Al-Ghamdi was spelling out what bin Laden had intimated a year earlier. Al-Qaeda was the long-foretold army of God. Not only did the group seek to defend Islam against unjust forces, but it regarded itself as the Mahdi's army-in-waiting. That was enticing because the Prophet had foretold that the Mahdi would emerge near the end-of-days and bring about a new order in which justice and fairness would rule supreme.[4]

But I still had questions.

'I don't know, brother,' I began uncertainly. 'I expected to be a soldier on the front lines defending the *Ummah*, not in the kind of war you are describing. I understand that the army of the black flags will come out of here and we'll end up in a big battle with the Israelis,' I said hesitantly. 'But maybe in a few hundred years' time.'

'No,' al-Ghamdi said quickly. 'It was no accident that the Jews returned to Jerusalem thirty years ago. That triggered the age of the final prophecies.' It was the first time I had heard it argued that Israel's capture of east Jerusalem and the West Bank in the 1967 war was such a 'trigger'.

'Recall also this *hadith*,' al-Ghamdi went on. I felt as if I was in a seminary.

> *'There will come a time when you shall fight the Jews. You will be east of the river Jordan, while they are to the west of it.'*[5]

'This prophecy refers to a war Muslim armies will wage against the Jews before the arrival of the Mahdi, the emergence of the Antichrist and the return of Jesus Christ.[6] The preconditions were fulfilled when the Jews took control of the West Bank and pushed Arab armies east of the river Jordan. The countdown to the arrival of our armies at the gates of Jerusalem and the arrival of the Mahdi has begun.'

He pressed home his advantage.

'Can it be a coincidence that just a few years later the Godless Soviets came to Khurasan, allowing us to raise the banner of jihad?

'Who else would carry the Black Banners into battle other than us? Martians? We have to do this for ourselves, even if many in our homelands have deserted us and we are few in number. The alternative is simply to be a bystander and watch history flow by.'

I was struck, amazed even, that to someone so senior in al-Qaeda the fulfilling of the prophecies and the arrival of the Mahdi was not some distant dream but something more urgent, even within our grasp.

As if I hadn't understood, he laid his hand on my wrist and added quietly: 'Either you honour your commitment to God or be a spectator.'*

---

* While the *hadith* relating to the 'black banners' were an intoxicating and effective form of recruitment, serious questions have been raised by Islamic scholars about their authenticity. Their doubts stemmed from the exploitation of *hadith* by the Abbasid dynasty, which adopted black as its colour in overthrowing the Umayyad dynasty and so had every interest in promoting *hadith* foretelling the emergence of such an army. The prophecies relating to the black banners are mostly found in less authoritative *hadith* collections.[7]

It was a calculated appeal to my faith and manhood, delivered with passion (and most likely not for the first time). But it also envisaged an entirely different form of warfare against those identified by bin Laden as our enemies.

'The war in defence of Islam is now *everywhere* between the earth's poles,' al-Ghamdi continued. 'Sheikh Osama was stripped of his Saudi nationality three years ago because he opposed the American military presence in Arabia.'

Those same soldiers I had seen defending my hometown after Saddam Hussein's invasion of Kuwait were now the enemy.

'If you search within yourself, you will feel this shift too,' al-Ghamdi said. 'Gone are the days when you were dressed in military uniform going from trench to trench in Bosnia. There are no uniforms or trenches anymore. These days you and your friends are training on explosives and urban warfare, so you're subconsciously aware of this shift.'

'But my plan is to train with Abu Khabab al-Masri,' I interjected. Abu Khabab was not formally part of al-Qaeda.

'This will not be a problem. We can put in a good word so that you can get a place on his next intake.'

It was a strange feature of jihadi life in Afghanistan in those days that individuals, even once recruited into al-Qaeda, had freedom to roam between camps and alternative centres of gravity.

There was one small issue, I said. How were we – with AK-47s and an explosives lab run out of a hut in the mountains – expected to challenge the world's undisputed superpower?

Al-Ghamdi's answer was swift and confident: America had grown soft.

'You remember Beirut in 1983? Somalia? The Americans have no stomach for taking casualties. You have to make them bleed, physically and financially.'

As I walked back to my lodgings that evening under a crescent moon I felt energized by the prospect of joining the struggle al-Ghamdi had described. Al-Qaeda had clearly embarked on a new strategy, putting flesh on the bones of bin Laden's declaration the previous year – and at the same time embroidering it with religious authenticity. It might seem impossible to anyone steeped in Western secularism, amid the irreligious cynicism of modern life, that Islamic prophecies should be such a powerful driver. But among millions of Muslims – and especially among jihadis – they are imbued with immense spiritual resonance. They are divine sayings vouchsafed to Mohammed by God himself. And they were central to al-Qaeda's ideological foundation.*

The thousands of overlapping *hadith* were fertile territory for theological debate. Handed down by word of mouth, they were scattered and disconnected; it seemed to me that the Prophet had never intended them as a complete picture of the future but as a glimpse into what it might hold. I believe in the purity of the Koran, a compilation of God's revelations to the Prophet which has been perfectly preserved. But the *hadith*, on which al-Qaeda and ISIS lean heavily, are sayings *attributed* to the Prophet, revised and in many cases corrupted in the centuries that followed, and adapted to suit particular moments in history. They provide therefore a minefield of argument.

Over the centuries Muslims' belief in the validity of some of these prophecies has been reinforced by events, including the conquest of Persia, Syria and Yemen in the early years of Islam and the capture of Constantinople in 1453.[9] But not all *hadith* are equal; many have been distorted and exploited for narrow ends.

Al-Qaeda leaders believed the Mahdi** would rule over a restored Caliphate after a period of strife and epic battles, and it was the mission of the Vanguard to work towards that Caliphate

* Bin Laden's Abbottabad diary, released by the CIA in late 2017, showed his fascination with eschatology.[8]
** Many Sunni Muslims believe the presence of the Mahdi on earth will set the stage for the return to earth of Jesus Christ (it is foretold to Damascus), who will then vanquish the Antichrist (foretold to first appear between Iraq and Syria). Jesus Christ, according to a prophecy, will then reign for forty years with the final Day of Judgment following some time after his death (Muslim: 2937).

and hasten his arrival by bringing about the circumstances foretold to precede it.* Bin Laden's commitment to liberating Jerusalem was not a rhetorical flourish designed to rally 'the base' but at the very core of al-Qaeda's mission.** Al-Qaeda's actions were all about accelerating progress towards what the Prophet had described as the glorious end phase of history. By presenting the searing defeat of Arab armies in 1967 as a precursor to the end-of-days, al-Qaeda was turning it into a rallying call for jihad.

Al-Ghamdi was one of the messengers, but the high priest of the prophecies was the head of al-Qaeda's Shariah College Sheikh Abu Abdullah al-Muhajir, the Egyptian who had provided religious instruction at Hekmatyar's camp in Darunta.[11] It was he who developed the theological arguments presenting the defeat of 1967 as the dawn of the age of prophecies.***

His Friday sermons were a weekly highlight for al-Qaeda recruits. I was one of well over a hundred young fighters to attend one of them at a training camp near Khost. The Nazi Holocaust and the creation of the state of Israel had been foretold by a passage of the Koran, he maintained, setting the stage for the 1967 war that was the 'mighty trigger' for the age of prophecies.[12] The mujahideen, the cleric said, had congregated in Afghanistan after years of scurrying to obscure campaigns in the far corners of the globe. I momentarily felt a little guilty about the Philippines. He repeated the Prophet's words about the Vanguard 'hurrying from one front

---

* Seventeen years later, Abu Bakr al-Baghdadi declared himself the first Caliph of a restored Caliphate. ISIS theologians cited prophecies to argue the Mahdi would be one of his successors. Al-Qaeda leaders argued the new entity did not have sufficient backing among Muslims and was not strong enough or geographically large enough to be a legitimate Caliphate.[10]

** It is not possible to understand al-Qaeda's strategy without understanding its fixation on fulfilling the prophecies. Creating the preconditions for the arrival of the Mahdi also explained the group's later establishment of affiliates in Yemen, Syria, Iraq and the Maghreb, which along with Afghanistan are the lands of the Five Armies of Jihad prophesied to fight in the epic battles.

*** Al-Muhajir, whose real name was (Sheikh) Abdulrahman al-Ali, had taught in various camps in Afghanistan. His profound influence on the Jordanian Abu Musab al-Zarqawi is discussed later.

to another, never harmed by betrayals, until God's command descends'.[13]

One young fighter stood up and exclaimed: 'I don't think I'm worthy of the Prophet's praise but now I know he was talking about us, comforting us when everybody was standing against us.'

Sheikh al-Muhajir was providing certainty and eliminating doubt. Certainty has been and will always be the most powerful weapon in the jihadi arsenal. He picked up his thread.

'We are now reaching a crucial phase: the preparation for the "Epic Battles" and the coming of Imam Mahdi. Divine interventions do not just fall into our laps; it is our duty to pave the way for such interventions, so as to meet God halfway.'

Al-Muhajir knew he was winning over his audience. We could advance the course of history. Perhaps the Mahdi might emerge even within our own lifetimes.

Sitting next to me was Abu Abdullah al-Maki, the young Saudi I had met soon after arriving in Afghanistan. He was enraptured. For hundreds – thousands – of young men like al-Maki, this was the message that gave their journey purpose, delivered by skilful speakers who could marshal religious texts in the way a brilliant attorney summons case law.

Nor was I immune. For so many of us – sitting cross-legged before him – al-Muhajir's elucidation of the Koran and *hadith* was irresistibly alluring.

The sense that the prophecies were coming true was the sunshine that cleared away the mists of doubt and illuminated beautiful mountains towards which the road was leading: eternal paradise.

Al-Muhajir was building towards his conclusion. Finally, in words that echoed Sayyid Qutb's parable of the unlit candles, he said:

'Each of you are bricks in the Caliphate, but these bricks will only be cemented into the building at the moment of martyrdom.'

Al-Maki burst into tears.

After the sermon, we congregated for lunch. Prodding the

congealed lentils around my plate, I felt a tap on my shoulder. It was the Sheikh.

'Can you spare a few minutes?' he asked. I was hardly likely to say no.

In his office-cum-library, he asked me what I thought about the sermon, knowing that I was one of a minority with a prior interest in theology.

'It was well delivered and very well received,' I answered, in an attempt to avoid any in-depth debate. To be honest, my mind was on the dwindling stock of Twix chocolate bars I had smuggled into the camp. Neatly hidden beneath my stack of books, one was waiting for me. And I found al-Muhajir to be somewhat intimidating.

The Sheikh asked me to carry the message to other fighters.

'You have the intellect to propagate this message wherever you go, to whoever you meet. Please take the opportunity,' he said.

In September 1997, al-Ghamdi sought me out again at the Jalalabad guest house.

'Abu al-Abbas,' he said. 'If you are ready and committed, it's time for you to make the journey to Kandahar and make the pledge.'

We both knew what my answer would be. He was smiling mischievously. Al-Ghamdi had fast-tracked me as part of his mission to dilute the Egyptian contingent. And so, on a warm morning I climbed into a battered minibus heading to Kandahar in the deep south of Afghanistan, the headquarters of both the Taliban and now its honoured guest, Osama bin Laden.*

Kandahar was hotter, dustier and more crowded than Jalalabad. I made my way through noisy alleyways crowded with donkeys and carts, boys yelling and running, and the ubiquitous white Toyota pickup trucks sagging under the weight of watermelons or bags of rice.

---

* The Taliban had asked bin Laden to move there in case the Northern Alliance under Ahmed Shah Masoud (yes, he was still in business) attacked Jalalabad.[14]

Al-Qaeda had a training camp at a place called Tarnak Farms on a sun-baked plain near the city's airport on the south-eastern edge of the city. Bin Laden's headquarters complex consisted of about eighty small concrete and mud-brick buildings which had been converted into offices and living accommodation for al-Qaeda fighters.[15] The now ubiquitous black flags fluttered over the facility to remind us all of our prophetic duty.

In the exercise area trainees dressed in flowing dark robes were conducting drills on monkey bars as an instructor barked commands at them in an Egyptian accent.* On the other side of the complex, shaded by the wall that surrounded the camp, a large group was sitting crossed-legged listening to a religious lesson. The sound of Kalashnikov fire reverberated off the walls.

As I was ushered into one of the larger buildings, I was nervous but not overwhelmed; bin Laden, after all, was just flesh and blood and I had met him once before. Perhaps my youthfulness helped. I had seen older men consumed with nerves before they met the Sheikh.

I entered the main prayer hall and was greeted by al-Ghamdi. He ushered me into a bare reception room no larger than the average living room, simply furnished with straw mats. Large, hard cushions were propped up against bare walls whose eggshell paint was peeling.

One of bin Laden's Saudi bodyguards, Abdulaziz al-Juhani, entered the room to announce that the Sheikh was ready. I was escorted into the inner sanctum. A small window and a naked electric ceiling bulb illuminated the room. The walls were book-lined – the quiet reading room of a serious academic. And the desk was piled high with papers; al-Qaeda had its own bureaucracy and bin Laden was renowned for micro-managing.

The Sheikh was sitting cross-legged on a large Afghan rug, leaning against scarlet-coloured cushions. He was barefoot, wearing a

---

* Footage of al-Qaeda operatives doing monkey bar drills at Tarnak Farms later became iconic.[16]

simple white *salwar kameez*, the Afghan *pakol* on his head and an Afghan scarf around his waist. He was buried in a book.

When he looked up I thought he seemed older than when I had seen him a year previously. Perhaps the Afghan diet and his more austere surroundings in Kandahar were taking a toll. I was expecting at least an assistant or guard to be present; I had not even been searched.

Al-Ghamdi made the introductions.

'Sheikh, this is our Bahraini brother. He has come to pledge *bayat* [the oath of allegiance].'

Bin Laden closed his book and stood up with a smile. I was again struck by how tall he was. He had the beady gaze of a hawk; I could almost feel him examining my every gesture and movement. He shook my hand and in a voice scarcely more than whisper bade me sit on the floor.

He lowered his long limbs, not without some stiffness, to join me. Al-Ghamdi sat opposite.

'Where are you staying?' he asked.

'At the guest house in the city,' I said, feigning a casual air as if I was talking to an uncle. 'But I hope to go back to train with Abu Khabab in Darunta.'

He nodded approvingly. He was clearly aware of the work of Abu Khabab's precocious team. Al-Ghamdi had told me about the dreams of al-Qaeda leaders in which the Prophet had urged training in explosives.* Perhaps we were the vanguard of the Vanguard.

Bin Laden seemed unhurried. He asked me about my family and was impressed that my oldest brother, Moheddin, had already been to Afghanistan to fight.

To show I was not overawed and to move the conversation along, I told him we had met once before, soon after he had arrived in Jalalabad the previous year.

'Ah, yes,' he said. 'I remember you now.'

---

* The dreams and visions of leading figures within al-Qaeda had an outsize impact on decision making because they were regarded as divinely inspired.

I had no idea whether he did – but preferred to think so.

'And tell me about your time with our brothers in the Philippines.'

I provided an optimistic portrayal of the struggle there. It would take time, I said, for jihad to take root in the rainforest, thinking of the welcome diversion the improvised volleyball court had provided. But I was anxious to move on to the real business of the meeting. Al-Ghamdi had persuaded me that al-Qaeda had been anointed to shape history. I had to be part of it.

Perhaps bin Laden sensed my agitation.

'You are about to enter into a sacred oath. You have been chosen as a mujahid,' he said. By whom went unsaid but was obvious: it was by God. I was one of a few hundred out of a billion Muslims chosen to fight for our religion.

The enemy was now America, he told me. Afghanistan was the crucible of jihad, the beginning of a global campaign. This was to me undoubtedly a call to *offensive* action, however much al-Qaeda might dress it up as a defence of Islam – light years from defending Muslims in the Balkans or Caucasus. Indeed, eighteen months later, in the very room where we were meeting, bin Laden would approve Khalid Sheikh Mohammed's idea of flying hijacked aircraft into targets in the United States.*

Bin Laden was never excitable; he seemed to relish the idea of struggle against the odds.

'This path you have chosen will not be easy. There will be times when it will become difficult, so you must always pray to God to make you steadfast,' he said. There would be many years of suffering ahead for the true believers, he added; the cause of jihad would not start nor end with him. But with God's help al-Qaeda would ultimately prevail.

The moment for my pledge of allegiance had arrived. He extended his right hand with his palm opened upwards and took

---

* Bin Laden also later spent time with the 9/11 hijackers at al-Qaeda's headquarters at Tarnak Farms.[17]

mine. I noticed how long his fingers were and how soft his skin. Clearly this was someone who had rarely endured physical labour.

The recital of the *bayat* can be compared to a wedding vow. Al-Ghamdi played the role of the priest, asking me to repeat every clause after him. I recall my exact words as I looked solemnly into the al-Qaeda founder's eyes.

'I give you my allegiance to obey, to follow orders during the good times and the bad without disobeying God on the path of jihad. I fight alongside you when you declare war and I make peace when you make peace. And God is the witness to what I have declared.'

There was a pause and he smiled.

'May God welcome you into the caravan of jihad and the mujahideen,' he said.

'What name have you chosen?' bin Laden asked. New al-Qaeda operatives frequently changed their fighting names for security reasons.

'Abu Abbas al-Sharqi,' I replied. Al-Sharqi referred to the Eastern Province of Saudi Arabia where I was brought up. Now I was joining al-Qaeda it would have been imprudent to carry on identifying myself as a Bahraini national.

Bin Laden had his first instruction for me.

'I understand you have had a good religious upbringing and are well versed in holy texts and religious history,' he said. 'I need you to bring some of this wisdom to our brothers from Yemen who have much less education.

'You should go among the camps and help them understand what God intends for us. They have not had the luxury you enjoyed of growing up with scholars and books.'

There were hundreds of Yemenis descending on the camps at that time: illiterate boys recruited by militant imams in that splintered, chaotic country that hugged the Arabian Sea.

As I took my leave and stepped out in the harsh sunlight, I felt euphoric. I had just been given serious time with the Sheikh; I had been praised and encouraged, welcomed as one of the *safwah* (chosen ones).

The bond of brotherhood was unbreakable, something to be celebrated. I was now inextricably tied to a group where absolute and indefinite loyalty to the cause and to the Sheikh was unarguable. Whatever other associations I might be allowed to keep up, I was ultimately al-Qaeda's property. When the call came, there could be but one answer.

I lingered in Kandahar for a few days while al-Ghamdi made arrangements for my training with Abu Khabab. It was a useful introduction to the al-Qaeda hierarchy. I had my first interaction with bin Laden's right-hand man Abu Hafs al-Masri.

I would have mistaken him for an Egyptian labourer; he was simply dressed, with a straggly beard that might have been borrowed from a bison. He had a working-class accent and had been a low-ranking policeman before coming to Afghanistan. Despite his modest background, he had a sharp mind with an unsparing attention to detail. There was an intelligence and alertness in his eyes. He was effectively al-Qaeda's Chief Operations Officer. If bin Laden was the inspirational driving force behind al-Qaeda, Abu Hafs was the one who made the trains run on time. When I met him he was preoccupied with spare parts for al-Qaeda's vehicles.

He was a man of few words but had a calm presence that inspired deference. He asked who I had known in Bosnia, especially among the Bahrainis. I was astonished by how many names he could recall.

'I actually grew up in Saudi Arabia,' I said.

'Ah, I thought the accent was not quite Bahraini,' he said in his deliberate, ponderous voice.*

I returned to Darunta on a cool, late autumn day. The Himalayan winter was foreshadowed by the speed with which the temperature dropped as soon as the sun slipped behind the mountains.

---

* Abu Hafs' real name was Mohammed Atef. He fought alongside bin Laden in the 1980s Afghan jihad and was a charter member of al-Qaeda. Over the years he hardened bin Laden's views, persuading him of the need for regime change across the Arab world.[18]

While I had been in the Philippines, Abu Khabab's reputation had only grown in al-Qaeda circles as an explosives alchemist. His camp was situated on two levels on a steep, barren hill above the artificial lake at Darunta. The upper level consisted of two small mud and straw buildings. One served as a kitchen and dormitory with room for just five occupants. The other was used as a laboratory and classroom and resembled an Ottoman apothecary. Its safety precautions, or, rather, their absence, would have induced a cardiac arrest in any Western chemist. The shelves were bent by the weight of Pyrex jars – some of them cracked – containing an assortment of highly toxic chemicals. Down the hill there was a shipping container which had been modified into storage space for chemicals, and by the waterfront a scorched area with several craters where Abu Khabab tested his concoctions. The buildings occupied perhaps fifty square yards, but the experiments there would change the face of the global terrorist threat.

Abu Khabab was an avuncular figure out of class but a demanding teacher. He only allowed four or five apprentices at his camp at any one time. One of them was Hassan Ghul, a baby-faced Pakistani in his early twenties. Ghul had grown up in the Saudi city of Medina and spoke Arabic with its unique twang. He had wanted to travel to Bosnia but had been denied a Croatian visa because of his Pakistani nationality. He told me he had applied to train with Abu Khabab after having a dream that he would become a master bomb-maker. He would indeed become skilled in handling explosives. His links to Medina and fluent Arabic, Urdu and Pashto would also make him a trusted courier.*

Within a few minutes of meeting him I knew we were destined to get along. He had an infectious sense of humour and we would joke about some of our more austere comrades, of whom there were plenty. Occasionally, we would jump in any truck heading for Jalalabad for provisions so that we could spend our precious

* Ghul's capture in northern Iraq early in 2004 would be a critical point in the long trail leading to bin Laden's hideout in Abbottabad.

pocket money on mango and banana shakes. When Abu Khabab needed more supplies from Peshawar, Hassan Ghul was often the shopper.

Another apprentice called Abu Nassim al-Tunisi was from Milan. He was lanky and awkward, with a prominent hook nose and receding hairline. He was also a sociopath. He had a gentle voice and shy eyes when in conversation, which was rare, but took great pleasure in torturing the animals on which we experimented and held extreme *takfiri* views. His only redeeming quality was an extraordinary ability to conjure mouth-watering pasta dishes out of whatever basics were available in Jalalabad. Al-Tunisi's real name was Moez Fezzani. After a misspent youth selling hashish on the streets of Milan he had found religion and decided to join the jihadi cause after attending sermons by Anwar Shaaban.[19] He'd fought in Bosnia (though I didn't meet him there) before coming to Afghanistan.[20] None of us knew much chemistry when we arrived, and in the first few weeks Abu Khabab taught us the basics.

'Brothers,' he announced at our first session, 'always remember: you are not dealing with potatoes here. These are dangerous chemicals. Your first mistake is your last. I only allow the best in this camp because making explosives requires exceptional care.'

Abu Khabab was speaking from bitter experience. Over the years, a who's who of jihadis had sustained injuries. Ibn al-Khattab, the Saudi commander in Chechnya, had lost two fingers. An Egyptian named Abu Hamza had made the mistake of inserting a detonator into nitroglycerine while it was still warm, when training at a previous facility run by Abu Khabab in Pakistan.*

Abu Khabab had told him to wait until the mixture cooled and

---

* Abu Hamza had trained with Abu Khabab around 1993. A Pakistani general had made a farmhouse available near Lahore to train Kashmiri militants. Abu Khabab told me the future Finsbury Park preacher had regarded himself as God's gift to making explosives after just a few days' training. When Abu Hamza moved to London he told a rather different story about losing his hands, saying that they'd been blown off while he was working to clear landmines. All the same, Abu Hamza raised considerable funds for Abu Khabab's Darunta camp.

went upstairs. Seconds later, Abu Khabab was blown off his feet by an explosion. He rushed downstairs to find Abu Hamza bleeding from his left eye and minus both hands, which were lodged in the rafters. The Egyptian's disability would become a trademark when he became a notorious preacher at the Finsbury Park Mosque in London. The ever-delicate British tabloids were quick to nickname him 'Captain Hook'.

Abu Khabab saw himself as an artist whose vocation was to create innovative weapons for the Jihadi cause.*

I have often asked myself why I so enjoyed learning with Abu Khabab. It is an uncomfortable question. I think it was the science, the experimentation and sense of discovery that attracted me. Perhaps I subliminally set aside the obvious consequences of our work, pushed them out of mind in my fascination with chemistry and engineering challenges. My motivation was certainly not to learn how to murder and maim as many people as possible. I had an innate aversion to civilian casualties, even as a headstrong teenager. I was constantly haunted by that scene on the bridge in Sarajevo; it would achieve nothing to mimic the Serbs' savagery.

Only much later did I appreciate how naive I had been to embrace and advance Abu Khabab's experiments without sufficient thought for why al-Qaeda regarded them as so important. These were not weapons for use on the front lines.

I found Abu Khabab an appealing, almost bewitching character. He looked after us, insisting we eat properly.

'You were taught how to be tough in the other camps,' he told us. 'But here I need you to be healthy and alert and your immune system at full throttle, otherwise you're not going to last long.'

And he was never short of surprises. He had a house at the university in Jalalabad, from which I went to collect some

* A large Algerian named Assad Allah, who had green eyes and the build of a weightlifter, was also providing training nearby, but Abu Khabab warned me off his courses, saying, 'He treats explosives like vegetables.' Indeed, there were plenty of tales of experiments gone awry at Allah's workshop and around this period he himself lost one of his hands in an accident.

chemicals one day. In the corner of one room there was a mattress resting on about a thousand neatly stacked grenades.

Abu Khabab laughed when he saw my look of astonishment.

'The Communists used this place as a store room. We found the grenades when we took over the house. They still have their explosives, but they won't go off unless their pins are removed.'

'That's good,' I said, laughing. 'Just don't have any violent nightmares.'

Abu Khabab was more than a master bomb-maker. Like me, he was fascinated by Islamic history. In a place where entertainment and recreation were in seriously short supply, we could while away an evening talking about some obscure historical figure or battle. Like many jihadis he was also deeply interested in the meaning of dreams and insisted I help him decode them, regarding them as messages from God.*

He was also a superb storyteller, and I liked to think that I was one of the lucky few to be told the inside story of this plot or another.

Abu Khabab's hatred of the Egyptian regime was visceral, and he had helped plan a truck-bomb attack on the Egyptian embassy in Islamabad in 1995, the one in which the preacher al-Muhajir had also been involved.

'I told two guys how to build the bomb. It weighed 750 kilograms and was made up of fertilizer, which was easy to get. The bomb was built in a garage in Rawalpindi, just down the road from Islamabad.

'Fate intervened to guarantee our success. A few weeks before the attack, there was a falling-out between the Egyptian and Pakistani security services. An Egyptian agent hit one of his Pakistani counterparts in an argument over what to do about a

---

* I witnessed many jihadis make decisions – sometimes life-altering ones – based on their dreams. I was often asked to interpret dreams because I had studied the meaning of them. I had read an old book called *Interpretations of Dreams and Visions* by a Muslim scholar called Ibn Sirin (died AD 728) who used the mindset of the dreamer.

detainee. They couldn't do anything; the guy had diplomatic immunity. Out of spite, someone in the ISI (Pakistani military intelligence) decided that security at the embassy should be lowered.'

He shrugged. 'Did they have an inkling there was an attack planned? We'll never know.'

It's impossible to know if Abu Khabab's story was true, but he was not known for embellishment. The attack was the first suicide bombing by Islamist radicals on Pakistani soil, and killed fifteen people. He told me several of the dead were officials working undercover as diplomats to help the Pakistani authorities track down militants. I wondered if they included the man who had lost his temper.

After being instructed in the basics of bomb-making in a forty-five-day course, I was taught how to set off explosive devices using a watch as a timer or a mobile phone as a remote detonator. I soon learned why the testing ground was situated at the water's edge. If the explosives blew up in our faces, we would be able to douse the flames with water from the lake (or so the theory went).

More than once, I felt that trial and error was not quite the right prescription for bomb-making. I will never forget the cold sweat and nausea as I tried to concentrate on perfecting a chemical formula or wiring up an experimental device. I was not afraid of death, or so I told myself, but if martyrdom came I wanted it to be on the battlefield surrounded by my comrades, rather than on an empty hillside after I had made a dumb mistake.

Abu Khabab's interests went well beyond conventional explosives. He began discussing experiments with chemicals and poison gases. He developed a procedure for extracting nicotine poison from cigarettes using a large supply of Marlboro Reds, a blender, a Pyrex jar and other easily obtainable substances. Over several days we drained and squeezed a dark brown liquid until it thickened to the consistency of treacle.

I was fascinated by the procedure but had deep misgivings

about the discussions that accompanied the experiments. Marlboros were a lot cheaper than missiles, but this was clearly a weapon designed to spread terror among a civilian population. Our resident psychopath, Abu Nassim, talked about lacing banknotes with the poison inside letters.

Abu Khabab viewed the crude chemical weapons and toxins he was developing at Darunta as adding powerful capabilities to the arsenal of jihad. Several Arab regimes had such weapons, so why shouldn't groups like al-Qaeda? Khabab was always adamant, however, that their use would require approval by the Shariah Committees of jihadi groups, and worried that hot-headed jihadis might use them without getting the necessary approval. For my part, I viewed these weapons as deterrents or at most weapons of last resort. Only later would I agonize over the research being done at Darunta and who would decide on how and when such weapons might be deployed.

We went through more than eighty rabbits and thousands of cigarettes in perfecting our nicotine poison recipe. Abu Nassim volunteered to take the lead on the testing; I had never seen him happier. Darunta was not a place for animal lovers: rabbits were frequently the victims of our experiments. For years afterwards I had dreams of being chased by rabbits as they avenged my cruelty to the species. I did not need to be a dream interpreter to figure out why.

'Join the club,' Abu Khabab confided to me one day. 'I see rabbits, puppies, kittens and donkeys. They are always chasing me.'

One day I took Hindh, the stray cat I had adopted at Darunta, to Jalababad and left her there. I didn't want her anywhere near Abu Nassim.

We also experimented with making botulinum, a toxin that attacks the body's nerves and causes difficulty breathing, muscle paralysis and, in high doses, death. The bacteria that make the toxin occur naturally when foods are stored improperly.[21] Abu Khabab found a way to make nature work to our advantage: sealing certain foodstuffs with human excrement and other easily available ingredients inside a container, and allowing the mixture to simmer.

It fell to poor Hassan Ghul to open the container weeks later to extract the active toxin. He wore kitchen gloves to protect his hands as he scooped out the appalling dun-coloured ooze. The rest of us donned wet scarves covered in charcoal to protect against the noxious fumes.

Abu Nassim added a few drops into the water bowl of a rabbit. It died about forty hours later from what was essentially extreme food poisoning. Clearly the batch we had concocted was not very potent. Botulinum quickly loses potency unless stored under laboratory conditions. Abu Khabab discontinued our experiments even as others in al-Qaeda dreamed of poisoning water supplies with botulinum. He calculated, correctly, that the chlorine in most drinking supplies would render it quite useless.*

After I subsequently started working for British intelligence, I would tell them all about these experiments,** and it would be no surprise to read the observations of the US Presidential Commission on Weapons of Mass Destruction in 2005: 'Information in the Intelligence Community's possession since the late 1990s indicated that al-Qa'ida's members had trained in crude methods for producing biological agents such as botulinum toxin and toxins obtained from venomous animals.'[22]

While fascinated by toxins, Abu Khabab was scornful of the nuclear 'boosters' among the al-Qaeda hierarchy.

'You know what I think about these so-called dirty bombs,' he said one mid-winter evening as we huddled round the fire wrapped

---

* Abd al-Aziz al-Masri, an Egyptian al-Qaeda bomb-maker who also sought to create WMD, wrote down in an al-Qaeda manual that sixty million people could be killed by poisoning water supplies with botulinum, a ridiculous assertion.
** At the Darunta facility we also developed techniques to extract venom from scorpions, which involved trapping them and making them sting an object, thus secreting the venom. Abu Khabab concluded that the significant amount of venom needed to kill even a small rabbit made it a pretty impracticable weapon.

in a cocoon of blankets. 'They're a waste of our time, more likely to kill us than anyone else.'[23] Even the materials for a primitive 'dirty bomb' would be hard to come by, he said, and the radiation from such a weapon would cause little harm.*

For others in al-Qaeda's orbit, the fear and panic that would be provoked by some sort of workable nuclear capability – however crude – remained the holy grail. And the group went to some lengths to play up its nuclear capability in an effort to sow uncertainty among the intelligence agencies. Abu Hamza al-Ghamdi had told me, in typically subversive fashion: 'It would be a good thing for our enemies to be afraid that we have them.'**

Abu Khabab also scoffed at attempts to produce biological weapons and nerve agents. An Egyptian bomb-maker and chemist in his early thirties called Abd al-Aziz al-Masri was talking a big game about producing anthrax[25] and even the nerve agent soman, but in Abu Khabab's view the lack of proper laboratories in the medieval surroundings of rural Afghanistan made such a goal implausible.

'Forget nuclear[26] and nerve agents,'[27] he said that same bitterly cold and silent night. 'There are alternatives and they are within our reach.'

I was instantly apprehensive, as much for my own wellbeing as anyone else's. I had tested the limits with explosives formulae and didn't feel like choking to death as an alternative.

'These are the critical chemicals,' he continued with evident relish, holding up a glass jar containing a white powder with a yellowish tinge.

---

* Experts on the threat from radiological devices say the biggest impact would be to sow panic. In many cases the blast from a dirty bomb would kill more people than the radiation.[24]

** Al-Ghamdi told me al-Qaeda operative Abu Leith al-Libi had suggested spreading the rumour that the group had several nuclear weapons at a meeting attended by Abd al-Aziz al-Masri and Abu Khabab. Abu Khabab also told me about the meeting. He told me that Chechens and Uzbeks linked to the Russian mafia had several times approached al-Qaeda offering nuclear warheads but they all turned out to be scams.

His breath shot bursts of condensation across the freezing room. He reached up to a glass jar plastered with ominous warning stickers perched precariously on a shelf. It had an acid inside.

'If you mix it with a strong acid like this you get what?'

'Hydrogen cyanide,' I said warily, not liking the direction the conversation was taking.

'Exactly,' he said, the professor proud of his A-grade student. 'That's what the Nazis used in the death camps. Another name for it is Zyklon-B,' he added, almost nonchalantly. 'And if you mix potassium permanganate with the acid you get chlorine gas. But now,' he stopped and raised his hand, 'put together all three ingredients, and you produce a gas.'

I was falling behind, but didn't want to show it.

'A very toxic one,' I said.

'To be sure, cyanogen chloride,' he went on, now in full flow.* 'It's two and a half times heavier than air. It gets into your bloodstream and cuts off the oxygen supply to your organs.'**

The biggest challenge, he said, was finding an effective delivery mechanism. The actual combination of ingredients was not complicated, but you didn't want to be standing over them as they mixed. Quite so, I thought.

Before I could give a lot of thought to the technical challenges I fell seriously ill, thanks to a visit from what was colloquially known in the camps as the 'Afghan visa'. As the days shortened and the cold seeped into our bones, I suddenly succumbed to a raging fever. Malaria and typhoid were simultaneously invading my body, already weakened by my slow recuperation from being wounded in the Philippines.

---

* The descriptions of all these chemicals do not go beyond well-known chemistry and details already in the public domain in academic studies, media articles, court documents, government reports and the like.
** Hydrogen cyanide and cyanogen chloride are what are called 'blood agents'. They 'achieve their effects by travelling through the blood stream to sites where the agent can interfere with oxygen utilization at the cellular level'.[28]

I lay on a thin mattress on the concrete floor of Abu Khabab's living quarters, slipping in and out of a delirious state, too weak even to sit up. Abu Khabab showed real concern and had a medic of sorts visit from a nearby camp. It didn't require too much expertise to realize that without proper treatment I might die, and even Jalalabad – a humming metropolis compared to most of eastern Afghanistan – had few medical services.

I probably owe my life to Abu Khabab. He organized antibiotics, an exotic treatment in that part of the world, and contacted Abu Zubaydah in Peshawar. I was loaded into the back of a battered van that smelled of diesel and animal manure and driven to Jalalabad over rough tracks that jolted my already shaking frame as if administering electric shock treatment. Clammy with a cold sweat, I was poured onto a bus in Jalalabad for the five-hour trip to Peshawar. At times I wanted to be allowed to get off the crowded, stinking bus to die in peace at the side of the road. But exhaustion shut my body down; I had to be woken from a deep slumber of psychedelic dreams in Peshawar.

I had a night of fitful sleep at the safe house. Abu Zubaydah told me he had called my brother Moheddin to let him know I was very sick. Like other Arab recruits, I had left a family contact number in Peshawar in case I was killed. Moheddin had immediately wired cash to the Faisal Bank account held by Abu Zubaydah, al-Qaeda's version of the Western Union.

Abu Zubaydah looked at me with a rare look of genuine concern. However his bedside manners lacked tact. 'You might be about to die so you should revise your will,' he said. Leafing through my passport, he said that Qatar was the only safe destination. But I would need someone to meet me. For a moment the fog of my addled brain lifted.

'Ahmed,'* I whispered. I was with him in Bosnia. I had a number somewhere.

'Use this phone,' Abu Zubaydah said, handing me a battered

---

* I'm not divulging his last name.

Nokia. It was a gesture that would ultimately change the course of my life.

Abu Zubaydah graciously relaxed his rule about no flights in and out of Peshawar and bought me a ticket to Doha.

It was the longest flight of my life: delirium at high altitude, high fever, dizziness mixed with anxiety about my reception by the Qatari authorities. Looking back at that day, I am astonished I was even allowed to board a plane. I could have been carrying any number of contagious diseases.

I was either not suspected or looked too sick to be any risk. Ahmed duly met me at the airport and took me immediately to a hospital, where two weeks of treatment restored my health if not my strength.

So perilous was my condition that I was told to return in a year's time for a series of checks. If I'm still alive, I thought as the doctor left the room. Another stamp on my 'Afghan visa' or too much cyanide would finish me off.

I moved to Ahmed's house to recuperate further, and Moheddin came to visit. We had not seen each other in three years – since I had left Khobar for Bosnia a few days past my sixteenth birthday.

'You look dreadful,' he said with a grin.

'Thanks very much.'

'I've seen it before; Afghanistan can suck everything out of you.'

'It's been a very long time,' he continued quietly. 'When you left that morning, I had a sense you were planning some big adventure. It wasn't a routine camping trip; your wild eyes told me that.'

He began to laugh; I did, too, though it hurt.

He had no idea I had been to the Philippines; I had told none of my family and suddenly felt guilty that my wanderlust had been so irresponsible. If Moheddin was hurt he didn't show it, and he peppered me with questions about everything from the snakes to operating a mortar.

He also wanted to know about the Taliban, by then into their second year of ruling Afghanistan.

'Well, their ideology really is medieval,' I said. 'It's nothing like the Ottoman Empire. But they have achieved one extraordinary thing. Before they came to power no one ever travelled at night in Afghanistan – too many bandits and rogue checkpoints. Now it's completely safe.'

It was in some ways a strange encounter. Here was the man I had always looked up to, now just shy of forty, listening agape to my stories of global travel in the service of jihad. I could tell he was both proud of me and a little jealous.

Eventually he asked the big question.

'Have you joined Sheikh Osama?' he asked, referring to bin Laden.

'I still have some reservations,' I lied. It was forbidden to reveal such information even to family members, and what Moheddin didn't know couldn't hurt him.

Just weeks after being discharged, I was back in the Afghan mountains at al-Qaeda's Faruq training camp on a barren ridge south of Khost. It was January 1998.

The panorama was stunning. To the north lay the distant snow-capped peaks of the Spin Ghar and Jaji, where Osama bin Laden had made his name in the jihad against the Soviets in the 1980s. Beyond that was Tora Bora, from whose caves he would escape after 9/11.*

---

* I was given a tour of the caves in 1998. Camp Faruq was one of four camps al-Qaeda maintained exclusively for its recruits. Two others – Zhawar (which locals called Jihad Wal) and al-Sadeeq – were part of the same camp complex south of Khost and the fourth was the group's administrative headquarters in Kandahar. Bin Laden provided significant funding for four additional camps. The group also maintained safe houses in places such as Kabul and Jalalabad. Other camps operated independently. One was the Khalden camp, whose interests were looked after by Abu Zubaydah in Peshawar.

One afternoon, I sat watching the pale winter sun as it dropped behind hills strewn with scree and boulders. The chill of dusk began to seep through the camp. I had begun to dread another long winter's evening. Suddenly there was a commotion. A convoy of SUVs roared into the compound, throwing dust into the clear mountain air. Heavily armed fighters jumped from the first and last vehicles and made a show of securing the area.

Osama bin Laden stepped from the middle vehicle, his saturnine smile greeting chants of '*Allahu Akbar*' from scores of al-Qaeda fighters. I was as enthusiastic as any to see him; he would only make such an appearance if he had some sort of announcement to make.

I was not disappointed. As the mustard evening light ebbed, bin Laden led the *Maghreb* prayer in our makeshift mosque. Then all the fighters were told to gather in the exercise yard. Bin Laden stepped up to a microphone. There was a hush of anticipation.

'Brothers, I bring glad tidings. We are unifying the mujahideen in a new global front against the Zionists and the Crusaders. We will soon announce this to the world.'

We cheered.

'Finally, we will now have unity. Unity among the Arabs here in Afghanistan and in the *Ummah* beyond. I have come here today to tell you we are at the beginning of a new era, an era in which we will triumph against the enemies of the Muslims.'

Bin Laden delivered this momentous news in his typically soft-spoken way. He didn't need to raise his voice to command the complete attention of his followers.

'We must focus on America, the head of the snake, rather than the tail, the Arab regimes! Cut the head and the tail will die,' he declared.

As if on cue, bin Laden's bodyguards pointed their AK-47s into the air and unleashed a long burst of automatic fire. The tracer lit up the night sky. There was a deafening chorus of cheers. He then led the camp in the *Isha* prayer, before bidding farewell under an ink-black sky dotted with stars.

We all knew his announcement was significant; we had no idea that it heralded a campaign of attacks that would change the world.

The following month, al-Qaeda declared 'jihad against the Jews and the Crusaders' and the creation of a World Islamic Front. The 'Far Enemy' was coming into focus: the *kuffar* regime of the United States and its allies, which sought domination over Muslims and occupied their lands.[29]

'The ruling to kill the Americans and their allies – civilians and military – is an individual duty for every Muslim who can do it in any country in which it is possible to do it, in order to liberate the al-Aqsa Mosque [in Jerusalem] and the holy mosque [Mecca] from their grip, and in order for their armies to move out of all the lands of Islam, defeated and unable to threaten any Muslim.'[30]

In hindsight, the declaration left little room for doubt. But at the time I could not have imagined how it would be pursued.[31]

As my health was still too delicate for me to return to Darunta, it was my job to explain to some of the fighters with very basic education (essentially the large and growing contingent of Yemenis) just what this declaration meant and on what it was based. After all, I had promised bin Laden.

My pupils were dull-eyed and uncomprehending; more than once I felt like yelling at them as they sat and fidgeted. All they wanted to do was ride in the back of pickup trucks with rifles.

I explained my frustrations one day to Abu Hamza al-Ghamdi, who laughed roguishly.

'You thought I was being less than literal about the Vanguard?' he asked, one eyebrow raised extravagantly. 'The Sheikh is guided by the words of the Prophet. Remember the *hadith*: "An army of 12,000 will come out of Aden-Abyan. They will give victory to Allah and His Messenger."'[32]

That mountainous region in the south of Yemen was indeed where al-Qaeda would soon build up its forces, with hundreds of foot soldiers trained in Afghanistan.*

As I came across jihadis from different backgrounds, I became fascinated by what had brought them to al-Qaeda's camps. Some had come to believe in jihad after years of thought and argument. Some – often the less stable – had been radicalized almost overnight, perhaps as a reaction against a form of addiction or in seeking redemption for some terrible sin. They were escaping demons or the tedium of a mundane existence. Still others (like the young Yemenis) were told by preachers that they were needed: hooked and drawn in like helpless fish by a silver-tongued imam. There were many personal journeys, but all sought one end: martyrdom.

I, too, had taken that journey. I still believed that it was worth dying for the right cause – to defend and protect Muslims. But the doubts were beginning to creep in, almost subliminally, and when I least expected them. There was a bloodlust among some fighters that was alien to my upbringing and beliefs. I had first glimpsed it in Bosnia; now I heard it expressed more often. Abu Nassim, the cruel Tunisian, was just one example. I began to wonder whether it fed on itself in the intense atmosphere of the camps, where adrenalin and testosterone met in a heady mix.

Some men had been hardened by torture and imprisonment. Among those who would eventually come through the Afghan camps was none other than Yusuf al-Ayeri, my instructor in the Islamist 'Scout' group. Since I had last seen him in Bosnia, he had done a stint in jail in Saudi Arabia, for extremist activities. Now, he

---

* In 2009 al-Qaeda in the Arabian Peninsula (AQAP) was founded in Yemen, led and staffed by veterans of al-Qaeda camps in Afghanistan. It was not the first time bin Laden had prioritized building up jihadi forces in southern Yemen. In 1989–90, after the withdrawal of Soviet forces from Afghanistan, he poured great energy into plans to liberate southern Yemen from Communist rule, but his hope to create a unified Islamic State in Yemen were stymied by a lack of support from some key clerics and the unification of the country in May 1990 under President Ali Abdullah Saleh.[33]

was on the fast track to higher things in al-Qaeda, carried by a burning anger.*

So was I, but thanks to entirely different attributes. I was the innocent who could carry money or get two weeks of hospital treatment without arousing suspicion. But I was also the intellectual who could improvise and find solutions, who could explain himself to hostile questioners. Which is why al-Ghamdi tested me with two sensitive missions.

The first was to meet with a 'brother' in Islamabad, who would take me to a money transfer office. I should ask for Karim. The message was: 'Doctor Mariam sent me to collect the fee for the operation.'

Karim turned out to be a middle-aged Pakistani who looked terrified when I passed on the word about 'Dr Mariam'.

'Come with me,' he said and led me furtively to a side room. He took a rucksack out of the safe and handed it to me. Inside, in bundles of crisp notes, was half a million US dollars.

I walked back to the car, sure that hidden eyes were watching my every step. We drove to an Afghan refugee camp outside Islamabad and in a dusty workshop the money was transferred into nylon bags and inserted in a space hollowed out inside the driver's door. We then made the two-hour drive to Peshawar, during which I was convinced we would be stopped and the loot discovered. We weren't and I was relieved to entrust the treasure to another courier. Much later I discovered that 'Dr Mariam' was a code word used for transfers to Osama bin Laden from one of his sisters, who really was called Mariam.**

That task accomplished, al-Ghamdi gave me a more ambitious

---

* After he was released in mid 1998, Ayeri made several trips to al-Qaeda's camps in Afghanistan. After the second Chechen war started in 1999 he was a key fundraiser for his friend Ibn Khattab's jihadi efforts there.[34]
** Bin Laden held his half-sister Mariam Mohameed Awad bin Laden in high esteem. His speeches often drew on her master's thesis, 'The role of Ibn Taymiyyah in the jihad against the Mongols', which she completed in 1983 at the Umm al-Qura University in Mecca. Her thesis presented the famous Muslim theologian's writings as providing theological justification for Sayyid Qutb's ideological arguments six centuries later.

one: go to London to pick up a satellite phone. My Bahraini passport meant I could get a visa for the UK in Qatar, where I had previously travelled without incident.

I flew into London's Heathrow Airport on a day of April squalls with slate-grey clouds scudding across the rooftops.

The immigration officer at the airport asked whom I was coming to visit.

'I have a friend who is a computer scientist,' I said in my halting English.

'Can you speak good enough English to get around?' he asked.

'I can order from McDonald's,' I said.

'That's good enough,' he said with a laugh. Another reminder from the age of innocence.

A quiet and grave Jamaican convert I had briefly encountered in Bosnia picked me up and drove me towards London. Despite the seriousness of my mission, I could not help staring agog at the greenery and the sheer size of the metropolis.

'This is it,' he said simply.

We had arrived at a large town house in one of the less salubrious streets of Gipsy Hill, a neighbourhood undergoing gentrification. A British Pakistani opened the door and ushered me in.

The house was empty apart from a British Egyptian man in his fifties who introduced himself as Safwat. He was elegantly dressed in a cotton suit and had an aristocratic bearing. He told me that he was soon leaving for Afghanistan, and at the recommendation of Abu Hamza al-Masri, the hook-handed cleric of London's Finsbury Park Mosque, he would train with Abu Khabab.

'You're making the right choice. I know Abu Khabab; there's no one better.'

The next day, the Pakistani gave me £200 and told me to head for the al-Muntada al-Islami mosque in Parsons Green, which had dormitories.

'Make sure you attend the *Fajr* prayer there every day,' he said, before setting me on my way. After a week of early morning prayers he finally showed up. We walked to his car and he took out a suitcase with the satellite phone in bubble wrap. It had been paid for in cash; it was not registered to anyone.

'Tell the brothers in Afghanistan there is £25,000 of credit on the phone. After that they need to send me funds to top it up.'

I enjoyed my brief time in London. Despite warnings that the English would be frosty or hostile I found them polite and helpful. I also delighted in the freedom to jump on and off buses in a random exploration of the city. And both Coke and chocolate tasted so much better than they did in Afghanistan. Cadbury's became my best friend.

At that time, jihadis did not see the United Kingdom as enemy territory. In fact, many were taking shelter in London. America was the enemy. But this was 1998, before 9/11 and the Iraq War broadened the battlefield and in so doing stoked a creeping anti-Islamic sentiment across the Western world.

In Peshawar Abu Zubaydah was very happy to receive the phone; I think it may have been the only time I saw him smile. But in my brief time away, the mood had shifted in the camps. There was talk of martyrdom operations, a first for al-Qaeda. Those who wished to volunteer, the word went, should seek out the group's operational chief Abu Hafs al-Masri.

While we all wished to die gloriously in battle, the notion of suicide attacks was hotly debated at a number of levels. Only once had a group affiliated with al-Qaeda carried out such an operation: the attack two years previously on the Egyptian embassy in Islamabad. To me, the Koran had an unarguable prohibition of suicide.[35] I believed Zawahiri's group had crossed a line and my unease deepened.

Perhaps the Egyptian cleric, a figure of fun in Baku just two years earlier, now prevailed inside al-Qaeda. I thought back to al-Muhajir's lecture glorifying martyrdom, to bin Laden's statement about taking the war to the United States, to Abu Khabab's description of the truck bomb he'd designed. Things were changing, and fast. But I had no inkling that the opening shot in this war was just weeks away.

# MY FOURTH LIFE: ESCAPE FROM AL-QAEDA

## 1998

A t 10:30 A.M. on 7 August 1998, a truck arrived at the entrance to the underground car park of the US embassy in Nairobi, Kenya. The occupants demanded the local guards at the barrier allow them access to the garage. They refused, at which point the two men in the truck opened fire and threw flash grenades.

In the offices above, people came to the windows to see what the commotion was about. For many of them curiosity proved fatal. Seconds later a massive bomb composed of a 2,000 pound mix of TNT and other explosive substances was detonated in the truck. Just four minutes later, a truck bomb exploded outside the US embassy in neighbouring Tanzania.*

In all, 224 people were killed in the two suicide bombings, but despite the targets only twelve Americans were among the victims. In the first explosion, most were ordinary Kenyans going about their business in one of Nairobi's busiest neighbourhoods. The force of the blast demolished an adjacent building and seriously damaged both the embassy and the twenty-two-storey Co-operative Bank of Kenya.

The intelligence community had picked up no chatter, let alone actionable information, about the plot. Nor had there been any

* I later learned the bombs were designed by Abd al-Aziz al-Masri, al-Qaeda's in-house explosives expert.

whispers in al-Qaeda camps about an impending operation that would declare, in action rather than words, Osama bin Laden's war against America.

That day I was at Camp Faruq in eastern Afghanistan, blissfully unaware of the carnage thousands of miles to the west. There was no Internet, no texting in those days. The first I knew of the attacks was when celebratory gunfire erupted. It had a pattern unlike hostile fire.

I ran towards the main office at the camp, where jihadis were gathering in the crisp mountain air, brandishing their AK-47s aloft and chanting '*Allahu Akbar*'. One fighter climbed into a pickup truck and urged fighters to rejoice.

'The largest CIA station in Africa has been destroyed, thanks to our martyrs,' he proclaimed.

Hours before the first indications came from the US that al-Qaeda was the likely perpetrator, there was no doubt among my fellow jihadis. At first I celebrated with them, imagining a surgical operation that had taken out a CIA office. How naive. As details trickled through, thanks to one short-wave radio, the scale of the destruction became evident and I was troubled.

If this was the war al-Qaeda planned to wage, I had serious misgivings about it. I could not ignore the callous disregard for the lives of innocent civilians. One of my fellow jihadis even dismissed the dozens of African casualties as 'something that happens' when you are at war. There was more than a tinge of racism in his attitude; many in al-Qaeda looked down on black Africans. Al-Qaeda's leadership had chosen mid-morning on a Friday to carry out the attack on the grounds that most Muslims would be on their way to prayers.

Almost as troubling was the use of suicide bombers in both embassy attacks. I could see no religious justification for the use of such a weapon. In my view the Koran explicitly forbade suicide. At the time I could see why the Palestinians would use such a weapon of despair against occupying Israeli forces. But we – al-Qaeda – had a choice. This was the first time the group had deployed suicide bombers: was this to be the way ahead?* Were suicide attacks to be the foundation of al-Qaeda's campaign? Under what circumstances – and supported by what theological arguments – could the deaths of civilians be acceptable?

I thought back to the growing discussions in the camps of martyrdom operations; and how the leadership had put out word that interested candidates should come forward. It began to come together. A few days later, it became intensely personal and even more distressing.

For several weeks I had been asking others at Faruq where Abu Abdullah al-Maki had gone. No one knew. I assumed he'd chosen to move to another camp, but we were close and I found it odd that he had just vanished without a word. While I wondered, al-Maki was already in Kenya. He had been hand-picked by bin Laden as one of the Nairobi bombers. I imagined him volunteering in a euphoric rush after that impassioned sermon by Sheikh al-Muhajir.**

Al-Maki had been the driver of the truck. When his co-conspirator had thrown the flash grenades and then fled the scene, he had detonated the bomb.

Within a couple of days, news footage of the bombing reached the camp. Dozens of fighters crowded around a dusty video recorder to watch it. Many of them cheered at the scenes of devastation and suffering. I was shocked and sickened, haunted by the image of an African businessman immaculately dressed in a khaki suit clutching a briefcase in one arm. His other arm had been blown clean off. One side of his suit was drenched in blood, the other untouched. The contrast was arresting and horrifying.

My mind was jolted back to my childhood and the videos I had seen of similarly well-dressed civilians in Sarajevo sustaining awful

---

* As noted above, Ayman al-Zawahiri's Egyptian Islamic Jihad carried out a suicide bombing attack on the Egyptian embassy in Islamabad in November 1995. But at the time his group had not yet formally joined forces with al-Qaeda.
** Al-Maki's birth name was Jihad Mohammed Ali al-Harazi and he also went by the name Azzam. His al-Qaeda alias was Abu Obeydah al-Maki. He was the cousin of Abd al-Rahim al-Nashiri, the future mastermind of the USS *Cole* attack, and a friend of two of the future 9/11 hijackers.[1]

injuries from Serb mortar fire. Those videos had pushed me towards jihad; now we – the jihadis – were inflicting such casualties.

The expressions on the faces of the dazed and traumatized civilians in Kenya immediately reminded me of the faces I had seen at the bridge in Sarajevo. They had the same look of numb disbelief at the cruelty of mankind as had the women and girls who shuffled across that bridge. I remembered just how I felt then, an infuriating clash of emotions: determination to take revenge but also a dispiriting sense that it would achieve nothing beyond another cycle of revenge.

I still felt that Muslim communities throughout the world needed defending against enemies with overwhelming superiority. That impulse had taken me to Azerbaijan, the Philippines and Afghanistan. If it brought martyrdom, God would be pleased. But I began to ask myself how that defence should be waged and when it might legitimately become attack. And what methods were allowable in what I still perceived as a just cause?

I still subscribed to the view that the US and the 'modern Crusaders' stood in the way of a victorious Islam illuminating a better path for humanity, as had been foretold in the prophecies. We needed to oppose their hegemony. But not this way – through suicide bombings and mass casualties. Did we – al-Qaeda – have the authority to decide on behalf of 1.6 billion Muslims what a just or legitimate war looked like?

Amid these doubts, the wrangling inside me, I did know one thing for certain. The moral clarity I had felt as a sixteen-year-old setting off for Bosnia was forever gone.

In the days that followed, I felt increasingly disconsolate, a mood deepened by the jubilation of everyone else. This was not why I had felt the call to jihad in Bosnia, dreamed of reaching Chechnya or even joined Abu Khabab's laboratory.

I recalled a heated discussion the previous winter in Abu Zubaydah's safe house in Peshawar. An article by a member of the Libyan Islamic Fighting Group, a jihadi faction committed to the overthrow of Colonel Gadhafi, had described how the group had once spared the lives of Libyan soldiers after extracting a promise they would 'return' to Islam. Several Algerian al-Qaeda members had argued that the soldiers should have been summarily executed; they were apostates who deserved no mercy. I had disagreed, arguing that in their humanitarian gesture the Libyan fighters had opted to persuade fellow Muslims rather than terrorize. But my perspective had made no impact.

'Why must they be so bloodthirsty?' I had asked the only fighter who had taken my side. Not for the first time, I felt that some of the men attracted to the al-Qaeda banner were driven as much by psychosis as religious conviction.

Six months before the embassy bombings, bin Laden had issued the now famous fatwah against the 'Jews and the Crusaders' in which he called for Muslims to kill American soldiers and civilians wherever they could find them. I had not taken him literally; perhaps American military personnel in Saudi Arabia would be targeted. But huge truck bombs 2,000 miles from Mecca and Medina? Were we going to fight the Americans in Africa to try to expel them from the Arabian Peninsula? Was this now a global campaign where any civilian – a woman and child on a beach, an elderly couple at an archaeological site – was a legitimate target? And were casualties among locals now acceptable collateral damage, really the 'cost of doing business'?

There was certainly historical and religious justification for offensive jihad. It was usually carried out against what the Muslim leadership of the time perceived to be a threat to the community, the *Ummah*. The Persian and Byzantine empires had constituted such threats. Had Muslim communities not taken desperate steps against both these empires, they would have been subdued or exterminated. Pre-emptive action to prevent defeat was entirely permissible. But such action had traditionally been the prerogative of the Caliph.*

* That prerogative had been loosely interpreted by the Umayyad Caliphs to justify wars fought for the sake of territorial expansion – expansion that would take them across North Africa and into Andalus, what is now southern Spain. In the end the expansionist behaviour of the Muslim empire was not much different from that of any other empire.

In Bosnia, Abu Ayoub Shamrani had preached to us that in the absence of a Caliph a Vanguard of mujahideen could wage a new form of jihad to spread Islam around the world. Eventually, Abu Hamza al-Ghamdi – in his guileful, charming way – had convinced me that Osama bin Laden was leading such a Vanguard. I had pledged allegiance to follow his orders so long as these did not disobey God. But in killing innocents in Africa was bin Laden disobeying God? This terrorist spectacular risked provoking an American response which would bring suffering to millions of Muslims and destabilize the Muslim world.

My unease grew when I spoke to Sheikh al-Muhajir himself. He was one of several figures who were highly influential inside al-Qaeda but known by very few beyond it. Years later he would collect his teachings in a book on the dogma of jihad which would make a deep impression on the founders of the Islamic State.

I caught up with al-Muhajir after Friday prayers and asked him if he had a few minutes. He probably imagined that I was coming to ask him for advice or flatter him about his sermon. I intended neither. Instead, as we sat on the carpet of his book-lined study, I had a few questions. I was careful not to express any doubts about the embassy attacks.

'Sheikh,' I said, 'how do we respond to criticism that we have killed innocent civilians while attacking the Crusaders?'

Al-Muhajir smiled. It was an invitation to show off his great erudition. He launched into a detailed description of the Mongol invasions of Muslim lands in the thirteenth century. The scholar Ibn Taymiyyah had issued a fatwah that clearly legitimized the deaths of Muslims and non-Muslims alike where the enemy is using them as a human shield.

'This fatwah is comprehensive; it gives us justification,' he said firmly.

Al-Muhajir probably assumed I would go away reassured and impressed. I didn't. Instead I took advantage of a long-planned trip to the villa which served as al-Qaeda's guest house in Kabul to consult its well stocked library of Islamic texts. I sought out the fatwah – in the twenty-eighth volume of a thirty-seven-volume encyclopaedia – and found that it had no relevance whatsoever.

It had been issued in response to Mongol attacks on Muslim cities in Central Asia. Every time the Mongols sacked a city, they took civilians – sometimes as many as a couple of thousand – and forced them to push siege towers towards the walls of the next city. The fatwah said the defenders of a city were permitted to kill Muslims being used as human shields – because otherwise they and their families would end up being killed, and the Mongols would go on conquering more Muslim cities.

But the fatwah (known as *al-Tatarus*) had been proclaimed in very specific circumstances.*

To me, there was no resemblance or parallel between Muslims being used as human shields by Mongol armies and the attacks in East Africa. Al-Muhajir's precedent was a castle of sand. Were al-Qaeda's other theological justifications, including its interpretation of the prophecies, built on equally shaky foundations? Was al-Qaeda really the Vanguard that would fight with the Mahdi or was it set on a path that future generations of Muslims would reject rather than celebrate?

As I stared at the dusty volumes spread around me, I felt a nauseating knot of doubt. In Bosnia I had worn a military uniform with the insignia of the Bosnian army and had passionately believed I was serving my religion. Despite my reservations, Abu Hamza al-Ghamdi had persuaded me that al-Qaeda offered the truest path to serve Islam in a looming clash of civilizations. But within months of pledging allegiance to bin Laden, I was beginning to feel that al-Qaeda might actually be harming our faith by offering specious justifications for abhorrent behaviour. If that was the direction the jihadi movement was shifting, how could I be a part of it? How

---

* In the view of the Jordanian scholar Marwan Shehadeh, al-Qaeda and other groups have abused *al-Tatarus*. 'Killings started to target innocent civilians without observing those restrictions and conditions or considering the preventions that guard against the spilling of "protected" blood,' he wrote.[2]

could I continue to teach young Yemenis and other gullible recruits that religious texts and prophecies justified a global jihad that included the maiming and murdering of innocents? If this new definition of jihad did not offer a path to paradise, then it offered no path at all.

Feeling dazed, I wandered out onto the street. I had an appointment to meet one of the most eminent jihadis in Afghanistan. I had longed to meet Abu Musab al-Suri[3] ever since reading his book *The Syrian Experience* while recuperating from typhoid and malaria. In over 900 pages the Aleppo-born jihadi had forensically examined the reasons for the outbreak and failure of the jihadi uprising in the city of Hama in 1982, which had been brutally put down by Bashar al-Assad's father, Hafez.

Al-Suri had joined the uprising before being forced to flee the country. He argued that its failure to reach out to different factions to create a broad and unified rebel movement and mobilize the wider population had been fatal. The book helped establish him as one of the most brilliant jihadi strategists of his generation, and years later greatly influenced jihadis trying to overthrow Bashar al-Assad.*

Al-Suri had a volatile relationship with Osama bin Laden. He joined al-Qaeda soon after it was founded but their paths had diverged after bin Laden decamped to Sudan in the early 1990s. In 1997 he had escorted CNN journalists to interview al-Qaeda's leader.[4] Soon afterwards he moved to Kabul where he built strong relations with the Taliban, whose 'emirate' he viewed as paramount to the future of the jihadi movement.

Over time al-Suri had become exasperated with bin Laden's provocative media statements, especially as the Taliban, faced with growing international pressure, had asked him to stop

---

* For example, the Syrian al-Qaeda aligned group Jabhat al-Nusra emphasized coalition building and building up support among the local population.

grandstanding.* Unsurprisingly, Abu Hamza al-Ghamdi had looked less than pleased when I asked for permission to meet al-Suri. I assured him, looking hurt, that I had no intention of breaking my *bayat* to bin Laden.

'Good,' he replied, and then with a twinkle in his eye added, 'let us know what he's up to.'

Informing on al-Suri to al-Qaeda was the last thing on my mind as I approached his villa in the Wazarak Khan neighbourhood. I hoped that if anybody had the answers to my doubts about the path al-Qaeda appeared to be taking it would be him.

I was immediately taken aback by his red hair, pale complexion and intense green eyes, a genetic legacy of the conquest of northern Syria by the Normans during the First Crusade. He escorted me to his study, shooing away his four young children so that we could speak.

And speak we did, for hours. Al-Ghamdi had been right to be suspicious. Al-Suri was looking for recruits and seemed impressed with my grasp of history and theology.

'You know, Abu al-Abbas, you're the first jihadi under twenty I've met in Afghanistan who has even heard of the Cuban Missile Crisis. I want to start teaching recruits here soon and I could do with your help.'

'But I have pledged *bayat* to the Sheikh,' I answered feebly, suddenly feeling like the customer who realizes he's been fooled into buying faulty goods. He rolled his eyes and I wondered if I heard him muttering 'the Sheikh' under his breath.

Al-Suri was by far the most interesting thinker I met during all my time as a jihadi. He had little time for Salafis, whom he accused of inflexible dogmatism. Instead he peppered his remarks with references to Che Guevara and Fidel Castro, from whom he said the mujahideen had much to learn.

---

* Al-Suri's anger was triggered, in part, by the May 1998 press conference bin Laden and Zawahiri held for a select group of Pakistani journalists to talk up their 'Worldwide Islamic Front for Jihad Against the Jews and the Crusaders'.[5]

'They built a broad coalition and waged a brilliant propaganda campaign to win the support of the masses. That was the key to the Cuban revolution. Overthrowing regimes requires strength in numbers.'

Until then his tone had been professorial. Suddenly he raised his voice. 'What we need, Abu al-Abbas, is to rouse the believers! Only then can we drive the Americans from our land and oust the regimes they imposed on us! Only then can we exterminate from this earth Assad, Mubarak and the corrupt imposters of the so-called House of Saud.'

I was taken aback at his eruption of anger towards the rulers of the Arab world. Al-Suri had a brilliant mind but also a taste for revenge and violence. It made him both captivating and frightening – and potentially more dangerous than bin Laden. After the devastation in East Africa, bloodshed back home was literally the last thing I wanted. It was one thing to target Americans, but I remained deeply uncomfortable with the idea of fighting our own rulers and dividing the population, especially in Saudi Arabia.

'What do you think will be the impact of embassy bombings?' I asked, anxious to change the subject.

He did not mince his words. 'Bin Laden is an idiot. I'm all for killing Americans but we need to build up our capabilities first. Bombing their embassies in Africa is not going to make a blind bit of difference at this point. You might as well go to fight them in Argentina.'

The trauma of Hama was still very real for al-Suri.

'Do they think the dictators and their American backers with their armies and their charming security services are going to suddenly wave the white flag of surrender? You can't launch a few attacks and hope the spirit of jihad will trickle down to the masses. You need to be on the ground, mobilizing every last Muslim for a rebellion from below.'

Al-Suri's strategy was not to carry out sporadic attacks worldwide, which seemed the direction in which al-Qaeda was going, but to *mobilize* worldwide. 'We need to start exploiting the Internet! We need to trigger a global jihadi intifada,' he said.

By now he was on his feet, pacing across the room. And his views were unvarnished.

'What makes bin Laden worse than an idiot is that he carried out these attacks with absolutely no permission from the Taliban. They told me that themselves. He's put the Islamic emirate here in jeopardy and he knows it. That's why he's not claimed responsibility.*

'The Islamic emirate of Afghanistan is the biggest success story in the entire history of the jihadi movement, but now this provincial from Hadramaut** who fancies himself as the next Caliph risks sabotaging the base we need to build up our strength. Now, the Americans will pressure the Pakistanis to put the squeeze on us. They might even intervene against the Taliban militarily.'

I sat back against the cushions, drained and deflated. Hearing a jihadi I held in such high regard denigrate bin Laden and speak so eagerly of exterminating the rulers of the Arab world made me feel lost.

The ideological edifice of my jihad was tottering like a house of cards. Earlier that day I had concluded that al-Qaeda's theological justification for the Nairobi attack was at best flawed, at worst fraudulent. Perhaps, even then, I could have justified the bombings as a means to an end. Now I was being told the strategic rationale was flawed, too. If the strategy and tactics had been mistaken but the theology sound, then maybe I could have accepted the attack. But if both the theology and the strategy were flawed, how could there be any justification at all?

My soul-searching was interrupted on 20 August. I was at Camp Faruq, using the latrines on the edge of the camp. It was about 10:00 P.M. The sky was suddenly illuminated by what seemed to be magnesium flares, descending rapidly towards me. Within seconds there was a series of detonations that shook the

* On 20 August 1998, bin Laden explicitly denied responsibility for the embassy attacks in a statement relayed to a Pakistani journalist.[6]
** Bin Laden's father's side of his family hailed from Hadramaut in Yemen.

entire hillside. Balls of fire erupted, and pungent clouds of smoke and dust enveloped the whole camp. Those few moments of privacy in the latrines probably saved my life. I ran back up the hill to see fires sprouting across the camp and fighters screaming in pain from horrendous injuries. A companion in my tent was severely injured.

The United States had fired back, declaring Operation Infinite Reach as retaliation for the embassy attacks.* Altogether some two-dozen people, including Arab and Pakistani fighters, were killed in the cruise missile attack on Camp Faruq and nearby facilities.

Fearing further attacks, and possibly a commando raid on the camps, al-Qaeda moved dozens of fighters, including me, to safe houses in Jalalabad.

After the initial shock, I noticed a hardening of resolve among al-Qaeda leaders and fighters alike. America had been dragged into a war, but its cowardice meant that it would only use missiles against us. It had confirmed al-Qaeda as the Vanguard of jihad, brave enough to take on the most powerful country on earth. But in my mind that bestowed on al-Qaeda even greater responsibility to be sure that its path was legitimate.

Spinning my wheels in Jalalabad, I visited Abu Khabab at his house at the university compound. Staying with him was the quiet British citizen of Egyptian background I had encountered in Gipsy Hill in London. Safwat** had swapped his fine suit for flowing robes to become a 'mature' student of Abu Khabab's.

---

* Weeks before the African embassy bombings, the camp leadership had relocated us 'for training purposes' from our usual sleeping quarters to tents which were put up on the edge of the camp. With the benefit of hindsight it is clear the camp leadership anticipated the United States would likely retaliate with air strikes. The fact the tents were hit illustrated the Americans had undertaken careful satellite reconnaissance. President Bill Clinton described the strikes as part of 'a long, ongoing struggle between freedom and fanaticism'. Few guessed how long that struggle would be, nor how quickly it would escalate.

** He was also known in jihadi circles as Tala'at. His real first name was Safwat but I never found out his last name.

Over the next few days he revealed to me that he had married and separated from an upper-class Englishwoman in London, with whom he had a daughter. He never made clear to me the reason he had so late in life suddenly decided to come to Afghanistan, but perhaps it was the problems in his personal life. I found him to be the essential geek, always working on formulae for explosives and devices.

When Safwat heard I was travelling to Peshawar (to replace reading glasses which had been incinerated in the cruise missile strike) he asked me to deliver something. Worried the Americans might hit Darunta, he had created an almanac of Abu Khabab's research on two floppy disks: hundreds of pages of computer-typed documents as well as scans of handwritten notes and diagrams.

'If something happens to us then this knowledge needs to be preserved,' Safwat said, pressing the disks into my hands. 'Take care of them,' he said, his sad, drooping eyes beseeching me.

My instructions were to leave the disks with an American Jordanian called Khalil bin Saeed al-Deek, who had a guest house in Peshawar.* I couldn't help thinking that if Western intelligence really wanted to go after al-Qaeda, they should spend more time wandering the streets of Peshawar than firing missiles at Afghan hillsides.

An IT expert and sometime resident of California, Deek had set up a website for al-Qaeda in 1997 and a sham charity to search out recruits. I had first met him at Darunta in 1996; he was just about to start at Abu Khabab's embryonic camp and had raised money for the Egyptian bomb-maker.

I arrived in Peshawar in a dark mood, still wrestling with the implications of al-Qaeda's new strategy. I looked at the disks Safwat had given me, realizing that the information they contained might one day give al-Qaeda terrifying destructive power. I also felt that I

---

* Deek was known in jihadi circles as Abu Ayed. He was close to the British jihadi Abu Hudhaifa and stayed with him in Birmingham for a time.

was responsible for much of that information, having worked closely with Abu Khabab.

I passed an Internet café in a busy commercial street and almost involuntarily stopped. Without thinking through the consequences, I instinctively went in and asked for copies of the disks. I assumed that the shopkeeper could neither speak nor read Arabic.

Why did I do it? Twenty years later, I still can't say for sure. Was I already subconsciously hatching a plan to alert the wider world, somehow, to al-Qaeda's plans? Probably not – but I did want to preserve the knowledge I had helped generate. After all the long hours in Darunta, that information was – in a sense – part of me. What I could not appreciate at the time was that for the princely sum of $20 I had bought my passage to another life.

I hid the copies deep in my rucksack and proceeded to Deek's house, where I dutifully handed over the disks with a brief explanation. Deek was, to put it mildly, extremely interested.

One evening at his home, my dinner companions included Ibn Sheikh al-Libi, head of the Khalden training camp, and none other than Khalid Sheikh Mohammed.*

While he had not yet sworn an oath of allegiance to bin Laden, KSM was now working closely with al-Qaeda.

'I had heard you joined our ranks. I'm glad you took my advice brother,' he said with a smile, embracing me.

I attempted a smile in return. It didn't seem the right moment to announce I was increasingly wracked with doubts. He was ebullient about the embassy attacks.

'Jihad has come of age. The attacks in Africa have energized the whole Muslim world and there is widespread fury over the missile strikes. We have more recruits joining than ever

---

* Also there was Abu Abdullah al-Scotlandi from Dundee in Scotland. His real name was James McLintock. He told me he had settled in Pakistan after working for Aramco in Saudi Arabia. He married a Kashmiri woman and began moving in jihadi circles in Peshawar. He had a reputation as a 'high society' jihadi. For those attending the camps in Afghanistan, Peshawar was like the 'Hamptons' – a place where the cream of the crop went to rest and recharge.[7]

before. Nairobi and Dar es Salaam was just the opening salvo, *Insha'allah.*'

Deek chimed in, 'The only thing the Americans understand is force.'

I chose my words carefully.

'But are we ready for the consequences? Think of all the charities that work among Muslim communities. And think of anyone who carries an Arab passport. It's alright for those with US passports. I'm a Bahraini.'

There was an awkward silence, before KSM fixed me with a gaze that said *you are but an apprentice.*

'As I said, jihad has come of age. The *Ummah* must be ready for suffering,' he said firmly.

In an effort to ease the tension, al-Libi took me to one side.

'I probably shouldn't tell you this,' he said, 'but the embassy attacks were meant to take place two years ago.'*

They had been postponed, al-Libi said, after one of bin Laden's top aides, an Egyptian called Abu Ubaidah al-Banshiri, had drowned in a ferry accident on Lake Victoria in May 1996. He was carrying plans for the attack.[9] Random moments where fate intervenes, I thought, can change an awful lot.

After dinner I found myself speaking late into the evening with Abdul Rasheed al-Filistini, a Palestinian al-Qaeda member married to Deek's sister in law. His favourite topic of conversation was

---

* According to US court documents al-Qaeda first sent operatives to conduct reconnaissance of the US embassy in Nairobi in 1993. Ibn Sheikh al-Libi told me one reason the embassy was targeted was because Zawahiri's Egyptian Islamic Jihad believed it was the biggest CIA station in Africa and had orchestrated the defection of the wives of two EIJ operatives in Sudan. Al-Libi would be detained in Pakistan after 9/11 and transferred to US custody. He was subsequently transferred to Egypt where, allegedly under torture, he stated (falsely) that Saddam Hussein had provided chemical and biological weapons training to al-Qaeda, information subsequently used by the George W. Bush administration to make the case for war in Iraq. He was later transferred to Libya where in 2009 he was found hanged in his prison cell in suspicious circumstances. Given his religious views it is almost inconceivable he committed suicide.[8]

selling honey, which he insisted could finance the future of jihad. He would provide unwitting but valuable cover for me in years to come.

The next morning, Deek instructed me to meet a new recruit and escort him into Afghanistan. Maybe KSM was right: more jihadis had been energized to make the trek to Afghanistan. During stays in California, Deek had taken a teenage Muslim convert and onetime Death Metal fan under his wing and had radicalized him. That youngster – the recently turned twenty-year-old Adam Gadahn – was now on his way to Pakistan. Deek didn't want to be seen out and about himself; he was worried about being identified by informants.*

'You go,' he said. 'You look young and Afghan.'

As I walked around Peshawar on my way to meet Gadahn's flight from Karachi, I was struck by the normality of the place: the street markets, the amiable doctor who gave me a prescription for new glasses, the bustle of people trying to make a living. This was reality for the vast majority of Muslims whose only goals were to take care of their families in relative peace, to choose how they lived and worshipped. It was a normality I suddenly craved. I passed a school and heard the excited chatter of a hundred children on their mid-morning break. Perhaps when all this is done, I thought, I could become a teacher. At the same time I was acutely aware that, with every passing month, I was more indelibly stamped as an al-Qaeda operative. The longer I stayed in the group, the less realistic a return to normality would be.

After a half-hour wait in the pandemonium of Peshawar airport, I spotted a callow young man emerging from the arrivals hall. He was wearing Afghan clothing and a round white cap but was unmistakably American. I walked up to him and offered the pre-arranged greeting.

Gadahn had greasy hair and there were traces of ginger in his

* Gadahn had made one previous trip to Pakistan the year before. After falling ill he had returned to California.[10]

short beard. His only notable physical features were his bright, cobalt-blue eyes. Nothing about him suggested the young American would one day become one of al-Qaeda's most recognizable voices worldwide.

I hugged him and welcomed him to Pakistan. He looked sullen and withdrawn.

'There's not much good food the other side of the border,' I joked as we climbed into a motorized rickshaw. 'How about a pizza before we go?'

He abruptly refused and said he wanted to eat local food. This was a serious young man, I thought. We went to a place in the Orkazay Plaza which served authentic Afghan fare.

'So when did you convert?' I asked him.

'I was seventeen. I found out about Islam online and went down to my local mosque. It was there that Abu Ayed [al-Deek] led me to the path of jihad.'

Gadahn was not remotely apprehensive, but composed and curious. He was pleasant enough on the journey if lacking in the humour department. There was an intensity about him that was slightly unnerving.

As we took a bus towards the Afghan border, he gazed out of the window while I thought about my route out of al-Qaeda's orbit. Simply quitting was not an option. I had sworn allegiance and knew too much about the organization's personnel and camps for them to allow me to 'retire'. I had also come to know – and be a part of – the ambitious programmes led by Abu Khabab.

The key problem was that Abu Zubaydah had my passport. I needed a way to extricate myself from al-Qaeda without provoking suspicion. The irony was not lost on me as I dropped off Gadahn in Jalalabad. He was arriving with the burning desire of the true believer; belief in al-Qaeda was seeping out of me daily.

I retreated to Abu Khabab's isolated Darunta camp to try to work out my next move. I was relieved to discover he had known nothing in advance about the East Africa bomb plots.

As always there were only half a dozen or so apprentices in the camp. I was reunited with several members of the 1997 intake, including Hassan Ghul and the psychotic Abu Nassim. The current class included Safwat, the British Egyptian who had entrusted me with the disks, and a stocky recruit in his mid-thirties by the name of Abu Bakr al-Masri. Abu Bakr was a member of Zawahiri's group and had developed a particular expertise in the electronics and circuitry of bombs. That had made him a useful foil for Abu Khabab, whose forte was bomb chemistry.

Abu Khabab had continued to experiment with poison gases and I returned just in time for some gruesome practical tests. The poison of choice was hydrogen cyanide, and one cool autumnal morning the experiments got underway.

With disturbing relish Abu Nassim placed a rabbit in a glass aquarium by the lakeside and started piping in the hydrogen cyanide. White fumes started to fill the aquarium, and within seconds the poor creature started furiously licking its lips. Its breathing quickened and it started scratching furiously at the side of the tank before losing muscle control, rolling onto its back and convulsing. Finally it was dead. The whole process had lasted a minute.

Subsequently Abu Khabab's team would use that same aquarium for tests on dogs and videotape the effects.* And it was filled with much more than hydrogen cyanide as the experiments evolved. We tested chlorine and then cyanogen chloride. Then came phosphine, a toxic gas based on a certain type of rat poison, and phosgene, a colourless gas deadlier than chlorine, which smells like musty hay.** It damages lung tissue, causing a build-up of fluid, and in high doses leads to suffocation.

---

* Al-Qaeda footage of a dog being exposed to what one expert said was likely hydrogen cyanide poison gas was obtained after 9/11 by CNN in Afghanistan and broadcast in a report by correspondent Nic Robertson. A leading chemical weapons expert advising the US government said at the time: 'The fact they were able to repeat tests or demonstrations on this tape indicates that they clearly have a way to produce a predictably lethal chemical.'[11]
** Phosgene was first used by the Germans against British troops in late 1915 and was responsible for up to eighty-five percent of the 90,000 deaths by gas in the First World War.[12]

A macabre contest accompanied the research, in which apprentices competed to kill the rabbits as fast as possible.* I stayed out of it. The technical challenge of assembling a viable delivery system for poison gas confounded Abu Khabab's apprentices. It was hardly practical to ask an al-Qaeda operative to mix the chemicals just before launching an attack, as they would likely be asphyxiated in the process.

Hassan Ghul was preoccupied with the problem.

'Abu Abbas – we've been thinking of it the wrong way,' he said to me one afternoon as we headed up the hill after a stroll to the lake. 'We shouldn't be thinking in terms of mortars but rather putting a device in a rucksack and then leaving. We should be treating chemical weapons like IEDs.'

He quickened his pace, entered the empty classroom, grabbed a piece of chalk and began drawing on the blackboard.

'We need some kind of cylindrical container to store the chemicals in, but the problem is the explosion will shatter or ignite the whole thing before the chemicals have had a chance to mix and react.'

I blurted out the answer.

'So you need a small charge to break glass vials inside the cylinder. Then the substances will mix.'

I should have remained a sullen, silent observer. I had no desire to add to al-Qaeda's arsenal if it planned indiscriminate attacks around the world. But for some reason my scientific curiosity and urge to impress had momentarily overcome my qualms. How many times since have I regretted that impulse to show how clever I was?

At that moment, Abu Khabab and his other apprentices walked in for class. Hassan Ghul blurted out the idea. Predictably, Abu Nassim was excited.

* According to the Robb–Silberman Presidential Commission on WMD, prior to the US offensive to remove the Taliban from Afghanistan, 'analysts assessed that al-Qa'ida "almost certainly" . . . had produced small amounts of World War I-era agents such as hydrogen cyanide, chlorine, and phosgene.' They knew this because I told British intelligence.[13]

'This will change everything. Imagine if we'd used poison gas in Nairobi and Dar es Salaam,' he said.

Abu Khabab responded with a sharpness I had rarely heard in him.

'It's one thing developing such weapons and quite another using them. The scholars will have to be unified in justifying with a fatwah any use of a device like this.'

From my conversations with him, it seemed clear that Abu Khabab felt he was developing al-Qaeda's equivalent of a nuclear device, for use in very defined circumstances. I had clung to the belief that these weapons would only be used as a deterrent, that somehow al-Qaeda would let the world know that it had developed a WMD capability but would hold it in reserve unless attacked. But my grip on that belief was loosening almost daily.

Ultimately, I realized that the Darunta team, for all Abu Khabab's prized autonomy from al-Qaeda's high command, would not be the arbiters. The question that lurked at the back of my mind was how soon such a weapon might spread deadly gas in a cinema in London or in the Paris Métro. Unless I could extricate myself I would have to answer to God.

One long and lonely night at Abu Khabab's camp, with a winter wind howling around our flimsy shack, I had what can only be described as a blinding realization.

'Of course,' I whispered to myself, metaphorically slapping myself on the forehead.

The doctors in Qatar who had treated my malaria and typhoid had told me to return for tests twelve months later. Abu Khabab had always known this; he would support my travel, not least because he needed me to be in good health as one of his assistants.

Here was a way out beyond suspicion. I rehearsed endlessly how I would broach the subject and one morning late in November the opportunity arose. Abu Khabab was busying himself rearranging shelves of chemicals.

'You know I'm meant to go back to Qatar for medical tests,' I said airily. 'Do you think it would be safe?'

'You should go,' he said. 'I don't need another episode like last year.' He was probably aware that the chemicals we were experimenting with were known to affect the liver.

As he spoke he absent-mindedly left a jar of something white hanging off the shelf. I moved quickly to restore it.

'Well, I'm in no hurry,' I lied, 'but perhaps you'd ask for permission for me to retrieve my passport.'

I began to make plans and wondered what bolt-hole would be safest. I was undoubtedly on the Bahraini security services' radar. According to intelligence gathered by Abu Zubaydah, my friend Khalid al-Hajj had been arrested in Saudi Arabia weeks after returning from the Philippines, during a panicky response to the embassy attacks. I wondered whether under interrogation he had given up my name; I doubted it. Kuwait looked like a better bet; it was more tolerant of hardcore Salafis. I could travel there easily from Qatar.

On an early winter's morning, I made the trip through the Khyber Pass to Peshawar once more. As I travelled from Jalalabad, the White Mountains away to the south were already powdered with snow. The brutal Himalayan winter was about to set in and I would not be sorry to miss it.

Abu Zubaydah handed me my passport, no questions asked. I felt a euphoric surge of freedom, tempered only by anxiety that some officious Pakistani official would detain me for questioning at Islamabad airport. But there, too, no questions asked.

On the flight to Qatar with my imaginary 'doctor's slip' I began thinking of the comforts of obscurity and routine – the very opposite of what I had yearned for just three years before. I thought of catching up with my brothers, doing a university course, becoming a history teacher. Perhaps I would find a devout young woman to marry and settle down. Just twenty, I still had plenty of time for a fresh start. Or so I thought.

*       *       *

Doha airport was the ordered, antiseptic opposite of my previous surroundings – all gleaming marble floors and bling-laden duty-free shops. It was an assault on the senses of a jihadi used to primitive mountain dwellings and isolation.

I put on a brave front at immigration control. I was here for routine medical tests.

'Where did you start your journey?' the officer asked.

Should I lie? What if they already knew?

'Er, Peshawar in Pakistan,' I said with a sigh, trying to sound like it was a weekly return trip.

I was treated to a stern look, but the loud stamp on my passport sent a wave of relief through me.

'Have a nice stay,' the officer said, not meaning it.

I was met in the arrivals hall by Ahmed, my friend from Bosnia who had looked after me during my medical emergency the previous year. I told him that the last year had been gruelling and I needed a rest. Over the next two days I sank into comfortable anonymity, grazing at shopping malls and catching a couple of films. It was a relief to pray at mosques untouched by the devious fanaticism of Sheikh al-Muhajir. Within a few days, I began to ask myself whether I had left al-Qaeda or al-Qaeda had left me. I was no longer wracked by doubt; I could follow my interpretation of what God intended and bin Laden could follow his. But normal didn't last long. As we drove back from dinner one evening, Ahmed received a call on his cell phone. The colour drained from his face. He looked frightened.

'That was state security,' he stuttered. 'They told me to drive you to their headquarters immediately and then come back with your belongings later.'

I was surprised that they knew how to reach him but then remembered that I had provided his name at immigration as the person I'd be staying with. A part of me had been preparing for this moment. Even so, the prospect of a visit to state security filled me with apprehension. What did they know and how did they know it?

'In my luggage,' I whispered, 'there's a leather pouch. Inside, two floppy disks. Please hide them somewhere.'

Those disks, copied on a whim, were now my insurance, something I could trade in case of trouble but not something I wanted others to find. Should the Qataris discover them, I feared I would never see the light of day again.

'Just be sure no one can find them,' I repeated.

Ahmed agreed. I trusted him absolutely.

Over the next nine days, I would get to know well the anonymous beige-brick building near a Sheraton Hotel on the outskirts of Doha. My host was Captain Ali Mohanidi, a courteous man who assured me I would be treated well. Even so, I realized the Qataris might be persuaded to transfer me to a less understanding regime.

I was given a couch to sleep on in one of the offices, guarded by Pakistanis, who did much of state security's grunt work.

Sleep took a long time to come that first night. As I lay curled up, I focused on the small, high window that allowed in the glow of the city beyond. I felt a shudder of claustrophobia; there was no guarantee I would ever leave detention.

I decided cooperation would be my best strategy. I was not going to be beaten to a pulp to protect a group that was veering towards some warped interpretation of a religion that meant everything to me. I wanted a normal life, and I would not let a misplaced sense of loyalty stand in the way.

Early the next morning, I was taken to a wood-panelled office in an adjacent building. In front of me was an array of pastries and juices. Killing me with kindness, I mused.*

I was questioned – 'interrogated' would sound too harsh – by five officers. It soon became clear they knew where I had been – and

---

* It was a smart move on the part of the Qataris, surprising and putting me at ease. Sometimes coaxing is much more effective than cajoling or threatening. Al-Qaeda and ISIS recruits expect to be brutalized and are trained to resist 'enhanced interrogation'. They believe the more they resist it, including by providing false information, the greater the reward in the afterlife. Good food, somewhere to sleep and shower, the prospect of rehabilitation, disorientates and destabilizes the detainee.

whom I'd met. It read like an al-Qaeda leadership chart: bin Laden, Abu Zubaydah, Ibn Sheikh al-Libi. I knew all the wrong people.

'Do you deny this?' one of the officers asked curtly.

'No,' I replied. They looked surprised. I had just spared them a lot of time.

'There was a call from a phone linked to Abu Zubaydah to your friend here once upon a time which has been of great interest to Western intelligence,' he continued. I suddenly realized why they knew about me; in the depths of delirium, when I was trying to get to Qatar for emergency medical treatment a year earlier, I had called Ahmed from Abu Zubaydah's phone.[14]

'Was it the French who were monitoring the phone?' I asked.

'We can't tell you that,' one of them replied.

'Was it because of his role in the Paris Métro bombings a few years ago?' I said.

I told them I had heard in the camps that Abu Zubaydah had provided fake passports to the network behind the 1995 attacks and was worried the French were onto him.

They were unable to hide their excitement.

'Why are you telling us this?' one of them asked with a hint of suspicion.

'Look, I came to Qatar because I wanted to leave the group. I wasn't exactly planning to talk to you. But here I am.'

As I caught the questioning look in their eyes, I realized that I needed this speech to be very persuasive.

'I went to Bosnia to defend Muslims, to prevent them from being massacred. I went to Afghanistan because I thought bin Laden wanted to defend Muslims. But it turns out he wants to attack the world. There is nothing in the Koran that justifies the embassy attacks. And I know there is more, and worse, to come.

'I just wanted to get out, disappear.'

I felt my voice trail away. It was an authentic and spontaneous epilogue to a speech I had rehearsed to order my own thoughts.

While I needed the Qataris to be convinced of my change of

heart, I also needed to be able to trade information for some assurance that they wouldn't leave me languishing in jail after extracting all they could. The routine was polite, orderly – but I was very much not free to leave.

On the third day of interviews they asked me for something 'big' they could take to their counterparts in French intelligence. I wasn't about to tell them about Abu Khabab and Darunta; that was my ace. But I had plenty of other baubles I could dangle.

Abu Zubaydah, I told them, had a fake Saudi passport – and he used it to open an account at Faysal Bank in Peshawar. I gave them the account number, which I had memorized after my brother had used it to send cash for my travel for medical treatment.

'How on earth do you remember the account number?' one of them asked.

'I have a photographic memory,' I replied.

Two days later, my inquisitors looked exceptionally pleased. They had passed the bank account details to the French, who had recovered a trove of information and even a photograph of the elusive Abu Zubaydah. Thanks to me the Qataris were playing at the top table and basking in the attention.

I knew I was an interesting case because every day a more senior official would come by to be briefed on the interrogation. They even asked me for a favour. Captain Mohanidi took me to small room stacked from floor to ceiling with books.

'We've gathered these from underground booksellers specializing in Shia tracts. But we really haven't had time to work out which are seditious and which are harmless.' He flicked through a couple of titles, detonating a small cloud of dust. Sheepishly he asked, 'Do you understand Shia theology? Would you mind taking a look at them? You're a learned man; you'll understand what might be risky.'

I agreed and within a couple of hours had established a small stack of politically provocative volumes and a much larger pile of purely religious works.

After nine days of courteous but insistent questioning at the state security headquarters I was told I would be allowed to leave. But first I had to see the boss: Colonel al-Nuami.

I expected a taciturn, humourless bureaucrat. You didn't become head of the security service in an Arab state by cracking jokes. So I was pleasantly surprised to discover the colonel was a jovial man who sprang from his enormous leather armchair to grasp my hand.

His office was the size of a tennis court – all mahogany furniture with the obligatory photographs of his meetings with various Royal Highnesses. He beckoned me to a sofa that I thought might swallow me and offered tea.

'Thank you for what you've done,' he began. 'Everything you told us about Abu Zubaydah checks out. The French are excited.' No wonder he was in such a good mood. He took a sip of tea and leaned towards me across the acreage of his green leather desktop.

'We'd be happy to keep you here but we can't protect you if any of your former comrades find out you've been talking. Regretfully, there are still a few here.' Another sip. 'Also, word may spread that you are in Qatar. There is a risk the Saudis or Bahrainis will demand your extradition for whatever offences you may have committed in their countries, and that would put us in an awkward position.'

The Qataris liked to show their independence from the Saudis, but there were limits. 'Your talents would be better served with a bigger organization. I can arrange a private jet tonight to take you to France. The DGSE [French overseas intelligence] would like to meet you.'

He set his expensive gold pen on the desk and waited.

'Do I have a choice?' I asked. I thought for a moment about asking whether anonymity was an alternative, but the gaze fixed on me did not encourage bargaining.

'The Americans, the British. I know what I'd do,' he replied.

I raised my eyebrows.

'Let's just say I wouldn't choose the Americans. They'll chew you up and spit you out. They don't have a history of looking after their people. Think about it. Come back and tell me in thirty minutes.'

So I had a whole half-hour in which to decide the rest of my life.

I felt little cultural affinity for the French and didn't speak the language. I didn't trust the Americans either, and, given my lingering anger over the Dayton Accords, the idea of talking to them was a step too far. I imagined (was it the spy films?) that the British were more professional than other intelligence agencies. They understood the Arab world; they had been here long enough. I had enjoyed being in London when I had picked up the satellite phone.

There was another reason. My grandfather had fought against the Ottomans for the British in the Mesopotamia campaign of the First World War. He had risen to the rank of major and become head of the Colonial Police in the Iraqi city of Basra. He had always spoken of British administration in glowing terms.

After my appointed half-hour was up, I was ushered back into the colonel's office.

'I'm ready to go to London,' I said. I was suddenly (and perhaps irrationally) excited about my new lease of life. My appetite for adventure and movement had briefly stifled any apprehension I might still have about such a sudden and drastic change of course.

The Qataris booked me on a British Airways flight and called Ahmed.

'You can come and collect your friend,' said the captain. 'Bring all his belongings. He's going straight to the airport.' My heart leapt. Would they discover the leather pouch? It might give them second thoughts about releasing me.

When Ahmed arrived my suitcase was carefully unpacked in front of me, its linings prodded, pockets minutely examined. I did my best to look uninterested but every second of the search felt like a long winter's night at Darunta.

To my relief Ahmed had taken the precaution of burying the

pouch in a flowerpot. As we left the building, he asked me with a smirk if I'd been worried.

'I wasn't exactly chilled,' I said with a laugh.

'You know me,' he said, 'I'm no amateur. You'll be glad to know that they warned me of serious consequences if I breathed a word of this to any of our jihadi brothers. As if . . .' he said, waving both his arms skyward.

On the way to the airport we stopped at Ahmed's villa. He lived in a quiet suburb of Doha; it had been easy to ensure we were not being tailed. He closed the front door and checked no one was within earshot.

'I knew they'd arrest you,' he said quietly, without looking me in the eye.

'After your last visit they came to see me, the security people. They somehow knew about the phone you'd used to contact me. Whoever it belonged to was of interest to them. I didn't want any trouble. I just told them that the only person to call me from Pakistan was an old friend from Bosnia known as Haydara al-Bahraini. I told them it was an emergency; you had come to Qatar for urgent medical treatment. Obviously they checked with the hospital and found out you'd be coming back for a check-up. So they came to me and said that if you returned I would have to tell them immediately. And that if I warned you, there would be consequences for me.'

We retrieved the pouch from the pot on his balcony. He paused as we got into the car and then looked at me. I was taken aback to see tears welling up in his eyes. 'I'm sorry; I didn't know what to do. I want to stay here. I have a fiancée.'

I clapped him on the shoulder.

'Ahmed; you kept the pouch away from them. That's all that mattered. Remember, I've been in the camps for two years; I'm quite hardened to adversity. They're allowing me to go to London to get medical treatment for this liver condition. Life's good.' I laughed. 'Well, it's better than my liver.'

When I arrived at Doha airport, I noticed that the flight had a stopover in Bahrain. Would the security services there know of my travel and march me off the plane? Colonel al-Nuami had indicated I was a wanted man there. I was apprehensive but had literally no one in the world to talk to; this was truly the meaning of limbo.

When the flight arrived in Bahrain, it seemed to sit at the gate forever. Or was that me just experiencing every minute as an hour? There were hushed conversations going on between the purser and one of the pilots. A Bahraini official came on board. My stomach turned over. Was I being stitched up?

'Ladies and gentlemen, captain speaking, apologies for the delay, but unfortunately we won't be leaving Bahrain tonight . . .' There was a chorus of groans. 'The air space over the Gulf has been closed due to military operations. We will have to wait till tomorrow, when I hope we'll have a better idea of what's going on.'

Operation Desert Fox, a four-day bombing campaign to punish Saddam Hussein for defying UN resolutions and obstructing weapons inspections, was in motion.

This was impossible. I couldn't go through passport control in Bahrain; I would be arrested. I motioned to one of the cabin crew.

'I would rather stay at the airport tonight,' I said. 'I need to do some duty-free shopping and really don't want to travel miles to a hotel.'

I was instantly aware that my excuse sounded beyond lame. Stay up all night to buy perfume?

'I'm afraid you'll have to leave the airport. We've made arrangements to fast-track everyone through immigration.'

Everyone but me, I thought.

'Look,' I said, leaning towards her confidentially. 'I am in the Bahraini opposition. I am based in Qatar. If they identify me I am in real trouble.'

It was a desperate gamble. She could see I was very anxious and looked sympathetic. Other passengers shot me quizzical glances as they filed through the plane.

She asked to see my boarding pass.

'Just remain in the terminal. I'll take care of it,' she said.

I spent an uncomfortable night wandering the brightly lit duty-free shops and trying to find a quiet corner at an unused boarding gate. The BA flight finally left Bahrain the following morning, and I was glad to see the sprawling metropolis shrinking beneath me.

In the gathering gloom of a December afternoon I finally arrived at Heathrow Airport.

Standing at the gate were one of the most senior counter-terrorism officials at MI5, who introduced himself as Tom, and an MI6 agent who introduced himself as Harry.* (It might have been because of his fleshy ears.) They welcomed me with broad smiles and firm handshakes, as if they'd been expecting me for months. In fact, the Qataris had given them just a few hours' notice that I was en route. Perhaps the welcome reflected their glee in putting one over on the French.

Tom was tall with a shock of white hair, which sat slightly uneasily with his much younger features. He had a ready smile and an air of casual authority. He spoke excellent Arabic and seemed to enjoy practising it.

They took me to an interview room.

'You must be tired, so we will try to keep this short,' Harry said, speaking slowly to accommodate my basic command of English. 'First we'll need your boarding pass. I've sent someone to collect your suitcase.'

After plenty of practice in Qatar I delivered a concise account of my story. They were sympathetic listeners. At one point Tom told me: 'We understand how difficult this is. These people, you fought alongside them, you shared a lot of experiences. But you're doing the right thing.'

---

* As is the practice of British intelligence, these were the invented names they used in handling me, rather than their real first names. While, after years of service, I learned the real identity of many of my handlers, this book uses their invented names or in a couple of cases pseudonyms to protect their privacy and security.

'Your medical condition gives us some cover,' he said. 'We'll work on a story with the Qataris,' he said. 'Like the Ministry of Health sent you to London for specialist treatment of your liver problem.'

I felt I needed to give them a token of goodwill.

'Can I speak in Arabic?' I asked. 'I want to be accurate.'

I was almost too exhausted to think in my native tongue, let alone English.

'You know I can't accept civilian casualties. Well, I'm concerned about a plan in Yemen that involves British citizens.' The change in their body posture assured me I had their full attention.

'In Jalalabad, before I left, I met a teenager. He's the son of a cleric here at a place called Finsbury Park, Abu Hamza al-Masri.'

'Oh yes,' Tom said, 'we are well aware of him.'

'Well, we got into conversation. He was impressed that I'd been at Darunta. His father provides funds for the camp.'

'We didn't know *that*,' Tom murmured.

'Anyway, his name is Mohamed Mostafa. He said that his father had big plans for Yemen. He recited a well-known prophecy to me:

*'From the region of Aden and Abyan 12,000 warriors shall rise to fight for God and His messenger.'*

'He said his brother had already gone to Yemen. And he said his father had warned Westerners to stay out of Yemen.'[15]

'Yes, he did, that's true,' Tom said in Arabic.

'He claimed that they're going to start an armed campaign to drive out the remaining infidels. They're planning to strike a missionary church and to kidnap Westerners.'

'Oh boy!' Harry sighed, after Tom translated.

'Keep talking: we need every detail on this you have.'

After three hours I was escorted through immigration control to a waiting car that would take me to a hospital in London.

'Rest up,' said Tom. 'I'm sure we have a lot more to talk about.' He added an almost mischievous grin.

'Oh! Before I go, you'd better have this,' I said and handed him the leather pouch still dusty with Qatari sand. He gave me a curious look as he gingerly took it. 'On the disks you'll find a lot of stuff on al-Qaeda, their camps and the formulas for some of the bombs the group's working on. Especially the work of Abu Khabab; he's very clever.

'Don't lose it,' I said, allowing my fatigue to release a whiff of impudence.

The car pulled away. As I glanced out of the back window, Tom was holding the pouch as if it had just emerged from Tutankhamun's tomb.

# MY FIFTH LIFE: UNDERCOVER

## 1999

I had travelled from the medieval surroundings of an al-Qaeda camp to a sofa in Qatar's intelligence headquarters to the hushed corridors and expensive sheets of a private London hospital – and all within two weeks.

It was enough to disorientate anyone, which as much as my inflamed liver kept me awake despite aching fatigue. I had left Jalalabad for medical treatment and a lifetime of anonymity, and ended up thousands of miles away in London as a guest of British intelligence. Christmas trees adorned every floor of the South Kensington hospital, their lights twinkling cheerily. As a Muslim who had until very recently been a fully pledged member of al-Qaeda and one of its up and coming bomb-makers, they were a source of surreal amusement.

My new friends had ushered me quietly into the hospital – no form-filling or check-in. As it turned out, I was there for good reason. I had failed to keep up a treatment regime for malaria and typhoid (no easy task at Darunta) and my liver had rebelled. The stress of the past two weeks had no doubt contributed.

The day after I was admitted, I was absorbing all these changes while gazing at the grey street below and following the ubiquitous white vans as they broke most traffic regulations in the space of a couple of hundred yards.

I realized this was a watershed in my life. I needed to cooperate fully with the British if I wanted to resume what might resemble a normal existence.

There was a knock at the door. Tom from MI5 entered with a cheerful smile.

'Rested?' he asked.

'Well, not exactly,' I said. 'It's quite a lot to take in.'

'So was the pouch you gave us for Christmas,' he said.

I smiled.

'I hope it's useful,' I said with false modesty.

'We are still going through it all. Our Arabic translators are at full throttle.'

'Tell them to focus on what's called the "Encyclopaedia of Jihad". It has years of practical information on how to wage terrorist and insurgent campaigns. It'll take them a while.'

'We're arranging a six-month medical visa for you,' he continued. 'That happens all the time for people from the Gulf who get private medical attention in the UK. Call it one of our invisible exports,' he said. 'And we're following up on the Yemen story. Wanted to check whether you had any more on that.'

I didn't. But the value of what I'd provided was demonstrated even as I lay in hospital.

On 24 December 1998, Yemeni security forces arrested five British citizens in the port city of Aden. In the process they also seized rockets, landmines and explosives. Those arrested were about to carry out devastating attacks on the five-star Mövenpick Hotel, the British consulate and a Westerners' club. The cell included the son of Abu Hamza I'd met in Jalalabad and his stepson.[*]

Another of their targets, as I had warned British intelligence, was Aden's only Christian church. The cell planned to declare the attacks were in retaliation for the recent British and American air strikes in Iraq (the same ones that had led me to spend an uncomfortable night at Bahrain airport).[2]

---

[*] Both Abu Hamza's son Mohamed Mostafa Kamel and stepson Mohsin Ghalain were convicted in a trial in Yemen for the Aden terrorist plot. After completing their sentences and returning to the UK, they were convicted in a fraud case in 2009.[1]

In a nod to the famous prophecy the group had called itself the 'Abyan Faction of the Islamic Army of Aden' and was a joint venture between the Finsbury Park cleric and a local militant called Abu Hassan al-Mihdar,* with funds funnelled from London by the former. Abu Hamza had provided his stepson with a satellite phone so that he could orchestrate their efforts from London.

Four days after the plot was thwarted, the remaining members of the cell, armed with machine guns and rocket launchers and led by al-Mihdar, kidnapped sixteen Western tourists in a convoy of SUVs in an attempt to win the release of their comrades. After they took the hostages into the desert, Abu Hamza himself provided them with guidance via the satellite phone. When the next morning Yemeni security services launched a rescue operation, the kidnappers used the hostages as human shields. Four British tourists and one Australian were killed.[4]

I don't know whether my intelligence was the only warning about the plot. The calls Abu Hamza made to Yemen were also intercepted (though whether by the UK or CIA I was never told).[5] But Tom told me my information had helped them understand just how serious the threat was.

It was a good start. But my new clients wanted more.

'It would be very interesting to see who you might be able to flush out here,' Tom said. 'Make a few calls perhaps. We're getting a bit tired of this Londonistan tag.**

Trouble is,' he continued with a grim smirk, 'we'd need to prove they are raging psychopaths about to blow up Buckingham Palace to get an English court to take notice.'

I nodded, but Tom wanted to reinforce the message, just in case it had been obscured by my sketchy understanding of English or medical condition.

* His real name was Zain al-Mihdar. He was known by the *nom de guerre* 'Abu Hassan'. He was executed ten months after the hostage attack.[3]
** British media and some commentators had begun dubbing the city 'Londonistan' because of the number of radical Islamists who had arrived to seek political asylum or raise funds and support for militant groups.

'It would be good to let some of your contacts in England know you are here in hospital, so the news gets round.'

It made sense: questions were sure to be raised when I failed to return to Afghanistan. I'd also be able to establish myself in the jihadi community in London.

Time to reach for the Bosnia rolodex.

My first call on what would become a meandering journey through the UK's militant scene was to Babar Ahmad, the British Pakistani jihadi I had helped down the mountain during that final battle in Bosnia.* I'd briefly encountered him in Baku when he visited our 'charity' offices in order to make contact with the mayonnaise-loving Ibn Khattab. We had sent a letter to the Saudi jihadi leader vouching for Ahmad and they had been in contact ever since.

I was taken aback by how much he had aged. Perhaps the head wound he'd received in Bosnia was in part to blame. Nearly bald, he looked less the youthful jihadi fighter and more the earnest technician. Which in a way he was – using his considerable IT skills to propagate the wonders of jihad.

He leaned down to embrace me.

'Not how I expected we would meet,' he said with a grin.

'Not where I expected to be,' I replied, laughing.

I spun him a story about how my routine check-up in Qatar had uncovered some sort of medical emergency – and now, at great cost to my family, I was in London for treatment.

'Can you let people know what's happened to me?' I asked. 'I don't want them to think that I've been arrested.'

Babar Ahmad readily agreed and invited me to visit his home to catch up.

Next on my list was 'Mohammed al-Madani', the Saudi who had teased me about my puny frame in Bosnia and had since moved to England. Al-Madani made an odd sight in central London in his

---

* Babar Ahmad had completed an engineering degree at Imperial College after coming back from Bosnia.[6]

black Afghan robes and carrying a shepherd's staff. I thought he was both cunning and perceptive so was more than a little apprehensive about meeting him. He was also in close contact Abu Qatada, one of the most influential preachers in Londonistan. Gaining access to the cleric depended on my making a good impression. I was not yet convinced that I could hide my change of heart, nor even sure that I wanted to work against some individuals who had been my fellow travellers for the previous four years and might even share my vision of jihad rather than al-Qaeda's.

I imagined that as my old friends arrived to see me in hospital a man in a raincoat waiting for a bus or fixing a phone box across the street was taking clandestine photographs. Al-Madani promised to get word to Afghanistan that I was getting emergency treatment in London. (Tom had impressed upon me how important it was to keep what he called my 'legend' intact.) Al-Madani appeared genuinely happy to see me again and we spent a surprisingly relaxed hour talking about the Bosnia campaign.

After a few days recovering my strength, I called my brother Moheddin in Saudi Arabia and explained recent events. He was shocked and wanted to come to London. I quickly dissuaded him; having my oldest brother in tow, asking awkward questions, was all I needed.

'You know the Islamic Centre here,' I said casually. 'If you have any contacts there, can you arrange a room? I want to get out of this hospital as soon as possible,' I lied, as an attractive nurse entered the room with lunch.

In fact I'd already stayed at the Islamic Centre (the al-Muntada al-Islami mosque in Parsons Green) the previous year when I'd picked up a satellite phone for al-Qaeda. It was a suitable first step towards familiarizing myself with the area's Muslim community. And my brother might just know some interesting characters.

I left the cossetted comfort of the hospital early in the new year. A plan had evolved in my mind: do a few weeks of sleuthing and spotting for my new friends at MI5 and then revive my dream of obscurity, perhaps scrape the cash together to go to college.

Her Majesty's Secret Intelligence Services had rather different plans for me. The famous pouch had provided many intriguing answers but provoked myriad questions. And it was not as though Tom could pop down to a café on the Brompton Road to catch up on al-Qaeda's plans for global terror.

On a grey and bitter January morning I was huddled inside a suite at a grand Victorian hotel a little way south of King's Cross. Tom was master of ceremonies – irrepressibly cheerful but also sensitive to my cultural background. No doubt ignoring the service's HR manual, he asked me if I preferred to work only with male agents. I reflexively replied yes. I still inhabited an all-male universe and wasn't sure how I would interact with a female officer, beyond being cripplingly shy.

Another MI5 officer introduced himself as Nick. He resembled the actor Sam Neill, who had played the palaeontologist in the *Jurassic Park* movies.

MI6's representative might have come from central casting, dressed immaculately in a double-breasted Savile Row suit, his tie dotted with the crest of some exclusive school or college. A gentleman's hat hung on the coat stand. This eminent member of the British establishment introduced himself as Richard. He was probably in his early forties but looked older. He had the cut-glass accent of the well-educated, and his bulging waistline, receding hair, hooded green eyes and majestic salt and pepper beard made him the spitting image of King Edward VII. I soon took to teasing him as 'Your Majesty', which he took in good humour.

Richard startled me by switching briefly to perfect Arabic with a Bedouin twang. In a previous incarnation, he had spent time visiting tribal encampments in the desert interior of Saudi Arabia. For the sake of his colleagues, he reverted to boarding school English to lay out the British government's needs.

'The information you brought – let's describe it as alarming. Those designs for bombs and chemical devices won't remain theoretical forever. You've seen this?' he asked.

He passed me a photocopy of a recent interview that Osama bin Laden had given *Time* magazine.[7]

'Quote,' he continued, '"Acquiring [chemical and nuclear weapons] for the defence of Muslims is a religious duty. If I have indeed acquired these weapons, then I thank God for enabling me to do so."'[8]

I thought of Abu Khabab and his prized independence. How long could that last?

'It's conceivable,' Tom continued, 'that you've spent much of the last two years in the most important fifty square yards in Afghanistan. So we're going to need your help – maybe for a few months.' He let the last three words sink in, perhaps inviting protest. His hawk's eyes peered at me from beneath heavy lids. 'If you help us, we can then help you transition to a normal life.'

The alternative was left unsaid.

And so began a series of meetings that stretched into the spring. I came to know a lot of hotel conference rooms in central London. The protocol was always the same, but I sometimes felt slightly foolish following it. Every time I met my handlers I would call a given number from a public phone, holding my nose in the stuffy, smelly booth and ignoring the various services on offer from silhouetted women. I would be told to proceed to another phone box via a particular route to place another call. Only on the second call would I be told where to go and when. The tortuous routine – not unlike a reality TV show – was to allow MI5 spotters to ensure I was not being followed.

I explained how the Darunta research team had been working on a delivery mechanism for poison gas and provided my inquisitors with every last detail about Abu Khabab's laboratory. They were not happy to hear that a middle-aged UK citizen of Egyptian origin (Safwat) was one of his most able apprentices.

I related my bomb-making experiments and my time in the Philippines and Bosnia, including my narrow brush with the Serbs' landmine booby trap and my leg wound in the jungle.

'Perhaps we should call you the cat,' Richard said. 'You're certainly using up some lives.'

The nickname quickly stuck among my handlers.

I also provided MI5 and MI6 with a detailed picture of how al-Qaeda was organized, the leading players and the relationships between them, the locations of camps and safe houses. I listed common jihadi travel routes and financing sources, support networks in Saudi Arabia, the Gulf, Pakistan and Turkey. I supplied or confirmed the identities of dozens of operatives from their photographs, details of bank accounts, phone numbers al-Qaeda operatives used and even the models of vehicles they preferred.

I was surprised that I seemed to be drawing on a blank sheet of paper. Literally everything I said was being scribbled down by my audience. British intelligence (and they were not alone) was awakening to a danger of which it knew little. For years, MI6 had been focused on the chaos that had followed the collapse of the Soviet Union and countering nuclear proliferation, while MI5 had focused on Northern Ireland. The Africa embassy bombings just four months previously had changed the calculus in London and Washington.

Of greatest concern to my new handlers was the emergence of suicide bombings as an al-Qaeda tactic and the 'suicide bomb squads' that Abu Hafs al-Masri had been organizing in Afghanistan.*

Senior jihadis in Afghanistan obligingly helped keep me up to date. Just weeks into my debriefings, I got a phone call from Afghanistan. Ibn Sheikh al-Libi, the head of the Khalden camp whom I'd met in Peshawar just months earlier, was on the line, along with Peshawar gatekeeper Abu Zubaydah.

They told me I should meet an Algerian by the name of Said Arif, who was the head of al-Qaeda's intelligence apparatus in London and right-hand man to the Jordanian Palestinian cleric Abu Qatada. Abu Qatada was raising serious sums of money for the

* MI6 also wanted my thoughts on where al-Qaeda might strike next. I told them of the flood of Yemenis being trained and sent home. Yemen would be the location for al-Qaeda's next big attack in October 2000, when al-Qaeda operatives approached the USS *Cole* in a skiff off the port of Aden and detonated a huge bomb, killing seventeen US sailors and crippling the destroyer.

cause of global jihad. While he was very much on the radar of British intelligence, he covered his tracks expertly. Everything he raised was helping 'Muslim civilians' in conflict zones. Like the Haramain Foundation, Abu Qatada and many others were using the guise of humanitarian causes to siphon money to militant groups.

I called al-Madani to arrange a meeting with Said Arif and Abu Qatada.

'You'll find them at the Four Feathers Club. I'll take you to see him after Friday prayers,' he said.

I found it amusing that the Four Feathers Club was not far from the fictional dwelling of Sherlock Holmes in Baker Street. There the similarities ended. Rather than the book-lined study of Victoriana's most famous investigator, the Four Feathers social club occupied several dingy rooms in a dilapidated building. But appearances were deceptive; it had become a nerve centre in Europe for international jihad. MI5 was aware of some of what was going on but badly wanted someone on the inside.

Al-Madani and I met Said Arif on one of those London afternoons where the lowering clouds send squalls of heavy rain into every corner. Arif was a lean man in his late thirties, whose searching brown eyes gazed through wire-framed spectacles. He had a long beard and a tidy, close-cropped haircut. Part of his job was to vet would-be jihadis from North Africa who wanted to go to Afghanistan. His intense expression suggested he was probably quite good at it. As he began to talk I quickly realized we had met in bin Laden's camps in Afghanistan, when I had known him by another name. It helped cement the relationship that we could reminisce about the 'good old days'.*

---

* Arif's *kunya* was Abu Sulaiman al-Jazari. He had contacts with extremist networks throughout Europe including in Bruges, Antwerp and Stuttgart. He was also connected to a cell in Strasbourg which in late 2000 plotted an attack on a Christmas market in the French city. In 2003 he was arrested and tried in France in connection with a plot to blow up the Eiffel Tower. After getting out of prison he travelled to Syria in 2013. He was killed in a Coalition air strike there in 2015.[9]

I noticed several long-bearded young men, some of whom appeared to have battlefield injuries, sitting on the other side of the room. And here they all are, safe and sound, sitting next to the radiator in a sanctuary in central London. The tolerance – or naivety – of democracies, I thought.

'Al-Ghamdi says we should take advantage of your medical visa so you can help us recruit and fundraise in London,' Arif told me. Al-Ghamdi, I thought – still watching over me after luring me into al-Qaeda, and with a direct line to London, too.

'Rather than return to Afghanistan?' I asked, feigning disappointment.

'First you should recover your strength, then we'll see.'

'I just don't want to be here too long. The filth and sin of London is too much,' I said self-righteously. I hoped I was not over-doing it.

'This way,' he said, and knocked gently at a cheap wooden door.

Inside was a grinning, generously proportioned man in his mid-forties. 'Sheikh Abu Qatada' had deep-set eyes that didn't always look in the same direction, and a fleshy nose. His bulging waistline and magnificent beard, like a ruff, gave him an almost Shakespearian air.

'Sheikh,' said Arif, 'this is Abu al-Abbas, who until last month was with the brothers in Afghanistan.'

'Welcome, my brother. We've heard a lot about you,' Abu Qatada said to me quietly.

Probably not as much as you need to, I thought.

Abu Qatada's surroundings belied his place in the global jihadi establishment. If his surroundings were modest, his self-esteem was far from it. He was rare among radical preachers in the UK in having serious theological credentials. He claimed he had a master's degree from the Jordanian university in Amman in the study of *hadith*. He had come to Britain illegally in 1993 after spending time in Afghanistan and Pakistan.[10] None other than Abu Zubaydah had provided him with a forged UAE passport.

Abu Qatada was known for being an extreme hardliner.* In a 1995 fatwah he had condoned the killing of the wives and children of 'apostates' by the militant Armed Islamic Group (GIA) in Algeria, which gave the group theological cover to massacre Muslim civilians.

He was thirsty for news from the camps and was impressed that I had been commissioned by bin Laden to 'educate' recruits. I quickly realized that he didn't suffer fools gladly.

'I look forward to more conversations about Shariah and the future of jihad,' he said as he bade me farewell. 'Most of the Algerians around me are no more intelligent than their family donkeys.'

Abu Qatada was the consummate performer. In private he was all calm authority, soft-spoken and smiling. In front of the faithful on a Friday morning his voice would rise to shrill anger as he pumped up the congregation, mixing a loathing of the perfidious West with glorification of jihad. A favourite target was the recently deceased King Hussein of Jordan, whom he pronounced 'would be spat out even from hell'.

Trawling the mosques and lecture halls of Islamist London was both illuminating and surprising. I also discovered plenty of petty jealousies among 'leaders' such as Abu Qatada and Abu Hamza al-Masri.

In presiding at Finsbury Park, Abu Hamza controlled one of the largest mosques in the city. He also garnered more publicity than Abu Qatada because of the loss of both his hands in that experiment gone wrong, and his piratical metal hook made him an irresistible draw for the British tabloids.**

---

* In Pakistan Abu Qatada had come under the influence of Sayyid Imam, an Egyptian cleric who was the intellectual architect of *takfirism*. In a treatise written in the early 1990s, Sayyid Imam argued that Muslims who did not follow his interpretation, even those in some jihadi groups, were lapsed Muslims whose lives were potentially forfeit. From London, Abu Qatada helped spread Sayyid Imam's hardline ideology, though he later distanced himself from the leadership of the GIA after they started killing fellow jihadis.
** By his own account, Abu Hamza was not a 'good Muslim' when he came to the UK and worked for a while as a nightclub bouncer in Soho. He

The story Abu Hamza told about how he had lost his hands and one eye was typical of the braggadocio among London clerics. He said he'd been disabled while clearing mines in Afghanistan, but I already knew from Abu Khabab about his bomb-making mishap.* He preached about the obligation of jihad to impressionable youngsters at Finsbury Park, and formed an organization called Supporters of Sharia (SOS) which peppered Muslim neighbourhoods with leaflets. On one visit, I went down to the mosque's basement to find rows of bearded young men in sleeping bags on the concrete floor. Some of them would soon be on their way to Afghanistan. I outlined to MI5 how the cleric was facilitating the travel of young men from the UK to al-Qaeda's camps.

To Abu Qatada, it was insufferable that he had to make do with preaching to acolytes in the drab surroundings of the Four Feathers Club, while the Egyptian 'pretender' – whom he described as an 'uncouth low-life' – preached to a congregation of hundreds. Abu Hamza for his part resented the fact that Abu Qatada was held in greater esteem by Salafis back in the Middle East. His Yemen project had been a failed attempt to eclipse the Jordanian cleric.

I was witness to their rivalry. At a wedding party to which both had been invited, Abu Hamza had proffered his elbow so that Abu Qatada could shake it in greeting, but such was the contempt the Jordanian felt towards the Egyptian that he had pretended not to see him and moved on.

'Abu Qatada is an unforgiving brute,' Abu Hamza said to me, rolling his one good eye.

I raised the subject of their rivalry with Mohammed al-Madani.

'It's like putting roosters in a cage,' he said with a shrug.

Abu Hamza's links to terrorism were more direct than those of the more guileful Abu Qatada. But he had not been arrested even after

---

became 'born again' after marrying a Muslim woman and travelled to Afghanistan in the early 1990s. He took over the Finsbury Park Mosque in 1997.[11]

* Abu Hamza admitted at his trial in New York that his injuries came from an experiment with explosives in Lahore.[12]

the hostage attack in Yemen. I was told the police needed more time to gather evidence. Under British law, the intercepts of Abu Hamza's satellite phone calls could not be used in court and any information I gathered could not be used without exposing me as a spy.

MI5 nevertheless pressed me to find out as much as I could. After prayers one day at Finsbury Park, Abu Hamza revealed to me he had constantly been in touch with the cell in Yemen. There had been no intention to harm the hostages, he said, but the plan had unravelled when Yemeni security services discovered the cell's desert hideout.

My intelligence contributed to Abu Hamza's arrest and questioning on 15 March 1999 on suspicion of 'the commission, preparation or instigation of acts of terrorism'. However, he was released without charge because of a lack of admissible evidence.* British security forces had wanted to rattle his cage.**

One of those held in the Yemeni desert was a slight, middle-aged Xerox executive, Mary Quin. Two years after the kidnapping, she travelled from New York to London to confront the cleric. Abu Hamza confirmed to her he had provided the group with a satellite phone. He declared the kidnapping was justified and would not have resulted in lives being lost had the hostage takers' demands been met. He also (astonishingly) allowed her to tape their conversation. This evidence, which corroborated the information I provided MI5, was used to convict him in a courtroom in New York many years later. The prosecutor described it as 'devastating evidence of the defendant's guilt'.[15]

Completing the north London triumvirate was another preacher given to bombast and double-talk, Omar Bakri

* In 2004, the British home secretary (interior minister) David Blunkett conceded that the prohibition of using phone tap evidence in UK courts had made it more difficult to try Abu Hamza in Britain.[13]
** During later court proceedings in the United States, Abu Hamza claimed that in 1997 MI5 and Scotland Yard's Special Branch opened a line of communication with him in order to 'keep the streets of London safe'. His defence team submitted documentation to the court which they argued backed up the claim. But nothing has come to light suggesting he ever wavered in his commitment to the broader jihadi cause.[14]

Mohammed. Detractors called him the Tottenham ayatollah. Abu Qatada described him as the biggest fraud in London, and it was clear from my one meeting with him that he had the theological intellect of one of Abu Qatada's 'donkeys'. But in the girth stakes at least, he easily surpassed Abu Qatada.

Despite their rivalries, this trio, surrounded by acolytes, were all capable of raising serious money for the Afghan camps and other 'worthy causes'. They were also adept at whipping up a crowd and knew where the dividing line between free speech and incitement to terrorism lay. To impressionable young Muslims looking for a sense of identity they were charismatic and persuasive, and that made them dangerous. Their followers came to believe what I had been led towards in al-Qaeda's camps just months earlier: that God had made the world for Muslims only.*

It was a dark and divisive view of the world that I found increasingly repellent. And it wasn't confined to a few mosques north of the Thames. After a number of weeks living at the Islamic Centre in Parson's Green I was nearly drowning in jihadi acquaintances. My handlers decided I needed new premises, though obviously nothing too grand. I was, after all, meant to be a struggling militant in Londonistan.

Those premises were a one-bedroom flat in a gloomy semidetached house on Brighton Road in Purley, a suburb south of London. Thanks to contacts at the Four Feathers and among the Bosnian alumni, my shabby pad became a dormitory for itinerant jihadis. The smell of fish fingers and Cornish pasties never quite left the place. There were listening devices in the ceilings and even behind the cistern, thanks to an 'electrician' who had come to update some wiring.

---

* Omar Bakri was allowed to spread his toxic message for far too long. He was banned from returning to Britain in 2005, but by then his organization – al-Muhajiroun – had hundreds of committed followers. At least a half of all terror plots involving British nationals since the late 1990s have had links to al-Muhajiroun.[16]

I paid the rent from the modest income* I earned from working part-time in an Islamic bookshop, topped up by a £1,500 monthly stipend from Her Majesty's Exchequer. The £18,000 a year I received in the early years I worked for British intelligence was a modest sum, but I was never motivated by the money.**

Among my guests at Brighton Road was Abu Zubayr al-Hayali, a Saudi al-Qaeda member known as 'the Bear' because of his large frame. He was from a prominent family and was married to a Saudi princess – a sign pre-9/11 of just how deeply embedded jihadis were in the Kingdom. We had first met in Bosnia.

Al-Hayali told me he had recruited four Saudis to carry out an attack on US soldiers in the BurJuman shopping mall in Dubai. The attack would have coincided with the August 1998 embassy bombings but had been aborted because he was unable to procure weapons in the emirate.***

Most of my visitors were earnest young men with romanticized visions of jihad. As we huddled around the three-bar electric heater, I spun stories of life in the Afghan camps. If only I had a working liver I might still be there, I complained. The yarns may not have been Rudyard Kipling but they bolstered my credibility.

There were some unintended consequences. Two young men of Egyptian and Sudanese extraction were so inspired by my stories that they resolved to travel to join al-Qaeda in Afghanistan.

---

* Being seen to do some form of paid work was necessary as otherwise questions might have been asked in jihadi circles about how I was sustaining myself. From 2002 the British gave me a raise, bringing my annual income up to £30,000.

** Still it grated when, much later, former British prisoners at Guantánamo reportedly received millions of pounds of compensation from the British government.[17]

*** Al-Hayali (real name Badr al-Sudairi) would be arrested in Morocco in 2002 for a plot targeting British and US warships off the coast of Gibraltar. I was told by MI6 his aim was to attack British nuclear submarines. Despite his royal connections he was short of funds. In 2000 he stole my Bahraini passport from the drawer in my bedroom so that he could leave the UK. In an ominous sign for Saudi authorities, al-Hayali was greeted by thousands when he returned home in 2013 after being released.[18]

However, to my MI5 handlers who were listening in, the value of the intelligence I was gathering far outweighed the risks of a few extra radicals walking the walk.

So rich was south London in jihadi contacts that I could jump off at pretty much any stop of the number 77 bus and find a 'like-minded' militant. The Tooting Circle, co-founded by my friend Babar Ahmad, was one of the most active – sometimes meeting at the gloriously named Chicken Cottage, a halal fast-food joint on Tooting High Street. I was often enlisted to talk about jihad to the youngsters who gathered around Ahmad. They were in many ways the poster children for a second generation of British Muslims who felt alienated both from their immigrant parents' traditional Islam and from mainstream British society. Their rootlessness made them vulnerable to radical interpretations of Islam and the call of jihad. Many of their parents had come to England from humble backgrounds in the valleys of Kashmir, the villages of the Punjab and the rice fields of Bangladesh.

The older generation was renowned for their hard work and efforts to co-exist in their new societies, even if assimilation was often beyond them. Their children had higher expectations. While first-generation migrants had hardened themselves to discrimination, many in the second generation did not feel British and resented the casual racism that was an almost daily experience. Some became involved in petty criminality and gangs, before confronting this identity crisis and seeking 'redemption' by turning to religion. It was a pattern that was beginning to repeat itself in dreary inner cities around Europe, in places like Molenbeek in Brussels, Aubervilliers in Paris, and Small Heath in Birmingham.

Salafism's rejection of modern Western values provided these kids with an alternative identity of rebellion (just as Sayyid Qutb had provided me with such a foundation) – a way to define themselves against not only mainstream society but the traditional Islam of their own parents. They reminded me of the nihilists in Ivan Turgenev's novel *Fathers and Sons*, who mocked their parents' traditional values as simple-minded.

Groups like the Tooting Circle allowed these young men to evade the authority of strict parents (how could they object to their children becoming more devout?) and plot their own lives. One of the group was an earnest nineteen-year-old called Saajid Badat, whose bookish reading glasses made him seem much older. He was entranced by my stories of working with Abu Khabab and nagged me to provide a letter of introduction. Within weeks of receiving it, he was gone.

The suffering of Muslims in Bosnia and then Chechnya had created not only a sense of burning indignation among these young Muslims but also a frustration that their own community was not doing enough to fight back. Into this mix stepped proselytizers like Abu Qatada and Omar Bakri Mohammed.

The result was a mood of bleak anger fed by a cynical message from the pulpit.* It was shocking to me because even in Saudi Arabia I had grown up in an Islam that was rich and compassionate, that celebrated its history and morality. The Islam I had found in Europe was all about hellfire and guilt. It was totally joyless. In many respects it was more puritan than Wahhabism. Imams shipped over from rural Pakistan or conservative parts of the Arab world with a warped view of Western culture and with few words of English warned their congregations they should avoid succumbing to the depravity that surrounded them. Our preachers in Khobar (with the notable exception of the Smurf-hating Yusuf al-Ayeri)

---

* Because I was seen as well versed in theological matters, I was asked by one of my Londonistan contacts to fill in for an imam in a mosque in Brighton down on the south coast. For a while I travelled there to give the Friday sermon. I tried to keep it orthodox and non-political. 'We can talk about jihad during the barbecue afterwards,' a Libyan jihadi who was on the mosque committee advised me. One day I stood up in front of the nearly 300 congregants and discovered that I had brought the sermon I had given weeks before. I improvised. 'I spoke to you about gossip, backstabbing and the need for brotherly love, but I've not seen any improvement so I'm going to repeat the sermon I gave a few weeks ago,' I complained to the faithful. Afterwards one of the elderly congregants came up to me and whispered, 'So the imam forgets his sermon and the congregation pays the price.'

had preached about Islamic compassion, but there seemed to be a snarl on the lips of many imams in the UK. Damnation, they shouted during Friday sermons, lay around every corner.

Young Muslims consumed by this message decided jihad was the surest way to avoid hell and be admitted to paradise.

Around the turn of the century, this anger was turbo charged by the Internet, by the likes of Babar Ahmad's website azzam.com, whose mission was to spur to jihad 'the Muslims who are sitting down ignorant of this vital duty'.

'Fight in the cause of Allah,' it said, and 'incite the believers to fight along with you.'[19]

I would sit next to Babar Ahmad for hours as he administered azzam.com in his bedroom. He had set up the website at the request of Ibn Khattab and adroitly used editing software to create short clips of mujahideen exploits in the Caucasus. Azzam.com would clock up hundreds of thousands of visitors from around the world. Babar Ahmad's presentation of 'martyrdom operations' by Chechen jihadis was the prototype for many online efforts by Islamist terrorist groups. And he wasn't just active virtually. Babar Ahmad would reveal to me he had 'sent' several of his circle in Tooting to fight in Chechnya.*

A few stops on the bus from Babar Ahmad's home was another group of extremists clustered around the black-robed Mohammed al-Madani, who lived in Balham, an area popular with Islamists. Al-Madani became an unwitting source of intelligence following a brief visit he made to Afghanistan in the spring of 1999.

The setting was quite bizarre. We were sitting on a low stone wall outside a house near Wandsworth Common where his in-laws lived. As we chatted, women walked by with prams or shopping; an ice-cream van with its familiar music-box jingle drifted optimistically down the road.

* Babar Ahmad was arrested in December 2003. After an eight-year extradition battle he pleaded guilty in the United States to providing material support to the Taliban at the time they were harbouring Osama bin Laden. He was released in 2015 and returned to the UK.[20]

Al-Madani revealed with barely suppressed pride that he had met bin Laden and formally joined the group. With a hint of *amour propre*, he confided to me that bin Laden had had a private landline installed between his headquarters outside Kandahar and the Pakistani city of Quetta. And he had the number. The significance of the information jostled with the absurd setting.

I informed MI6 and imagined GCHQ analysts in Cheltenham or the United States National Security Agency at Fort Meade in Maryland monitoring the number. I never found out if they heard anything useful.

I was rapidly getting the sense that MI5 was ill-equipped to deal with the panorama of jihadi agitation across London (and also in places like Birmingham, Luton and Manchester). The resources and focus were elsewhere, and the counter-terrorism laws were much weaker than they would be after 9/11. The law before the turn of the century made it difficult to prosecute anyone not actively planning an attack on British soil. Asylum laws were generous; extradition both difficult and time-consuming. Jihadis flocked to London from all over Europe and North Africa, knowing that arrest was unlikely so long as they did not announce plans to bomb Piccadilly Circus.

British intelligence were delighted with the information I provided and worked diligently to reinforce my change of heart and probe for any doubts. One afternoon in a grand hotel room Richard and I had one of our long chats. We shared a love of Arabian history and I enjoyed his dry sense of humour. I had been devouring some of the classics of Arabic literature in between playing host in Purley.

'You know, Richard, our great writers had compassion for all of humanity. Think of Naguib Mahfouz. That's what gave them such powers of observation and the ability to tell such wonderful stories. When I look back now, I think I was in danger of losing all empathy in Afghanistan. I started to see anyone who was not a jihadi as a brainless grazing animal, no better than a sheep.'

Richard was sitting upright in a mahogany chair which was a little too small for his generous frame and puffing on one of his beloved Cuban cigars.

'And we all know what happened to Mahfouz,' he said drily. The Nobel Prize-winning author had been stabbed by an extremist in 1994. He survived but suffered permanent nerve damage.

'Exactly. When you start to dehumanize non-Muslims, and even Muslims you don't agree with,' I went on, 'attacks like the bombings in Nairobi and Dar es Salaam become thinkable, desirable even. Al-Qaeda is unleashing the inner psychopaths in its recruits.'

Richard nodded and rested his cigar on an ashtray.

'I fear what a certain Saudi millionaire has set in motion is not going to end well for any of us,' he said through threads of blue-grey smoke.

'The irony, Richard, is that he's going to provoke a backlash and Muslims around the world will end up suffering the most. This violence they are inflicting is senseless.'

Richard eyed me closely.

'I take your point,' he said. 'But we use violence, too. We went to war with Saddam Hussein to remove him from Kuwait. Those were Muslims we were fighting. How do you feel about that?'

He was trying to goad me. And I was conflicted. I'd been appalled by Western inaction in the former Yugoslavia, but equally by Russian atrocities in Chechnya. At least NATO had ultimately moved to protect the Muslims of Kosovo from Serbia. And to me the British Prime Minister Tony Blair had shown real leadership in confronting the Serbs.

I thought for a few seconds.

'It's about legitimacy – the just war,' I said with deliberation. 'I don't have to tell you that to many Salafis violence is the monopoly of the state, that politics is beyond or beneath them. So what authority does Osama bin Laden have when he goes beyond defending Muslims? He has set out on a path of chaos and disorder.

'I used to think the old scholars of Islam who preached moderation and obedience to the state were fools and cowards. I thought they knew nothing of the world. But they were the wise ones and I was the foolish one.'

'But don't you feel guilty sometimes working for us?' Richard asked. 'After all, your targets here are all Muslims.'

'You know what? I really don't,' I replied truthfully. 'I hear them say that you should never betray your Muslim brother to the *kuffar* [disbelievers], that only Muslim lives matter, regardless of the circumstances. So this is what I'd ask them now: what are you meant to do if a Muslim is about to commit a murder which could result in the *kuffar* killing many more Muslims in retaliation? Stay silent or act to protect the community?'

Dusk crept across the room. It was a question that would soon resonate throughout the Muslim world.

As the weeks went by, my old acquaintances, even a few I had come to call friends, gradually metamorphosed into adversaries and even targets. I saw them as misguided, bent on gambling with the fate of the Muslim world. I may have been only subconsciously aware that MI6 was grooming me through a well-calibrated mixture of persuasion, empathy and encouragement. The subtext was: 'We think you're beginning to see the world as we do, and that would be good for you and us.'

From the mountains of Afghanistan, the world had looked black and white. It was us – the Victorious Vanguard – against all comers, in a pressure-cooker atmosphere where the cause occupied your every waking moment. Now, as my English improved and I immersed myself in a thousand contrasting views, the world looked much more complex. I would spend hours in public libraries and watch the television news. And every night, the last thing I would do as my head hit the pillow was press play, and wait for the Sandman while listening to an audiobook: British history, the great artists of Renaissance Europe, the Shinto religion in Japan.

The effect was both disorientating and liberating. I questioned the orthodoxies that had become ingrained in me: that there was a Jewish/Crusader conspiracy against Islam and that the struggle could only end in an end-of-days battle. Facts were beginning to eat away at ideology and the tendentious interpretations of *hadith*.

What had begun for me as an attempt simply to extricate

myself from al-Qaeda had become a mission to destroy it. Certainly, in the view of MI6, I was the perfect double agent: once highly committed to both an ideology and an organization but then struck by a moment of moral crisis – a moment expertly disguised from my 'brothers'. My handlers seemed impressed by my mental agility and analytical skills, as well as my ability to penetrate networks while keeping my cool. I was not a one-off treasure trove but a continuing asset, invaluable because my 'legend' was intact.

It helped that I felt comfortable living in London. I found the British tolerant and open-minded and unlike some Muslims experienced no racism. Like many fresh arrivals in London, I got to know the city through its public transport. Londoners are always complaining about their commute, but for me the extraordinary network of Tube lines and bus routes was a thing of wonder. Public services were nonexistent or haphazard in the Middle East and it was strangely liberating to be able to travel with such ease around such a huge city. It was, I now tell my wife, a case of intellectual liberation by public transportation.

I was struck by how multicultural London was. My fellow commuters were from every race, ethnicity and religion, all going about their daily lives in a country in which they were free to express themselves, worship and work. There was a broad tolerance in society – compared to much of the Middle East – that I found refreshing and impressive. It was a sign of confidence in a way of life that had absorbed migration better than most – if by no means perfectly. It made me smile that fish and chips had been replaced by curry as the national dish, that Caribbean music had been woven into the mainstream of British pop. And while others complained about hooliganism, I saw countless examples of common courtesy: the student giving up his seat on the bus for an elderly Indian woman, the station manager explaining patiently how I could best reach Marble Arch, and of course the national pastime of queuing patiently. On the very first page of his manifesto *Milestones*, Qutb had written, 'Western civilization is unable to present any healthy values for the guidance of mankind.' As a teenager I'd lapped up these words, but now I saw a different reality.

He had also written, 'In all systems [apart from Islam] human beings obey other human beings and follow man-made laws . . . it is the duty of Islam to annihilate all such systems.'[21]

Civilization was more complicated than that. And I was now in a society where laws passed by an elected parliament were paramount – and gave everyone equal rights if not equal opportunities. It was, I soon came to accept, more just and free than any back home in the Arab world.

I also developed the greatest respect for my handlers in the intelligence services. Consummate professionals, they understood the Arab world better than I imagined. They had studied the rise of Salafism and were not beyond criticizing the Western response.

And then there was a very personal discovery. Ever the historian, I began to investigate my grandfather's time as the head of the police in Basra during the colonial period. He'd been granted a British passport. So had my father, in the 1960s. But why?

I raised this family history with Richard, who was as intrigued as I was. He did a little homework and told me at one of our meetings that my father had 'done some work for the Foreign Office once upon a time'.

'I'm sure there's much more in the archives,' he said, 'but finding it would take an eternity, and so would the paperwork to get access.' Could my father also have been a spy? Whatever the truth, it seemed the Durrani family had a long line of service to HMG.*

At the beginning of April, when the strange notion of a Fool's Day fell a couple of days before the Easter holiday, I was summoned to a meeting. My handlers were looking forward to a few days in the countryside or a short break in Europe. I knew which I would prefer; bands of heavy rain were sweeping in from the west.

---

* I also found out that my father and uncle, who worked for the Saudi–American oil company Aramco, had known the British spy and adventurer Harry St John Philby. Philby had worked as a British colonial administrator before converting to Islam in Saudi Arabia in the 1930s. His son Kim would become a notorious double agent inside MI6, fleeing to the Soviet Union in 1963.

'Time for a status report,' said Nick as we settled into another unassuming hotel suite. 'Your medical visa lasts just three more months: if you stay here how do we explain that away to your new friends?'

I'd been so busy I had given it no thought.

'One idea: you tell people your father had a British passport, which is true. You are wanted in Bahrain, which we can make true,' Nick said with a smirk. 'For now your health precludes an early return to Afghanistan, which is sort of true. Hence, you are applying for British citizenship.'

'But Said Arif and the rest of them think I hate Britain.'

'So you'll have to take one for the team,' laughed Richard. 'Offer yourself as a sacrificial lamb, wallowing among the *kuffar* in the service of jihad. But let them have the idea.'

They really were looking forward to a few days off.

I spent hours pacing about my apartment on Brighton Road rehearsing the gambit before meeting several of the Four Feathers crew for a kebab at a tiny café that was all chipped Formica and steamed-up windows. They included Said Arif and Abu Walid al-Filistini, a wiry Palestinian sidekick to Abu Qatada who fancied himself a theologian.* I said a silent prayer that I would not muff my lines. Arif was sharp; this had to be good.

'I'm thinking of my next move,' I told him. 'My medical visa runs out soon.'

Arif briefly removed and polished his spectacles. As he replaced them, he fixed me with that cold stare.

'Can you get it extended?'

'No. The only thing I could do is apply for a passport. My father had one because he worked for the colonial government.'

Arif raised his eyebrows.

---

* He was a leading ideologue supportive of al-Qaeda who also had been a staunch defender of the Armed Islamic Group (GIA) in Algeria, despite its many atrocities against civilians. Al-Filistini was also known as Abu al-Walid al-Ansari.[22]

'I know,' I mumbled. 'I'm not proud of my family history but it was apparently quite common.'

'It makes sense to me. We need you here and I'm sure it will come in handy. There will come a time when certain other passports get greater scrutiny,' he said.

Abu Walid leaned forward.

'Becoming a British citizen would involve swearing an oath to the Queen,' he said with unveiled disgust. 'This is completely *haram* [forbidden].'

Arif appeared annoyed at being contradicted but merely said, 'Let's give it some further thought.'

As I stood in the drizzle waiting for a bus, I worked through my dilemma. It was something of a catch-22. If I accepted Abu Walid's stricture, people in my circle might grow suspicious if I was able to stay in the UK beyond the end date of my medical visa. But rejecting his command might also attract suspicion, and that, too, would damage my contacts within the jihadi community.

Nick lit on a brilliant solution.

'I think we can work around this. You are claiming British citizenship by descent, so would not need to swear any oath to Her Majesty.'

Even Abu Walid could not object now. *Phase one complete*, I thought to myself as I waited at a rain-swept bus stop.

Phase two was to make myself indispensable to Abu Qatada and Said Arif. This involved ostentatious deference to Abu Qatada's wisdom and becoming Arif's errand boy.

Arif masterminded a network of Algerians in Europe using credit card fraud and other schemes to raise six-figure sums for various jihadi groups in Afghanistan and elsewhere, including Ibn Khattab's jihadi outfit in Chechnya. They called the proceeds *ghanima* – the loot or spoils of war – and were not using them to buy blankets for suffering refugees.

On one occasion Said Arif handed me a bag with £6,000 in cash and a slip of paper with one name on it: 'Abu Sarah'.

'Go to the Costcutter store next to King's Cross and ask for "Malik",' he said.

As I left the Four Feathers, I felt a shot of exhilaration. Arif must really trust me.

'This is for Abu Sarah. Suleiman sends his regards,' I told Malik.

He took the money without a word and scribbled a receipt for Arif.

This was how terrorists moved money, in cash and in envelopes. No deposit account at Barclays. It was the *hawala* system, introduced by Arab traders over a thousand years ago to transfer money along the Silk Road. The *hawala* allows funds to be transferred outside the banking system but without money physically moving. It is based on the honour system, so there is no paper trail lodged with third parties.

Malik was a *hawala* broker. After I dropped off the cash, I imagined him placing a phone call to a counterpart in Peshawar instructing him to pay out the £6,000 to 'Abu Sarah'. The Peshawar *hawala* broker's confidence that Malik would eventually settle the balance between them meant they only needed to send actual money to each other if their account became lopsided.*

British intelligence didn't intercept the payment. It was much more valuable to them to tap into the financial arteries that provided terrorism with its lifeblood. Throughout the spring, I helped MI5 map out the impressive money-spinning operation run out of Baker Street. My shocked handlers used a word other than 'impressive' as we learned more of the operation.**

---

* The US Treasury would devote a great deal of time and effort to persuading Gulf authorities to rein in the *hawala* system.
** One of the main recipients of Abu Qatada's largesse was the Khalden camp in Afghanistan run by Ibn Sheikh al-Libi. As always, funds first needed to be transferred to Abu Zubaydah, the camp's gatekeeper in Peshawar.

My employers were beginning to get a sense that Europe had an expanding and multifaceted problem: radicalization, recruitment and fundraising in what was essentially a continent-wide sanctuary. I soon had first-hand evidence of the way jihadi networks saw themselves as pan-European even as the national security services arrayed against them worked in silos. A man called Abu al-Fidaa was coming to town from the German city of Stuttgart. He was a key associate of Abu Qatada and Said Arif, and like the latter an Algerian.

Nick was intrigued, although his way of showing it was nothing more than a raised eyebrow. Al-Fidaa was on MI5's radar, but a faint blip. They wanted me to meet him.

Amid the bustle of people hurrying for trains and muffled announcements of cancellations to Haywards Heath, I sat down at a coffee shop on the upper floor at Victoria Station. I remember it as a crystal-clear May morning, when even the traffic fumes of central London seemed to have been banished.

Al-Fidaa was a thickset man in his late thirties, whose face seemed squashed flat. I wondered if he'd been a boxer. He wore a sour expression as he shook my hand, looking quickly towards the surrounding tables.

'Abu Qatada suggested we meet,' I said, 'in case I can help your operations, especially as I'll soon have a British passport.'

His Arabic was guttural and streetwise.

'I'm sending people from Germany and Austria to Khalden,' he said. 'I need money.' He wasn't a man for courtesies. 'They're mainly Algerians and Moroccans; they don't have much money. Flights, sometimes forged documents, it's expensive. Look,' he said, stirring his espresso vigorously, 'there are hundreds and even thousands of young men in Germany ready to go. Thirty years of migration as guest workers – now a second generation that hate their parents and hate being called German.'

There was a grim relish in his voice, but I recognized the scenario.

'Düsseldorf, Cologne, Stuttgart, Munich, Hamburg – I could

be on the road all the time. Let's just say there's no shortage of recruits. And the BfV are useless.* They have no idea what's going on, they're too busy hiding information from the BND. I'm building a support network but I have to be careful. I don't work with fools.'

We talked for half an hour – al-Fidaa was not a man to shoot the breeze – and then he left abruptly. But the impression he left was that the exodus of young Muslims from Germany amounted to an underground railway, including converts and men of North African and Chechen descent.

As I stood on the escalator to the Tube, I wondered why he'd said nothing about plots inside Germany. Perhaps there were none, because it was more important to ship recruits to Afghanistan. More likely, he didn't trust me enough to talk about them.

Nick from MI5 had told me to catch the Underground to High Street Kensington after the meeting. If I thought I was being followed, I should stop by a fruit stall at the exit. If not, I'd be picked up by the pedestrian crossing. I was very careful on the way there, stopping to read an advert in one of the tunnels, pretending to confuse east with westbound platforms. Any tail would have been exasperated by my indecision.

A black van picked me up at Kensington. Nick was inside.

'We'll feed everything back to the Germans,' he told me as we swept into Park Lane. 'They have to put a stop to this.'

Unfortunately, the BfV and other agencies were as redundant as al-Fidaa had asserted. A short while later they lost track of him; and at some point he, too, left Germany for Afghanistan. The British established that he was raising hundreds of thousands of pounds through various fraudulent schemes and uncovered a network with major nodes in Stuttgart and Sheffield in northern England.

---

* The Bundesamt für Verfassungsschutz, or BfV, is Germany's domestic intelligence agency. It is overseen by the Interior Ministry, while the foreign intelligence service, the BND, or Bundesnachrichtendienst, is tasked with overseas intelligence gathering.

In the course of five hectic months, I had provided British intelligence with a manual of jihad unrivalled in its detail. I was told some time later that the services regarded my information as gold dust as they grappled with a new threat on which they had little solid information and within which they had precisely zero sources. While the Americans were ratcheting up their surveillance of al-Qaeda by 'national technical means' (in other words electronic eavesdropping) the British were much stronger in human intelligence. What I provided added a great deal to the very basic picture of al-Qaeda they had. My information was ending up – regularly – at Number 10 Downing Street. And much of it was being passed on to the American cousins (suitably amended to try to keep the source protected) where on occasion it was included in the president's daily intelligence briefing.

It was time for a reward – the subtle British way of making me feel 'family'.

'How about escaping Brighton Road for a few days? Perhaps a trip to the mountains?' Nick asked.

A few days later, he picked me up at Glasgow railway station. We drove through the Scottish Highlands to Oban and took the ferry to the Isle of Iona, where Nick told me about the ancient convent and its nuns. They had followed the teachings of St Augustine of Hippo, an early Christian teacher who had lived in what is now Algeria.

The haunting and windswept beauty of the place deeply affected me. I read of how Columba, an Irish missionary, had built a monastery here in the sixth century, and how the Vikings had plundered it in 795, not long after the Prophet had struggled to establish Islam in the deserts around Medina. The parallel was not lost on me.

There's something about the ocean, its vastness and timeless power, the monotonous crash of the waves, that always makes me brood. Standing on the shore of Iona, facing the soft westerly wind, I watched the gulls swoop and catch the breeze.

Nick had slipped into the hotel for a warming beverage, and I fancied it was not coffee. I had told him that I wanted to take some photographs, but in reality I wanted a few minutes to walk among the heather and try to make sense of things.

I felt a deep affinity for St Columba and the monks who had come to the Scottish islands in the sixth and seventh centuries to do God's will. Monks had remained here despite endless pagan raids in which many died a brutal death. An Irish monk called Blathmac had stayed because he 'wished to endure Christ's wounds'. He was ready to embrace martyrdom for his faith. The Vikings would grant him his wish.

Blathmac was to me the definition of faith. His medieval biographer, Walafrid Strabo, had written a poem about his death, imagining the monk's last words: 'Barbarian, draw thy sword, grasp the hilt and slay; gracious God, to thy aid commend me humbly.'

How different was this form of self-sacrifice from the bombing of Nairobi.

Incongruously, my mind leapt back to Khobar, and the years when I was finding my faith. The Omar bin Abdelaziz mosque – a sand-coloured, modern building – had none of the remote mysticism of Iona, but it had been my sanctuary as a child, especially after the death of my mother. There, I had been taught that Islam demanded much in the way of sacrifice but that it was also a religion of compassion and charity. It was not the language of Qutb, but he, too, had stressed obedience to God. I recalled his words: 'There is either commitment to Islam as a religion, as a way of life and as a social order, or unbelief – *jahiliyya* – ignorant desires, darkness, falsehood and misguidance.'

Was there more in common between the fidelity of Blathmac and the principles of Qutb than I might have imagined?

I wandered back to the hotel.

'You look deep in thought,' said Nick, his hands warming a glass of single malt.

'It's this place,' I smiled. 'It makes you think of the bigger things, what unites us as human beings, and what destroys us.'

'Goodness,' he laughed. 'I might need another drink.'

Not once during the few days we spent in Scotland did we talk 'shop'. Nick was instead the personification of kindness, gently coaxing biographical details from me but more than that showing that British intelligence valued me. I found myself telling him what a misfit I had been at school, how I had never ceased to miss my mother. I wondered aloud whether my anger with the world at the age of thirteen, deprived of parents, had pushed me towards more militant beliefs.

The trip was a bonding exercise, but it wasn't purely altruistic. I was not altogether surprised when in June 1999, a mere six months after sitting down for what I had fondly imagined would be a couple of debriefing sessions, Richard put a proposition to me.

We were in the George Washington suite at the hotel of the same name off Green Park, enjoying tuna and roast beef sandwiches.

'Ali, you've served us tremendously well,' Richard began, stressing the word *tremendously* like a district commissioner in the Colonial Service. 'I know we promised you that after all the debriefings we would give you the opportunity to go back to university or settle down somehow.'

It sounded like there was a 'but' coming.

'I know we made you this promise,' he repeated. 'But would it be stretching your tolerance to remain with us for another six months and make a trip back to Afghanistan? There are many gaps we'd like to fill in.'

It was an appeal to my restlessness as much as anything. By now the British were convinced of my bona fides.

'I was wondering when you were going to ask me that question. The answer is yes,' I replied.

I was confident that my handlers would – to the best of their ability – keep my cover intact. Amid periods of inaction between briefings, I was getting restless. As much as I felt settled in London, I knew there was unfinished work. Al-Qaeda's camps were evolving. New figures were being elevated; and who knew what advances

178

Abu Khabab had made? I was in a unique position to fill in the gaps. There's nothing like being 'wanted', in the positive definition of the word.

Richard's normally laconic demeanour erupted into a broad smile, which for him bordered on euphoria. MI6 would have its own asset deep inside al-Qaeda.

'But there is one problem,' he said, exchanging a look with Nick. 'You made a big song and dance about applying for a UK passport to help my dear friend here from Thames House, and al-Qaeda's intelligence chief in London seems to have grown rather fond of having you around.* Now suddenly you tell them you want to go back to Afghanistan. Does it make you look – er – a little mercurial?'

I looked a little puzzled.

Nick picked up. 'In other words,' he added, 'will they think you've lost the plot?'

'I can tell them I need to recharge my spirituality. I have already told them I can't stand it here and I'm longing to return,' I said. Richard raised an eyebrow. 'Or I could go into the luxury food business.'

They both looked at me as if to check on my sanity. I laughed.

'Some of the best honey in the world comes from the lower slopes of the Himalayas. There's great demand for it in the Gulf, as well as pink salt and saffron. Anyway, last year someone with al-Qaeda called Abdul Rasheed suggested we set up a business. He knew producers in Kashmir; I knew the wealthy markets in Saudi.'

'And how would al-Qaeda view this enterprise?' asked Richard sceptically.

'They'd be very happy. They like members who are financially independent. They like them even more if they contribute to the cause. There's another bonus: my brother Moheddin is perfectly placed to sell whatever we can get.'

Richard looked almost excited.

'I like it,' he said. 'Covers a lot of bases – allows you in and out of Afghanistan to attend to business. At the same time, you get a

* MI5 has offices at Thames House.

British passport – it makes you useful in terms of the financial flows and allows you to be the go-between between head office and the London mullahs.'

It was like a game of three-dimensional chess: anticipating your opponent's needs and decisions, preying on his weaknesses, thinking several moves ahead. My handlers were brilliant at exploiting such advantages, looking for vulnerabilities and temptations.

They also knew that even one clumsy remark to jihadis I encountered had the potential to trip me up. That made it essential to stick as close to the truth as possible. In London I had the grand-masters close at hand but once back in Afghanistan I would be on my own for months at a time.

'We'll provide a number for emergencies or if it's vital you get in touch,' Richard said, 'but we understand that won't be a lot of use where you are going. To be honest, we wouldn't know if you came under suspicion and could do nothing to retrieve the situation even if we did. It's not like we can just drop the SAS into Darunta to see if you're okay.'

Not for the first time he asked me whether I really wanted to go ahead with the plan.

'It's very rare for us to send someone on their own into such a situation. Even when we dropped agents in to help the French Resistance, they had a network.'

I said that I appreciated the risks – and the intelligence services would have to be patient.

'I certainly won't be calling from a payphone in Afghanistan, and I can hardly ask to use one of their satellite phones to call home. I might as well kill myself. So I hope the handlers are patient, because they won't hear from me until I'm at the airport in Doha or Dubai on my way home.'

I was reminded of an Arabic phrase about hopeless and damned places: 'Those who enter disappear; those who come out are born again.'

I knew I would have to commit every detail to memory;

nothing could be written down or sent, unless I wanted to risk execution.

'Just as well you have that famous photographic memory,' Richard told me. 'Let's hope that there's plenty of space left in it,' he laughed, clapping me on the shoulder.

Before leaving, I was taught counter-interrogation and counter-surveillance techniques. I was shown a variety of ruses for checking whether I was being followed – such as bumping into someone so that I could turn round, or dropping a handkerchief as I took out my wallet. I was told to avoid eye contact with anyone who might be following me but focus on the details of their clothes, to go into a shop to buy something and use reflections in windows to survey my surroundings.

'Street food,' said one of my instructors, 'is one of your best defences. It's impulsive and natural to stop. And in Peshawar,' he added with a grin, 'I imagine there's quite a lot of it.'

Then I was sent onto the streets. During three exercises I only identified one of my pursuers, even though at one point he crossed the road and was almost ahead of me. I failed in the other two exercises – probably because my tails were women. It was a useful reminder: don't make assumptions. I was told that my moderate pace was difficult for a tail to mimic; most people, apparently, walked more quickly or slowly than me. To this day I feel myself checking on my walking pace.

Most of the training was done on a sofa; it was like visiting a shrink. A variety of MI5 and MI6 instructors, some of them former military and police, drilled into me one thing: be yourself at all times. Don't start asking too many questions but don't become withdrawn. Let information come to you. Immerse yourself in your environment; try to recall what made you join in the first place, the injustices against Muslims, the perfidy of America.

In mock interrogations I was asked about my finances, which mosques I had attended, friends and relatives. Consistency was everything. I should always tell as much of the truth as possible rather than indulge in outright fiction. It was too easy to trip up when telling (and trying to keep track of) lies. And I was told always to get plenty of sleep; fatigue was the surest route to mistakes.

Another technique suggested was ingenious. If I felt that I was coming under suspicion, or someone was asking me too many probing questions, I should take it up with the local commander or emir, complain that such intrusive questioning was unnecessary and suspicious. Why would my inquisitor need such information? It would help restore my integrity and shift suspicion to whoever was being too inquisitive.

I was taught to read facial expressions and whether they suggested trust or suspicion. Those who insist on constant eye contact are trying to probe for uneasiness or guilt; those who keep bringing the conversation back to a certain topic after you have changed the subject are fishing.

'What can you do if you really need to leave or if you hear about an imminent attack being planned against Britain?' one instructor asked me.

I thought for a while.

'Take off your glasses,' he said. 'How short-sighted are you?'

'Very,' I laughed. 'Let's put it this way – you are three feet from me but a blur.'

'So,' he said, 'don't take a spare pair of glasses. Arrange for these to be broken, properly broken. I imagine there are not too many opticians around Darunta.'

I remembered the cruise missile strikes.

'That's brilliant,' I said. 'I'd have to go all the way to Peshawar to get the right glasses.'

'But this is your joker,' he said. 'You get to play it once.'

One thing I was not taught: handling weapons. As one of my handlers put it, 'We don't want to teach you any techniques that would be at odds with al-Qaeda's house style.'

In June 1999, I told Said Arif that I wanted to escape London and start a food business on behalf of the brothers. He wasn't displeased. It showed – he thought – where my heart lay, and he had some comms equipment that he wanted carried to the camps.

I accepted it, and British intelligence discreetly modified it before I left.

My first stop in Peshawar – as always – was Abu Zubaydah's guest house. I trudged towards the villa with some trepidation, thinking of the torture techniques for suspected spies I'd learned in the camps the previous year. If anybody could sniff out a spy it was Abu Zubaydah.

When he greeted me he put his hands on my cheeks and tugged at the skin. I tried to appear relaxed. It wasn't easy.

'I can see you've put on some weight. This is good. The brothers in England informed me you got treatment for your liver.'

I called Abdul Rasheed.

'The Kashmiri food business,' I said, 'let's make it work.'

He was delighted.

'Come over,' he said. 'I need to take you somewhere.'

The following morning I gazed from a Fokker Friendship aircraft as it threaded a path above thickly forested hills and indigo rivers. In the distance were the towering peaks of the world's highest mountain range; they looked almost frightening. Abdul Rasheed was taking me to Muzaffarabad, capital of exotic honeys. The flowers of the region had great medicinal benefits.

The business model was simple. We'd agree contracts among the Kashmiri suppliers; Moheddin would sell our produce at a rough mark-up of 1,000 percent. The more worldly-wise among wealthy individuals in the Gulf would be happy to pay a premium for the best delicacies and help the cause of jihad in doing so.*

We met a group of beekeepers the next day on a hillside covered in cedar trees in the Neelum valley – and bought our first tonne of

---

* Honey had long been a key source of funds for jihadi groups, including al-Qaeda and Kashmiri militants. Al-Qaeda welcomed self-funding recruits as it reduced their payroll costs. I did not funnel any proceeds to the group. Instead I used my earnings to pay for my own travel and for the rent on my UK apartment. Abdul Rasheed's brother-in-law, the Jordanian-American Khalil al-Deek, also became involved in the business that Abdul Rasheed and I founded.[23]

honey. Over the next several years the little company we founded in Peshawar sent Moheddin a good deal of the best Himalayan produce. My role was to manage the book-keeping and the paperwork for shipments, which conveniently required occasional trips to Islamabad and other places where I could be debriefed.

Muzaffarabad was a pleasant diversion but the real business of becoming a jihadi again awaited. By the time I made my way through the twisting Khyber Pass, I had clothed my mind in the persona of a Holy Warrior engaged in a war against the West. My method acting was a matter of survival. 'After the Torkham Gate, you'll be on your own,' Richard had said. If I was to come under suspicion, there was no way to escape and no possibility of rescue. I would be found within 500 yards of the camp if I tried to sneak away. Al-Qaeda's guards knew the terrain.

Despite the risks, I felt at peace as the bus rumbled its way towards Jalalabad. The training and the drills in London had boosted my confidence. To reduce the risk that counter-intelligence operatives like Abu Zubaydah would figure out I was a mole, Richard had assured me the British would only act on information from me if they could corroborate it with other sources. I trusted him. By volunteering to come back to Afghanistan I was showing my commitment to British intelligence. When the day came to move on with the rest of my life, that commitment would put me beyond reproach. I also believed strongly it was the right thing to do. Bin Laden was – pure and simple – a threat to my religion and to humanity.

I had been propelled into swearing *bayat* partly because I had wanted to be part of history, for my life to make a difference in the grand scheme of things as the 'age of prophecies' dawned. I felt a similar sense of purpose now. For a short while, a combination of emotional and physical fatigue had led me to want to retreat into quiet obscurity, eschewing risk. But that wasn't the real me. Deep down nothing frightened me more than the absence of a challenge or the sense of being surplus to requirements. Staying in the UK would have seen my value as an intelligence asset gradually atrophy. I was propelled by a need to be relevant, needed.

I was pleasantly surprised by the warmth of the welcome I received when I arrived at the safe house al-Qaeda used in Jalalabad. No one asked me much about my time away. The good thing about belonging to a group like al-Qaeda is that on the whole members don't ask too many questions. The camps seemed to have filled out; the cruise missile strikes against al-Qaeda the previous summer had served only to rally more followers to the cause.

It was not difficult to return to the familiar routine of camp life in Afghanistan. When I prayed with my fellow al-Qaeda members, I felt a sense of strength rather than shame. The message I took from those prayers was very different from that understood by the Holy Warriors kneeling to my left and right. I often muttered a saying of Imam Ali, the son-in-law of the Prophet Mohammed and fourth rightly-guided Caliph. 'Loyalty to the treacherous is treachery in the eyes of God. The betrayal of the treacherous is loyalty in the eyes of God.' It became my mantra, the bedrock of my conversion.

Soon after returning, I was summoned to bin Laden's compound in Kandahar to see Abu Hafs al-Masri, the COO. I tried, not altogether successfully, to quell my nerves. Could they, against all odds, have found out that I had betrayed them?

I was struck again by Abu Hafs' piercing intelligent eyes. There seemed to be more flecks of grey in his immense beard. He was still in charge of the day-to-day decisions in al-Qaeda, including training and the planning of attacks. He began with a note of congratulations, which put me at ease.

'The Egyptian and Sudanese boys who met you in London; they were so enthused they came here full of praise for you.'*

I told him about my time in London and the food business.

'Why did you choose Abdul Rasheed as a partner?' Abu Hafs asked.

'Because of his connections in Kashmir,' I replied.

'Ah, yes, yes,' Abu Hafs replied, seemingly satisfied. He picked

---

* Both men eventually left the al-Qaeda fold and neither became involved in terrorist attacks.

at his teeth. 'Just remember, if you make a good return on your investment you should not forget our brothers here – especially those with families.

'I was glad to hear you applied for a British passport,' he said, changing the subject. 'Very useful.'

News travelled fast, I thought. Headquarters must have had a note from Said Arif about my 'progress'. But rather than suspect me, it seemed that Abu Hafs – and others in the higher tiers – had come to consider me an asset, a savvy investor and one of the few mujahideen likely to have regular access to Western capitals and technology, apparently unsuspected.

In my interactions with al-Qaeda leaders it was as if I was now listening to them with a different part of the brain. No longer was I seeking counsel on jihad. Instead I was filing away every last detail to take back to my handlers. I was careful not to appear too inquis- itive, but thankfully had one skill that generated plenty of information.

I was the 'dream-whisperer'. I had begun to develop a reputa- tion as an interpreter of dreams in Bosnia and had further refined the skill in my first Afghan 'tour'. Fighters would provide me with all sorts of supplementary information to try to help me make sense of their dreams.

I was genuinely surprised to hear that my old friend Khalid al-Hajj – whom I had last seen in the Philippines – had just arrived in Afghanistan and was staying at the Kandahar compound. The last I had heard he had been detained in a Saudi sweep of militants after the embassy bombings. I had mixed feelings about seeing him. It was one thing to spy on al-Qaeda's high command and quite another on a man who for years had been my best friend. But he was a target now. His photograph was in the dossiers I had gone through with my intelligence handlers in London. I had watched him behead a man in Bosnia and was under no illusion he would follow orders, including torturing and executing me if I was suspected as a spy.

I found him at the shooting range, blasting away at a target on which had been scrawled the features of President Bill Clinton.

When we embraced I could not but feel happy to see him. He told me he had left Saudi Arabia almost immediately after being released from prison. He was now one of bin Laden's personal bodyguards, travelling with him around the country. Khalid was reluctant to speak about his treatment in jail, except to say that he had 'scars that will never heal'. I had no doubt about what he meant.

'I'll tell you one thing. If I ever go back to Saudi Arabia it will be to wage jihad against the House of Saud. They are a cancer that needs to be cut out,' he said. The bitterness in his voice was unsettling. Here was a young man whose optimism had been snuffed out; his mistreatment in jail had hardened him. The light I had previously seen in his eyes now had the glint of cold steel. He had never previously spoken about overthrowing the Saudi royal family. The change in him mitigated the unease I felt in spying on him.

My next stop was the fifty square yards of Afghanistan that most worried British intelligence.

At Darunta Abu Khabab greeted me like a lost son, and strangely – despite all that had happened in the previous eight months – I still felt some affection for him. I remembered London's advice: be yourself, let him talk.

Over the inevitable green tea and basking in the summer sun, Abu Khabab filled me in on experiments and personnel and asked me about the 'brothers' in London. I was just about to tell him about my chat with his former and handless student, Abu Hamza, when he grasped my forearm.

'Saajid Badat,' he said. I hesitated – and then remembered the serious teenager in the Tooting Circle. 'A good student – thank you for sending him. And his recitation of the Koran: beautiful.' He swept his arm into the thin air as he made the compliment.*

---

* I was later reunited with Badat in the camps. A few weeks after 9/11 he and Richard Reid were given shoe bombs and instructed by Abu Hafs al-Masri and Khalid Sheikh Mohammed to blow up aircraft over the United States simultaneously. He pulled out of the plot at the last moment but was later convicted by a British court after components of the device were found at his

In the months I had been away, Abu Khabab and his apprentices had been experimenting with delivery mechanisms for poison gas, based on Hassan Ghul's concept. I was relieved to find Hassan was still alive, and his good humour still irrepressible.*

The camp had become quite the finishing school for aspiring bomb-makers. Its guests included two members of the radical Palestinian group Hamas.** Jihadi groups were already mixing, learning from each other and collaborating.

Abu Khabab's priority that summer was the potent but very sensitive explosive TATP. For years, terrorist bomb-makers had been making the explosive by mixing particular quantities of acetone, hydrogen peroxide, and acid.[25] Despite the dangers, Abu Khabab produced the stuff as if he were brewing a pot of tea. So much for his stricture that our first mistake would be our last.

One afternoon he had accidentally changed the ratios and been surprised by the results. A solid mass of TATP formed in the solution after twenty-one hours rather than the normal twenty-four – and there was more of it.

He gathered us around and suggested we take advantage of his error and try to create even more TATP. The new ratio was both daring and foolhardy.

'My bet is that the standard formula has a significant safety margin,' he said.

I would have preferred greater precision than a bet. But to demur might invite a lack of confidence from my mentor – or worse, stir suspicion.

So for my new Queen and country, and with my heart

parents' home in Gloucester. He subsequently gave evidence against other al-Qaeda plotters.[24]

* Abu Bakr al-Masri was firmly established as Abu Khabab's deputy. There were some new faces in Abu Khabab's camp, though unfortunately Abu Nassim – the sadistic Tunisian – was still there.

** Over the years Abu Khabab's trainees became more diverse. In the early days at Darunta he had mainly trained Arabs, but as his reputation grew Pakistani, Uzbek, Chechen and Palestinian militants started training with him.

pounding, I helped Abu Khabab and the other apprentices make a new batch of TATP. We decided to produce it in the dormitory rather than the laboratory, which held all sorts of other explosives. A chain reaction would blow much of Darunta skyward. I was in a cold sweat as we mixed the ingredients, my mouth dry with apprehension.

The TATP solidified in just six hours and there was significantly more of it.

'Okay, so tomorrow lets see how far we can take this,' Abu Khabab said with a glint in his eye, every inch the mad chemistry professor. For a moment I thought he was teasing us; it was soon apparent he was not.

I prayed fervently that night that his scientific curiosity wasn't about to kill the cat.

The next morning, we wrapped damp scarves around our faces and put on spectacles and any other eyewear we could get our hands on. We must have made a comical sight, like short-sighted clowns moving clumsily at a lakeside. Extraordinarily, just a few minutes after we mixed the further enhanced formula, almost the entire solution became TATP.*

I was more an observer than leader in the process, focused on my survival and the challenge to chemical conventions. But the two Hamas members were ecstatic. Abu Khabab's experiments had yielded a recipe to make TATP on an industrial scale. Previously, TATP had generally been used to make detonators and was considered very expensive and labour-intensive to produce in large quantities. Now, bigger batches could be produced more quickly, making TATP the terrorists' explosive of choice for the 'main charge' in bombs.

* This description leaves out critical information on making TATP and does not go beyond information already in the public domain in academic studies, media articles, court documents, government reports and the like. While the recipe to make TATP is well known and all too easily found on the Internet, it is exceptionally tricky and hazardous to make. It involves a complicated and intricate set of steps with very little margin for error. Jihadi terrorists in the West who have successfully made TATP tend to have received hands-on training in how to make it.[26]

During the Second Palestinian Intifada, between 2000 and 2005, almost five hundred Israelis would be killed by suicide bombs,[27] some of which, I was later told, used the new formula. No wonder the Israelis referred to the explosive as 'mother of Satan'.*

I'd only been at Darunta a couple of weeks when a courier arrived ordering several fighters in the camp to report to Kabul.

'That can only mean one thing,' said Safwat. 'Front-line duty.'

Bin Laden regarded providing military support to the Taliban as an important part of al-Qaeda's mission and required members to help in the defence of Kabul. The Taliban had held the capital since 1996, but Ahmed Shah Masoud and other enemies had reorganized under the banner of the Northern Alliance and held on to positions not far from the capital. Arab fighters were made responsible for guarding a stretch of front line on the northern approach to Kabul.**

I was not happy. How ignominious would it be to become cannon fodder on the gridlocked front north of Kabul? After dismissing the idea of a medical excuse (malaria?), or a critical

---

* The new formula also produced TATP that was even more sensitive than before. Even a small impact or friction could set off the explosive. This made it even easier to set off but also likely contributed to dozens of Hamas bomb-makers accidentally blowing themselves up. The British explosives expert is my only source that the new formula was used to make the bombs in these attacks. Investigators have not released sufficient information to make this determination independently. TATP has more recently become an explosive of choice for ISIS and was used as the main charge in the terrorist attacks in Paris in November 2015, Brussels in March 2016 and Manchester in May 2017. Investigators have not yet revealed the preparation ratios in those devices.[28]

** The Taliban wanted to break through this front line because it would open the road to the Panjshir valley where Northern Alliance forces were headquartered. Al-Qaeda fighters were drafted in part because bin Laden wanted to curry favour with Mullah Omar. Participation on the front line was also seen as good for morale because it provided an outlet for recruits desperate for 'action' and 'martyrdom'. Perhaps most importantly, it allowed al-Qaeda to build up its capability as a military organization.[29]

moment in Abu Khabab's experiments (I'd only just got back), I realized I had no option but to go.

I had discussed the possibility with Richard in London before I left. 'If you can't find a way to avoid it, please be careful and *Allah Ma'ak* [God be with you],' he had said helpfully. I would later be commended by senior officials in MI6 for going to the front lines. In reality I had no alternative.

Kabul was at least no longer a city in anarchy. The hawkers had returned to the streets; battered taxis threw out noxious fumes. The heavy hand of the Taliban's Religious Police was everywhere. The Department for the Promotion of Virtue and the Prevention of Vice was at the zenith of its power. In the shimmering summer heat – laced with the odour of rotting garbage – one occasionally witnessed shapeless blue forms escorted by bearded men. They were rare evidence that women still existed under Taliban rule. For those guilty of one form of vice or another, there were regular stonings in the football stadium.

Al-Qaeda's Kabul guest house was a large villa in the Wazir Akbar Khan district, which by Kabuli standards was an upscale part of the town. It was just a few hundred yards from the presidential palace.

Abu Hafs al-Masri greeted the few dozen of us summoned from the provinces.

'I have news which will fill you with joy. *Masha'Allah* [by the grace of God] you have been selected for deployment on the front lines.'

The room was filled with a chorus of '*Alhamdulillah!*' (Praise be to God.)

We were provided with basic weapons – mine was an AK-47 that had seen plenty of action – and given a rota of duty. Just before dawn on a dusty July morning, we set off towards the front line at Murad Beg in a convoy of Toyota pickup trucks.

As our flags thrashed above the vehicles and dark shapes could be seen trudging along the roadside towards morning prayers, I felt something unfamiliar: fear.

I thought back to Bosnia and the Philippines and my readiness to embrace martyrdom. The world then had seemed so dualistic; the righteous path so obvious and undeniable. Doubt is a cruel thing, but it had seeped and then flooded into my heart in the past two years. I could not expect martyrdom in the service of a cause I had abandoned because it perverted Islam. In short, I had no desire to die; to the contrary, I felt that I had much work to do before being called to the next world. My faith was not in question but my perception of serving God was very different from that of the fighters sitting opposite me, as the truck bounced and jolted up the hill. I was somewhat comforted by the fatalism that is ingrained in Islam. In the words of Imam Ali: 'Cowardice never prolongs life and bravery never shortens life.'

But if a bullet or mortar round extinguished my life I hoped God would look on me kindly. While I could no longer be assured of the heavenly rewards of the martyr, surely He would not consign me to hell for trying to save lives?

Al-Qaeda's forward operating base at Murad Beg was situated on a high, flat, fertile plain bordered by mountains twenty miles north of Kabul. A bunker served as both command post and sleeping quarters. Taking shifts, fighters manned positions in a trench lined with sandbags. Northern Alliance fighters were dug in around some abandoned farm buildings 500 metres away.*

At sunset on the day we arrived I could hear the call to prayer being sung by a fighter on the enemy side. A young al-Qaeda fighter on our side began the *adhan* at almost exactly the same time. Al-Qaeda had taught its fighters that the Northern Alliance were godless mercenaries doing the bidding of Western powers, but hearing the soulful voices of the duelling front-line muezzin echo around the valley – as if in a duet – reminded me that this front was a civil war between Muslims. The enemy now was not the Serbs or the

---

* The front-lines were fluid and not neatly defined. I was told that at various points that year the nearest Northern Alliance fighters were further to the north.

Russians, or even Christians in the Philippines army, but others who turned to the same god that I did. It was not so long ago that Ahmed Shah Masoud had been proclaimed 'Lion of Panjshir' by the mujahideen for his exploits against the Soviets.

I knew that the following morning I might be called upon to kill those praying in the opposing trenches and felt deeply uneasy.

Our commander at Murad Beg was Abdul Hadi al-Iraqi.* He was dressed in camouflage and had strong symmetrical features, intelligent eyes and a beard that was just beginning to turn grey. He had been a major in the Iraqi army before coming to fight jihad in Afghanistan in the early 1990s and had won a reputation as a brave and capable military leader. He asked me what fighting experience I had and I was quick to stress my expertise on mortars.

'Very good, you will travel to the Bagram front tomorrow to join the mortar team there,' he said.

I was relieved. Being part of the mortar team meant I would be stationed a little way behind the front lines. My chances of survival during my two-week rotation to the front had improved.

The following evening, as the setting sun ringed the mountains in a crimson glow, those assigned to the Bagram front piled into the back of a Toyota pickup truck. The vehicle lurched and jerked along the track out of our rudimentary base.

Suddenly, there was a pinging of impacts and the vague sighs of bullets that had missed their target. Then came the much more definable clatter of machine-gun fire from a distance.

'Ambush!' one of the Saudi fighters screamed. 'Turn around.

---

* After the fall of the Taliban, Abdul Hadi organized the al-Qaeda resistance in Afghanistan. He also had contact with a group of British jihadis in Pakistan, who were encouraged via his deputy to launch an attack in the UK. Their plot to attack UK targets including possibly the Ministry of Sound nightclub with fertilizer bombs was thwarted by Operation Crevice in early 2004. Abdul Hadi later became a key liaison between al-Qaeda central and its Iraqi affiliate. He was captured en route to Iraq in November 2006 and transferred to Guantánamo Bay, where he faces a trial by military commission.[30]

Back to the base!' he shouted, hammering on the cab. Our driver slammed on the brakes and began an arduous turn that seemed to go on forever. We were now at our most vulnerable, a stationary target, broadside.

I clutched my AK-47 and trained it on what I thought was the origin of the fire, desperately searching for muzzle flashes in the fields below. A shell hit the road nearby, sending rocks and dust flying.

At last our driver completed his turn, the gears crunching. Next to me now was Safwat, the Egyptian from London. He nodded towards a small group of fighters creeping up the hill towards us. I turned to look and in that instant heard the crack of an impact that seemed inches away. I looked towards Safwat and was stunned to see blood pouring from his head. A round had gone straight through his skull, exiting at the temple. He slumped forward onto the muzzle of his AK-47 as the truck accelerated away.

At that moment I knew he was dead – even in the darkness – but I prayed otherwise. As I tried to prop him up I felt desperate. A lifeless body has a gravity all of its own. I had felt the difference in Bosnia; now I felt it here. In the few hundred metres back to the camp, I felt sure the truck's suspension or its rear axle would collapse. More than once I was sure one or more of us would be ejected by the pinball effect of our frantic retreat. But all the time, I had a mental picture of Safwat's ex-wife, the genteel Englishwoman, receiving news of his death in her London kitchen. It was an image that I found hard to shake in the following weeks.

The camp was a whirr of activity. Mortars were being mobilized and within minutes I was manning one of them, unleashing volley after volley in the direction of the Northern Alliance. There was no time to think; only time to act. But when Abdul Hadi ordered a ceasefire, and an eerie quietness descended, the adrenalin drained from my body.

I did not need to be told that, had one of our enemy trained his gun just a fraction differently, the body slumped in the back of the truck would have been mine.

In Bosnia I had felt despair at not being welcomed among garlands into paradise. In Azerbaijan, I had felt exasperation about not reaching Chechnya; in the Philippines infuriation at the lack of desire among local fighters. Now I felt just the ache of relief, an enervating emptiness.

I thought of Richard's wry remark that I was gambling away the lives of a cat. I had just used my fifth.

# MY SIXTH LIFE: JIHAD FOR A NEW MILLENNIUM

## 1999–2000

S hortly after midnight on 9 September 1999, a massive bomb
exploded in the basement of an apartment building on Guryanov
Street in Moscow. Much of the structure collapsed; over ninety
people were killed. At dawn, the full horror of the scene was apparent: children's clothes scattered across the street, a sofa perched on
a ledge that had been a sitting room.

Terrorism had come to Moscow, in the most shocking form its
citizens could remember. There was a climate of fear; whose building would be next?[1]

The city's mayor, Yuri Luzhkov, told Russian television: 'I am
sure Chechnya is to blame. It was a promised expansion of hostilities and terrorist acts by Chechen warlords.'[2]

In the three years since a truce had been declared between
Russian forces and Chechen separatists, the situation in the
Caucasus had slipped towards anarchy. Kidnapping was the
main industry amid a broader social disintegration, and foreign
jihadis were beginning to scent opportunity in the mist-covered
mountains. Separatism was now clothed in Islamist radicalism.

In August 1999, some 2,000 jihadis had crossed from Chechnya
into Dagestan and captured several mountain villages. The Russians
had responded with air strikes and ground operations. But the
rebels, led by Shamil Basayev and Ibn Khattab (no doubt galvanized by mayonnaise), carried out more incursions.[3]

Yet the Chechen warlords, normally quick to claim any

success against Russia, professed ignorance of the apartment bombing.

'The latest blast in Moscow is not our work, but the work of the Dagestanis,' declared Basayev hours after the bombing. 'Russia has been openly terrorizing Dagestan, it encircled three villages in the centre of Dagestan, did not allow women and children to leave.'[4]

Four days later another huge bomb – also planted in the basement – demolished an eight-storey apartment building on the southern outskirts of the Russian capital. One hundred and twenty-four people were killed; debris was hurled 300 metres from the scene.

Before anyone claimed responsibility for the second attack, the story took the strangest twist. On 22 September in the city of Ryazan, some 100 miles south-east of Moscow, individuals were seen loitering by the basement of an apartment block. The police arrived to find what appeared to be a detonating device and wires among sacks of powder in the basement.

A witness who had called the police swore that the men were undoubtedly Russian, not from the Caucasus. Tests on the powder showed it was hexogen, the same Second World War-era explosive that had been used in the Moscow bombings.[5]

Police detained two suspects, who turned out to work for the FSB. They were quickly ordered released and Nikolai Patrushev, chief of the Russian FSB internal security service, appeared on television to announce that the sacks had contained only sugar. The whole thing had been part of a public safety drill, he claimed. The FSB quickly cleared the basement in Ryazan of all evidence. The headlines were by now dominated by news of Russian military action in Chechnya. The previous evening Acting Prime Minister Vladimir Putin had announced that Russian aircraft had bombed Grozny airport.[6]

Questions began to swirl, not least among my handlers in London. Had Chechen jihadis really decided to provoke war with the Kremlin? And had Russian intelligence cynically co-opted a budding terror campaign to whip up hysteria and justify a Russian crackdown against Chechnya?

Astonishingly, it began to look as though the Russian security services – and perhaps others in the Moscow hierarchy – had fore-knowledge of the plot. Conspiracy theories multiplied. Why would they do such a thing, and where did responsibility truly lie?

The bombings occurred against a fevered political background in Russia in the waning days of Boris Yeltsin's presidency. Sick and suffering from alcoholism, Yeltsin presided over a failing state where corruption was endemic, reaching deep into his own family. Inflation was destroying the living standards of ordinary Russians; democracy had become a byword for chaos. Many subsisting on pensions were literally going hungry.

There was a growing feeling Russia's humiliation needed to be avenged, just as a succession struggle was shaping up in Moscow. The recently appointed acting Prime Minister Vladimir Putin was determined to exploit one to win the other.

Putin had been the head of the FSB and a long-time KGB operative in the Soviet era; he knew the dark arts of sabotage and blackmail. But as a relatively unknown figure, with presidential elections a year away, he needed recognition as the man who would drag Russia out of its mess. He grasped the opportunity presented by the bombings, laying to rest his image as the colour-less bureaucrat.[7]

'Those that have done this don't deserve to be called animals. They are worse . . . they are mad beasts and they should be treated as such,' Putin said. Lapsing into street jargon, he promised: 'We will waste them . . . we will bury them in their own crap.'[8]

It was an enormously popular message for a frightened people. His approval ratings rocketed, as did support for a scorched-earth assault on Chechnya. But questions about the bombings lingered.

In the weeks after the bombings, I was in London on what might be euphemistically called 'home leave' after my close brush with death on the front line north of Kabul. Richard told me the clumsy cover-up in Ryazan and the rapid clearance of the bomb sites in Moscow had prompted UK intelligence to wonder whether the Russian authorities had themselves carried out the bombings to create a pretext for invading Chechnya.*

'It looks as if they did it. That's their nature, that's the way they approach things,' Richard said, 'in complete secrecy as if they are covering up something. Any news on the grapevine?' he asked, more in hope than expectation.

Babar Ahmad, who was usually in contact with Ibn Khattab even from Tooting, told me he had not been able to find out whether the jihadis had carried out the attack. Abu Qatada, a major fund-raiser for Chechen jihad, told me he was convinced Putin had ordered the bombings to justify an all-out offensive on Chechnya, one that was indeed announced on 1 October.[9]

There were plenty of theories but no conclusive evidence, just a maelstrom of dark rumours fed by dubious sources. Even on my next trip into Afghanistan, influential figures like Abu Zubaydah shrugged their shoulders in what seemed genuine bemusement.

Illumination would finally come when I had an invitation from Abu Qatada to his home. My ceaseless flattery of his religious wisdom had paid dividends.

'Please,' he said, 'Come tomorrow, after *Iftar*. We'll have a call with your old friend Abu Said al-Kurdi.'

I was keen to find out what al-Kurdi, the former deputy of Abu Zubaydah, had been up to. I knew he had relocated to the former Soviet republic of Georgia and carved out a role as the logistics chief for the Chechen jihadis. Astonishingly, he seemed to operate unhindered by the Georgian authorities. Perhaps he was a tool for them in their rift with Moscow.

When I arrived at his home on a dank winter's evening, several associates of Abu Qatada, including Abu Walid al-Filistini (the stickler over my passport application earlier in the year), were already sitting in a semi-circle on the floor. Abu Qatada had laid

---

* The high number of Russian soldiers killed during the previous Chechen war (1994–6) had led to popular backlash in Russia which had forced Yeltsin to end hostilities.

out dates, biscuits and coffee. Somewhat incongruously, Ricky Martin's 'Livin' La Vida Loca' was wafting through the wall from a neighbouring house.

'We're going to get a first-hand account of events in Chechnya,' Abu Qatada said. By now the Russian offensive was in full force.

Using a scratch card for international calls, he dialled the Georgian number and placed the call on loudspeaker.

Al-Kurdi greeted us all in turn.

'It's a long time since we swam in the lake in Jalalabad,' I told him.

'Yes, my friend. Too long,' he replied.

He then gave us an update on the state of combat in the Caucasus. There had been heavy casualties among fighters and civilians. Putin had delivered on his threat.

Abu Qatada chipped in.

'So Putin killed his own people in Moscow so he could kill hundreds and thousands more of ours.'

There was a pause.

'No,' al-Kurdi replied. 'There's been a lot of talk about the bombings in Moscow. All of it is wrong. The Islamic Emirate was responsible.'

There was a stunned silence.

His brow furrowed, Abu Qatada asked: 'But why? Didn't it invite Putin to attack?'

'It was revenge,' came the curt reply.

Al-Kurdi said that members of the brutal Moscow Region OMON militia unit had been involved in previous atrocities in the Caucasus. The jihadis had tracked a few of them to the Moscow apartment buildings that had been bombed.*

'We have our informants; there are plenty of Chechens in Moscow,' al-Kurdi added. 'It took us nineteen months of

---

* A Moscow-based OMON unit had been involved in a massacre of Chechen women and children in April 1995.[10]

surveillance, preparations and bribes, because we smuggled all the bombs and materials and trucks. This is Russia. People will sell you their mothers for $100.'

Perhaps he could sense the doubt in the silence at the other end. 'I want you to remember that we as mujahideen on the ground assess the situation better than you because we are here, so trust us that we made the right choice. The war was coming whether now or in a year or two. So when we took vengeance we knew what we were doing.\*

'Believe me, it was ridiculously easy.'

I wondered who might be listening to the call besides the small party in Abu Qatada's living room. The British? The Russians? The Georgians?

'All were in agreement,' al-Kurdi continued, 'except Maskhadov, who didn't know. But Shamil Basayev and Ibn Khattab were in on the plan.'\*\*

Al-Kurdi's line from Tbilisi was muffled at times, but clear enough for me to hear a very precise figure: $180,000. That was the amount al-Kurdi said had been received in foreign donations for the Chechen cause, for which he was immensely grateful. And much of that sum had been raised and distributed by the mild-mannered cleric sitting opposite me. I nearly asked al-Kurdi to repeat the figure, such was my disbelief: the sums being raised were way beyond those handled in Peshawar by Abu Zubaydah. How had their movement never been detected?

After the call, Abu Qatada seemed preoccupied.

'I think they miscalculated,' he said.

He was probably right. Putin may not have ordered or even been aware of the plan to bomb Moscow. But it was a gift – whoever wrapped it – to the new hard man of Russian politics. In the

---

\* The jihadis were eventually driven deep into the mountains and Chechnya 'pacified'. Putin would install a pro-Kremlin regime.
\*\* Aslan Maskhadov was president of the Chechen Republic between 1997 and 1 October 1999, when Putin declared his authority illegitimate. He fought in both Chechen wars against the Russians.

smoke-and-mirrors secrecy of Moscow Rules, he didn't need to be complicit.*

One of the leading Russian authorities on the story wrote later that 'the world of terrorism and the world of the secret services are not divided by a wall so impassable that they are prevented from merging into one landscape. And a police provocation can take different forms: for instance, the police may fail to act when they receive threatening information – if, that is, someone thinks that inaction more closely corresponds to the unspoken desires of the higher-ups.'[12]

That night, against normal protocol, I scribbled down everything I had heard on the call. I had to get this right because al-Kurdi's information flew in the face of a widespread perception that the Moscow bombings were a false-flag operation staged by Putin.

Richard was taken aback by al-Kurdi's account and shocked by the money flows.

'There are plenty of people at Vauxhall Cross** who think this was an inside job,' he said when we met in an almost deserted café in Victoria. London was in limbo in that period between Christmas and New Year when offices are empty and commuter trains silent. More so this year, as the countdown to the new millennium reached fever pitch.

Within a couple of days Yeltsin quit and handed the keys of the castle to Vladimir Putin. It was New Year's Eve, hours before the advent of the third millennium, but I soon had a call from Richard. He demanded 'every detail about the call at Abu Qatada's house down to the brand of slippers he was wearing'. British intelligence wanted every last scrap of information about the Kremlin's new occupant, and that included anything on whether he was the cynical killer of his own people. The 'PM' wanted to develop a personal relationship with Putin.

* Just how the bombings occurred and who was responsible will probably never be known for sure.[11]
** The MI6 Headquarters building at Vauxhall on the south bank of the Thames.

Months later, when Tony Blair travelled to Moscow, he and Putin were photographed at the Pivnushka restaurant, dressed casually and talking animatedly.[13]

'You're responsible for that picture,' Richard said, poking at a newspaper. It was hyperbole, but he probably wanted me to feel that my contributions were significant. The information gleaned from the al-Kurdi call had at least raised questions about the bleakest appraisals of Russia's new leader.

The war in Chechnya became ever more brutal, with Russian forces razing the capital, Grozny, to the ground. The United Nations called it 'the most destroyed city on earth'.[14] As for the bombings, two men were convicted in 2004 of carrying them out. But their trial was held in secret, and several people who dug deeper into the case died in questionable circumstances.[15]

Al-Qaeda's gatekeeper eyed my freshly minted British passport, its gold-emblazoned coat-of-arms not yet dulled by wear.

'Most useful. It's a shame you did not tell us about your eligibility sooner,' said Abu Zubaydah as I checked in at his Peshawar way station a few weeks after the Moscow bombings.

He did not even try to hide the fact that his agents had done some vetting. My brother Moheddin had received a visit from a Saudi I knew to be a member of al-Qaeda. Was it true that our father had been a British citizen?

'It seemed a strange thing to ask,' Moheddin had told me in a phone call. 'I told him that while we don't exactly advertise the fact, Dad did have a UK passport.'

Abu Zubaydah caressed my passport and looked at me.

'I was very surprised when I heard your father was British.'

The subtext was obvious. We do check. Don't think you are too smart and don't try to hide anything. The same applied to the food business, for which I said I needed to keep the British passport.

'I hope it will soon be profitable,' he said, handing me back the passport, 'for all our benefit.'

I had promised to return to Afghanistan with 'supplies'. It was the downside of my freedom to travel. A few bits of communication equipment, suitably adapted by technicians at MI6, were buried deep in my suitcase. But in the depths of winter, amid sudden scrutiny of my story, I was apprehensive and agitated. Even though I thought my tradecraft was impeccable, I could not afford a 'bad day at the office'.

One piece of equipment was a phone for a training camp which al-Qaeda had set up in Logar province to replace the one destroyed by cruise missiles in Khost.* Fighters there were complaining that they could only contact their families if they went to Kabul, some fifty miles away. I was assured that detecting the tracking mechanism was beyond all but highly trained engineers. There was 'no way in hell' the device would be discovered, as one of them put it.

On the trek into Afghanistan, snow and ice covered every mountain crag; a bitter wind swept across the barren scarps. Clouds and mist obscured the peaks either side of the winding Khyber Pass.

The camp commanders were delighted with the 'satphone' – but not as much as British intelligence would be. For the next two years, MI6 was able to track calls into and out of al-Qaeda's main terrorist training camp. Calls were made to the UK, Sweden, Italy, Spain, Canada, the US and elsewhere. The British built a matrix of al-Qaeda's networks, its recruitment process and security – as well as the recruiting grounds that were proving most fertile. They were also able to get a sense of morale in the camps and movements in and out of Afghanistan. In effect, they built an organic structure of the group. The intelligence mined was more valuable than the arrest of any would-be jihadis.

The camp, hastily set up in an abandoned copper mine far from the site of the previous year's missile strikes, had over fifty fighters. Among them was the American Adam Gadahn. He had

---

* The camp in Logar was called Faruq, as it had been in Khost. The camp was later moved to near Kandahar and again called Faruq.[16]

filled out and was a head taller than me. He had also grown in self-assurance and spoke excellent Arabic.*

I made mental notes of the camp's size, buildings and location, a few mountain ridges from the forbidding outlines of the Pole Charkhi prison, before setting off for Darunta. British intelligence badly wanted to know about any technical progress and personnel changes there.

The journey took me within sight of the ridge of hills – now coated in snow – where Safwat had lost his life a few months earlier. I wished I had had the time to visit his burial site, and suddenly thought that his grieving widow would never know where he was laid to rest, in a cemetery outside Kabul where the flags of the dead fluttered among plastic bags that swept across the open land and snagged on bushes.

Safwat had been killed by other Muslims in a war that was going nowhere. Now I was about to re-enter global jihad's 'research establishment' as it looked for ever more inventive ways to kill people. Yet again I would need to be on my guard against any slip of the tongue, even while absorbing every minute detail about Abu Khabab's research and apprentices. Not one normally given to stress, I felt a suffocating apprehension.

Trucks coming north barrelled past the little minibus into which I was crammed, sending clouds of dust through cracks in the ill-fitting windows. More than once I thought about jumping into another minibus in Jalalabad and escaping into Pakistan and away from everything. But even had I succeeded, the guilt of moral surrender would have followed me. I treated myself to a banana milkshake in Jalalabad and walked for an hour to clear

---

* I saw Gadahn in the camps again the following year. He was learning Shariah law with one of al-Qaeda's leading clerics, Abu Hafs al-Mauretani. By the time Gadahn was eventually killed in a US drone strike in the tribal areas of Pakistan in 2015, he had emerged as al-Qaeda's chief spokesman and the driving force of al-Qaeda's media outlet as-Sahab. Another American al-Qaeda operative I met briefly in the camps before 9/11 was Adnan Shukrijmah, who was killed by the Pakistani military in 2014.

my head before haggling with a taxi driver over the fare to Darunta.

Abu Khabab welcomed me back warmly. He told me his team had made significant progress in solving the challenge of designing a simple device to spread poison gas, but he had paused in his work because a number of jihadis were visiting the camp to get training.

One of them was a short, heavy-set Jordanian. There was an intensity to him that was both compelling and somewhat disturbing. In a past life he had been the feared thug in a street gang. His name was Abu Musab al-Zarqawi, and he had just completed a five-year prison term in Jordan. He intrigued me because British intelligence had suggested I keep an eye open for Jordanians in the camps, especially any that might have done time in jail.

Zarqawi's background could not have been more different from that of the wealthy, highly educated bin Laden. He had grown up in a grim industrial town in Jordan and had a criminal record before he was out of his teens.[17] Barely literate, his rough-hewn street Arabic made him sound less than articulate.

On his first trip to Afghanistan in 1989 he had sought to escape a troubled life, in which multiple criminal cases against him piled up as he drifted from one calamity to the next.[18] To coin a phrase, he had needed jihad more than jihad needed him.

In 1994, after returning to Jordan from Afghanistan, Zarqawi had gone to jail yet again. He was arrested along with a militant (and highly influential) preacher, Abu Mohammed al-Maqdisi,* in connection with a plot to attack an Israeli border post.[20]

Zarqawi made up for his lack of schooling and intellect with

---

* Al-Maqdisi embraced the most extreme school of Salafism. In the mid-1980s he published *The Creed of Abraham*, which depicted Muslims who obeyed secular laws as apostates and worse than infidels. It had a huge impact on Salafi-jihadis in later decades. Al-Maqdisi would become al-Zarqawi's ideological mentor. His tracts were smuggled out of the Jordanian prison where he was he held with Zarqawi, and published online by Abu Qatada in London. It was an early example of the Internet's potential in disseminating ideas banned by oppressive Arab regimes.[19]

a ruthless determination and unwavering commitment to jihad. He had memorized the Koran while in prison and set about recruiting other prisoners. He had developed leadership skills that used fear and loyalty in a charismatic combination. Even in jail, Zarqawi and al-Maqdisi built a group that gained in numbers and notoriety.

The world might have been saved a lot of trouble had the Jordanian authorities not declared a general amnesty for prisoners in March 1999. Months later Zarqawi booked his passage to Pakistan, telling security officials at Amman airport he was starting, of all things, an international honey business.[21] It was astonishing to me that a man with his record was allowed to leave. Perhaps the Jordanians hoped for his untimely martyrdom in a foreign field; they would be disappointed.

Zarqawi arrived at Darunta with a companion and for long hours they were huddled with Abu Khabab in his makeshift laboratory or at the lakeside testing ground. Their focus was on basic but powerful bombs made from fertilizer. Once they had mastered the art, they assembled one tonne of ammonium nitrate. Abu Khabab called everyone to a viewing point above the lake as Zarqawi, a look of manic intensity in his eyes, detonated the device by remote control.

Such was the shock wave that reverberated around the hills, some locals thought there had been an earthquake and ran from their homes.

Zarqawi was also fascinated by experiments with gases and toxins. He spent part of his sixteen-day visit poisoning rabbits in the aquarium – using hydrogen cyanide and chlorine and taking detailed notes in the process. It would be an abiding interest for the Jordanian.

I wanted to know more about this driven individual, but he had not exactly integrated into camp life. Then one morning he emerged though the mist carrying two glasses of tea. I had just given the lesson at dawn prayers.

'The brothers here told me that you're our young preacher,' he said, sitting down next to me on a rock. It was quite the compliment.

'Thanks,' I replied, 'that's very kind of you.'

'Can I ask you a question? I was told by Abu Khabab that now and then you interpret dreams.'

'Yes, but I'm not an expert. I use a lot of the dream interpretation methods in old Islamic books.'

I didn't want to be labelled as selling a false bill of goods and was conscious of my youth in the presence of an experienced and by all accounts courageous fighter.

'Last night,' he continued, 'I dreamed that the Prophet Mohammed came into the camp. He shook hands with all of us. Then he extended both his hands and gestured to two of the group to follow him. They left with him. What does it mean?'

'Did you recognize them?' I asked.

'No.'

'All I can tell you, Abu Musab, is that generally in dreams when you see someone who is dead but who was dear to you – and they invite you to come with them – it means that your death is near.

'As for your dream, if it was a genuine vision, then two of our number here in the camp will meet their deaths soon,' I said.

Even as I spoke, I thought the interpretation outlandish. We were far away from any front lines here.

He started narrating to me his many vivid dreams while in jail in Jordan.

'I can only classify you as a prolific dreamer,' I said with a smile.

His expression barely changed.

He went on to describe his time in jail and his determination to build a force of Jordanian-Palestinian jihadis that would overthrow the Hashemite monarchy in Jordan, which was in his view an apostate regime. Zarqawi – like many jihadis – saw Afghanistan as the platform from which great armies would set out to topple the Arab regimes, recapture Jerusalem and establish the Caliphate.

'This land is blessed with the blood of thousands upon thousands of martyrs and it's the land mentioned in the prophecies, where the black banners shall rise,' he told me. How many times had I heard that before?

'Remember the words of the Prophet,' he said, momentarily forgetting that I was the preacher:

*'The era of Tyrannical Rulers shall last among you for as long as God wills to last, then it will end when God wills to end. Then comes the era of the righteous Caliphs.'*[22]

Our discussion was punctuated by the sound of muffled explosions at the lakeside. A few Pakistanis were testing devices they had built under Abu Khabab's supervision.

A short while later, a much louder explosion interrupted our conversation, accompanied by the unmistakeable whiff of sulphur.

I looked at Zarqawi.

'That's not right,' I said.

We ran down the hill and saw the bodies of two young Pakistanis, horribly mutilated by an explosion. Their comrades were crying and beseeching Allah to receive the two men in martyrdom. If anything, al-Zarqawi was more shocked than I was – less at the gruesome sight than in recalling our conversation.

'What you said was true. This is the dream I had. You must speak of this at their funeral, so others will know that the Prophet himself was waiting for them to arrive in Paradise.'

The incident made a deep impact on Zarqawi. But not long afterwards he left on the next phase of his quest. And I had to get back to 'business'. Before I'd left London my handlers had set aside a window when they would be in Islamabad, waiting to debrief me should a suitable excuse to leave Afghanistan materialize.

Abu Khabab looked at me with a hint of annoyance.

'We have things to do here that are more important than buying saffron,' he said.

'I understand,' I said, 'but Abu Hafs [al-Masri] and the others really like the business. I have to keep it going.'

Secretly I was delighted to escape Darunta, for my own mental health but also because I knew my handlers would be intrigued by Zarqawi's visit. As soon as I was in Pakistan, I alerted MI6 that I was on my way to Islamabad, using a Pakistani phone number that I had memorized when leaving London.

Al-Qaeda had its spies in the Pakistani capital and agents of the powerful ISI intelligence service were on almost every street corner. There was an elaborate protocol for me to be 'landed'. Under cover of darkness I should visit a specific phone booth to dial a number I had memorized. I was then given another number and received directions.

The male voice said simply: 'Walk south along the road. Five hundred metres. A vehicle will be there.'

A few minutes later a van pulled up alongside me. Two Pakistanis took me by the arms and shoved me – rather unceremoniously, I thought – into the back. I could see nothing as the van stuttered its way through the traffic, but I could hear the screams of the two-stroke mopeds and the growl of trucks. Then the roads grew quieter; there was some shouting and the sound of the metal rollers of a gate.

Someone opened the cargo door and I was blinded by bright fluorescent lighting. I seemed to be in a suburban garage. At the doorway to the adjoining villa was a familiar figure.

'Ah! If it's not the cat come to meet the kittens,' he laughed, holding up two mewing balls of fur. My eyes were still getting used to the light, but there was no mistaking Richard's voice.

'Welcome, welcome!' he said, and for the first time he put an arm round my shoulder.

'Sorry about the undignified arrival. The house belongs to one of ours. We've got a long night ahead of us. Come and meet the rest of the troops,' he said.

I was introduced to two British 'diplomats' stationed in Islamabad. They were both Scottish and one was the current occupant of the villa.

'And this is Alan, he's from the opposition,' Richard said.

A bald man with a pronounced beer gut, who might easily have been cast as Friar Tuck in a Robin Hood film, offered me a Coke – clearly he'd been briefed on my addiction.

'Alan's your new handler from MI5. He's taking over from Nick.'

'Heard a lot about you,' Alan said with a smile. He had a disarming manner that immediately put me at ease.

We sat around a large kitchen table.

'Plenty of Coke for you tonight, and there'll be food soon,' said Richard, heaving his frame onto a chair that looked as if it might not sustain the burden.

'But first, notepads at the ready, gentlemen.'

MI6 enjoyed its reputation of having better intelligence inside Pakistan than any other Western agency. The colonial legacy helped, as did the fact that both the political and military elite gravitated to Britain for education and training. But the emergence of Islamist militancy – and its infiltration of the armed services – had made the picture altogether more difficult to read.

My questioners wanted to know about the Pakistani factions represented at Darunta.

'Abu Khabab told me that he'd been asked to train members of Harakat [al-Jihad al-Islami] by old contacts inside the ISI,' I said. Harakat al-Jihad was a Pakistani militant group whose leaders' close relationship with the Taliban was allowing it to flourish in Afghanistan. It had also been involved in a plot to overthrow Benazir Bhutto in the mid-nineties.[23]

There was feverish note-taking as I sipped at my can. I suddenly felt very tired.

'At least two of them have died training on explosives,' I added, and then related my long conversation with Zarqawi.

'We had a feeling you might run into him,' said Richard, now very interested. 'Tell us more.'

It seemed that Jordanian intelligence, which worked very closely with MI6, had kept tabs on him in Pakistan. They may have asked for help from the British once he crossed into Afghanistan.* I told them about our long conversation and about the colossal bomb that he built and detonated.

More note-taking and another swig of Coke. Zarqawi's stay in Darunta appears to have been a crash course in learning to build powerful bombs and chemical weapons for what became known as the Millennium plot. It was an ambitious plan to attack tourist sites in Jordan and the Radisson Hotel in Amman in a blitz to greet the New Year.

The man who was CIA director at the time, George Tenet, later wrote that Jordanian intelligence discovered that the plot included using hydrogen cyanide in a cinema.[25] The conspirators hoped the bombings would destabilize the economy and undermine the monarchy.

The Jordanians would arrest sixteen people after learning about the plot in late November 1999. Zarqawi was not among them. Some intelligence suggested Zarqawi had returned to Jordan; the bomb-making ingredients seized by the Jordanian security services were similar to those he used at Darunta.** Certainly, the massive bomb he assembled on the hillside at Darunta would have brought down the Radisson.

To this day, I can't be sure whether my intelligence about Zarqawi played any role in thwarting the Millennium plot, but circumstantial evidence suggests it may have done. The Jordanians had discovered the plot after intercepting a phone call in which none other than Abu Zubaydah told the plotters 'the time for training is over.' It later emerged that some of the plotters had also trained in bomb-making in Afghanistan.***

* According to one account, Zarqawi had been trailed by an informant after he left Jordan and arrived in Peshawar in September 1999.[24]
** Seized documents and surveillance indicated that Zarqawi was a participant in the plot, though possibly only in an advisory role. He was later convicted in absentia in connection with the plot.[26]
*** As investigations continued, it was revealed that the attack plans in Jordan were part of a broader 'Millenium plot' linked to Abu Zubaydah to hit Western targets, including Los Angeles airport. Khalil al-Deek, the former resident of California

Richard's interest in Zarqawi was prescient. This was a young man in a hurry. At some point that autumn he tried to get an audience with Osama bin Laden in Kandahar. According to one account, Bin Laden was 'unavailable' but dispatched a key aide, Saif al-Adel, to meet him.[28] Al-Adel sensed an opportunity in Zarqawi's determination to cause mayhem in Jordan; it would mark another front in al-Qaeda's expanding war.

Bin Laden might have found the Jordanian uncouth and obstinate, but once more the power of prophecy intervened. According to the *hadith*:

> *'There will come a time when you shall fight the Jews. You will be east of the river Jordan, while they are to the west of it.'*

Expanding jihad to Jordan would create a showdown with Israel and thus fulfil the divine preconditions for the establishment of the Caliphate, the return of the Mahdi and a last glorious Islamic era in history. Or so they thought.

Saif al-Adel provided Zarqawi with start-up money for a camp in Herat in western Afghanistan.[29] A few dozen jihadis – mostly Jordanian, Syrian and Palestinian – joined him. So did Sheikh al-Muhajir, head of al-Qaeda's Shariah college and chief apologist for suicide attacks, to preside over the religious training of new recruits. When Zarqawi had been in Darunta, Abu Khabab had suggested he meet with al-Muhajir. Zarqawi and the cleric had clearly seen eye-to-eye in what would become a cruel alliance of brawn and extremist theology.*

---

who had dispatched me to Peshawar to meet Adam Gadahn, had helped arrange training for the Amman conspirators. He had even provided the plotters with a CD-ROM of the 'Encyclopaedia of Jihad' with instructions on bomb-making that I had passed to him via disk. That may have compromised his security. He was arrested in late 1999 in Peshawar and extradited to face charges in connection with the Millennium plot. He was released in the spring of 2001. He returned to Afghanistan and was killed in 2005, according to his wife.[27]

* Al-Muhajir's views were becoming increasingly radical. At Herat he began drafting a lengthy book called *The Jurisprudence of Blood* in which he

Zarqawi also continued to leverage his relationship with Abu Khabab. I learned that once established in Herat he sent a number of his men to train with the Egyptian so he could start his own research and training courses on unconventional weapons. Herat would not be Zarqawi's final destination. When he left Darunta he was a bit player with grand ambitions. Neither I nor anyone in al-Qaeda (nor British intelligence) had the faintest idea that he would become so influential and ruthless, nor that he would ultimately challenge bin Laden and Zawahiri and lay the foundations for the even greater horrors of ISIS.

The day after our kitchen meeting in Islamabad, I had another long and very personal chat with Richard. He'd noticed that only an almost intravenous supply of Coke had kept me awake the previous evening.

'You're a young man, but you have to pace yourself,' he said as we wandered through a garden tinged with frost. 'What's the word? Knackered, isn't it? That's how you look. You have to do better at protecting yourself from your own impulses. The last few months have been non-stop.'

'Yes,' I said, 'I'm tired.'

'And it's in our mutual interest,' he continued, 'that you are fit for purpose. I don't want it on my conscience if fatigue leads you to make a basic mistake.'

He set off back towards the villa, and then turned back.

'A week's bed rest. Doctor's orders.'

It was only halfway through that week that I realized how right he was. I was reminded of my original tradecraft training:

---

provided a sweeping justification for suicide bombings and argued it was justifiable to kill all infidels, including women, children and the elderly, and preferably by beheading them, unless Muslim authorities had granted them protection. He had an equally murderous disposition against the Shia. Zarqawi lapped up his teachings and ISIS later made the book a key part of its curriculum. As one close associate of the Jordanian put it, 'Our Shaykh al-Zarqawi, may Allah bless his soul, adored his Shaykh Abu Abdullah al-Muhajir ... [Zarqawi] told me that he had studied [*The Jurisprudence of Blood*] under [his] supervision.'[30]

good sleep was my best weapon. I slept long hours, mooched around the villa, made endless cups of tea and got to know Alan better.

'No!' I heard him exclaim one evening as the furry short-wave sound of the BBC World Service drifted through the villa. I thought for an irrational moment a jihadi had penetrated the villa and rushed downstairs.

'Can't believe they lost.' he said to no one in particular, pouring out the words in exasperation.

I looked puzzled.

'Everton, my team in England,' he said, 'though sometimes I wish they weren't.'

It turned out he rarely missed one of the team's games, home or away, when he was in England.

I realized in watching the low clouds swallow the hills above Islamabad that the rain here would mean snowstorms at Darunta. Another few days in a warm room snug amid crisp sheets would not go amiss.

I still needed a legend for my stay in Islamabad. It came in the shape of £4,000 in rupees, dropped onto the kitchen table by Richard in a brown envelope.

'This'll cover your second shipment, though God knows how I'm going to report it to Accounts. Not sure that "Exports, al-Qaeda Inc." will cut it.'

I had other concerns.

'In a few days I'll be back at Darunta yet again,' I told Alan and Richard as I prepared to leave. 'You know we are getting close to a device that really will work in spreading poison gas. How can I put this? How enthusiastic should I be?'

Alan and Richard understood the dilemma.

'From what you've told us,' Alan said, 'you're a significant player in this. You can't suddenly become insignificant and withdrawn. But we can't offer you a play-by-play. When you're there, your instinct for self-survival has to be paramount. We'd want you to be as passive as possible – responding to suggestions rather than coming up with solutions. But we know it's not as simple as that. The most important thing is to remain part of the team, and to have Abu Khabab's confidence.'


'I imagine business must be a little slow at this time of year; nothing grows in this weather,' Abu Khabab exclaimed when I arrived amid sleet and freezing rain. Whatever his surroundings, his sense of humour rarely deserted him. Thick mist obscured the lakeside. I had a sudden image of my tawdry flat on Brighton Road; it seemed like luxury now.

I found a corner of concrete floor for my sleeping bag and pretended I was glad to be back.

'We need your help,' Abu Khabab said as he brewed a kettle for tea. 'It's difficult to focus on developing the device and training new recruits in explosives at the same time, especially now the days are so short.'

I only wished they were shorter.

For weeks Abu Khabab's team tinkered with different designs before settling on one that was crude but seemed to answer the remaining technical problems. The device itself was not particularly impressive to look at – taped together from parts you might find in a tool shed, with holes that would allow – according to a later detailed description of the device publicly posted by American authorities – the 'violent spewing' out of cyanogen chloride.*

The detonator could be triggered by a timer or cell phone so

---

* A variation on this mixture produced instead hydrogen cyanide. Abu Khabab's team experimented for weeks to figure out how to disperse the gas in the most lethal way. We have omitted some details that appear in academic studies, media articles, court documents, government reports and the like. The device was described in detail in a 18 November 2004 joint FBI and DHS Bulletin which was obtained by a major US media organization and published in its entirety. To help first responders, at least one government body in the United States posted significant detail about the device.

that the attacker could deploy the weapon without sharing a choking, excruciating death.

It was time to put the invention to the test. On a gloomy afternoon down by the lake we rigged up a prototype and inserted a timed fuse to set off the detonator. We then put five rabbits inside wooden cages positioned at regular intervals, with the furthest fifteen metres away from the device. The fuse set off the detonator as planned, and from a safe distance we heard a crack and a rush of air. A translucent yellowish fog drifted towards the cages.

Through binoculars I saw the most exposed rabbit almost immediately flip onto its back and shake violently. Within a minute it was still. The rabbit furthest from the device endured thirty minutes of agony before it expired. We waited an hour before approaching the cages to confirm all five animals had died. Through our makeshift masks we could still smell the remnants of the acrid gas.

I joined in the inevitable chants of 'Allahu Akbar', hugging my fellow apprentices Hassan Ghul, Abu Nassim, and the camp's deputy, Abu Bakr al-Masri.

Predictably, Abu Nassim was ecstatic. 'Imagine seeing the enemy suffer like this. It brings joy to our heart. Several at once could kill many people in a confined space – like a subway or cinema.'

I felt sick to my stomach. Whether I liked it or not, the 'unique invention' – the *al-mubtakkar-al farid*, as it quickly became known – was born. Abu Khabab asked us to keep the successful test to ourselves. Perhaps he was perturbed by Abu Nassim's glee. But the genie was out of the bottle. A new class of terrorist weapon had been created.

After several weeks in the frigid camp, I was desperate to escape the psychotic Abu Nassim and further contributions to the perfecting of the *mubtakkar*.* I wanted to visit Kabul to see Abu

---

* I was later told that after I left the camp, Zarqawi returned for a brief spell to Darunta. As related above, in late 1999, Jordanian security services

Musab al-Suri again, not out of any devotion to his intellect but to see whether he had grown any closer to al-Qaeda's leaders, some of whom were gravitating to the Afghan capital.

The future of international jihad and al-Qaeda's relationship with the Taliban was entering a crucial phase. The Taliban's only backers in the international community at the time – Saudi Arabia, the UAE and Pakistan – wanted jihadi camps closed or at least scaled back. The Taliban had made a show of closing some camps around Jalalabad but allowed their occupants to relocate discreetly closer to Kabul where they could be better 'supervised'.

Al-Suri had made good on his plans for a training centre. The Taliban had given him a barracks in an old Soviet base at the Qargha reservoir on the outskirts of Kabul.[32] He was recruiting those he regarded as the most promising Arab jihadis, including from al-Qaeda, much to bin Laden's consternation.[33] Abu Khabab had told me in Darunta he would himself soon relocate to the same base.*

Al-Suri allowed me to attend a lecture in his draughty classroom. About forty young jihadis were in attendance, mostly Saudis, Algerians

thwarted a plot linked to Zarqawi to release hydrogen cyanide in an Amman cinema. Few details have been released about the device they planned to use but one possibility is Zarqawi planned to build and deploy a *mubtakkar*. Perhaps the decision to target a cinema was inspired by Abu Nassim.

As already noted, once Zaraqawi established himself in Herat there was a significant transfer of knowledge on unconventional weapons from Abu Khabab's facility to Zarqawi's facility there. Zarqawi's group would later morph into ISIS. A direct line can be drawn between Abu Khabab's Darunta experiments and the Islamic State's current capacity to unleash chemical terror.[31]

* The location of the camp was a reflection of al-Suri's strong relationship with the Taliban. Al-Suri told me about a heated exchange he had with bin Laden in front of Mullah Omar in the aftermath of the Africa embassy bombings. Al-Suri by his account had reminded bin Laden he had sworn an oath of allegiance to Mullah Omar as commander of the faithful and needed to keep him in the loop. Al-Suri also told me that in the summer of 1999 Mullah Omar had personally complained to him about bin Laden's activities in Afghanistan. Al-Suri told me the Taliban leader announced to him: 'We will never give Osama bin Laden up but we need to know what he's up to.'

and Syrians. His performance was equally brilliant and disturbing. Standing in front of a whiteboard, al-Suri outlined his vision for the future of the jihadi movement, his thick black marker pen soon filling the board. The lectures formed the basis for his 1,600-page *Call for Global Islamic Resistance*, which would be published online in 2004 and make a deep impact on jihadis around the world.

His arguments advanced what we had discussed the previous year. 'Open fronts' like Afghanistan and Chechnya were crucial bases upon which international jihad could build. But he was controversially dismissive of the structure of groups like al-Qaeda and Egyptian Islamic Jihad. Time and again their operations had been depleted and dismantled by security services in the Arab world and the West.

Modern communications technology provided a different opportunity to incite and provide strategic guidance to waves of 'individual jihad' by small cells connected only by ideology.[34] The lecture was a tour de force that in many ways predicted the evolution of jihad after 9/11.*

Al-Suri believed Islamists already living in the West should be the shock troops of terrorism in the future. Having himself lived for years in Europe, he believed there was already significant sympathy for the jihadi cause there.[35] More than any other jihadi leader I met, he had an unbridled hatred for European secularism and lassitude. While bin Laden obsessed about the United States, al-Suri had called on Algerian jihadis to 'strike deeply in France', and he hated Britain just as venomously.[36]

Al-Suri's other critique of bin Laden and Zawahiri was that their campaign of terrorism was making little difference. If terrorist

---

* *Inspire* magazine, a publication founded in 2010 by the late American terrorist cleric Anwar al-Awlaki, played a key role in circulating al-Suri's ideas on 'individual' terrorism. Finding it difficult to organize complex plots, groups like al-Qaeda and ISIS increasingly called on their followers in the West to launch terrorist attacks in their name. The 2013 Boston bombers, the 2015 San Bernardino shooters and the 2017 London Bridge attackers were a few of the many who responded.

outfits were going to attack the West, they should go big or go home. (On this point, of course, he would be spectacularly wrong.)

'Warfare in their countries should be based upon the infliction of large human losses. We have to start thinking about using weapons of mass destruction,' he told his students. He paused. 'You understand? In their countries we have to use these weapons. You have to kill civilians indiscriminately.'*

And Abu Khabab would soon be relocating here, I reflected. No wonder my handlers wanted to know more about how well he and al-Suri got on.**

Nobody did more than al-Suri to lay the intellectual foundations for the terrorism that erupted in Europe over the following decade. This one-time resident of Neasden in north London, living in Kabul with a Spanish wife, was a clear and present danger.

After the lecture, al-Suri offered to drive me back into town. Sleet danced around his mud-caked 4x4. It was so cold he gave me a *battu*, a garment for men made of thick wool, which helped to restore my circulation. He gazed out of the window at the mud-brick neighbourhoods, made even more desolate by the winter chill.

'Abu al-Abbas, all of our plans will fail unless we rouse the believers,' he said, citing a famous injunction of the Koran.[39] 'We can only be the detonators. We need the masses to be the main

---

* An audio recording of this lecture, part of al-Suri's 'Jihad is the Solution' lecture series in the autumn of 1999, was subsequently posted online. In his 2004 book, al-Suri said that 'Strategic Operations Brigades' should be established and given 'very high-level financial capabilities' to acquire an 'operational knowledge and potential to use WMD'. Then Americans, he argued, could be subjected to a 'back-breaking policy of collective massacres'.[37]

** Despite calling for massive attacks against the West, al-Suri was initially critical of the 9/11 attacks because they led to the removal of the Taliban and intensified counter-terrorism operations. But he eventually changed his mind, writing, 'I feel sorry because there were no weapons of mass destruction in the planes that attacked New York and Washington on 9/11.' After the US invasion of Iraq energized the jihadi movement he came to believe the 9/11 attacks had helped mobilize the jihadi movement by creating a confrontation between the West and Islam.[38]

charge. How are we going to do this? Complex theology won't move them. You need to give them a sense of destiny through the prophecies.'

He changed gear.

'The era of the Prophet shall last among you for as long as God wills it to last, then it will end when God wills it to end.' The same *hadith* Zarqawi had recited so earnestly when we had sat on the hillside at Darunta. He continued:

> 'Then the era of the righteous Caliphs shall last among you for as long as God wills it to last, then it will end when God wills it to end.
>
> Then the era of benign Kings shall last among you for as long as God wills it to last, then it will end when God wills it to end. Then the era of Tyrannical Rulers shall last among you for as long as God wills it to last, then it will end when God wills to end.'[40]

Al-Suri was in full flow.

'Hafez al-Assad, Hosni Mubarak, Saddam Hussein. What Muslim could deny we have lived through all these stages and are now in the era of tyrannical rulers? What Muslim does not want to enter the era of righteous Caliphs? We must appeal to the souls of the *Ummah* with the mystical forms of our religion. That's what Khomeini did in Iran.[41] His simple message was that the revolution was the first step towards the return of their Mahdi.'

Al-Suri was obsessed with the prophecies, not least because they foretold that both the Antichrist and Jesus would emerge in Syria. The descent of the Mahdi to Mecca and a new glorious age of Islam had been written, so it would come to pass.

I had once believed the same. I still believed in the prophecies but now the likes of al-Muhajir were abusing and twisting them. The notion that jihadis could hurry God's divine plan was, to me, a blasphemous conceit. But I was in a minority, and al-Suri's soliloquy was itself prophetic of the evolution of terrorism. The jihad of the early twenty-first century would be drenched in an apocalyptic contortion of the prophecies.

Before I left Kabul I had the opportunity to meet the 'great and the good' of al-Qaeda at a reception thrown by one of its wealthier members to celebrate the birth of his daughter. Many nationalities were present: it was like a United Nations cocktail party minus the alcohol, the women and the discussion of Manhattan property prices. Abu Hamza al-Ghamdi, who had used the prophecies to such good effect in recruiting me into al-Qaeda, was there. A lamb was slaughtered and the guests retreated upstairs. Platter after platter was brought in. It was a rare feast in a country where many went hungry every day.

It was odd to see Abu Hafs al-Masri and Abu Musab al-Suri in the same room together – another case of roosters in the same cage. Al-Masri (with some justification) believed al-Suri was trying to poach al-Qaeda recruits and was bad-mouthing bin Laden to the Taliban leader Mullah Omar. Al-Suri, for his part, believed the Egyptians in al-Qaeda had hijacked bin Laden for their own ends, shown a complete lack of respect to the Taliban and persuaded bin Laden that a few bombings in far-off places could reorder the Middle East.

'It's interesting bin Laden is not here today,' al-Suri said to me.

'He's like the absent Mahdi of the Shia. The Egyptians only reveal him when it suits their interests.'

Al-Masri and al-Suri did have one thing in common – hatred of the West.

'Our generation started the war, the next generation will fight the war, and the generation after that will win the war,' al-Masri declared. 'You know there's a group in America that wants to overthrow Saddam Hussein?* But they say the American people won't support a war in Iraq unless there's an event on the scale of Pearl Harbor.'[42] Then, with a rare flash of amusement in his eyes, he added, 'We should – with

---

* It was known as the Project for the New American Century, a neo-conservative group whose members would be prominent in the administration of George W. Bush.

God's help and grace – give them a Pearl Harbor! Let them come into Iraq, let them come into Afghanistan, let them come into Somalia.'

'Unlike the Japanese we don't have aircraft carriers,' retorted al-Suri.

'Maybe we don't need aircraft carriers,' Abu Hafs replied with a smirk.*

It seemed like idle jousting at the time, but years later Khalid Sheikh Mohammed would tell US interrogators that in March 1999, some eight months before this Kabul gathering, bin Laden and Abu Hafs had approved the outlines of the 9/11 plot.[43]

That night, in the dormitory of al-Qaeda's guest house, I fell into conversation with a pleasant young Saudi who had the mattress next to mine. His name was Abdul Aziz al-Omari. He had refined features and looked altogether too gentle to be a jihadi.

Al-Omari had recently arrived in Afghanistan from Asir, a Saudi province bordering Yemen, leaving his wife and daughter at home.[44] He was soft-spoken and thoughtful but clearly burned with desire to expel the Americans from the Arabian Peninsula and topple the House of Saud. He was twenty years old – just a few months younger than me – and had been moving towards life as an imam before deciding he was one of Sayyid Qutb's unlit candles.[45]

My journey had seen many twists since that fateful decision; there would be more to come. His would be a short one.** On the morning of 11 September 2001, al-Omari would be the lead hijacker on American Airlines Flight 11. He and the three other 'muscle' hijackers used box cutters to slash those who stood in their path, breached the cockpit door and overpowered the pilots, allowing Mohamed Atta to pilot the plane into the North Tower of the World Trade Center.[46]

I left Kabul, as keen to escape the long Afghan winter as I was to debrief my handlers in London. As I travelled the rutted highway towards the border, Atta and several others were arriving in Kandahar

* I reported the conversation, and much besides, the next time I was debriefed by my British handlers.
** I again met al-Omari in 2000 at bin Laden's Tarnak Farm headquarters near Kandahar.

after a long trip from Hamburg in Germany. Bin Laden and Abu Hafs al-Masri would personally recruit them into the plot that would change the world.[47]

Torkham Gate beckoned. Al Qaeda had a rule that operatives only cross into Pakistan in discreet pairs. My companion was carrying a bunch of letters that I was due to hand-deliver to 'brothers' in London. As we approached Torkham Gate, he fell back a little way to watch whether I would make it through. I had passed through into Pakistan many times before and never had anybody requested to look at my travel documents. I credited my father's Afghan heritage as helping me to pass for one of the hundreds of Pashtun who streamed through the crossing each hour.

This time, a Pakistani soldier who took his duties with uncommon gravity demanded to search my bags. I realized I had made a small but stupid mistake: I had forgotten to take my glasses off. Local tribesmen did not wear spectacles. I might as well have had a sign over my head shouting 'foreigner'.

The soldier addressed me in Pashto, asking where I was heading.

I replied in my best Pashto that I was on my way to Peshawar.

He broke into Arabic.

'You think I'm stupid? I worked in Saudi Arabia for ten years. I know an Arab when I see one.'

Things did not improve when he searched my luggage and found my British passport.

'An Arab with a British passport. That's interesting. They're giving out bonuses if we catch foreigners. I think I just earned myself one.* What were you doing in Afghanistan?' he asked.

---

* The new scrutiny at the border had no doubt been mandated by Pakistan's new military ruler, General Pervez Musharraf. His coup had been widely condemned in Western capitals, and he had every incentive to present himself as a constructive counter-terrorism partner. Although he intensified such cooperation in the face of withering American pressure after 9/11, he would prove to be a fickle partner.

'I'm a food exporter,' I said.

He cut me off. 'You must have got lost then,' he said. His moustache twitched. 'You're definitely one of bin Laden's people. I know them when I see them.'

'How on earth can you say that?' I protested.

'They're all just like you. Well-educated. Well-spoken. Clean. Tidy.'

He hadn't met some of the Yemeni boys, obviously.

Soon afterwards, two well-dressed officers from Pakistan's Inter-Services Intelligence agency arrived. The ISI had a reputation for brutality and duplicity in equal measure and inside Pakistan was a law unto itself. People in its custody would disappear for years, maybe forever. Depending on how the winds were blowing, an al-Qaeda member might be given a VIP escort or summarily executed along a dusty highway. British intelligence, despite regularly cooperating with the ISI, profoundly mistrusted it.

It had been drilled into me that nowhere and to no one should I ever admit to being a British spy. It was a statement of the obvious but, faced with an uncertain fate at the hands of the ISI, it was a tempting card to play. Then again, what would they do to me if they thought I had useful intelligence? I felt very much on my own.

My custodians escorted me to the back of a van and we set off from the border. But after a few miles the van pulled into a compound in a straggling settlement of low brick-and-mud houses. This was Landi Kotal, where the ISI brought visitors from Afghanistan who had aroused suspicion. I was let into a squalid cell to join several others chained to the wall.

With a start, I realized I recognized one of them, a Saudi al-Qaeda member I had known in Bosnia, who had set off for Pakistan a few days before me. He flashed a warning look at me. Acknowledging we knew each other would only dig us into deeper trouble.

I began to imagine all sorts of scenarios. I would perish of pneumonia just as my handlers concluded that I had gone back to the 'dark side'; I would be shot after blurting out something stupid.

For several days we all sat there, a miserable collection of drug traffickers, alleged terrorists and people whose faces didn't fit. We were fed rice and gruel twice a day and drew the tattered blankets around ourselves at night. My morale began to sag; I began to see myself as expendable to British intelligence, forgotten by al-Qaeda. And I felt desperately sick.

Days after being detained, one of the ISI officers who had been my original escort arrived at the door and told me to get up. I was bundled into another van. I could smell the body odour and damp that I exuded. I felt filthy and tired beyond measure. I began to shiver uncontrollably and begged the officers to turn on the van's heater. Perhaps anxious that I might die on them, they obliged.

I gazed through droplets of rain running down the grimy window at the grey-brown of Pakistani rural life, occasionally interrupted by the high walls of a feudal pile. In their piteous state you might expect these people to be Maoists or Marxists. But they were devout Muslims to a man, woman and child. Perhaps religion was the only comfort and explanation for a life of monotonous hardship.

I knew we were on the road to Peshawar and not surprised when we turned into a large, well-guarded barracks. A sign in Urdu and English announced that I was at the ISI's regional headquarters in Peshawar.

I was taken to a bare interrogation room, where I tried to edge my chair as close as possible to a paraffin heater, even though it was emitting more fumes than heat. A middle-aged man who appeared to be a major walked in with a file that contained just one piece of paper. At least they didn't have a dossier on me, I thought.

'So,' he began, sitting ramrod straight opposite me. 'You are a member of al-Qaeda, and you have a British passport. Interesting combination.'

He pushed his chair back, waiting for me to protest. I did not disappoint.

'Wrong,' I said, sticking to my story. 'I am a luxury food trader. You can check with my office in Peshawar.'

The major smiled.

'We shall see,' he said.

Perhaps more brutal methods would be used to elicit information.

My new accommodation was less draughty than that at Landi Kotal, but the chef was no better and the company no more inspiring – apart from a Pashtun opium smuggler with an irrepressible sense of humour. His offence was that he owed several million dollars to another smuggler with rather better connections. He had travelled the world and spoke good English and was optimistic that he would soon be freed if the appropriate commission were paid to the right party. Spending time in the company of the ISI was the cost of doing business across the border.

Our conversation was interrupted by the arrival of a visitor to see him. Even in my debilitated state I saw an opportunity.

'How do you get visitors?' I asked.

'Special relationship,' he laughed.

'Can you ask the next one to do me a big favour – to go to the British embassy and tell them Mr Durrani is being held in Peshawar. I am a British citizen and I'm exporting honey from Afghanistan.'

'Ah, so am I!' he laughed again, slapping me on the shoulder. 'Don't worry! I'll take care of it,' he said.

Four days later the major stormed into my cell.

'Why are the British asking about you? You're not British; you're Pakistani,' he said angrily.

'You know perfectly well I'm British,' I replied, adding an expletive for good measure. He was clearly not used to being addressed in such a way. 'In any case, if I was Pakistani, you would have hit me by now.'

He would have to let me go, but not without a final humiliation. I was shoved onto the open trailer of a pickup truck and nearly froze to death as I was transported through the mountain passes back to Landi Kotal.

A Land Rover sent by the British embassy in Islamabad was waiting. Inside was the First Secretary and a Pakistani Christian called Aziz.

'You look rough,' the First Secretary said.

'I feel a lot worse than that,' I said. 'Let's go, please.'

If my current streak of luck held, the al-Qaeda guy detained with me would tap on the window at any moment and ask for a lift.

'Islamabad,' said the First Secretary to the driver.

'But first Peshawar,' I said. I had to collect the letters that my travelling companion at the border still had. I had no idea of their contents, but one was from al-Suri to Abu Qatada. I doubted it was family news.

The First Secretary acquiesced reluctantly; the last thing he wanted to do was to spin his wheels in Peshawar while I trotted off to find a jihadi. I was exceptionally careful to leave the vehicle unobserved and recovered the letters.

When I was escorted through the staff entrance into the High Commission (embassy) in my filthy *salwar kameez* I felt a little like Lawrence of Arabia entering the officers' mess in Cairo after crossing the desert dressed as an Arab. The looks I encountered ranged from bewilderment to faint horror, but that may have been the odour.

One of the Scottish spooks I had met months previously was less than charitable about my vanishing act.

'You disappeared from the face of this earth,' he said. 'We thought you'd bailed on us – gone back to the dark side.'

For a few weeks after being extracted, I was mostly left alone to graze and recover, first in Islamabad and then back in London. Richard was as good as the promise he'd made about letting me rest – an agent comatose with fatigue was a liability.

When I went to meet Richard and Alan, I was still smarting from the doubts expressed by the unsmiling Scottish agent in Pakistan.

'Did you really think I'd defected?' I asked both men at our first meeting.

'Of course not,' Alan said. 'But in our job you see everything. We had to ask ourselves whether we could have done something to upset you.'

'Even if I was upset with you personally, there's no way I would change my convictions,' I replied.

They believed my cover was still intact. They weren't happy the Pakistanis had fingerprinted me but surmised the ISI hadn't a clue that I was a spy. Perhaps British diplomats had told the Pakistanis I was wanted back home for 'questioning'.

It was soon my favourite season in London – carpets of daffodils and crocuses illuminated St James's Park and the plane trees were in bud. To escape the long Afghan winter, the privations of camp life and ISI detention was a tonic in itself.

At a meeting with my handlers at a hotel near the park, talk turned to the Olympic Games, due to begin several months later in Sydney.

'I don't have much time for sport. Besides, we Bahrainis rarely cover ourselves in glory.'

Richard was staring out of the window.

'Well, our friends in Australia are worried,' he went on, gazing at the London traffic edging along Piccadilly. 'They're asking if there's any chatter about an attack on Sydney.'

I'd heard no whisper of al-Qaeda taking aim at the Olympics. I promised to keep my ear to the ground when I returned to Afghanistan.

It was weeks before I felt physically and psychologically fit enough to return to the fray. Eighteen months behind enemy lines, in Afghanistan and Londonistan, had taken a toll that I was only beginning to understand.

I arrived in Jalalabad, rejuvenated, in early summer, less than three months before the XXVII Olympiad was due to begin. When I reached the al-Qaeda guest house, I came across Abu Hamza al-Ghamdi. He saw me as one of his protégés and invited me to visit the Taliban's regional governor. It just so happened that the governor had another visitor – the Taliban's Sports Minister (if such an oxymoron is allowed), Abdul Shukoor Mutmaen. I decided to ask Mutmaen whether Afghanistan would be represented at the Olympics. After three years of rule, the Taliban wanted international recognition.

'All we want is to be invited to the opening ceremony. We are being treated like a pariah,' he said. 'The foreign minister wanted to use the Games to show we are the legitimate government here. But the International Olympic Committee in their wisdom invited the Shura-e-Nazar instead.'*

'That's ridiculous,' I replied sympathetically.

'This racist prime minister in Australia said: "No Taliban here – over my dead body,"' Mutmaen continued. 'They're always talking about the women, women's rights all the time.'

I decided to go for broke – a freelance initiative.

'I have an idea, but you may think it's crazy.' He looked at me quizzically.

'My mother's family is Lebanese. I have relatives in Australia, and a cousin is on Australia's Olympic Committee.' It wasn't true, but I took the risk that he would neither ask for his name nor check with the Committee. The Taliban could be surprisingly naive at times.

'He knows I'm in Afghanistan and thinks I'm involved in humanitarian work. I'd be happy to convey some sort of goodwill message, any assurance you could offer that groups here will not be allowed to target the Games. Break the ice, as it were.'

Keep it vague, I told myself. Let him have the idea.

'We can't declare that groups which take shelter with us can be turned on and off like a tap,' he replied.

'Some private message? From the foreign minister?' I had to stop leading the witness, but the seed was sown. Short of dictating a note for him, there was no more I could do.

As we parted, I played my final card. 'I may have to go to Australia to settle some inheritance issues. I'd see my cousin if I go.

---

* Shura-e-Nazar was the term used by the Taliban to describe the 'rival' government led by Ahmed Shah Masoud. I do not know if they were actually invited.

Let me know if I can help. But please keep this private; some of the brothers would not understand that sometimes there is a place for diplomacy,' I added with a sheepish grin.

A few days later Mutmaen returned to Jalalabad, in a convoy of 4x4s. The Algerian who ran the guest house looked at me wide-eyed and asked what I had done to deserve such attention.

'The minister knows I interpret dreams,' I said with a straight face.

Mutmaen escorted me to a part of the compound away from prying eyes and ears.

'On Mullah Omar's authority,' he said with gravity, 'Foreign Minister Muttawakil is entrusting you with a message that all groups with safe harbour in Afghanistan are under strict instructions not to launch any operation that would interfere with the Olympics.'

'I understand,' I replied, 'and I will do my very best.'

Two weeks later I travelled again through the Khyber Pass at the start of the long journey to Sydney. On a stopover in Dubai, I contacted Alan at MI5.

'I can't say much more,' I said, 'but I'm on my way to Sydney to discuss the Games.'

He arranged for me to be 'taken aside' at immigration in Sydney for further questioning.

In a conference room not unlike the one at Heathrow Airport eighteen months earlier, a senior MI5 official was waiting for me, along with a tall officer with chiselled features from the Australian intelligence agency.

I told them the full story.

'I'm sorry if you think I went rogue. It just seemed an opportunity too good to let pass.'

They were agape.

'That's brilliant, mate,' the Australian said quietly. The MI5 man wore a smile of quiet satisfaction, as if to say, 'It's the quality we have.'

'Does that mean we have the pledge of bin Laden and every-one?' he asked incredulously.

'Yes,' I said, 'and Mullah Omar is guaranteeing that.'

On 19 August 2000, news broke that the International Olympic Committee would be inviting observers from the Taliban to the Games, with the approval of the Australian government. The Australian agent I'd met told me that my initiative had led to visas being issued for two Taliban observers.[48]

Abdul Shukoor Mutmaen told the media in Kabul that after talks with Taliban delegates, 'The IOC have offered invitations to two of our Olympic Committee members for the Sydney Games, and this means that they recognize us. I am thrilled by this.'

So was I, but the Taliban could not help overplaying their hand. Mutmaen's boast that the IOC recognized the Taliban as Afghanistan's legitimate government was too rich for the Committee. Additionally, there was an outcry, especially from women's groups, that even observers had been invited. Within a week, IOC spokesman Franklin Servan-Schreiber announced that the Committee had reversed its decision after Taliban leaders had misrepresented the offer.

'They have turned this into a political issue by making a statement that this is recognition, there is no longer a problem with the IOC,' Servan-Schreiber said. 'Those arguments are completely wrong and totally outside what was agreed orally in the meeting. They are no longer invited.'[49]

It was an opportunity so nearly grasped and then squandered – one that could have brought the Taliban a step closer to being readmitted to the family of nations and even strengthened moderate elements in Afghanistan.*

---

* MI5 and ASIO (Australian intelligence) asked me to spend time in Sydney and Melbourne introducing myself to radical circles. Abu Qatada had provided me with contacts for several of his 'students' in Australia. But most radicals I met were keeping a low profile because of aggressive surveillance in the run-up to the Olympics. What I did encounter was bitter alienation among the younger generation of Lebanese Australians. It was my introduction to what would soon become known as 'gangster jihadism' – young gang members justifying petty crime with jihadi ideology and infusing that ideology with street violence.

At least, I consoled myself, the Taliban had apparently obtained guarantees from al-Qaeda and other groups in Afghanistan that they would not attack the Games. Perhaps that might be a precedent for other international events to which Afghanistan was invited.

But I was deceiving myself. Al-Qaeda's planning for the 9/11 attacks was well underway. I would play an unknowing part in their preparations.

# MY SEVENTH LIFE: SOMETHING BIG

## 2001–2004

In June 2001, I received an unusual summons. At the time I was at al-Qaeda's Tarnak Farms complex near the airport in Kandahar and was due to leave for the UK within days. The summons came from Abu Hafs al-Masri, bin Laden's right-hand man, which made me distinctly uneasy. Did the leadership somehow suspect I was working for the British? I couldn't imagine how, but ahead of the meeting I spent hours trying to work out whether and where I might have slipped up.

Al-Masri had a way of pursing his lips that only underscored his severity. One of the Egyptian group around bin Laden, he was not given to levity.

He was sitting behind a desk in a library that doubled as an office.

'When exactly are you travelling to England?' he asked.

'In four days,' I replied.

He did not invite me to sit down but stared at me for a few seconds in a way that turned my stomach.

'I want you to take a message to some of our brothers,' he said. He spelled out the four names slowly and clearly, as if I was an imbecile.

'They must leave the country and come here before the end of August. Something big is going to happen and we expect the Americans to come to Afghanistan.'

I failed to find words to respond as I tried to take in the enormity of what he was suggesting.

'Do not be tempted to come back to fight alongside us here. Stay in England; do not leave your post. We will contact you.'

It was clear the meeting was over. It had lasted two minutes, but set my nerves jangling and sent my brain into overdrive. Why these four men? Why now? What was 'something big'?

I was not stupid enough to ask. Al-Masri was obsessive about operational secrecy. He had literally drafted a 'need-to-know' policy and posted it prominently in the camps.

At least I was beyond suspicion; he would not hint at 'something big' unless he had complete confidence in me. It seemed that to al-Qaeda's leadership my ability to travel, apparently unsuspected, continued to make me a precious commodity. On several occasions I had been given letters for al-Qaeda supporters then in the UK – letters expertly unsealed and resealed by MI6 before reaching their recipients. But this time the message was simple, verbal and direct: get out.*

I knew three of the four individuals well. One was Mohammed al-Madani, who had introduced me TO Abu Qatada's circle in London. The second was 'Abu Hudhaifa al-Britani',** who had been in Afghanistan and knew Abu Khabab and many others within al-Qaeda. The British intelligence services had Abu Hudhaifa under surveillance but were frustrated by his expert navigation of the line between militant free speech and explicit involvement in a terrorist organization. I knew just how closely he had been involved with al-Qaeda because I had seen him in the camps, but that was hardly admissible in court.

---

* When I met Abu Hafs, the date for the terror attacks in the US had not been set according to information uncovered by the 9/11 Commission.[1]
** An alias. Both Abu Hudhaifa and Mohammed al-Madani left the UK for Afghanistan before the deadline. The only one of the four I did not know went by the name Abu Aisha and lived in Birmingham.

The third was Abu Walid al-Filistini, the Palestinian cleric close to Abu Qatada who had almost blocked me from applying for a British passport. *

The weather was muggy in London when I arrived five days later. At Heathrow I noticed the news stands were full of headlines about Tony Blair, who less than two weeks previously had been re-elected for a second term as prime minister. Within hours of arriving I was ensconced in another conference room with bad coffee and a car park view.

I told Alan and Richard of the cryptic message from Abu Hafs, and about his ominous phrase: 'something big'.

'I don't like the sound of that,' said Richard. 'Were there any other clues at all?'

'It was a two-minute conversation,' I replied.

'Was anyone else in the camps talking about a big operation?' Alan asked.

'No; like I said, the words came as a shock to me.'

'Go through it one more time,' Richard said. 'Every tiny detail, even if they don't seem relevant right now.'

I repeated Abu Hafs' instructions.

There were a few moments silence.

'We'll see what else, if anything, is being picked up and of course raise this with our colleagues across the pond,' Richard said, referring to the Americans. 'In the meantime, go ahead and deliver the messages,' Alan said as he closed his briefcase. 'Obviously, it's absolutely vital for us to know exactly how they react.'

I never found out. When I met Mohammed al-Madani, he curtly thanked me for the message and said he would tell the others.

There were other straws in the wind. I told them munitions and other equipment were being transported from the camps to

---

* When he moved to Afghanistan Abdul Walid al-Filistini would become of of the leading ideologues within al-Qaeda. He had previously made at least one trip to Afghanistan because I saw him in the camps in 2000. He is still at large.[2]

secret locations in Afghanistan and possibly into Pakistan, but I had no idea why.*

I reminded MI6 that influential figures like al-Suri were arguing that a confrontation with the Western powers was inevitable – and that large-scale attacks, ideally with weapons of mass destruction, were necessary. The one man who might be able to deliver such weapons – Abu Khabab al-Masri – had relocated to a facility next door to al-Suri alongside the Qargha reservoir. I had seen them both at a sprawling Taliban base on a recent trip to the Afghan capital. Abu Khabab revealed that he had developed a final blueprint for the poison gas *mubtakkar*, one that could be built by someone with no more than basic training. Al-Suri had told me there was an urgent need of a fatwah permitting the use of such weapons.**

'Abu Khabab told me that Zawahiri and others in the al-Qaeda leadership were interested in the technology,' I told Alan and Richard.***

'That's not good,' Alan said drily.

'No, it's not good,' I replied. 'The only glimmer of hope is that he won't hand it over to al-Qaeda for free. He's always complaining to me about how al-Qaeda never paid him enough to train recruits.'

'It's not much of a glimmer,' Richard said. He doodled on a notepad for a few moments. 'Is anyone missing from the camps?' he asked.

I didn't know – people were moving in and out all the time.

---

* We came to the conclusion that much – but not all – of the equipment was probably destined for the front lines north of Kabul. In the spring of 2001, the Taliban was preparing a major offensive against the Northern Alliance.[3]
** There was a great deal of debate within al-Qaeda about the deployment of WMD. Abu Hafs al-Masri purportedly wanted not only to possess WMD but also store it in the United States to be used in retaliation if the United States struck al-Qaeda camps. Bin Laden, who had declared in a 1999 interview that obtaining WMD was a religious duty, was more cautious about using such weapons, but let Abu Hafs take charge of the WMD file, according to one account.[4]
*** After 9/11, evidence emerged of some cooperation between Abu Khabab and Zawahiri.[5]

The camps were like a luggage carousel. Bags are added and taken away, but there are always bags. Their body language suggested my handlers had also heard people were on the move. But I could hardly go back. Abu Hafs al-Masri had told me to stay put; to reappear without permission would be insubordination and might, my handlers believed, provoke suspicion.

It was already abundantly clear that al-Qaeda was ready to intensify its war against the West. The previous autumn it had carried out a suicide bomb attack on the USS *Cole*, a naval destroyer, as it was moored in Aden, killing seventeen American sailors. Then, in late June, the Arabic television channel MBC reported bin Laden's 'pleasure with al-Qaeda leaders who were saying that the next weeks "will witness important surprises" and that US and Israeli interests will be targeted'.[6]

We all wondered about the magnitude of an event that would 'bring the Americans to Afghanistan'. It suggested to us a plot of greater ambition than the bombing of the USS *Cole*.*

At lunchtime on 11 September 2001, I was walking along Oxford Street in London. It was a bright and breezy day, and central London was breathing again after the hordes of summer tourists.

A small crowd had gathered at a store window. It was a branch of Dixons, the electronics retailer. Curiosity slowed my pace, and, as I reached the store, a large television screen was playing on repeat an image of a plane hitting a skyscraper. Black smoke was billowing into the blue sky above.

---

* According to the 9/11 Commission report, US intelligence saw a surge of reports in June and July 2001 suggesting al-Qaeda was planning attacks against US and Israeli interests. There were 'few specifics regarding time, place, method or target. Most suggested that attacks were planned against targets overseas; others indicated threats against unspecified US interests.' I am not sure how my intelligence affected the overall picture being formed by the Americans. In his memoir the then CIA director George Tenet referenced 'Late June information that cited a "big event" that was forthcoming.' Tenet wrote that by June 28, 2001 the CIA had ten specific pieces of intelligence about impending attacks.[7]

'New York,' said a man, glancing in my direction. It's a strange thing about the British that they rarely talk to strangers unless provoked by a crisis – a snowstorm or road accident. 'Seems like an airliner hit the World Trade Center,' he continued.

This was no catastrophic accident – rather, the most spectacular act of terror in the modern era. I knew it instinctively, and I knew it was al-Qaeda.

Immediately, my thoughts returned to Kandahar and my brief encounter with Abu Hafs al-Masri. 'Something big'. The vague, teasing phrase reverberated in my head.

In the preceding weeks, some of the best minds in British intelligence had tried to discern what 'something big' might be. I myself had repeatedly gone over the meeting with Abu Hafs with my handlers, until they had extracted every last drop of information. In our brainstorming sessions we had guessed that it might be another embassy attack or the bombing of a US military facility in Europe. The idea that al-Qaeda was planning to hijack and crash multiple aircraft into the towers of the World Trade Center, the US Capitol and the Pentagon was beyond our wildest imagination and our worst fears.*

I stood transfixed by the live images from New York, wracking my brain for clues I might have missed. And then I saw the second plane streaking towards the South Tower. It was exactly 2:03 P.M. in London; I thought of all the people arriving for work in the 110 storeys of the World Trade Center.

Mesmerized for what must have been half an hour, I eventually broke away from the crowd of whispering viewers and stepped into a quiet side street.

I dialled a number on my cell phone. The usual bland answer.

'It's Lawrence. Let me know if there's anything I can do.'

---

* The 9/11 Commission famously called the failure to anticipate such a spectacular attack 'a failure of imagination'. On 6 August 2001, the Presidential Daily Brief for President George W. Bush contained an item entitled 'Bin Ladin Determined to Strike in the US', but contained no specific information about any active plot.[8]

Lawrence was then my code name – a play on the name of the famous Englishman of Arabia.

As I thought of all my interactions in Afghanistan, only one small, opaque clue came to me. It was when Abu Hafs had talked about presenting America with another Pearl Harbor at the reception in Kabul in late 1999.

In the days after 9/11, we raked over old ground: the personalities, the camps, the connections. Targets were identified inside Afghanistan. I assumed that as we worked British Special Forces were being prepared for action. What had we missed that now – with the searing clarity of hindsight – looked obvious?

In fact, the plot had been brilliantly concealed within a very tight circle. Short of being selected as one of the hijackers myself, I could not have picked up the scent. The 9/11 mastermind, Khalid Sheikh Mohammed, later told US interrogators that the plotting was kept so compartmentalized that even senior figures in the group were in the dark. The 'muscle' hijackers – like the young Saudi I'd met in the Kabul guest house – were only told of their targets after they had arrived in the United States and just weeks before the attacks.*

I had come across the so-called twentieth hijacker, Zacarias Moussaoui, in London before he left in February 2001 (it later emerged) to get flight training in the United States. Surly and secretive, he used to attend prayers at Abu Qatada's Four Feathers Club. Moussaoui was confident that I was also a committed member of al-Qaeda but he never told me of any plans to travel to America.

Immediately after meeting him I told my handlers that I'd encountered a French jihadi called Zacarias and that he'd been in the al-Qaeda camps in Afghanistan, but I only knew his first name and nothing suggested he was a significant player. Only after 9/11 was I shown his photograph and learned his full name and connection to the conspiracy.**

---

* KSM also stated that bin Laden had only notified al-Qaeda's Shura Council in late August that a major attack against unspecified US interests would take place over the coming weeks, without disclosing additional details.[9]

** Moussaoui was arrested in Minnesota on 16 August 2001. According to

British intelligence asked me to game al-Qaeda's next move. Were more attacks in the pipeline? Where would the leadership go? Would this have been sanctioned by bin Laden himself? On that last question, I had no doubts.

I found it bitterly amusing that suddenly our meeting rooms were larger and invariably packed with attendees from both agencies scrambling to get up to speed on a subject that had been something of an intelligence backwater. Richard and Alan were having their moment in the limelight. For years, they'd been 'down the agenda' – behind nuclear proliferation, Russia and Northern Ireland. Now they were on the front page, their knowledge of the abstruse suddenly mainstream. They would soon earn promotions.

There were further questions about al-Qaeda's WMD ambitions. On 7 November 2001, weeks after the US-led offensive to topple the Taliban had begun, bin Laden told the Pakistani journalist Hamid Mir: 'I wish to declare that if America used chemical or nuclear weapons against us, then we may retort with chemical and nuclear weapons. We have the weapons as a deterrent.'[11]

I was as sceptical as ever. Al-Qaeda would have loved nothing more than some sort of nuclear capability. But nothing I had seen – or heard from Abu Khabab – suggested they were anywhere close to acquiring it.*

My work in London intensified as arrests were made in Pakistan and the first batch of detainees were shipped to the hastily prepared prison camp at Guantánamo Bay in Cuba. I went through hundreds of photographs trying to identify anyone I might have known, anyone who mattered. But few were of any interest; they were mostly young Yemeni, Afghan and Pakistani foot soldiers who had tried to

---

CIA director George Tenet, US intelligence was notified by French intelligence eight days later that Moussaoui had jihadi terrorist connections. He was subsequently sentenced to life in prison.[10]

* I reminded my handlers that the leadership had already decided to exaggerate (or fabricate) such potential to sow uncertainty. While much effort was devoted to testing al-Qaeda's boasts, US agencies in 2002 concluded there was no credible information that the terror group had obtained fissile material or a nuclear weapon.[12]

escape from Tora Bora through the mountain passes into Pakistan.

I was sure al-Qaeda had launched the attacks with the goal of provoking the Americans into invading Muslim lands. Abu Hafs had said as much at the Kabul gathering in late 1999. The aim was to spur US reprisals that would resurrect the spirit of jihad among the masses. The turmoil could then be leveraged to overthrow Arab governments seen as puppets of the West.*

The 9/11 attacks had also demonstrated to me the power of the ideology that was being spouted at mosques in London, camps in Kandahar and classrooms in Kabul. I had seen and heard it at first hand, from Abu Qatada and Abu Musab al-Suri among others. Exhibit A was eighteen tapes of Abu Qatada's lectures found in a Hamburg apartment used by 9/11 attack cell leader Mohamed Atta and two more of the hijackers.[14]

In the months after 9/11, al-Qaeda was scattered to the winds by a US-led coalition that bombed and occupied Afghanistan. By the end of 2001, its last redoubt at Tora Bora was once more an empty warren of ravines and caves. Many of al-Qaeda's leaders escaped, including bin Laden and Zawahiri. The organization they led fractured as if thrown into some centrifuge. But if it was reeling and diminished, it was far from extinct.

By the autumn of 2002, Osama bin Laden's gaze had turned to his homeland. US intelligence had intercepted a message sent to the

---

* To some in al-Qaeda the strategy worked. In 2005 Saif al-Adel, a senior Egyptian al-Qaeda operative I had known in Afghanistan, wrote: 'Our ultimate objective of these painful strikes against the head of the snake was to prompt it to come out of its burrow ... Such strikes will force the person to carry out random acts and provoke him to make serious and sometimes fatal mistakes. This was what actually happened. The first reaction was the invasion of Afghanistan and the second was the invasion of Iraq ... Our objective, therefore, was to prompt the Americans to come out of their hole and deal powerful strikes to the body of the nation (Muslims) which is in slumber. Without these strikes there would be no hope for this nation to wake up.'[13]

mysterious leader of al-Qaeda's Saudi 'branch' – known only as Saif al-Battar (Swift Sword) – instructing him to prepare for a campaign of attacks in the Kingdom.[15] Hundreds of Saudi al-Qaeda fighters had returned home from Afghanistan and the worry was they might be stockpiling weapons.* Nor were the Saudi security services organized for the task of confronting them.

Bin Laden might have been on the run, but he still had a grasp of the wider world. It seemed increasingly likely that the United States would invade Iraq. Bin Laden expected that would ignite Muslim anger across the region, providing al-Qaeda with the chance to lead an insurgency in his home country.**

There were, in short, a lot more intelligence opportunities in the Gulf than there were in London, where my work involved surveying jihadi websites and trawling round improvised mosques in warehouses, listening to execrable Arabic and half-baked slogans.

Abu Qatada had gone on the run, only to be found in a council house (public housing) in south London. One of my handlers told me he'd been found clean-shaven and awaiting fake travel documents. An earlier police raid had found the equivalent of £170,000 in cash underneath his bed, but no charges were brought, partly because MI5 didn't want me testifying in court but also because existing counter-terror laws made it difficult to win convictions.*** For several years he would remain in a legal limbo, but his freedom of movement (and fundraising) was radically curtailed.

---

* Since 1998 I had heard reports of al-Qaeda smuggling weapons into Saudi Arabia from Yemen and Kuwait, where Saddam Hussein had left an arsenal of weapons after being forced out in 1991.[16]
** Bin Laden had not been in Saudi Arabia in ten years, and the adoration of al-Qaeda's Saudi recruits had made him overestimate al-Qaeda's appeal in the Kingdom. He was right in believing a US attack on Iraq would spur an insurgency, but it would be in Iraq rather than Saudi Arabia.
*** Abu Qatada had finally been arrested in south London in October 2002 after new anti-terror laws were adopted in late 2001. Successive governments would place him under various forms of detention and house arrest before he was eventually deported to Jordan.[17]

I also had personal reasons for wanting to relocate. My brother Moheddin had just been released from jail. Once upon a time he had helped a Palestinian resident in Saudi Arabia reach Afghanistan – in those days an honourable calling that brought a family respect. After 9/11, the man had returned home and blown himself up – killing an American – in Khobar.[18] For that long-forgotten connection, Moheddin spent nine months in prison.

After serving his sentence, Moheddin had been expelled to Bahrain. I wanted to see him; we had not seen each other for five years. I also wanted to see what I might do to protect him from himself. If he were to become more active in militant circles, what might politely be called a 'conflict of interest' could pose a real dilemma for me. But at the same time his contacts could put me on a fast track to intelligence about al-Qaeda's plans in the Gulf.

It was ethical torture, and my employers knew it. On a bright October morning in 2002, I received a call from someone identifying himself as George. He was one of MI5's psychologists and he wanted to talk. Part of his job was to watch for agents and assets who were under stress or confronted with doubt.

'Fine,' I said. 'But I'm in the middle of packing. I'm not even sure I could find the teapot.'

George turned out to be a tall and strikingly handsome man in his early forties. Funnily enough he had more than a passing resemblance to George Clooney, though his accent was more northern England than New England. His empathy soon changed my generic image of his profession.

Unmoved by the state of my apartment, he found a place to perch.

'So, Bahrain,' he began. 'Will it be a little awkward with your brother?'

The subtext was obvious: can we trust you? Family or the Firm?

'I think it will work out,' I said, more out of hope than expectation. I felt he noticed the uncertainty in my voice. 'At least I can try to keep him out of jail,' I added with a touch of black humour.

'There'd be nothing wrong if you feel a bit conflicted,' George said. 'That's just human, healthy. Nobody is asking you to spy on your brother.

'I want to be straight with you,' he went on. He was leaning forward and watching me closely. 'There are some in the service who are worried about all this "with us or against us" bullshit. Bush and bin Laden are both at it and we accept it might – just might – introduce . . .' he paused to find the right expression, 'issues for some of our agents.

'I think we all accept that you are with us for the right reasons. It's not money; it's not revenge. It's conviction and your hatred of wanton violence. Fair?'

'Fair,' I said. I suddenly wished that he'd been with me when the dour Scotsman in Islamabad had challenged my bona fides.

'Even so, you are headed to a place where for some inform- ants it would be tempting to rejoin the cause. We need to do due diligence, and that's why I'm here.' I nodded. But he could see I was restless and anxious. 'Look, you need to understand that you have a very unusual story. You've been through more in your twenty-four years on this earth than the vast majority of mankind ever see.'

He quizzed me about Bosnia and being in the Afghan camps. Without even realizing it, I was soon pouring out every last detail – my narrow escapes, my doubts, the strain of working undercover.

'For God's sake,' he said – more in astonishment than exas- peration – 'a week before your seventeenth birthday you were drag- ging bodies down a hill in Bosnia, slipping in pools of blood and expecting to meet your maker at any second. That's not normal for a teenager. It damages you, whether you know it or not.'

There was a long pause, the sort he was probably used to and I found excruciating.

'Do you have anyone you can confide in – a partner? Have you ever had one?'

I could tell he was fishing.

'No – my career path sort of precluded that.'

He could tell from my tone, which verged on scornful, that he had struck a nerve. The discipline required of being a jihadi and then a spy had helped me deal with both temptation and the melancholy of being single, but the truth was that I badly wanted a companion with whom to plan a life.

'Has it occurred to you that you might be stifling your sexuality?'

I wasn't ready for that and reacted angrily.

'Oh great,' I said. 'I'm about to depart for a mission that's not exactly risk-free, and you want me to think about whether I'm gay. Sure, I come from a culture where men and women simply don't mix, where sexuality is repressed, but looking at the birth rate they do apparently get together at some point. And one day, I will leap at the chance if the right woman comes along. It will also be my last day working for British intelligence.'

I couldn't tell whether George thought my protests a little too loud. But he laughed and swiftly changed the subject.

'Goodness. You are in your early twenties. I can scarcely remember my early twenties. And I certainly didn't know a fraction of what you know, nor did I have a fraction of your experiences. You're not exactly a late starter. And, believe me, the Service will be very happy if Miss Right doesn't appear just yet.' Another long pause. The low timbre of a passing truck vibrated through the building. 'How are you sleeping?' he asked.

'Honestly, like a baby,' I replied. 'Ever since I was seven I've listened to the radio or cassettes to lull me to sleep. Anything: history, fiction, biography. I didn't learn the kings and queens of England to prove my loyalty to the Service. I learned them to get to sleep.'

'Oh shit,' he said with a smile, 'now we'll never know whether you are going back to the dark side.'

I burst out laughing.

'But seriously,' he said, 'the fact that you give your brain something entirely different to chew on every night is important. It's helping you not to have nightmares about some of the things you've witnessed, in Bosnia for example, and some of your very own close shaves.'

Two days later, a package arrived in the mail. It was a Sony Discman, with best wishes from George. We were destined to be friends and allies. George would help me through some dark times in the years to come.

Despite his worries, MI6 was enthusiastic about my moving to the Gulf and regarded Bahrain as an important conduit between Saudi Arabia and Iran (where some in al-Qaeda's upper echelons had taken refuge). The authorities in Bahrain had a lenient attitude towards conservative Sunnis and Salafis – and there were more than a few al-Qaeda sympathizers among them. The royal family and a minority of Bahrainis were (and still are) Sunnis and controlled the levers of power, while the Shia majority simmered and fumed (and still does).

MI6 believed it was safer for me to operate in Bahrain than Saudi Arabia because British and Bahraini intelligence had a long and tight relationship. While MI6 would not have dreamed of telling the Bahrainis I was a British spy, they worried that if I reconnected with my al-Qaeda circle in Saudi Arabia it would be difficult to get a message to Saudi security services not to kill me.

Even so, I needed a good explanation if I was to relocate. British intelligence helped me concoct one from, of all places, Paddington Green Police Station in west London.

An MI5 official met me there and took me into an interview room. I called my brother Omar.

'I'm in trouble,' I said to him after the usual salutations. 'The police have detained me because of some of the people I know here.'

'What did you expect?' he asked, with scant sympathy. It was just the response I was hoping for. 'I'll get a visa and come to help. I bet you don't have a lawyer, or any money.'

'Just wait till I find out what's going on,' I said. 'But it's become impossible to survive here. All my friends have been put in jail or deported. People look at me as though I have a bomb strapped to my chest. Someone asked me whether I was here to study flying!'

Had Omar checked the number, he would have discovered that it belonged to a London police station.

Having set the mood, I called back a few hours later from my own phone.

'They let me go,' I told Omar, 'but it's enough. I'm coming home.'

The moist warmth of Bahrain was a shock to the system after the brisk autumn breezes in London. It felt strange to be back in the Arabian Peninsula after so long away, my hometown just twenty miles across the King Fahd Causeway linking Bahrain and Saudi Arabia. Apart from that week being questioned in Qatar, this was my first return to old stamping grounds.

I had left Khobar as a starry-eyed sixteen-year-old. Now, at the grand age of twenty-four, I was a veteran agent of British intelligence. And I was back in the field. The thought sent a shiver of adrenalin through me. London had made me stale. Now I was on my own again, and there was no margin for error. I had to immerse myself in the persona of a jihadi striving for revenge against the West and Saudi Arabia. But I also had to be patient.

Moheddin and Omar greeted me at the airport. We embraced and were all embarrassed by the tears. My oldest brothers had both changed so much physically; I was almost alarmed to see the first flecks of grey hair around Moheddin's temples. Even Omar's suave looks were beginning to do battle with the creases of ageing. But they were in good spirits, and it felt like a family reunion.

On the way to Moheddin's home we drove past the brightly lit hotel bars and nightclubs along Exhibition Road and the al-Juffair district. These places were allowed to serve alcohol to non-Muslims, put on shows by go-go dancers, and were popular with American sailors from the Fifth Fleet based in Bahrain, as well as with Saudi men coming across the causeway for brief escapes from their puritanical existence.

'I see why it's called Exhibition Road,' I said, making a show of displeasure. Even among family it was necessary to keep up appearances.

Moheddin's residence in the Sunni neighbourhood of east Riffa was a world away from the carnal lure of Exhibition Road. He had taken over the first floor of a three-storey villa next to a beautiful mosque lit by floodlights. We dined long into the night, catching up on family stories, the exploits of cousins and nephews, memories of our mother. It all felt so long ago.

'It's high time that we find you a wife,' Moheddin said to me, a mischievous smile on his lips. 'My wife has several good candidates in mind.' But she was in Saudi Arabia; she regarded Bahrain as a den of debauchery.

'First I need to figure out my plans,' I replied with whole-hearted non-commitment. There was no way I could marry a Saudi or Bahraini woman and lead a double life – pretending to be a teacher or academic while spying for Britain. Ever since I'd been recruited as an agent, I'd decided that celibacy was the only option, though George had exposed the raw nerve of loneliness that had begun to eat away at me.

In any case, I hadn't the faintest idea how to make the right moves in female company. I had less small talk than a Cistercian monk. Call it the price of dedication to jihad: you didn't get to meet, let alone form any relationships with the opposite sex. In fact, it had always been seen as a virtue in the camps. A jihadi could not devote himself to the cause as a married man. In Afghanistan, few fighters had a family in tow. Some had left wives and children at home; the vast majority were determinedly single and awaiting martyrdom. Only then – surrounded by the virgins of paradise – would we give up celibacy. This perspective was common throughout al-Qaeda, though it would be turned on its head with the emergence of the Islamic State, where sex slaves were permitted and young girls were enticed from Europe to Syria. More than once I reflected that repressed attitudes towards the opposite sex stoked the anger and alienation of so many jihadis.

Moheddin had rented two apartments in the villa and insisted

I live in the one above his. I was very willing to accept the offer. It helped that the apartment was modern and comfortable and looked out onto palm trees, a rare privilege in the humid concrete jungle of Manama. But it also made it easier for me to keep tabs on him.

We spent many hours filling in the gaps of the past few years. I finally told him about my oath of allegiance to bin Laden; he was wide-eyed. For all he knew, that oath was still very much in force. I was struck by Moheddin's anger at the world. He recounted in greater detail his arrest and time in jail in Saudi Arabia. He had only been released a few weeks before my arrival. His wife and children would come across the causeway from Khobar most weekends to see him. He raged about the prospect of US forces invading Iraq and I worried that he was edging towards some rash action.

'I understand why you feel so angry,' I told him late one night as we sat on his balcony, 'but if you decide to do something you should at least wait until the kids can stand on their own feet. They need you now, even if they only see you once a week.'

He was already hanging out with the wrong crowd. I just didn't want him leading it.

Sunni militancy thrived in mosques around the sprawling capital. I attended some of the more radical places of worship to get a feel for the mood. I did not advertise my presence but waited for opportunity to come my way. Within just a few weeks, thanks to someone I met through Moheddin, it did. And it was no accident.

His name was Akhil and he was a chemistry teacher.* A Saudi in his mid-thirties, Akhil was working in Bahrain. He was balding and slightly overweight, with a forgettable face but intense, excitable eyes. He had fought in Afghanistan in the early 1990s.

'You must have dinner with me. I know a great place on Exhibition Road,' he told me.

Days later we were sharing grilled lamb and Bukhari rice. But I sensed this was not just a social event; Akhil had something to ask

---

* I am not revealing his last name.

me. As the plates were cleared away he leaned forward his eyes searching me.

'Are you by any chance also known as Abu Abbas al-Bahraini?' he asked quietly.

'Yes,' I answered, 'that was the name I took in Afghanistan.'

'Were you by any chance working with Abu Khabab on certain programmes?' Akhil continued.

I had to tread carefully. I hardly knew this man.

'I knew Abu Khabab, yes,' I whispered.

'So you are aware of something called a *mubtakkar*?'

He now had my full attention.

'Yes, I am,' I responded, and as casually as I could gave him the barest details about the device.

'I have an urgent message from your friends in Saudi Arabia who are looking for you.'

The friends turned out to be none other than Khalid al-Hajj, with whom I had travelled to Bosnia and the Philippines, and Yusuf al-Ayeri, my Smurf-hating instructor in the Khobar Islamic Awareness Circle. It was difficult to fathom that a single Scout troop could have produced so much trouble.

The last time I had seen Khalid had been in Afghanistan in the spring of 2001. He had subsequently travelled to Yemen before being smuggled into Saudi Arabia, where he was helping build the al-Qaeda network. I recalled the expression on his face that afternoon on the shooting range in Afghanistan, when he had promised revenge against the Saudi state.

In tones barely audible amid the restaurant chatter, Akhil continued.

'We have your notes from the *mubtakkar*. But we can't understand your handwriting.'

His tone was intensely serious, but the remark was almost absurdly funny.

'That's understandable,' I replied, enjoying a moment of light relief in what was now an alarming conversation.

Akhil slid a stack of papers with diagrams and formulae across the table. Not smart tradecraft, I thought to myself, unable to observe our fellow diners.

'Have we got it right?' he asked.

'Let me look,' I said, shielding the papers from view.

They had. Akhil knew his chemistry, and I could not lie to him for that very reason.

'You get an excellent grade for your tests,' I said cryptically. 'In fact, a hundred percent.'

A week later we met again at the same restaurant.

'Abu Hazim [Khalid al-Hajj] sends his Salaams,' he said with a smile. 'He wonders if you could join them in the desert.'

That would not be possible, but not for the reasons he thought. I told Akhil that the Saudis might be looking for me; it would be foolish to try.

'I have great news,' he went on, his eyes glowing. 'Our brothers built the *mubtakkar* in the desert. There was a successful test.'

How he loved being the go-between, at the centre of the web.

I had to slow the process down, find out more, but at the same time appear enthusiastic. For a second, I wished I had taken drama classes.

'That's great news,' I said. 'But Akhil,' I went on with all the solemnity I could muster, 'this device belongs to five people, the five of us who developed it in Afghanistan.* It was designed for a specific purpose, its use to be cleared at the highest level. You can't just go ahead and use the *mubtakkar* in Saudi. In fact, it was agreed it would never be used in a Muslim country.'

This wasn't true, but I was confident he would not know any better.

'I assure you that this is not for use in Saudi Arabia,' he replied.

I was momentarily lost for words. It implied that targets had

---

* I was referring to myself, Abu Khabab, his deputy Abu Bakr al-Masri, Hassan Ghul and Abu Nassim al-Tunisi.

been identified or at least discussed, most likely in the West. I let his answer hang in the air, scooping up some rice with my fork.

'I'm reassured,' I said.

I resisted the urge to ask any more questions. Let information drip out in the course of the conversation. And Akhil was full of information – a good chemist, but a naive operative.

'When you guys were developing the device did you ever talk about the sarin attack in Tokyo?'* he asked.

'Yes.'

His eyes flitted conspiratorially. For a moment he looked like a squirrel.

'Remember I asked you to confirm that cyanogen chloride was 2.47 times heavier than air?' Now he was into his chemistry teacher mode. 'How will that affect how quickly it spreads in the ventilation of a subway system? Should we use it or hydrogen cyanide?' he asked.

He had used the English word 'subway'. He hadn't said metro or underground.

For a moment I forgot my training.

'Subway, as in New York?'

He smiled but said nothing.

'Well,' I went on, trying to sound as if I was mixing a spray for the lawn, 'the two gases behave differently.'

'But which is more deadly?'

I had to cooperate, to sound as if I, too, wanted to maximize casualties. The best approach, I quickly decided, was to provide him a mix of information and disinformation. I would have to provide straight answers on anything easy for him to check but that left opportunities to throw some metaphorical sand in his eyes.**

It was perturbing to be discussing the relative merits of gassing

---

* The March 1995 sarin gas attack in Tokyo metro trains by the Japanese death cult Aum Shinrikyo killed twelve people and made thousands sick.
** I was indeed able to make a number of suggestions which I hoped would slow down or sabotage their plans.

New Yorkers with what was in effect Zyklon B or the equally nasty cyanogen chloride. Both are asphyxiants and can kill quickly. They are known as blood agents because they affect cells' use of oxygen[19] – and at high doses lead to rapid organ failure.

'What can happen with both gases,' I continued, 'is that the lungs are flooded with fluid. Your last moments can include cardiac arrest, choking and violent seizures. It's a ghastly way to die.'[20]

The rapt attention on Akhil's face is an image I still remember.

It was time to request an urgent meeting with British intelligence. When I had set off from London the previous October we had agreed that our rendezvous point would be Dubai, but to have left Bahrain immediately after my first meeting with Akhil could have invited suspicion.

The phone was answered by a woman whose calm, polite voice had inevitably led me to nickname her Miss Moneypenny.

'It's Lawrence here,' I told her. 'I need a meeting.'

A couple of days later, two representatives of Her Majesty's Intelligence Services were staring wide-eyed at me in a room at the Dubai Meridien hotel.

MI6 was now represented by Freddie. In his thirties, he sounded and looked like Prince William. He was a sympathetic listener and a good conversationalist with whom it was easy to relax. An economics graduate from Loughborough University, he didn't have the snobbery of some of the Oxbridge crowd. It helped that we were both big fans of *The Simpsons*.

The new MI5 man, Kevin, had spent most of his career in Northern Ireland and had been reassigned to Islamist terrorism like so many other officers after 9/11. He had sandy hair and deep-set green eyes. Kevin was from northern England and was less patrician than the average British intelligence officer. They made a good team and I would get to know both of them well. But on this first encounter overseas after our introductory meeting in London, the urgency of the agenda left little time for small talk.

I related my meetings with Akhil and his links with al-Qaeda in Saudi Arabia. After I was done, Freddie finished scribbling notes and tucked his pen inside his jacket.

'We're going to have to take this back to London.'

Kevin picked up. I noticed how he would narrow his eyes when things got serious.

'But the controller will want to know why you confirmed to Akhil the designs worked. Shouldn't you have played for time?'

I made no attempt to hide my annoyance.

'Come on, guys. I was dealing with a chemistry teacher, for goodness sake. They had the recipe right. They had the engineering right. I was on the spot and had to improvise. Don't you think he would have become rather suspicious if I'd asked for time to figure it out. They know I was one of the creators of the device.'

There was an awkward pause.

'We need you to stay here. We'll be back within forty-eight hours,' Freddie said.

As I sat nursing an ice cold Coke by the hotel's neon-blue swimming pool that night, I imagined the lights burning in the MI6 building at Vauxhall Cross. Within hours, though I did not know it then, the Americans had been informed.

When Freddie and Kevin returned they looked worn out. They had clearly not slept much in their brief trip home.

'This has become an urgent priority,' Freddie said.

We went over my dinners with Akhil again, checking every detail.

'We need you to stay on the inside. More dinners, I'm afraid,' Freddie said. 'But the higher-ups are a bit anxious that you might end up providing Akhil with information to improve the design. We know you're in an impossible situation, but try to keep that in mind.'

Kevin handed me a comms device.

'We'll need you to use this to keep us informed. There's a software program buried inside to encrypt and decrypt messages. It's no substitute for meeting in person, but you can use it to request meetings and send critical information.'*

After a quick tutorial they departed again for the airport.

There followed more dinner meetings with Akhil.

'I have a question for you,' he said one evening. He was annoyingly cheerful. 'Your notes don't say anything about means of delivery. In the camps in Afghanistan did you discuss a martyrdom mission or to leave the device behind?'

'It depends on the situation. If you use it in a cinema, you can have two brothers come in and set off one device near the entrance and one near the emergency exit. In between you'll have a kill zone.'

My callous words made me feel nauseous, but they were a necessary evil. I needed to find out more about their plans.

He cut me off.

'It's not a cinema. We're talking about inside the trains or next to the ventilation shaft in the subway system.'

'If you use it in trains you're going to get some casualties,' I said. I was only stating the obvious. In fact Abu Khabab's team had estimated that half the occupants of a subway carriage could perish if a device was timed to go off between stations.

Akhil nodded non-committally and then repeated his original question.

'Did you discuss a martyrdom mission or put-and-go'?

'Put-and-go,' I replied. 'It's not like a bomb blast in which the brother will instantly be in paradise. It's an extremely unpleasant way to die.'

'Well, we have four Saudi brothers already in Morocco and someone there who will teach them how to build the *mubtakkar*. They all have ten-year visas for the United States and can go anytime,' he said.

The operation had clearly moved beyond the planning stage. The enormity of what I was hearing was slowly sinking in.

---

* The system encrypted messages into garbled text which could then be sent to an anonymous email address. My handlers could then decrypt this using the same software. Ironically, al-Qaeda itself would later use similar technology to swap encrypted messages through a system called Mujahideen Secrets. This was well before the days of smartphones and encrypted messaging apps.

'What is your passport?' he continued.

'I have a UK passport.'

'So you can fly to Morocco without a visa?'

'Yes, of course.'

'Would it be dangerous for you to go? Do you think you are on the radar screen?' he asked me.

'I don't know,' I replied. If he was testing me I could not afford to sound too keen, nor too reluctant.

I risked raising an obstacle.

'You need a fatwah for this.'

'Sheikh Yusuf has commissioned a fatwah,' he said. He meant my former community group instructor Yusuf al-Ayeri. 'And we are waiting for the final clearance from Sheikh Osama. It will be a matter of weeks before we have a go-ahead,' he added with a note of triumph.

I feigned confusion in case it should unearth another lead.

'Why would Yusuf commission a fatwah? Shouldn't it be the leader of the group Saif al-Battar [Swift Sword]?'

That knowing smile again.

'Yusuf al-Ayeri *is* Saif al-Battar.'

'Oh my God,' I felt like shouting as the penny dropped. Western intelligence agencies had been trying to fathom out the identity of Swift Sword for months. Now it had been casually tossed to me over chicken and rice, and it was someone I had spent many hours with in Saudi Arabia, Bosnia and Afghanistan. I could scarcely believe the ammunition Akhil had given me. Not only did we have a chance to thwart the plot against New York, but an opportunity to dismantle al-Qaeda's network in Saudi Arabia.*

---

* In the lead-up to 9/11 al-Ayeri and his associates recruited a significant number of young Saudis to train with al-Qaeda in Afghanistan, including the 9/11 'muscle' hijacker Abdul Aziz al-Omari I met in Kabul. After 9/11 al-Ayeri focused on building up the group's operations in Saudi Arabia. He had originally disagreed with bin Laden's orders to start an all-out war in Saudi Arabia, fearing the organization was not yet ready, but as a loyal soldier had accepted his orders. I was subsequently told this by an al-Qaeda operative in Bahrain.[21]

A week later, in the incongruous setting of the Holiday Inn near Victoria Station in London, I was debriefing Freddie, Kevin and a young officer called Nish over sandwiches.

'You have to be absolutely sure about this,' Freddie said. 'Even the Saudis don't know who Saif al-Battar is.'

'I'm sure,' I said as I prodded a rather tired looking sandwich. 'Akhil is very much part of this plot; he would know.'

My colleagues were excited; this was serious information to trade. Freddie allowed for a moment of levity.

'Excellent,' he said, steepling his fingers in his best impression of Montgomery Burns. 'So now we're going to have to call you Chemical Ali.'

We all laughed.

'So it was al-Ayeri that wrote *The Truth about the Crusader War*?' asked Nish.

'Correct,' I said. The tract had appeared weeks after 9/11 to justify the attacks. It and other publications had made the mystery writer a subject of great interest to Western intelligence.[22]

I was warming to Nish, who had clearly been doing his homework since joining MI6. It seemed he had immersed himself in the subject, reading jihadi output and studying biographies.

'We have two problems,' I said, stifling the brief interlude of good humour. 'Akhil told me they're training recruits in the desert and stockpiling weapons for attacks against the security services and foreigners in Saudi Arabia.

'As for the *mubtakkar* plot, it could go operational within weeks. If Akhil is to be believed, Swift Sword has four Saudi operatives sitting in Morocco about to be taught how to make the *mubtakkar*. They have ten-year US visas. I don't know how they'll get hold of the materials but once they build the devices they'll cross into Manhattan with their backpacks and set them off in the subway.'\*

---

\* I subsequently learned that MI6 later corroborated from other sources that the target was New York.

My handlers looked not a little anxious at the thought of four operatives setting off multiple *mubtakkar* under the streets of New York.

MI6 shared my intelligence with the Americans. It was inevitable and necessary but also like buying a lottery ticket. You had no idea who would gain access to the information and what they'd do with it. Given the stakes, I imagined the CIA had demanded more detail about the source. How much they were told I could not know. It was one of those moments when an informant's life is in the hands of others more than one step removed from his welfare. In the febrile and competitive world of US intelligence gathering, that was not necessarily a good thing.

Even in the aftermath of 9/11 it is unlikely the British would have revealed my identity to the 'cousins'. It is conceivable that the CIA gradually built up a picture of my identity (if not my name) through the drip-feed of answers from British intelligence. I imagined at the time that the sort of specifics I was providing – imminent and actionable – had inspired a torrent of further enquiries.

My information was fed quickly up the chain to the White House. President George W. Bush was briefed in the Oval Office; according to one account there was stunned silence when the implications of the *mubtakkar* were absorbed.[23] Bush in particular was very concerned.[24]

Despite the fact that the invasion of Iraq was weeks away, the plot was discussed at length, with CIA Director George Tenet stressing the need to 'chase down' the threat.[25] The mood among some officials was later described as 'just shy of panic'.[26] Might the cell already have been dispatched to the United States? Was there a plan to attack the New York subway the moment the invasion began?* When the NYPD police chief Ray Kelly was eventually briefed he worried 'the damage could be catastrophic.'[28]

---

* Tenet wrote in his 2007 memoir that the operatives 'were already staged in New York'. I do not know why he wrote that. Nothing I heard suggested they were.[27]

But al-Qaeda had another surprise in store.

'It's not going to happen,' a crestfallen Akhil told me when we next met. 'Zawahiri has cancelled the operation.'

I tried to appear desperately disappointed despite the relief coursing through my veins.

'But why?' I asked. 'We were so close.'

I might as well squeeze the last details out of him; it wasn't likely to be difficult.

Al-Qaeda's deputy leader Ayman al-Zawahiri had consulted al-Qaeda's Shura Council. He was concerned that an attack in New York would be used to claim that Saddam Hussein had given al-Qaeda WMD so that the Americans could legitimize the invasion of Iraq, however ridiculous the link.*

'Zawahiri thinks this would be a gift to Bush, Cheney and Blair and that the *Ummah* will not forgive al-Qaeda. He thinks it will feed conspiracy theories that al-Qaeda is an invention of the Americans,' Akhil said gloomily.**

The way he spat out the words suggested he thought Zawahiri's logic was at best convoluted. He said al-Qaeda's leadership also feared the use of the *mubtakkar* might prompt the United States to use tactical nuclear weapons against al-Qaeda. I found that hard to believe.

---

* Akhil said that all communications destined for bin Laden had first to pass through Zawahiri. In the years after 9/11, al-Qaeda used a mixture of electronic communications and couriers to transfer messages. Messages were sent by courier within Saudi Arabia and then electronically to Pakistani cities such as Peshawar before again being transferred by courier to al-Qaeda's leaders.
** Of the cancellation, Tenet wrote that the cell had requested 'permission from al-Qa'ida central leadership to conduct the attack. Chillingly, word came back from Ayman al-Zawahiri himself in early 2003 to cancel the operation and recall the operatives, who were already staged in New York – because "we have something better in mind." Tenet added: 'There was endless speculation at the highest levels as to the proper interpretation of al-Zawahiri's cryptic comment. We still do not know what he meant.' One aspect of Tenet's recollection makes no sense to me. While I informed the British that Zawahiri had called off the plot, I never heard the rationale was that al-Qaeda had 'something better in mind.'[29]

'So what are Zawahiri's instructions?' I asked.

'To keep knowledge about the *mubtakkar* under tight control,' Akhil replied.

He leaned towards me and lowered his voice.

'Perhaps if we can't use it against the Americans we should use it against the Israelis. Now we have all the notes, we can share it with Hamas.'

His arrogance finally touched a nerve in me.

'You have no right to do that,' I replied sharply. 'They said don't disseminate it. You don't own this technology.'

For the first time I saw Akhil moved to anger. No doubt he was still smarting from cancellation of the project that would have made him a household name.

'The fucking Jews are killing our people in the West Bank. It's no less than what they deserve.'

When I returned home I encrypted a note to MI6. A message that looked like a jumble of letters and symbols was soon on its way to London. Given the apparent imminence of the threat, my handlers had wanted regular updates. Once decrypted at the other end, the response came quickly. *Come to London.*

'But why?' were Freddie's first words when we met. 'You sure it's not a ploy, that they've decided to spread word that the operation is off, even among their own?'

I believed Zawahiri's message was genuine. He had a reputation for being extraordinarily sensitive to other Muslims' views of al-Qaeda.

When my intelligence reached the White House, Vice President Dick Cheney was perplexed and worried that something bigger was in the works.[30] For British intelligence, the priority was to prevent the *mubtakkar* blueprint from finding a wider audience.

On 13 February 2003, as a result of intelligence I provided to the British, Bahraini police stopped a group of men as they drove across the King Fahd Causeway to Bahrain. It was made to look like a random security control. If they believed the security services had stumbled upon them by accident, they would be less likely to suspect the existence of a mole inside their ranks. One of those detained was Bassam Bokhowa, an IT technician in his mid-thirties. On his laptop they found blueprints for the *mubtakkar*.* I knew from spending time with both of them that Akhil had tasked him with converting my handwritten notes into an electronic document complete with diagrams.

Bokhowa was a friend of Akhil and a painful narcissist, constantly boasting about his computer skills and embellishing his role in the jihadi cause. He had tried but failed to reach Afghanistan to join bin Laden's jihad. Now he worked for a telecoms company.

Unfortunately, my brother Moheddin was caught in the net. Like Akhil, Bokhowa had been less than discreet about the enterprise and told Moheddin about the *mubtakkar*. My brother was not a little surprised to discover that I was one of its architects. Once again Moheddin was on the fringes of the wrong crowd; his degree in chemical engineering only added to the suspicion.**

The official Bahraini news agency trumpeted that the security forces had 'broken up a cell that had been plotting terrorist acts . . . targeting the kingdom's national interests and endangering the lives of innocent citizens'.[33]

The cell did try to upload the *mubtakkar* blueprint for Hamas. My handlers later told me the Israelis had intercepted the messages before they could reach their intended recipients: operatives within the al-Qassam brigades, Hamas's military wing.

Within hours of Bokhowa's arrest, MI6 and the CIA were poring

---

* I was told this afterwards by my British handlers. In his 2015 memoir, Ray Kelly, the NYPD police chief at the time, wrote that 'the plot talk' was 'confirmed in early 2003 when Bassam Bokhowa, a jihadist from Bahrain, was captured in Saudi Arabia. On his laptop, Saudi security forces discovered detailed plans for building what the terrorists were calling a *mubtakkar*, the Arabic word for "new invention".'[31]
** Besides my brother and Bassam Bokhowa, the security services named those arrested as Bassam Ali, recently arrived from Iran; Issa al-Baluchi and Jamal al-Baluchi. Both of the al-Baluchis would serve time as they were caught in possession of weapons. Issa was a lieutenant in the Bahraini National Guard. Neither had anything to do with this plot though they were not innocent in other instances.[32]

over the blueprints.[34] Any remaining scepticism that a real plot had been in the works was banished. The CIA arranged for a prototype of the device to be built and estimated that a coordinated attack involving multiple *mubtakkars* would undoubtedly be lethal. The agency was so disturbed by the outcome that they took the device to the Oval Office.

President Bush is said to have picked it up, saying quietly: 'Thing's a nightmare.'[35]

The device obviously generated huge interest among the experts. Some time later, two of them said it was 'perhaps the most nefarious and dangerous' of all the chemical and biological weapons designs produced by jihadi terror groups. 'Equally troubling', they concluded, 'it is relatively easy to assemble and deploy if terrorists are able to acquire precursor chemicals of suitable potency', even if 'it is doubtful that deploying such a crude device would truly produce mass casualties.'* Of greater concern was the panic that would follow a poison gas attack under the streets of Manhattan. If successful, it could shut down the New York transport system for weeks and dent the US economy.[37]

Akhil was not immediately detained as the risk to my cover would have been too great.

His eventual arrest in Saudi Arabia weeks later was wrapped up in a general sweep of al-Qaeda sympathizers.** Moheddin, who had been released, called me with the news and said we should go immediately to Akhil's apartment in Bahrain to remove any incriminating evidence. The risk to him was considerable but I could hardly refuse. I was not surprised to find the place ransacked and Akhil's computer gone. Bahrain's intelligence service had already paid a visit.

Saudi security services later recovered a large quantity of cyanide salts and potassium permanganate in a desert retreat near

---

* They noted the poison gas attack in Tokyo, when 'Aum Shinrikyo members disseminated the deadlier sarin nerve agent' that 'resulted in only 12 deaths' despite being carried out on five subway cars during the morning rush hour.[36]
** He would spend about five years in prison before being released.

Riyadh, apparently acquired to test the *mubtakkar*.* As for the four Saudis waiting in Morocco for their orders, they just vanished. None was identified, let alone apprehended.

Although the immediate danger had passed, Western intelligence continued to worry that another plot using the technology was in the works.** After US and British troops entered Iraq, Zawahiri's key reason for holding back no longer applied.[39] My handlers told me later that for years US border agencies were under instructions to look out for Saudis coming into the United States with multi-year travel visas and Morocco entry stamps.

They had every reason to worry. Weeks after the *mubtakkar* plot was called off, Nasir bin Hamid al-Fahd, chief theologian in al-Qaeda's Saudi wing, published a twenty-five-page fatwah seeking to legitimize the use of weapons of mass destruction against the United States. The fatwah was very probably the one Akhil had told me was being prepared to justify a poison gas attack. Part of it read: 'If those engaged in jihad establish that the evil of the infidels can be repelled only by attacking them with weapons of mass destruction in a surprise manner, they may be used even if they annihilate all the infidels.'[40]

Above all, it was about an eye for an eye. Al-Fahd argued the United States was responsible for the deaths of millions of Muslims and so 'it is permissible [to strike them with WMD] merely on the

* I was told this by my British intelligence handlers. In his memoir CIA director George Tenet stated cyanide was found in a terrorist safe house in Saudi Arabia during raids by Saudi security forces in the spring/summer of 2003 making clear 'their interest in using cyanide weapons in future attacks'.[38]

** On 26 March 2003, the FBI issued an intelligence bulletin on the threat from chemical dispersal devices. This bulletin was updated in November 2004 and published in full by a major US news organization. It described the *mubtakkar* in detail and provided a photograph of its component parts. Its conclusion was consistent with other analyses: 'Little or no training is required to assemble and deploy such a device, due to its simplicity. [...] One or more assembled devices could easily be brought aboard a train or subway. These gases would also be effective when released in confined spaces of buildings or other indoor facilities. It is difficult to judge the number of casualties that would result from the use of multiple devices; however, such an attack will likely generate fear and panic among the local population.'

rule of being treated as one has been treated.' He made explicitly clear that women and children were potentially legitimate targets.* For those intent on carrying out WMD attacks, al-Fahd's fatwah was valuable theological cover.**

Bokhowa spent just a few months in prison. It seemed like sympathy for Sunni militants in Bahraini security circles had only increased as a result of anger over the US invasion of Iraq. When he got out he had the temerity to spread the word that he was the inventor of the *mubtakkar* technology. The electronic blueprints he had created – a step-by-step guide for building a chemical weapon – were eventually posted online by the cell and found their way like a virus from one al-Qaeda online forum to the next.*** There was no chance of bottling them once jihadi webmasters had their hands on them.

I spent many hours agonizing over my role in developing the *mubtakkar*. On good days, I would tell myself that I had had no choice but to help Abu Khabab's team perfect the means to develop and deliver it, and that, had I not been there, others would have readily solved the technical challenges that arose. On bad days, I asked myself whether there was anything I could and should have done to delay its progress.

The life of a double agent is rarely simple and never pure; it's one of often unpalatable compromises.

Yusuf al-Ayeri and Osama bin Laden were right about one thing: the US invasion of Iraq would galvanize the global jihadi cause

---

* The fatwah defined WMD as including nuclear, chemical and biological weapons. It was the first time a leading jihadi cleric had provided explicit theological justification for all forms of CBRN weapons.[41]
** Al-Fahd was arrested in Saudi Arabia in May 2003. After six months in custody he appeared on Saudi television annulling his fatwah and expressing remorse for the 'error' of his religious interpretation. Hardline jihadis are likely to dismiss his recantation as extracted under torture. ISIS later claimed the cleric had pledged allegiance to them from prison.[42]
*** The document posted online (file modified date: 2 November 2003) was an eight-page manual with thirty-four diagrams providing instructions on creating the device and possible targets.[43]

across the Middle East and beyond. It would draw in my family in countless ways, inflict doubt and depression on me and even land me in jail. And for the next three years, a squat, streetwise Jordanian who had sat on the hillside at Darunta and marvelled at my interpretation of his dream would be at the heart of it all.

In the early hours of 18 March 2003, hours before US air raids on Baghdad began, there was an unusual visitor to Iraq's Central Bank, an austere cube-shaped building rising several storeys above al-Rasheed Street. His name was Qusay Saddam Hussein.

Qusay was carrying a letter from the Iraqi dictator which instructed the bank to hand over a cool $900 million in cash. In an operation that lasted several hours the money was carried from the vaults. It was presumably intended to finance resistance to US forces.[44] Intelligence reports suggested the trucks travelled north towards the Syrian border. But somewhere along the way, one was either intercepted by, or handed over to, a resistance group led by Abu Musab al-Zarqawi.*

Zarqawi later boasted he had witnessed the heist of the heist and that his men had removed more than $340 million from Qusay's convoy.** That was probably an exaggeration, but with even a fraction of that money, Zarqawi was able to merge dozens of embryonic insurgent groups in Iraq. In the world of Terror Inc., he was the CEO when it came to mergers and acquisitions.

Zarqawi used his millions to buy businesses and farms in Sunni areas of Iraq, part of a plan for a long-term insurgency.[46] He also received invaluable and inadvertent help from the US-run Coalition Provisional Authority. Its dismissal of Baathist civil servants and disbanding of the Iraqi military provided a pool of recruits for Zarqawi's group – now rebranded as *al-Tawhid wa al-Jihad*, or Monotheism and Jihad.

---

* After the US invasion of Afghanistan, Zarqawi had decamped to Iraq's Kurdistan region to prepare for what he believed would be 'a forthcoming battle against the Americans'.[45]
** That was the sum mentioned to me by jihadi contacts.

Zarqawi turbocharged the insurgency. A suicide bombing against the Jordanian embassy in Iraq was followed by a devastating attack on the UN headquarters in Baghdad and the beheading of American citizen Nick Berg. The surge in suicide bombings owed much to the influence of Sheikh Abu Abdullah al-Muhajir, whom I had challenged about the embassy bombings.* In his sermons in Herat, al-Muhajir, Zarqawi's Rasputin, had provided the Jordanian with the religious justification for an unlimited suicide bombing campaign.[48]

Al-Muhajir's 'thesis' would take the form of a treatise ominously entitled *The Jurisprudence of Blood*, which asserted that all forms of suicide in the name of jihad brought martyrdom. It also called for the killing of Shia, arguing they were a greater threat to Islam than all other enemies, and maintained Islam did not differentiate between the military and civilians in warfare. He wrote that 'the brutality of beheading is intended, even delightful to God and His Prophet,' just one of the many aspects of his teaching that would be embraced by ISIS. After the declaration of the Caliphate, the group made the *The Jurisprudence of Blood* a key part of the curriculum at training camps.**

Zarqawi took sectarian loathing to new depths in Iraq just as the Shia majority reasserted themselves. His group assassinated Ayatollah Muhammad Baqir al-Hakim in a car-bomb attack on 29 August 2003. Al-Hakim was the leader of the Supreme Council of

---

* It was indeed the jurisprudence of blood. According to database maintained by the University of Chicago between 1974 and 1997 about 2,000 people were killed in suicide attacks around the world by a variety of groups. But between 1998 (the year al-Muhajir provided theological cover for the Africa embassy bombings) and 2016, more than 50,000 were killed by suicide attacks, according to the database.[47]

** Copies of *The Jurisprudence of Blood* (also titled *The Jurisprudence of Jihad*) began circulating in Iraq around 2004, just as Zarqawi's insurgency was finding its feet. Also popular among the jihadis in Iraq was another of his books, *The Pioneers of the Victorious Vanguard*. Al-Muhajir escaped to Iran after 9/11, where he was detained. It's not clear what happened to him next. There were reports in the Egyptian media that he was freed in 2011 and returned to Egypt.[49]

the Islamic Revolution of Iraq and one of the most influential Shia figures in Iraq; the driver of the truck bomb was Zarqawi's own father-in-law.[50]

Zarqawi monstrously expanded the definition of Muslims who were apostates, or *murtad*. His followers regarded Shia customs such as worshipping at the graves of imams and public self-flagellation as contrary to the Koran. They also saw the insurgency as validating the prophecy about an army of jihad arising in Iraq.

In targeting the Shia – seen by many Gulf Sunnis as the agents of Iran – Zarqawi appealed to many donors who had abandoned al-Qaeda. Many of them were wealthy Kuwaitis who took advantage of exceptionally lax financial regulation. Clerics and businessmen in Saudi Arabia also sent donations.

Bin Laden was horrified that al-Qaeda in Iraq should expend so much effort on killing other Muslims. But Zarqawi's fighters were battle-hardened – taking on coalition forces in urban combat, designing ever more powerful IEDs, carrying out assassinations and kidnappings. They were the poster boys of jihad, just two years after 9/11.

Al-Qaeda central – by contrast – was hemmed into a corner of Pakistan and running out of money. Friends who had stayed with the group after 9/11 told me stories about selling weapons for food and fuel. Soon the tail was wagging the dog; the smell of money began wafting from Iraq.

Thanks to an unusual family connection, I was able to follow that money as it travelled from Iraq through Iran to the tribal territories of Pakistan and al-Qaeda central's treasury. One of the main couriers was named Abu Hafs al-Baluchi.

Al-Baluchi was an extraordinary character. As the name suggests, his family was from Baluchistan, a wild border region straddling the Iran–Pakistan border. The Iranian part was largely Sunni, dirt-poor and sparsely populated, producing alfalfa and little else.

Al-Baluchi came from the mountainous area of Qasr-e-Qand in the far south-east of Iran. Its hundreds of caves were perfect hiding places for opponents of the security forces. The most promising enterprise for any ambitious teenager in Qasr was smuggling across the Pakistani border, with petrol the product of choice and drugs a close second.

As a young man, al-Baluchi had crossed the Gulf in pursuit of a better life. In a region where the concept of the nation-state is young and often unconvincing, Bahrainis, Baluchis, Saudis and Omanis have mixed and moved for generations. He was given a Bahraini passport and became a police officer before getting into trouble for possession of drugs. He'd also become a devotee of Bob Marley and Rastafarianism and knew the lyrics of all the Jamaican star's songs (surely the only Baluchi who could recite the lyrics of 'One Love').

He'd then mixed with the wrong crowd in Saudi Arabia and in the panic-stricken response post-9/11 ended up in one of the Kingdom's crowded cells. It was there that he met my brother Moheddin.

Jails around the world were (and still are) breeding grounds for militancy; networks were built and relationships formed. Saudi Arabia was no different. In the months before I moved to Bahrain, Moheddin and al-Baluchi were able to call me from prison occasionally, thanks to sympathetic or negligent prison warders, and sometimes asked to have their dreams interpreted. In the few months they were inside together, they became fast friends.

As soon as he was out of jail, al-Baluchi decided he would be better off back in Qasr. He was also aware that a number of senior al-Qaeda figures had been smuggled from Afghanistan into his home province. He began to help with the smuggling operation, but not just to make a profit. By now al-Baluchi was committed to the cause of jihad. Moheddin also got to know some of al-Baluchi's relatives in Bahrain, a connection that only made him even more of a 'person of interest' to the Bahraini authorities.*

Al-Baluchi was always on the move. He knew many of the smugglers who operated between Iran and Pakistan. He also had contacts with Iranian Kurds, another group at odds with the

* Abu Hafs al-Baluchi's brother Jamal al-Baluchi and cousin Issa al-Baluchi were among those arrested in February 2003 after I alerted Western intelligence to the *mubtakkar* plot against New York. To my knowledge they had nothing to do with the plot.

Shia-dominated state. There was essentially a tried and tested rat run between the mountains of Waziristan and Zarqawi's heartland in northern Iraq. Al-Baluchi was the traffic cop – lapping up information that he would share with my brother, which my brother would share with me, which I would share with British intelligence.

Al-Baluchi was one of the conduits through whom a stuttering dialogue was evolving between Zarqawi and Ayman al-Zawahiri. Zarqawi sent a stream of requests – for everything from explosives experts to authorities on Shariah law.* These exchanges were not exactly a meeting of minds. Al-Qaeda's more cerebral leadership was suspicious of the streetwise Jordanian whose group murdered Muslims with the same ferocity that it attacked occupying forces. But there was a larger goal. Jihad had already erupted in Iraq, and US troops had returned to Saudi Arabia, a launching pad for the invasion to topple Saddam Hussein. The efforts of the Saudi government to distance themselves from the preparations were unconvincing amid almost universal public hostility to the war. Bin Laden perceived an historic opportunity.

Late in the evening of 12 May 2003, teams of al-Qaeda gunmen attacked three Western expatriate compounds in the Saudi capital, Riyadh. They first fired on the compounds' gates, allowing vehicles each laden with high explosives to penetrate residential areas. In just a few minutes of carnage thirty-five people were killed, including Americans, an Australian and a Briton.[52]

Yusuf al-Ayeri and Khalid al-Hajj had launched their campaign of terror in earnest. Bin Laden probably imagined it was the first

---

* Not all the couriers made it safely. My friend from Darunta, Hassan Ghul, would be detained in early 2004 as he made his way through northern Iraq carrying correspondence between bin Laden and Zarqawi. The discovery was an early breakthrough in the long road to tracking down bin Laden. Ghul told the CIA a jihadi with the *kunya* Abu Ahmed al-Kuwaiti was an important courier close to bin Laden. The name had already been mentioned by other al-Qaeda detainees, but Ghul's information made the CIA more interested in the name. Identifying, locating and tracking this courier eventually led to bin Laden's Abbottabad compound.[51]

shot in a campaign that would bring down the House of Saud. He would be bitterly disappointed. Al-Ayeri was killed in a shootout with Saudi police just three weeks after the Riyadh attacks, and Khalid took over as leader.[53]

Under his command al-Qaeda launched attacks on Saudi security forces for the first time.[54] As I watched the unfolding insurgency in Saudi Arabia and wondered where Khalid was hiding, I thought continually about our shared childhood. Just over a decade previously, we had celebrated being awarded a poetry trophy by a Saudi prince. Now Khalid was the most wanted man in the Kingdom.

Khalid lasted all of nine months. On 15 March 2004, he was killed in a highway shoot out with Saudi security forces in Riyadh.[55] Saudi Arabia had ramped up its counter-terrorism capabilities and was progressively dismantling al-Qaeda's networks across the country. The wave of violence was not over, but bin Laden had lost his gamble that al-Qaeda could spark an insurgency to topple the monarchy. A new generation of 'unlit candles' angered by the Iraq War had mostly flocked to join Zarqawi's insurgency in Iraq rather than turn their guns on their own people.[56]

I was shocked to see images of Khalid's body riddled with bullets in a black SUV. I thought briefly of our many experiences together, but we had taken different paths. If I felt sadness, it was because his life had been worse than wasted.

A few days after his death, there was a meeting of about a dozen al-Qaeda supporters in Bahrain, and I was asked to offer a few thoughts about his life. I spoke fondly about the romanticism of his jihad, his love of poetry. It was an act, but I felt that I owed my old friend a warm tribute.

'He pursued martyrdom like a lover chasing the object of his desire,' I told them. 'I remember him telling me in Afghanistan that there was an elixir about jihad that sometimes made him think of castrating himself to avoid temptations of the flesh.'

As I spoke, the words echoed in my mind. They could have been a eulogy for me years earlier. But I had come to believe that subscribing to al-Qaeda demanded a blinkered dedication, a lack of inquisitiveness. Khalid's elixir was now a poison to me. I felt I was the true jihadi for turning against al-Qaeda. Once again, Imam Ali's phrase came back to me: '*Loyalty to the treacherous is treachery in the eyes of God. The betrayal of the treacherous is loyalty in the eyes of God.*'

As we ate together afterwards, I was introduced to a young Bahraini called Turki Binali. Only nineteen years old, he would soon enjoy the distinction of being expelled from university in the United Arab Emirates for his militant views.[57] He sneered about the Mujahideen Brigade in Bosnia, which he described as pointless. Somewhat emotional after delivering the eulogy for Khalid, I shot back.

'Brother,' I said, 'I was fighting to defend Muslims at the age of sixteen. You were at school at that age, a pre-pubescent.'

'That doesn't matter. Facts are ageless. Bosnia was not a jihad to establish God's sovereignty over Earth.'

'Of course not,' I retorted. 'It was about saving Muslim lives. The Koran tells us to fight for those who are oppressed and exiled from their homes.'[58]

I thought Binali an arrogant sociopath; later events would validate my perspective. But there was no doubting the anger among militant Salafis on the verge of crossing from word to deed. Thanks to the Iraq War the 'street' across the Middle East was boiling.

One of the men who had attended the memorial for Khalid was Yasser Kamal, the Bahraini militant who would plot to kill me at my nephew's wedding more than a decade later. He had a lithe frame, symmetrical features dominated by large arching eyebrows and a groomed beard which betrayed a certain vanity. His small, dark eyes could flit from friendliness to anger in an instant. For all his charm there was an underlying menace about him. His voice was raspy, as if had smoked forty unfiltered cigarettes in short order.

Kamal was a fishmonger, selling the catch of the day in a van he drove around Manama. But his vocation was jihad, and besides hawking fish he was visiting like-minded members or followers of al-Qaeda.

I had first met him at the al-Nisf mosque in early 2003, weeks before the US invasion of Iraq. He smelled of fish. Within an hour we had established that we had a lot of associates in common, including Abu Zubaydah.

Kamal's journey was a familiar one. He'd been a small-time drugs dealer and petty criminal before finding redemption in jihad, just like al-Zarqawi. He had fought in Kashmir against the Indians, and then moved on to Afghanistan, where he had joined al-Qaeda. But if Zarqawi was an enforcer, Kamal was a salesman and wheeler-dealer. He liked to persuade. He was a bundle of nervous energy and networked like a politician. When we walked outside after prayers, he popped into all the stores, greeting everybody by name. He was constantly befriending people from all walks of life.

Kamal thought he had found a kindred spirit in me; I thought I had found someone who might well interest my handlers. He invited me to his home several times, where I met his brothers Omar and Hamad. Omar had been deported from Saudi Arabia for militant activities; Hamad had been at Tora Bora for al-Qaeda's last stand.

A few weeks after Khalid's death, Kamal arrived at my apartment unannounced.

'Abu al-Abbas,' he greeted me effusively. The salesman was pitching. 'I have thought so much of what you said about Khalid.'

After a few minutes of idle chatter, he surprised me with an invitation.

'Let's go for a drive.'

All of twenty kilometres long, Bahrain didn't offer much in the way of road tours, but we drove out of Manama beyond one of the poorer Shia fishing villages. We reached a stretch of deserted road and he pulled over. The Arabian Gulf merged into the offshore mist; ripples lapped onto the soft sand.

'Leave your phone in the van,' he said.

'Abu al-Abbas,' he said, staring out at the sea, 'do you know how many Americans celebrate New Year's Eve in the cafés and nightclubs in Juffair and on Exhibition Road?'

I didn't need to answer. Maybe hundreds of sailors from the Fifth Fleet would be out on the town. Some hotels had tables set aside for US personnel and expats who worked in Aramco's oil installations across the causeway. Bahrain was also one of the few places in the Gulf where foreigners could find alcohol easily. There was no shortage of targets.

'Look what they're doing in Iraq, massacres in Fallujah.* It's time to hit back. We need to cleanse our lands of the Crusaders,' he said, those dark brown eyes flitting excitedly. 'Brother, I asked you to come here because I have some exciting news. We are in touch with Hamza al-Rabia. He is now head of external operations.'

I was astonished. Neither I nor British intelligence knew that al-Rabia, a veteran Egyptian jihadi, had succeeded 9/11 mastermind Khalid Sheikh Mohammed, who'd been seized in Pakistan the previous year.

Kamal enjoyed a moment of self-importance.

'He's in Iran and is in touch with Sheikh Osama and Zawahiri. He is considering a big operation here and has authorized me to seek your help. He will be sending an envoy soon to provide us with funds and instructions, the same guy he uses to communicate with our brothers in Saudi Arabia. You were with Abu Khabab. We need your expertise on bombs and chemicals. Are you with us?'

'Of course,' I replied immediately.

I did not need to feign excitement. This was a plot that could potentially reveal a much bigger network running high into the al-Qaeda leadership. But at the same time the word 'chemicals' screamed at me. Would I never escape the shadow of the *mubtakkar*?

'Yasser, I just need to ask one thing. This is to target military

* The Americans had just launched a large offensive in the Sunni town near Baghdad after insurgents had strung up the charred bodies of US security contractors on a bridge.

personnel, right? We would try to avoid civilian casualties. I know I am in a minority, but I still struggle with the religious justification for killing civilians, especially our brothers and sisters.'

It might seem counter-intuitive, but I felt that it sometimes helped to show a little independent spirit.

'That is our plan,' he said.

'Then you can rely on my help.'

Kamal stepped forward and hugged me.

'Wait here,' he said, walking back to the vehicle.

He returned with a Koran and asked me to swear on it that I would manufacture the devices for their plot and swear obedience to him as our local leader. I complied without hesitation. I had no problem making the devices. Whether they would work was an entirely different question.

When I got back to my apartment, I encrypted a note requesting a meeting with Freddie and Kevin in Dubai.

'It's never good news when you summon us to Dubai,' said Kevin, giving me a hug as we met in my hotel room.

I explained Kamal's plan, stressing the possibility that chemicals might be involved and warning that although Kamal had spoken about an attack on New Year's Eve it might be fast-tracked. I also revealed al-Rabia's role and the likelihood that he was now based in Iran.

'Wow,' said Freddie. 'I think that trumps your Swift Sword ID.' I thought for a moment he was going to do a *Simpsons* impression.*

'We thought we might at least get a swim in this time,' Kevin said drily. 'But you keep sending us scuttling back to London with your latest discoveries. I can't imagine how the Americans are going to react,' he sighed. 'Probably overreact.'

We talked about the Iranian dimension. There was growing apprehension that Iran was becoming a logistical hub for al-Qaeda, even though it seemed illogical that a Shia Islamic Republic should

---

* After I informed MI6, al-Rabia rocketed up the most wanted list. An FBI official said later that year: 'If there is an attack on the US [then] Hamza Rabia will be responsible. He's head of external operations for Al-Qaeda – an arrogant, nasty guy.'[59]

shelter a Sunni extremist group. Regional enmities could make for strange bedfellows.[60]

MI6 saw the value of spinning out the line and showing patience. The controllers at Vauxhall Cross felt that as the plot was not imminent and I was the bomb-maker there was a measure of insurance. Letting the conspiracy play out could reap a rich crop of intelligence, especially if al-Rabia's envoy were detained when he arrived in Bahrain. Western intelligence might then be able to get crucial information not only on al-Rabia but even on the location of others in al-Qaeda's leadership. The unspoken hope was that some breadcrumb might fall about bin Laden's whereabouts.

It was a relief to spend forty-eight hours in Dubai. It felt like weekend parole. Bahrain was suffocating, emotionally and literally. It was so small that I constantly expected to meet people I would rather avoid. The thousands of concrete buildings held the heat and humidity; their drab uniformity was in stark contrast to the glittering towers of Dubai. And it had been months since I had seen my handlers. I needed reinforcement and encouragement; the stress of being alone and undercover was beginning to weigh on me. Whereas in Afghanistan I had been able to walk alone among the hills to renew my spirits and my sense of self – my true self – working undercover in Bahrain was like being a spy in a goldfish bowl.

As I wandered around one of the Emirate's glitzy air-conditioned malls, it also occurred to me that living on the floor above my brother was making things worse. Even with him – especially with him – I had to be careful never to let my guard drop. The constant need to deceive him and other family members was gnawing at me.

My brother had a growing brood of children. Every weekend his wife came with them across the causeway from Khobar to Bahrain. I had grown close to their third oldest, Ibrahim, who was a lively and generous spirit. Often there would be an impatient knock at the door followed by an excited stream of high-pitched chatter about events at school or his heroics in a game of street football. I indulged his passion for playing hide-and-seek and answered his torrents of questions.

Ibrahim was always inquisitive about the wider world. Even at the age of nine, he was talking about events in Afghanistan and Iraq and begging me to tell stories about my time with the mujahideen. I told him those would have to wait for another day. Given the broiling anger in the region, I feared he might be vulnerable to taking the same path I had, but I was helpless to tell him that the jihadis were now distorting our religion.

I entered a multiplex cinema inside the mall and bought a huge bag of popcorn. I had started to stress-eat without realizing it. For a few glorious hours I watched one movie after another. The tension drained from my body. But after the last credits rolled and my thoughts turned to the early morning flight to Manama, my nerves began to jangle again.

Through the spring of 2004, Kamal introduced me to the other members of the cell. There were about half a dozen in total. His brothers were going to be the suicide bombers. When I asked them over tea after Friday prayers whether they were ready, the older of them said serenely: 'It's our dearest wish.'

Events in Iraq were deepening their yearning to die for their faith.

'Who can deny Abu Musab al-Zarqawi's jihad is but a fulfilment of the prophecies?' Kamal said one day. He quoted the *hadith* I heard many times in the camps of Afghanistan.

*'There will come a time when three armies of Islam shall simultaneously rise, one in the Levant, one in Yemen and one in Iraq.'*[61]

'Next will be Syria and then Yemen,'* he said, matter-of-factly. I was reminded of the same utter certainty of Abu Abdullah al-Maki

---

* It turned out to be the other way around. Al-Qaeda took over large parts of Yemen's tribal areas between 2011 and 2012. Subsequently, al-Qaeda militants, as well as ISIS, established a major presence on the ground in Syria.

when we were listening to Sheikh al-Muhajir speak about how prophecies were being fulfilled.

We hung out like a little gang – praying and eating together. Kamal forbade the cell from talking about the plot while we were in the city. He was obsessive about operational security. Being with the cell was exhausting. I knew one slip could expose me, and the mental energy required to match their level of fanaticism was starting to take a toll.

In mid-May Kamal and I drove out to the quiet beach again. This time he had something even more startling to say.

'Brother, you remember the chemical devices that Yusuf al-Ayeri, God bless his soul, wanted to use?'

'Yes,' I replied.

'What do you need for them?'

'Cyanide salt and acid,' I replied before telling him which kinds. I was alarmed but not surprised at the turn. There was no point lying. He knew Bokhowa, who was now out of jail, and it was likely he had viewed the *mubtakkar* blueprints.

'The acid will be no problem. And I think I can get you the cyanide,' he said. 'What I'm thinking is we set off multiple *mubtakkar* at the entrances and emergency exits of the bars in the Juffair district and on Exhibition Road. We'll kill people as they rush away from the fumes at one entrance to the other. When the survivors flood out and the emergency services arrive, that's when we hit them again – by detonating our explosives on the street. This will maximize the number of Americans we kill, *Insha'allah*,' he said.

'What about Muslims in the area?' I asked.

He had an answer for everything.

'No true Muslims will be in such a place on New Year's Eve.'

His small eyes had darkened, draining them of life, as if anticipating his own death. It was clear he had every intention of being one of the suicide bombers.

It was fortunate that Kamal had come to me. Had I not been in Bahrain he might have asked someone else to build the *mubtakkar* without Western intelligence ever knowing.

As soon as I got back to my apartment, I updated my handlers with a terse, encrypted email. Stay the course came the reply.

Kamal and I met again on the night of 20 June. By now the Gulf summer was at its worst. Beyond the air-conditioned malls, there was scarcely any movement in the daylight hours.

He was unable to contain his excitement. 'I have two pieces of news,' he told me. 'Number one: Hamza al-Rabia's envoy is arriving this next Sunday to bring us funds and to get clarification on the targets we are going to hit. He's coming in from Kish.' Kish was an Iranian island in the Gulf, a short hop by plane from Manama.

I was seized by a sense of urgency. The envoy would likely need to travel back to al-Rabia to get the plans approved. Tracking the unnamed envoy's movements after he came to Bahrain might lead all the way to al-Qaeda's top leaders.[62]

'Number two: I've obtained fifty-five kilograms of cyanide.'

I made an instant calculation: fifty-five kilograms of the cyanide salt I requested would be enough to build ten *mubtakkar*. The only upside was that I would soon get to test the chemicals. I was still in control of the plot, if I could hold my nerve.

I was too astonished at that moment to ask how he had acquired that amount of cyanide. But above all Kamal was an operator. He combined salesmanship with a vast contact list that included the criminal underworld and jihadis in Bahrain and elsewhere. He kept a tattered notebook full of hundreds of phone numbers, which I itched to borrow and photograph.

'Make sure you stay at home on Sunday so I can pick you up. No phones, or anything – you have to come completely clean,' he said. 'Then you can start testing on the chemicals. What will you need?'

'I'll need rabbits and an aquarium. The first thing we'll need to test is if the cyanide you've obtained is poisonous enough. And we do that through digestion,' I said.

'You will have what you need,' he replied with unnerving confidence.

I imagined my encrypted note with the latest information setting off alarm bells in London and probably Washington. Yet it would still be weeks, maybe months, before the plot came to fruition – even if al-Rabia's emissary approved its outlines. As long as I was entrusted with building the devices, we had time.

That night, I lay on my bed trying to work out ways that the cyanide could be seized and Kamal arrested without tipping off al-Qaeda that I was the mole. Without the cyanide, convictions (especially in Bahrain) were unlikely. I even toyed with the idea that Bahraini authorities could pretend that some of the customers for Kamal's fish had gone down with cyanide poisoning as a pretext to make arrests.

An email pinged into my inbox. I took out the comms device, copied and pasted the email and decrypted it.

*Note received. Try find location cyanide ASAP.*

The following day I met Kamal again. I decided that flattery was the smartest approach but expected his well-developed paranoia about security would overcome any fawning.

'Yasser, I'm really impressed. How on earth did you get that amount of cyanide?'

He smiled.

'I have a friend at a shop that makes paint for cars. I'm keeping the barrels at a place near the sea where nobody will find them; the smell of fish would fool any sniffer dog.'

He abruptly stopped talking. His expression suggested he had already told me more than he meant to.

But events were about to overtake us all.

I returned to my apartment to find an encrypted email with instructions to call a UK number from a payphone as soon as possible. Kevin took the call.

'Lawrence, thank goodness.'

'You sound surprised that I'm alive,' I replied.

'No, we needed to let you know something. You and your associates will be getting a visit early tomorrow morning. It's not going to be a social call. Your brother will also be detained. Obviously, don't resist. Rest assured, we will be across everything. But you need to make sure that both apartments are clean – no evidence.'

'I don't understand. I know we can't discuss this now, but it just makes no sense.'

There was a pause at the other end.

'Nor do we, to be honest. Just hang in there, get rid of everything, we'll figure out what's next.'

And that was it. They were less than reassuring words. To be told to 'hang in there' as the Bahraini security services moved to arrest us was hardly a plan, and clearly my handlers were at odds with the decision. So was I: why arrest the cell just days before Hamza al-Rabia's envoy was due in Bahrain? And before I could get access to the cyanide?

The answer to both questions was many thousands of miles away, in the office of the vice president of the United States. Ever since taking office, Cheney had run a parallel intelligence operation to the professionals at the CIA and National Security Agency. He ensured that almost anything related to terrorism, post-9/11, came across his desk.

Informed that a terror cell was plotting an attack against US military personnel in Bahrain, Cheney had personally called the King to demand arrests.* What he apparently did not know was that the British had an informant inside the plot.**

I walked home in the stultifying heat, at first dazed by the

---

* Cheney had close ties with King Hamad al-Khalifa of Bahrain and had visited the country in March 2002 in one of his rare forays abroad. According to another account, the then CIA director, George Tenet, also paid the King of Bahrain a personal visit to pressure him to make arrests.[63]

** I learned about Cheney's phone call from British intelligence later. A Bahraini intelligence official confirmed to me that the arrests had been ordered after Cheney's call to the King. I was told the British had not informed the Americans that the source in Bahrain was actually a double agent inside the terror cell; to do so would have revealed my identity to the CIA. MI6, like any intelligence service, has always been very careful to protect the identity of its sources.

message I had just received, and then focused – almost manically – on what I must do next. Fortunately, Moheddin was not in his apartment. I let myself in with my key and gathered up all the USBs and CD-ROMs I could find. I was reminded as I crept around of my conversation with the MI5 psychologist George. Family or the Firm? Thankfully, my handlers' instructions had resolved the dilemma.

I ran upstairs and extracted the hard drive from my computer, found the comms device with the encryption software and smashed all the electronics into small pieces. I put everything in refuse bags and then went downstairs. Harath, one of Moheddin's young sons, was at home.

'Harath,' I said, trying to sound casual. 'Ice cream if you help your uncle. Take these bags to the garbage dumpster.' I thrust the bags into his hands. 'And don't put them all in the same dumpster.'

He looked somewhat puzzled but didn't complain.

I showered and changed and then brooded, glancing out of the window for signs of police activity. What if the Bahrainis detained me indefinitely and the British were unable or unwilling to persuade them to let me go? I worried, too, about Moheddin: would he be caught up in this dragnet? He had hated his prison spell in Saudi Arabia so much I was concerned he might resist arrest and be shot.

I dozed fitfully through the night, the orange sodium light of the streets printed on the ceiling of my bedroom, the comforting whirr of the air-conditioning drowning out any noise below. Before dawn I wandered into the kitchen and grabbed a large bottle of Coke from the fridge. I might as well have a last drink of something other than water before being arrested.

Something told me that the police operation was imminent. I wandered to the balcony to see about a dozen SUVs swing into the parking area of the apartment complex and disgorge some fifty heavily armed men wearing Kevlar protection and helmets.

But there's just one of me, I thought – this is all a bit excessive. That gentle mockery gave way to a more perturbing thought.

Perhaps they wanted to stage a gun battle in which I was finally brought to justice. In turn, that anxiety gave way to incredulity as the police began demolishing the ground-floor apartment.

What followed was (in retrospect) almost comical. A police captain caught sight of me leaning out of the window and started shouting at me.

'Stay inside! We're arresting dangerous people!'

I was tempted to yell back: 'You've got the wrong apartment! It's me you want.' But I resisted the temptation to humiliate them and instead opened my door so that when eventually they figured out who they wanted they wouldn't need to break it down.

Next I heard a commotion downstairs. It seemed like they were arresting Moheddin. A minute or two later, the same police captain walked in, his hand resting on a revolver in its holster. He asked me to confirm my name. There was no point lying.

'You're under arrest,' he said cuffing me. 'You're going to have to wait outside while we search your apartment.'

To add insult to injury, one of his subordinates had the nerve to say: 'He looks harmless enough.'

Moheddin had been forced to wait further down the stairwell. We exchanged glances of bewilderment. As he had no role in the plot perhaps it was a case of guilt by family association.

For three hours I sat in the stairwell while they ransacked the entire apartment, opening up the sofa and mattress with knives. I knew they'd find nothing.

'Where is your evidence?' I shouted loudly at the senior police officer, playing the part of an angry fundamentalist, though the anger did not demand much acting.

The Bahraini security services had made six arrests.[64] Yasser and his brother Omar were among them. Also caught up in the sweep was the IT engineer Bassam Bokhowa. We were placed in separate cells to await interrogation. Yasser and Bokhowa were in my prison cell. Bokhowa, like my brother, had not been involved in the plot. *Round up the usual suspects*, I thought to myself.

Yasser Kamal was staring at me.

'You look pale and you're really sweating. Are you okay?'

I realized I was soaked with perspiration. I felt a terrible thirst and was overcome by drowsiness. The room started spinning.

The next thing I heard was a loud banging. I was lying on the ground and Yasser Kamal was kicking at the door.

'We need a medic urgently!' he was shouting.

I came round in a hospital bed. My arm hurt; I looked and saw it was connected to an IV drip. My other arm also hurt: it was handcuffed to the bed. I still felt terribly weak. When the room came into focus, I saw no fewer than five heavily armed members of Bahraini's security services standing guard. Some even had their fingers resting on the triggers of their machine guns. Did they think I was Hannibal Lecter? I was hardly in a position to lift myself out of bed, let alone escape.

A doctor walked in. His stern expression suggested that he either loathed treating me or was about to tell me I was dying.

'You're at the King Hamad Military Hospital. We've run blood tests; you have diabetes.'

'I had no idea,' I said.

'It needs to be brought under control. Your blood sugar levels were so high you were in danger of going into shock. We wouldn't want you dying in detention. The human rights people would have a field day,' he said drily.

I lay there, slipping in and out of consciousness, imagining – hoping – that Kevin and Freddie were working the phones and raising hell. But for someone so used to controlling his destiny, not knowing what would come next was worse than the diagnosis of diabetes.

The purgatory lasted thirty-six hours until a police officer entered my hospital room and told me I could go while investigations continued. I wasn't about to tell him that I didn't feel well enough. Dizzy and beyond exhausted, it took me ten minutes to put on my clothes.

I was puzzled about the whole operation. If we were as

dangerous as the Americans asserted, surely we would be held longer than a couple of days. Perhaps the Bahrainis thought they'd rounded up the wrong people. Perhaps MI6 had brought them into the picture and asked for a softly-softly approach, though that seemed unlikely. There were too many mysteries, but one certainty. Unable to reach Kamal, al-Rabia's envoy would abandon his visit. Hopes of detaining or tracking one of al-Qaeda's most important envoys were in tatters.

But at that moment I was too tired to care.

Oblivious to the extensive damage to my apartment, I collapsed onto my mattress; it sagged sadly as some of the stuffing came out. When I woke up, I realized I had no way to send encrypted emails to my handlers; I had smashed all my equipment.

I'd have to be old-school.

I went to a payphone and called an emergency number in London, after wandering the streets to ensure I wasn't being tailed.

'Can you get me out of here? I'm sure you've heard I had a slight health issue.'

Freddie was at the other end, trying to slow me down.

'We need to handle this carefully. You've been put on their no-fly list. We don't want the whole of Bahraini intelligence suspecting you're working for us. Hang in there. We're working on it.' Before ringing off, Freddie said they would contact me on a particular website British intelligence believed was unlikely to be monitored by the Bahraini security services. While the messages would not be encrypted, we could get essential information across by choosing our words carefully.

It was a frustrating limbo. It took me two days to restore my apartment to a liveable state and I was forbidden by the conditions of my bail to leave the country. Nor did I have any sense whether my fellow conspirators suspected me.

On the evening of June 25 our defence lawyers organized a press conference at the headquarters of the Bahrain Society for Human Rights to claim we had been wrongly arrested. I had little choice but to attend. Each of us addressed the reporters in turn. I kept my remarks as brief as possible, imagining how nervous my handlers in London would be when they saw all the coverage. I was now a double agent pretending to be a terrorist and denying being one at the same time. It was enough to make your head spin.

My moods over the next days veered between anxious, angry and sad, punctuated by a sense of relief that at least I was no longer locked in a cell with Yasser Kamal. I was unnerved by the diabetes diagnosis and it took days to find a doctor who could give me decent advice. At times I felt perilously close to losing my self-control, overwhelmed and suffocated by the sheer speed and gravity of events.

There was at least some welcome news. My lawyer was able to recover my British passport from the authorities. I badly wanted to use it.

After two weeks of purgatory, a post on the website said simply Need to leave. It was followed by a jumble of six letters: a flight reservation. I fumbled my way to the British Airways website and plugged in my name and the code. It was for that night.

I am normally quite fastidious when it comes to packing. Not on this occasion. I raced to Manama International Airport, checked in and headed to security.

The immigration officer frowned as he scrutinized my passport.

'You are a Bahraini citizen and you are banned from travelling,' he said.

'Under what authority?' I asked.

He repeated himself and asked me to step away. I returned to the BA desk and explained what had happened before finding a payphone. I was desperate and blew the normal protocols to the wind.

'We'll sort it out. Watch the website,' was the curt reply.

A few hours later, the message came through. 'It's handled.'

For the second time in as many days I presented myself at

passport control. The sound of a stamp in my passport could have been symphony. Almost light-headed, I walked through the concourse and with a rush of relief onto the waiting plane.

I would later learn that, under huge pressure from the Americans,[65] the Bahrainis were about to rearrest the cell and my handlers needed to get me out of Dodge. Having me out of circulation for a few weeks was tolerable; losing me for months to the vagaries of the Bahraini legal system was out of the question.

Freddie and Kevin met me at Heathrow. They looked anxious and even a little sheepish. They were clearly expecting a tirade from Lawrence. By the time we were in a hotel suite in west London, I was ready to deliver it.

'I thought I was working for a professional organization. Why was my brother arrested but not Yasser's brother Hamad, who was going to be one of the suicide bombers? Why did this happen when I was just days away from meeting Hamza al-Rabia's envoy?'*

I rarely swear – at anyone – but this time the gloves were off. 'Could you not have waited five more fucking days? It was six months from being carried out and I was the one tasked with building the bombs. We had total control over the plot.'

Freddie attempted to explain.

'Our liaison people in Bahrain were doing everything we could to get the Bahrainis to hold off. We knew there could be a treasure trove of information and wanted to let this play out. But Dick Cheney picked up the phone and called the King of Bahrain and demanded the arrests.'

'Why did you tell the Americans about the plot if you knew they were going to overreact?'

'There are rules and conventions about intelligence sharing,' Freddie replied. 'You can only pick and choose so much.'

---

* Al-Rabia would be killed in a US drone strike in Pakistan in late 2005.[66]

Kevin was studiously examining his notepad and remained silent. MI6, he clearly thought, owned this one.

Freddie pressed on: 'We can't sit on information like this. And we can't control the intelligence once it reaches them.* Yes, they overreacted and compromised our operation. Representations will be made, but if the White House decides to take action it's way beyond the pay grade of even our director.'**

'Well, thanks at least for the warning,' I shot back. 'I hope no one minds that fifty-five kilograms of cyanide is sitting by the sea in Bahrain.'

To the best of my knowledge, the cyanide was never found. I still brood about the missed opportunities to this day.

Kamal and the others were rearrested on 14 July. The conspirators had computer files on how to 'make weapons, explosives, poison and chemical substances', the Interior Ministry said. The files, I was later told, had been recovered from Kamal's computer.

Anonymous sources briefed the media that a British citizen had been sent to the UK for 'medical treatment' and Bahrain would 'ask Britain to either extradite Ali or try him there'.

Yet within a few months, a judge ordered the release of the suspects, dropping terrorism charges against two and releasing four, including my brother, on bail,[68] prompting the US embassy to complain that the decision 'sends the wrong signal on [Bahrain's] commitment to fighting the war on terrorism'.

US diplomatic cables also said that senior Bahraini officials 'have complained of the lack of hard evidence against the suspects'.[69] This was scarcely credible given the Bahrainis' earlier declaration about the computers.

Nevertheless, I enjoyed the irony. The White House itself had

* Under the 'Five Eyes' agreement, the intelligence agencies of Britain, the United States, Australia, New Zealand and Canada share a significant amount of intelligence.
** When details about the operation were later leaked, the leaker had the temerity to describe the informant as a CIA asset.[67]

demanded arrests before sufficient evidence could be gathered. Only Yasser Kamal went back to jail, and that was because he had fled the court house during a September hearing (amazing in itself), rather than on terrorism charges.*

The Americans were apoplectic about the judge's decision. A secret diplomatic cable sent on 6 November complained that 'Bahraini officials from Prime Minister Khalifa and Crown Prince Salman down have told us that the GOB [Government of Bahrain] would conduct a thorough investigation and aggressive prosecution of the case.' The releases had 'shaken our confidence that Bahrain is with us in the global war on terror', the cable stated.

US Deputy Secretary of State Richard Armitage was dispatched to Bahrain to warn the Bahrainis that 'by not aggressively pursuing this case, they will put into jeopardy further progress' on everything from a free trade agreement to cooperation on counter-terrorism.[71] The Americans were playing hardball with the Bahrainis, as they did with other Gulf States seen as insufficiently determined to stamp out terrorism.

I took time to recalibrate. The intelligence services had found me an apartment in Oxford, in a quiet side street near the railway station. Part of me still yearned to become an academic, and I felt a real affinity for the city and its air of learning. I walked its cobbled streets, through the Covered Market and the meadows along the river Isis, peered with envy into the cloistered quadrangles.

It took time to recover from the intense stress of the Bahrain operation, and I worried about Moheddin. I was still learning to cope with diabetes. Waves of anxiety troubled my nights as I slowly released myself from immersion in conspiracies and chemical weapons. The intelligence services were happy to let me graze for a while. They occasionally checked on my wellbeing but realized they were close to burning out an asset.

My respite would not last long.

---

* Kamal was released in January 2005. The terrorism charges against him were only lifted on constitutional grounds the following year.[70]

# MY EIGHTH LIFE: NICOTINE

## 2004–2005

The fiasco of the US occupation of Iraq had become a recruiting sergeant for al-Qaeda. It was breeding a second generation of jihadis, two decades after the first Arabs had gone to Afghanistan, ten years after Bosnia. Deep networks of militancy now spanned the globe. I was beginning to find out just how deep.

When I wasn't in Bahrain my work for MI5 took me to mosques in poorer parts of England – mainly in London and the West Midlands. I was careful not to look as if I was sniffing around. I would wait for an invitation from someone I had known in Bosnia or Afghanistan.

In late 2003, there was a buzz among militants in the English Midlands. Anwar al-Awlaki was coming to speak, and I was invited. I thought I should take stock of this rising star of the jihadi movement.* Awlaki at that time was not a priority for British intelligence, even though he had left the US complaining of harassment after 9/11.

Born in New Mexico to Yemeni parents, Awlaki had spent most of his college years in the US, and had developed a slick intellectual justification for jihad in the face of 'Judeo-Christian

---

\* It's difficult to overestimate the influence of Awlaki. He returned to live permanently in Yemen in 2004 and would go on to play a key role in al-Qaeda's affiliate there, masterminding terrorist plots against American passenger jets. Over the next ten years, his online sermons and lectures would inspire literally dozens of terrorist attacks and plots in the West.

hegemony'. His honeyed tones and careful reasoning made the argument even more persuasive to his doting audience.

And so I ended up one damp evening in the scruffy town of Dudley. In a large room above a shop that had closed long ago, Awlaki gave a performance that both impressed and alarmed me.

'I want to make it very clear,' he began, his rimless spectacles glinting in the lights, 'that anything I say is not an exhortation nor an invitation to violence against an individual or society or state.'*

Except that it was; he'd just played his 'Get Out of Jail Free Card' first before whipping up his audience by selectively quoting Islamic scholars.

'Muslims will never experience peace unless jihad is established because the harm of the enemy can only be stopped through jihad. No peaceful means will deliver that,' he said. There were murmurs of agreement.

Awlaki talked about a medieval scholar, Ibn Nahhas, who had lived in Egypt at the time of the 'later Crusades' in which he had fought and died for his faith. Ibn Nahhas had essentially written the manifesto for jihad, over five centuries before Qutb refocused the Muslim world's attention on it. I had read passages from the book before battles in Bosnia, seduced by his descriptions of heaven and eternal bliss, the virgins of paradise and rivers of honey and milk.

'His writing is really fabulous,' Awlaki said in his mellifluous tone. 'As Sayyid Qutb said, "Our words are dead until we give them life by our blood." Ibn Nahhas' book is considered the best book on jihad because it's written by a man who walked the talk.'

Awlaki drew parallels between Ibn Nahhas' struggles and the invasions of Iraq and Afghanistan. Several times, he pointed to his audience as if to say: 'These are the rewards that could await you.'

Among Awlaki's audience were three young men at the back of the room. Two were British Pakistanis and the other was of Caribbean descent. They had taken copious notes. I met them briefly as the congregation mingled after the lecture. The most

---

* I later obtained a recording of the lecture in Dudley.

confident of them had slightly plump features and a trimmed beard. He spoke in a Yorkshire accent and introduced himself as Mohammed. He said he'd driven from Leeds, at least 100 miles away, to hear the Sheikh. He was clearly enraptured.

There was nothing especially interesting about the trio, but less than two years later they would together kill dozens of people.[1]

I returned to my car at the end of that evening, past the fish and chip shops and the vandalized bus stops, in a despondent mood. I was beginning to understand why second- and third-generation Muslims in dilapidated inner cities were seduced by Awlaki's message. They felt they were neither English nor Pakistani; they were rootless and probably the victims of real discrimination that made it more difficult for them to find jobs or respect. They were a small minority, but they were an angry and impressionable minority. The mosques and meeting halls they frequented were invariably basic – above shops and warehouses in poor neighbourhoods; no gleaming domes or minarets reaching for the sky. And like Awlaki, the clerics who preached in these places were clever at navigating the line between the rhetoric of condemnation and a call to action. The intelligence services were well aware they had a growing problem – but were playing catch-up.

I told MI5 just how spellbound Awlaki had left his audience and said they'd be well served monitoring the lectures he was giving across the UK.

'At the risk of sounding like a cracked record,' I told Kevin, 'people are fired up by events in Iraq and they're all watching the flood of videos that groups like Zarqawi's are uploading. Everybody in that room has the potential to become a suicide bomber.'*

Throughout 2004, those videos became more commonplace and more grotesque, and authorities seemed to have no way of blocking them. For Zarqawi's group, no outrage seemed too outrageous.

---

* MI5 conducted surveillance outside of Awlaki's remaining lectures in Dudley as a result of what I told them.[2]

On 16 September, his fighters abducted an elderly British engineer, Ken Bigley, and two American colleagues, in Baghdad. They soon posted a video of the three men. The demand for their release was impossible for the Coalition Provisional Authority to meet. They wanted Muslim women held in Iraqi jails to be freed. Amid rumours that female prisoners were being tortured and raped in prison, Zarqawi's group could claim that it was standing up for the 'sisters'.

Within days the terrorists killed the two Americans because the United States refused to negotiate with them. Al-Zarqawi then released another videotape in which Bigley, manacled in a cage, pleaded for Tony Blair to meet the hostage takers' demands.

The British intelligence services launched an intensive operation to locate and rescue Bigley, but at the same time, a parallel initiative to engage the kidnappers through an intermediary began.* A unit within MI5 called G6, which was dedicated to what are known as 'psyops', involved me in efforts to prolong negotiations with Zarqawi's lieutenants. One idea was to recruit Abu Qatada – by then in custody in the UK – in an effort to exploit Zarqawi's admiration of him.

George, the MI5 psychologist, had been assigned to the unit and was liaising with the team in Baghdad leading the negotiations. We had long and often circular discussions about messages sent by al-Zarqawi's group and how the British should reply. As George put it, 'We need to understand their state of mind and for that we need to understand their mindset. You've spent time with Zarqawi so your insights here could make all the difference.'

The wording of the responses was approved by the prime minister and the foreign secretary.

It was surreal, sitting in Oxford on countless calls about how to engage the kidnappers. Did their language indicate they were serious? Were they agitated or angry? What sort of Koranic verses,

---

* This was subsequently acknowledged by then Foreign Secretary Jack Straw.[3]

George asked me, could we cite that might make them think twice about killing an unarmed hostage or an elderly civilian?

MI6 also had an informant inside Zarqawi's group – a priceless asset. A plot was hatched to smuggle Bigley a gun so he could escape. He would be told of an extraction point where he would be picked up. I wasn't informed about the plan till weeks later but would have strenuously argued against it. The negotiations were beginning to gain momentum, and the idea that Bigley – then sixty-two – could have evaded capture and reached a rendezvous point seemed far-fetched.

Sadly, the plan was given the go-ahead. Bigley received the gun from the informant and instructions on where to go. But he was being held in a town called Latafiya, near Baghdad, that he did not know. It must have been confusing for him; eyewitnesses later described him running along a ditch and trying to use walls for cover. But he didn't get far before he was bundled into a car by his captors. No doubt beaten, it seems Bigley told them who had given him the gun.

On 8 October, news broke that Bigley had been beheaded.[4] The informant who provided the gun was also killed.[5] A video showed Bigley sitting in front of his captors in an orange jumpsuit before being gruesomely murdered. It was soon all over the jihadi forums. Judging by the comments being posted, it was being viewed with almost pornographic excitement. With a shudder I was reminded of that dreadful day in Bosnia.

I was appalled; the negotiations had begun to gain momentum only to be shattered by the high-risk rescue mission. I thought a lot in the weeks that followed about the asset whose life had been sacrificed. The world would never know his name.

The episode shook my faith in British intelligence, for which I'd developed the greatest respect over the previous five years. I had a growing sense that they just didn't understand the nature of the 'second-generation' threat at home, nor just how dangerous the situation in Iraq was becoming thanks to the foolhardy invasion. Not only was Zarqawi's insurgency lashing out in all directions, but he was moving towards a Faustian bargain with al-Qaeda central. His money was talking.

I had warned my handlers, based on Moheddin's conversations with Abu Hafs al-Baluchi, that a deal was in the offing: Al-Qaeda would formally back Zarqawi's leadership in Iraq in return for substantial donations to the mothership. For bin Laden, establishing al-Qaeda in Iraq was also key to his ultimate ambition of liberating Jerusalem.[6] For Zarqawi it served two purposes. He was fulfilling a religious obligation to support jihad wherever it was fought, while funnelling money to al-Qaeda and the Taliban would bog down US forces in Afghanistan, distracting Washington from the insurgency in Iraq.

The deal was announced on 17 October 2004. Zarqawi pledged allegiance to bin Laden and al-Qaeda in Iraq was born.[7] The announcement electrified al-Qaeda's rank and file because of the prophecy that an Islamic army would emerge in Iraq near the end of time.

Worse was to come.

'Do you recognize this voice?' a man asked in Arabic.

My stomach turned. It was the last voice on earth I had expected to hear.

'How on earth did you get hold of this number?'

Had my reply sounded anxious?

'You gave it to me in Bahrain.'

It was Yasser Kamal. He had taken his tattered notebook of phone numbers to jail with him. The Bahrainis had apparently not seen fit to examine it, let alone share it with UK intelligence.

'I have to keep this call short. The brothers smuggled a phone to me in jail. There's someone I need you to meet.'

'What's his name?'

'Here's his number. His name is Abu Muslim,' he said. He was either confident that his call was not being monitored or ready to take the risk.

It transpired that Kamal's connection with this Abu Muslim went back several years to when they had fought together in Kashmir against Indian rule of the largely Muslim region. Bonds endured among the far-flung jihadi brotherhood. Abu Muslim, who had tried and failed to join the insurgency in Iraq, had somehow managed to get a question to Kamal: did he know a good bomb-maker or a specialist in poisons and chemicals?

I did not rush to make the call. I needed to think, put together an approach. When I eventually dialled his number, Abu Muslim's voice – alternately gravelly and squeaky – reminded me of the dog Mutley in the cartoon series *Wacky Races*.

'Bruva, I'm glad you called. I want to visit you, soon as possible.'

The accent was pure West Midlands – a thick, almost mournful rendering of the English language.

The next day, two men pulled up outside my apartment building in an old BMW. Abu Muslim was very short with a thick beard and bushy eyebrows that were only magnified by his wire-rimmed spectacles. He seemed to be in his mid-twenties. He excitably embraced me as he walked into my apartment, trailed by a sullen sidekick called Javed.*

'Bruva, before we talk, let's sort the phones, yeah,' Abu Muslim said. Shades of Yasser Kamal, I thought, who was equally obsessive about phones. I wondered how long it would be before I became irritated with 'Bruva' at the beginning of every sentence.

With our cell phones separated from their batteries and SIM cards, we sat down to a meal of lamb and Bukhari rice which I had prepared.

'Bruva, we need your help.' I winced. 'We want to do something in England. It's time to hurt the *kuffar* at home for what they are doing in Iraq.'

---

* Javed is not his real first name.

'It's awful,' I replied.

And I meant it. I was disgusted by events in Iraq, and especially the US Marines' recently launched offensive to take back Fallujah, in the heaviest urban fighting by US forces since Vietnam. Once known as the 'city of the mosques', many of its domes and minarets were being destroyed in the fighting.* Civilians were fleeing and dying.

I had been viewing footage posted online from Fallujah, growing increasingly angry. The Americans were doing what the Serbs had done in Bosnia, I thought bitterly.

I didn't know whether to curse or bless Yasser Kamal for bringing this oaf into my life. He was unbearable but at the same time potentially of great interest to MI5.

Some of the rice had caught in his beard and I was nearly overcome with the urge to laugh. But his next words quickly doused the temptation.

'I'm not interested in bombs. It's poisons I want to do. We heard you were a student of Abu Khabab, and are good at poisons.'

Javed looked on blankly. I wondered if he would react even if I stuck a pin in his cheek.

I took my time to respond, the old tradecraft instinctively coming back to me. Never seem too enthusiastic; don't ask too many questions. After a few seconds shuffling some rice about my plate, I looked at Abu Muslim with as much gravity as I could muster given the state of his beard.

'I need to consider this; let me pray the *Istikhara*,' I said.** 'If my heart is clear I will do it.'

'Of course, of course,' Abu Muslim replied. 'Bruva, we have huge respect for you; we have heard of everything you've done.'

---

* The destruction of many of Fallujah's mosques caused a global outcry. The Coalition blamed the insurgents for using them as firing positions during the fighting. This would become known as the second battle of Fallujah, fought in November and December 2004.[8]
** The *Istikhara* is a prayer seeking God's guidance and for Him to show you the way.

I seriously doubted that.

'We have a place all ready to begin, in a flat in Dudley.'

Dudley again; could life get any better?

As they took their leave, wandering out into the drizzle amid the matted brown leaves, I sighed and rested my forehead against the front door. I knew that events in Iraq were energizing the global jihadi movement. Dismantling a conspiracy in the West Midlands was like using a cork to plug a leak in a dam about to collapse. Was I ready for this?

Three days later, I took the train to London to meet my handlers. As usual I walked a pre-arranged route so that the services' spotters (or probably spotter singular in this time of budget cuts) could be sure that I wasn't being tailed.

After circling Victoria Station twice, I received a text on my phone to tell me it was safe to proceed to the nearby Holiday Inn.

In a bland room copied a million times worldwide, Freddie from MI6 and Kevin from MI5 stood to welcome me. I accepted a Diet Coke and told them of my recent visitors.

Kevin looked as though he wanted to be sick.

'So this happened three days ago? Don't you think you should have told us immediately?'

'I don't think there's much to worry about now. It's not like there's any immediate danger – they want *me* to make the poisons.'

My tone bordered on flippant, and he didn't look persuaded.

'First, we need Abu Muslim's phone number and the exact time he came to visit you. We'll be making some calls,' Freddie said as he reached for his overcoat. 'You're staying the night in London.'

I snapped.

'Actually, I'm not staying the night. I'll give you what you need then I'm getting out of here.'

In truth I was feeling jaundiced; I needed a break.

Suddenly, I found myself berating colleagues I had come to see as friends. I could scarcely understand the tone and force of my own voice; it seemed beyond my control.

'Are you watching what's going on in Fallujah – the civilian casualties? What's the point of me working to prevent these guys from launching an attack when there will be dozens more like them in the weeks and months ahead? Everything America and the UK are doing is simply recruiting more trouble. Do none of you see that?' It was an unfair accusation to level at Kevin and Freddie, but it didn't matter. 'Honestly, I think I'm done.'

To their credit they let me finish. But before I took my leave, Freddie had some parting words.

'Honestly, I understand where you are coming from. There are many people inside government who think it was stupid to invade Iraq. And it's got worse ever since. Take all the time you need. But if there's one thing I'd advise, just for your own health and sanity: stop watching those videos.'

When I returned home that night, I didn't bother turning on the lights. I fell into an uneasy sleep. A mood of deep brooding and utter loneliness set in; for several days I scarcely left home.

A week later I received a house call from George, the shrink from MI5.

'So it seems like the Iraq clusterfuck has produced a bit of a situation,' he said. He'd obviously received a call from Kevin: someone was going off the rails.

'You could say that,' I replied, smiling weakly. Seeing him lifted my spirits, but I also felt embarrassed. I didn't want to be seen as a prima donna. 'I just don't know if I can continue doing this.'

He looked sympathetic.

'I've put my life on hold these last few years to work for the British government. The work has literally made me sick. I have no social life, no friends or colleagues – apart from you and Kevin and Freddie and a few others. The rest of the world thinks I'm a jihadi, which hasn't exactly enhanced my marriage prospects.'

He nodded sympathetically. He must have heard the lament before: *The Service has sucked all the life out of me.* While stewing in my apartment I had even gone so far as to contact my brother

Omar in Khobar to ask him if the family knew of a good marriage match.

'And when I say single I mean very single. I just turned twenty-six and I've never been with a girl. Sure, some of the jihadi lot have offered their sisters in marriage, but there's no way in hell I could bring myself to do that. Lying about who I really am would be cruel and I'm not sure I want to marry into al-Qaeda.'

I was hitting my stride, and like the best of his profession George knew when to listen.

'Being a spy has been a lonely life. It was a price I was willing to pay, but I've really started to question that. Has anybody been listening to anything I've been saying? There are ten thousand British troops in Iraq and all the focus is there. That means Afghanistan's a disaster in waiting, and it plays right into bin Laden's narrative of a war on Islam. I'm monitoring the extremist forums and they're red hot. George, I've never seen jihadis around the world energized like this.'

'A lot of us agree with you,' he replied.

I reprised the theme I'd taken up with Kevin and Freddie.

'It's all so futile. What's the point of me risking my neck to identify terrorists, when Fallujah and Abu Ghraib are creating so many more?'*

George felt he needed to intercede before I disappeared down a rabbit hole.

'Hold on. Futile is the last adjective I would choose to describe your work. You're one of the most important assets in British intelligence. But if you don't feel like you should go on, then don't. I shouldn't really be saying this but you don't owe anybody anything. They owe you.'

There was a long silence. I walked to the window and watched leaves drift from the trees opposite.

'And then,' I said, turning to George, 'there's the Bigley fiasco.'

---

* The full extent of the mistreatment of Iraqi detainees at the US detention facility in Abu Ghraib had become clear earlier that year.

'Believe me, I'm upset, too,' he said. 'I had no idea about the rescue mission. They kept that on a need-to-know. I forced myself to watch the video. It's awful but there's nothing we can do about it now. We were faced with impossible choices. If we hadn't kept them talking, Ken might have been killed before even having a chance to escape.'

We talked for hours. A few days later, when he came to visit again, I asked him if he had any news about my new friend from Dudley, Abu Muslim.

'That's interesting!' he said with a knowing grin. 'You're not ready to quit just yet, are you?'

He studied my reaction for a few moments.

'No,' I replied sheepishly, 'I guess I'm not.'

I realized that without my help Abu Muslim might end up taking innocent lives. Something about him unnerved me.

I might not be able to change the world, but as the Koran says:

'Whoever saved one life it is as if he saved mankind entirely.'[9]

The following day, there was an encrypted message from Freddie.

'Heard you had a good talk with our friend. Come down to London on Tuesday evening. Important meeting – 66 Trafalgar Square.'

66 Trafalgar Square turned out to be the address of Albannach, an expensive restaurant with the finest Scottish menu in London. Freddie and Kevin were sitting with a third man out of earshot from other diners.

I'd never met my handlers outside of hotel rooms in London. After a few years working for the British, I'd told my handlers that I felt such precautions were over-elaborate.

Freddie must have noticed the surprise on my face.

'Don't worry. Vauxhall Cross signed off. Extensive reconnaissance by one particular representative of Her Majesty's Secret

Service has established the Albannach is not a known watering hole for al-Qaeda,' he said, before taking a sip of wine.

'We know you love Scottish food and a dinner out was long overdue,' Kevin said.

Their colleague was called Alastair and was taking over the task of handling me for MI5 from Kevin. He was short, had a ginger goatee and a friendly face, and came across as nerdish.

'*As-Salaam-Alaikum*,' he greeted me.

In near-perfect Arabic Alastair told me how he had taken Arabic studies and fallen in love with the language and culture of the Arab world. He had a particular fascination with medieval Muslim philosophers, but also a deep understanding of the history of the region. That history, he confessed at one point in the conversation, suggested the current British expedition to Iraq might not have been very well thought out.

In the coming years we would spend many hours discussing the more esoteric and obscure aspects of Islamic philosophy. British intelligence had chosen well if it had sought someone who would restore my confidence in the mission.

The pampering did me good. Meeting my handlers in public eased my claustrophobia by expanding the space in which I didn't have to pretend to be a jihadi.

Examining the wine list, Freddie quipped that choosing one particularly fine burgundy would fulfil a life's ambition.

'And what's that?' I enquired.

'Drinking my income tax.'

'That sounds like the ultimate tax refund,' Alastair retorted, laughing. 'But I fear the ladies in accounting would make this your last supper.'

I enjoyed seeing Freddie's enthusiasm and knowledge of vintages, but I was on Diet Coke.

At the end of the evening, Freddie said: 'The top brass would very much like you to come down to Fort Monckton to address the troops.'

Fort Monckton had near-mythical status in the field of

espionage: the training base for Britain's spies for nearly a century. By inviting me they were sending a message: you are one of us. And I had begun to realize that the British government was not a monolith; at least some of the professionals were aghast at the conduct of the Iraq campaign and the missteps of the coalition authority and were prepared to say so. It was the politicians who were screwing it all up.

Fort Monckton had been built to protect the naval harbour of Portsmouth towards the end of the eighteenth century and retains its bastions, moat and drawbridge. It also boasts high razor-wire fences, floodlighting and CCTV cameras. Richard, my first MI6 handler, was there to greet me. He now had a senior role in the agency and had organized for a select group of officials to hear me speak about my missions. We swapped stories and the old camaraderie flooded back.

I stayed in the private quarters of Sir Mansfield Cumming, the legendary early twentieth-century British intelligence chief. I noticed some of his jottings were indented on the green leather top to his mahogany desk. Richard told me I had been given a rare honour, accorded only to Britain's most valuable agents over the decades.

The next day, I went up to London to see Freddie and Alastair with a fresh sense of resolve. It turned out that my living near Oxford railway station was more than just convenient. There were plenty of surveillance cameras in the immediate area – aimed at car thieves and loiterers rather than would-be terrorists. My handlers had obtained CCTV images of the Midlands duo. Abu Muslim's real name was Hamayun Tariq. He was a car mechanic born and raised in Dudley after his family had emigrated from Pakistan. Alarmingly for MI5, he was not on their radar screen as a likely extremist, but West Midlands police were investigating him and his circle for financial fraud.

'It looks like we'll need you to spend some quality time in Dudley,' Freddie told me. How come none of my assignments took me to the French Riviera or the Algarve?

On a bleak winter's morning I took the train north and met Abu Muslim near his home. He was in conspiratorial mood, glancing around him exactly like a secret agent doesn't.

'We have a safe house,' he whispered. 'I'll take you there now, bruva. You'll meet the others.'

He relished uttering the words 'safe house' – as if it made him the real deal. It turned out to be the same cavernous space in the centre of Dudley in which Awlaki had given his lecture the year before. Abu Muslim told me he'd obtained recordings of the 'great Sheikh'. Large bookcases with Islamic texts lined the walls. Dominating the far end of the room was the largest television I had ever seen, on which Abu Muslim's co-conspirators Javed (whom I now called 'Silent but Deadly' for my own amusement) and an equally taciturn 'bruva' I will refer to as Ahmed* were killing each other in some video game.

They reluctantly put down their control pads to greet me. Ahmed, a lanky specimen in his late teens, seemed even surlier than Javed. With the television turned off, I now heard a *nasheed* – a jihadi hymn – on the CD player. The contrast with *Soldier of Fortune* was poignant.

We sat down on some expensive leather couches. I noticed they had what looked like the latest Apple computer sitting on a desk. All purchased from their fraudulent activities, I reflected, which would no doubt also finance our terror plot.

'What's the plan?' I asked.

Abu Muslim held court.

'Sheikh Osama has instructed the Muslims to launch attacks that hurt the West's economy. We want to make an attack with poisons. But we want to do something that will terrify the dirty *Kuffar* bruva. Are you able to make poisons from nicotine?'

'Yes, brother,' I replied.

---

* Not his real first name.

I cast my mind back to Darunta and our experiments with Marlboro Reds. It was a time-consuming process that required several rounds of purification, until the liquid became a paste.

Just a tiny quantity of pure nicotine could kill a person.

I outlined to my trio of collaborators how we had experimented with nicotine poison in Abu Khabab's facility, and gone through more than eighty rabbits in the process.

'I still dream of being chased by rabbits to this day,' I told them. No one laughed.

'So how do we do it?' Abu Muslim asked quickly. He was like a boy about to enter a chemistry lab.

'Well, first,' I said, 'we'll need to buy a lot of cigarettes – the really strong ones. We'll need to mash them in a blender, the biggest we can find,' I told him, before outlining a series of bogus steps that would stand zero chance of producing any poison. 'We'll also need gloves and protective clothing for the next stage, which is to extract the solidified nicotine and refine it.' Just how went deliberately unsaid. I didn't want any freelance efforts in my absence. 'Then the process is repeated. I will recognize the final product when I see it.' (And you won't, I thought.)

There was a moment of silence. Even Javed was paying attention.

'How deadly is it?' Abu Muslim asked, barely able to contain himself. The word 'psychopath' popped into my mind.

'Within two minutes a victim would have breathing problems. Within ten to fifteen minutes they'll likely start to experience organ failure – we're talking lung failure, seizures, cardiac arrest, really painful stuff. Within half an hour to an hour, unless they get the right medical treatment, they'll be dead.'

Abu Muslim's eyes gleamed with excitement.

'Bruva!' he said predictably. 'This is brilliant. The *kuffar* will suffer before they die. It will serve them right for supporting Blair's war.'

In the first weeks of 2005, the nicotine poison plot took shape. Abu Muslim would drive from Dudley to Oxford to pick me up. In his eyes, my stature within al-Qaeda made me a VIP and there was no way he was going to let me take the train. He might be a budding psychopath, but he was sweetness personified with me, enquiring about my diabetes, whether I'd taken my medication and generally fussing over me. Every time he picked me up there was a can of Coke in the cup-holder in case my blood sugar levels dropped.

He had married a Moroccan and his broken Arabic and claims to religious knowledge clearly impressed Javed and Ahmed. After enduring each two-hour car journey listening to him butcher the language of al-Mutanabbi, I considered demanding MI5 double my pay.

The three of them constantly asked me to talk about my days in Afghanistan. I provided snippets about my time in bin Laden's camps, careful to make it seem like I was reluctant to talk about it. Javed and Ahmed were spellbound, their computer games briefly forgotten.

Their plan was to apply nicotine poison on the door handles of expensive cars. Abu Muslim thought it was the perfect way to undermine the British economy as bin Laden had called for.

'Let's go after the fucking rich pricks: Ferraris, Bentleys, Jaguars and Mercedes. If ten or twenty dirty *kuffar* drop dead, it'll drive the price of the cars down and insurance up,' Abu Muslim suggested. It took all my self-control to keep a straight face. The maniacal mechanic seemed to have a rather strong case of car envy as well as pretensions as an economist.

Abu Muslim dispatched Javed and Ahmed to London to select targets and they came back with video footage of expensive cars parked on streets in Chelsea, Knightsbridge and Mayfair. The plan was to recruit additional foot soldiers for the plot. In the first wave, a small group would use the cover of darkness to apply the nicotine poison with a brush to the door handles of expensive cars. A few victims might die the next morning, and more if the medical professionals failed to recognize the very unlikely symptoms. Panic would set in. And then the cell would strike again, creating a crescendo of fear.

Abu Muslim wanted to make enough poison for ten waves of attacks, and to provide other British Islamist extremists with the nicotine poison.*

'If we want to test the poison before we use it what will be the best way?' Abu Muslim asked me on the way to Dudley one frigid February afternoon.

'The same we used in Afghanistan: rabbits,' I replied.

'Then we'll get pet rabbits,' he replied. There was something Pythonesque about the conversation.

'Soon the rich are going to be swapping their Mercedes for Minis. It's gonna cause panic, bruva.'**

In early March the group purchased a large quantity of cigarettes, Pyrex glass containers, protective gloves and other items necessary to prepare the nicotine poison. Alastair from MI5 told me to cut off all contact.

'To protect you the police are going to arrest them for financial crimes,' he told me.

It was rather like prosecuting Al Capone for tax evasion, but the British did not want to expose me. A few days later, Alastair confirmed to me the trio had been arrested and charged with defrauding banks and the post office.

The nicotine plot was thwarted, but just a few weeks later – on 7 July 2005 – terror came to London. Like millions of others I flicked between the live news networks as the horror beneath and on the streets of the city emerged. When MI5 established the identities

---

* The plan was similar to an aspirational poison plot broken up by British security services in 2003. At a flat in London police found traces of an attempt to make nicotine poison and the raw material for ricin, along with equipment needed to produce it. They also found recipes for these two poisons as well as for cyanide and botulinum. Police said the jihadi convicted in connection with the plot discussed smearing nicotine poison on the door handles of cars in London.[10]
** It was not clear whether the senior leadership of al-Qaeda was aware of what was in the works. During the preparations for the attack, Abu Muslim was sometimes in touch with Yasser Kamal, but I don't know how much he told him.

of the plotters they realized that several had been on the edge of their radar screen, but they'd not been seen as dangerous.

When I was shown their photographs, I recognized Mohammad Sidique Khan, Shehzad Tanweer and Germaine Lindsay as the three young men I'd met at the talk given by Anwar al-Awlaki. Both Khan and Tanweer had cropped up during the surveillance of another British terrorist cell that had been broken up but had not been judged priority targets. Khan and Tanweer had left the UK in 2004 to be trained to make explosives by al-Qaeda in the tribal areas of Pakistan. The explosives instructor who taught them how to make the devices used in the London bombings – Marwan Suri – had been another student of Abu Khabab.*

'What you have witnessed now is only the beginning of a string of attacks that will continue and become stronger until you pull your forces out of Afghanistan and Iraq,' Tanweer said in a martyr-dom video.[12]

It was the clearest indication yet that al-Qaeda central was regenerating in the Afghanistan–Pakistan border region. Not long afterwards, al-Qaeda would task another group of British extremists they trained with blowing up over half a dozen trans-atlantic airliners leaving from Heathrow with liquid bombs. The plot, which rivalled 9/11 in ambition, was thwarted the following summer – but a string of other conspiracies using Western recruits trained in the Afghanistan–Pakistan border region would follow.**

Zarqawi had been right. The diversion of US resources away from Afghanistan and his largesse had allowed al-Qaeda to recover. The Taliban had begun what would prove to be a sustained comeback and were now using suicide bombings, having seen

---

* Mohammad Sidique Khan had already made several trips to the Afghanistan–Pakistan region when I encountered him at the Awlaki event, including attending a jihadi training camp in the summer of 2003.[11]
** These plots included the plan by Najibullah Zazi and two other al-Qaeda recruits to bomb the New York subway in 2009.

how devastatingly successful such attacks had proved in Iraq.[13] I summed it up to my handlers: 'Instead of fixing Afghanistan we went into Iraq. Then we broke Iraq. Then Iraq broke Afghanistan.'

Were there missed signals? Western intelligence soon suspected that the brains behind the London bombings was Hamza al-Rabia, who'd been guiding the plot to attack the Fifth Fleet in Bahrain in the summer of 2004. We had, of course, missed the opportunity to capture al-Rabia's envoy; it was an old battle scar that still irritated me. It might have led Western intelligence to al-Rabia and other senior al-Qaeda operatives, perhaps even have disrupted plans for the London attack.*

The British government responded to the attacks by placing Islamist terrorism at the top of its agenda. Prime Minister Tony Blair announced a twelve-point plan to protect the country from further terrorist atrocities. Several of those points, my handlers told me, were developed from brainstorming sessions I had with the services in the immediate aftermath of 7/7. Whether real or imagined, the praise did little to ease my fears that we were now fully immersed in a new era of home-grown jihadi terror – and that Europe was especially vulnerable given its large migrant populations from North Africa, the Middle East and South Asia.

There was also growing evidence – to me – that the security services were overstretched and the court system too lenient in grappling with the problem. I learned within weeks of the July attacks that my Dudley sidekick Abu Muslim had skipped the country and was now believed to be in Pakistan.

After his arrest he had been released on bail without any control order.** At some point MI5 had delegated surveillance to

---

* Hamza al-Rabia's training of foreign recruits 'resulted in the blessed attacks on the British capital', according to a subsequent academic review of al-Qaeda martyr biographies.[14]
** I later learned the Dudley trio had been arrested and bailed on fraud charges weeks earlier than my handlers had led me to believe and had continued plotting with me as they awaited trial. The control order system was introduced in March 2005.[15]

the West Midlands police. The sullen sidekicks, Javed and Ahmed, were both given two-year sentences for fraud. But Abu Muslim failed to turn up for his trial at Wolverhampton Crown Court.[16] He still had his passport and had simply absconded. MI5 blamed the police for not keeping tabs on him. I had not heard the last of him.

On a beautiful autumnal afternoon a few months after the London bombings, I was out walking amongst the fallen leaves on Oxford's Port Meadow when I received an unexpected call from my brother Moheddin in Bahrain. Thankfully he'd stayed out of trouble for more than a year, but he still kept some interesting company. I still struggled to separate loyalty to Moheddin from my role in passing on much of what he told me to MI6. Sometimes I was less than transparent about my sourcing with British intelligence. I was not going to tell them anything that would implicate him.

'Ali,' he said, 'there's someone who'd like to meet you. He says it's important.'

'If it's Yasser Kamal,' I replied, 'that's not smart. It would put all of us on the radar again.'

As far as Moheddin knew, I was still devoted to the cause, living among the *kuffar* under sufferance.

'No, no,' he said. 'Abu Hafs al-Baluchi.'

Zarqawi's courier and sometime Bob Marley fan. Of all the people I wanted to meet, al-Baluchi was up there.

'Really?' I didn't have to feign surprise. 'I don't think I can get to Baluchistan without getting into trouble.'

'No, no,' Moheddin laughed. 'He's coming to Bahrain – the week after next.'

I told MI6 I had the opportunity to meet one of al-Qaeda's Iranian couriers, and they were all too happy to prise me away from domestic duties. The insurgency led by Zarqawi had turned the Sunni 'triangle' north and west of Baghdad into a state of war.

The US occupation, supported by an increasingly anxious British government, was unravelling.

'But,' I asked Freddie from MI6, 'how about my going back to Bahrain after a less than dignified departure last year?'

'The slate's clean,' he replied. 'You won't be harassed. Words have been exchanged.'

Even so, passing through immigration in Manama, my palms felt rather moist.

Moheddin arranged for me to meet al-Baluchi discreetly in a suburban mosque. Al-Baluchi was an elegant if stocky man, with a dark beard that was just beginning to show traces of grey. I guessed he was in his mid-thirties. I was impressed by how calm and relaxed he was. He had an impish sense of humour, frequently cracking jokes about his itinerant existence (an occupational necessity) and slapping his thigh in the process.

'What about Bob Marley?' I asked, joining in the levity.

A wistful look crossed his face.

'*Haram*,' he said with a note of regret. In the astringent world of Sunni jihadism, 'No Woman No Cry' was beyond the pale.

He told me about his job quite openly. He clearly had no doubts that I was still a committed jihadi. The traffic he supervised spent days or even weeks crossing Iran. At one end were remote border posts into Pakistan or Afghanistan, places with mysteriously exotic names like Taftan or Zaranj. At the other were mountain passes between Kurdish parts of northern Iran and Kurdish parts of northern Iraq. The city of Isfahan, a historic crossroads in central Iran, was the hub – where messengers would meet and transfers of money, letters and people would take place in smoke-filled coffee shops and safe houses. The security services of the Islamic Republic were unable or perhaps unwilling to interrupt the traffic.

'You would not believe the money passing through,' he told me mischievously. 'Large bags of cash, almost always dollars – is coming from Zarqawi's people on their way to Zawahiri and al-Qaeda's treasury.* Millions of dollars are flowing in from private donors in the Gulf to the Iraqi brothers, but I don't know how they have so much money left over while fighting the Americans.'**

This was a cue for another burst of laughter. But the consequences were deadly serious. From what I could gather, well over a million dollars had been transferred from Iraq to al-Qaeda 'Central' in the previous eighteen months; it had helped revive jihad in Afghanistan and was laying the foundations for al-Qaeda's operations in Yemen.

After a while I felt it prudent not to seek any more details.

'But tell me, what did you want to see me about?'

Al-Baluchi knew plenty about me.

'You worked with Abu Khabab, right? There may be some interest in your experiments in poisons.'

I looked puzzled; I was. But al-Baluchi had ambitions for the Baluchi cause. Two years previously, a young Baluchi nationalist called Abdul Maliq al-Rigi had formed a militant Sunni group called Jundullah to fight the Iranian state. Now he was looking for unconventional ways to take on the enemy.***

'It's very difficult to be successful with poisons unless you are qualified and experienced,' I told al-Baluchi. 'But I'll give you some formulae.'

---

* The degree to which al-Qaeda's senior leadership in the Afghanistan–Pakistan region had grown dependent on Zarqawi for funding was made clear in a letter Zawahiri sent al-Zarqawi in July 2005: 'Many of the lines have been cut off. Because of this, we need a payment while new lines are being opened. So, if you're capable of sending a payment of approximately one hundred thousand, we'll be very grateful to you.'[17]
** According to a classified June 2006 US government report, insurgent groups in Iraq relied in part on funds coming into the country from foreign donors and other sources until 2004, but in the years that followed became self-sustaining financially. The report stated that by 2006 insurgent groups were raising up to $200 million a year from oil smuggling, kidnapping and other forms of criminal activity in Iraq, potentially providing them with 'surplus funds with which to support other terrorist organizations outside of Iraq'.[18]
*** Al-Rigi was later captured and executed.[19]

I did, and al-Baluchi scribbled down the details. But each one of my recipes omitted a crucial step. I wanted to be sure Jundullah never devised its own WMD programme.

'There's another matter,' said al-Baluchi before we parted. 'Zarqawi is looking for you.'

For a searing split second I imagined he had somehow suspected that I was a spy.

'What?' I asked, stepping back with an incredulous look.

'He remembers a young Bahraini who wore glasses and was good at interpreting dreams. We worked out it must be you. He wants you to join him in Iraq, as a spiritual adviser.'

I was flattered and appalled in equal measure. The invitation made me seriously important in the eyes of al-Baluchi and burnished my jihadi credentials. But it also posed a delicate problem. The answer: play for time.

'You'll excuse my surprise,' I said. 'I'd have to sort out a few things here and then work out how to get to Iraq. It may take a few weeks.'

While joining Zarqawi would have given me the sort of access that Western intelligence craved and possibly brought his murderous sectarian campaign to an end sooner, it would have also used up my remaining lives as 'the cat' – and more besides. I thought immediately of the informant who had lost his life – no doubt after being tortured – in the failed attempt to rescue Ken Bigley.

I had no intention of spending my last days holed up in a safe house in Iraq's Sunni Triangle, with people who made my old acquaintances in al-Qaeda look like reasonable moderates. I just hoped that al-Baluchi would forget about the invitation and move on to more pressing business.

When I returned to London, my British handlers were obviously fascinated and not a little tempted by the Zarqawi offer but agreed that the risks were hideous. As one of them put it, 'There's no way we could extricate you; and you could be killed by any one of a dozen parties. We'd never know.' Events would soon prove that in this instance discretion was indeed the better part of valour.

Over the next few months, Zarqawi's campaign of sectarian murder reached new heights. The number of Iraqi civilians killed rose eighty percent in the first six months of 2006,[20] and the attack on one of Shia Islam's most revered shrines, the Askari Mosque in Samarra, threatened to tear Iraq apart in an orgy of bloodletting.

On the morning of 7 June 2006, a US Predator drone picked up a 'person of interest' being driven through Baghdad. His name was Sheikh Abd al-Rahman and he was Zarqawi's spiritual adviser. He was heading north out of Baghdad into Diyala province. The car stopped and he climbed into a truck. Al-Rahman, an interrogation of a detainee had revealed, visited Zarqawi every ten days or so – and the available intelligence put the AQI leader in Diyala, a province towards which the truck was now travelling.

In the town of Baquba, al-Rahman changed vehicles again – getting into a white pickup truck that drove to a nondescript square house near the town of Hibhib. By now dusk was approaching – but not before a US drone observed a man of heavy build in front of the house. It was Zarqawi.[21]

Minutes later, an F-16 dropped laser-guided bombs on the house. Zarqawi was mortally wounded. His young second wife was also killed in the strike. (His first wife, a Jordanian, did not even know of her existence and was reportedly very displeased.) Zarqawi's death did not mean the end of the insurgency that had taken so many American and Iraqi lives. But it was a major breakthrough: Zarqawi was beyond doubt the most dangerous and powerful terror leader on earth in 2006.

There were other signs of progress. Many of al-Qaeda's senior figures were scattered to the four winds or dead; others languished in US detention at Guantánamo Bay. Few of what I called the 'Bosnia generation' posed any further threat. In the UK, Abu Qatada and the hook-handed Abu Hamza al-Masri were in detention. Abu Musab al-Suri, whose strategic acumen and fascination with WMD had so concerned Western intelligence, was under lock and key after being arrested in Pakistan.\* I had disrupted one potentially dangerous plot – the nicotine conspiracy – and provided plenty of intelligence on other militants in Britain.

My handlers suggested I take a few days off to celebrate Zarqawi's demise. I planned my first real vacation since becoming a spy.

It would not go according to plan.

Eleven days after Zarqawi's death, I was on a pleasure boat easing through the rippling waters of the River Seine. Ahead was the majesty of Notre-Dame Cathedral, on each bank the bustling café society of Paris on a summer Sunday. I leaned against the railings of the upper deck. Children chattered or gazed at the churning wake of the boat; the usual cast of tourists from around the world brandished cameras or lazed in the warm sunshine. It all felt vaguely surreal. Just weeks earlier, I had been tracking large sums headed to al-Qaeda's coffers from Iraq and eavesdropping on Britain's jihadi fraternities. But nearly eight years working for British intelligence had left me drained.

Soon we would be docking near the Hôtel de Ville. I anticipated watching the world go by sitting on the terrace of a café, a leisurely stroll through the flower market. I was still getting used to having nothing on my schedule.

I felt my phone vibrate and pulled it out. The text, black on green, was difficult to read in the bright sunlight. I cupped my hand over the device.

*Brother go into hiding there is a spy among us.*

I scrolled down.

*Go read Time website now.*

I immediately recognized the source from the number: someone closely associated with al-Qaeda in Bahrain. He was someone I had fought alongside in Bosnia, someone I trusted and who (I

---

\* Al-Suri was detained in the Pakistani city of Quetta in October 2005. He was held in secret by the CIA and then transferred into the custody of the Assad regime in Syria. His current status is unknown.[22]

thought) trusted me. I was puzzled but also alarmed; there was an urgency about the text that worried me. I read it again – perhaps it was a sick joke. Not likely: this was not someone given to pranks. And here I was, stranded on a boat making its unhurried way to moorings some fifteen minutes away.

I turned over the possibilities in my brain – too quickly to give any one of them real scrutiny. I read the text again, grasped at the reassurance that at least I wasn't being accused of being the spy. Then again, perhaps it was a ruse to flush me out. Every possibility spewed more.

The passengers descended the stairs to the cobblestone dock in slow motion. They would go on with their vacations, laugh over dinner and a glass of wine, sleep soundly. I had to get out.

I almost ran in search of a café with Internet access: this one closed, the next occupied. Finally, after what seemed an odyssey, I found a quiet place in a side street off the Voie Georges-Pompidou. Such was the rush of my fingers that it took three attempts to access the *Time* website. The bold type of the headline leapt from the screen.

> ### Exclusive Book Excerpt: How an Al-Qaeda Cell
> ### Planned a Poison-Gas Attack on the N.Y. Subway

A wave of nausea swept through my body. I had to slow down, read carefully, and above all think clearly.

'Al-Qaeda terrorists came within 45 days of attacking the New York subway system with a lethal gas similar to that used in Nazi death camps,' proclaimed the opening sentence.

The 2003 *mubtakkar* plot.

'Over the previous six months,' the report went on, 'US agents had been receiving accurate tips from a man the writer identifies simply as Ali, a management-level al-Qaeda operative.'

Ali was my birth name. Sure, there were a few Alis among the dozens of al-Qaeda sympathizers in Bahrain and Saudi Arabia. But

I was probably the only one with intimate knowledge of the *mubtakkar*.

The *Time* report was an extract from a book, *The One Percent Doctrine*, by Pulitzer Prize-winning American journalist Ron Suskind, to be published just two days later.[23]

'US intelligence got its first inkling of the plot from the contents of a laptop computer belonging to a Bahraini jihadist captured in Saudi Arabia early in 2003,' the article continued. That was the laptop found on Bokhowa when he was stopped on the causeway. I grasped for comfort. Plenty of others also knew him, I calculated, and a few had been less than discreet in discussing the details of the plot.

I was astonished that such sensitive intelligence could have been leaked. But my surprise was soon overtaken by shock and disbelief, and a deep sense of foreboding.

The excerpt continued that Ali was 'aware of the plot [and] identified the key man as bin Laden's top operative on the Arabian Peninsula, Yusuf al-Ayeri, a.k.a. "Swift Sword"'.

I had indeed identified al-Ayeri.

Suskind had described 'Ali' as an informant in four different respects. It was like one of those police sketches of a suspect, I thought. Every paragraph provided another detail about Ali, until the full picture emerged – looking distinctly like me. Even though Suskind's account contained several errors,* in all these strands I was the common denominator. As for whoever had leaked this intelligence, I was stunned that of hundreds of names they could have chosen, they had opted for mine.

I wasn't afraid. Twelve years as a jihadi or spy had bred a

---

* It was of little consolation that the account provided to Suskind by his source or sources contained several factual inaccuracies. Firstly, I worked for British intelligence not the CIA. Secondly, Western intelligence was first alerted to the poison gas plot against New York by me weeks before the blueprints were found on Bokhowa's computer. Thirdly, Zawahiri had already called off the plot by the time Bokhowa was arrested and those blueprints were found. Fourthly, I had been told in some detail about the reasons why Zawahiri called off the plot, and provided this information to my handlers.

certain sangfroid. But I was angry. I looked up from the computer screen and traced the delicate ironwork of the balconies across the street. In three short days I had been captivated by the City of Love, by the bistros and boutiques of its side streets, the wide, leafy boulevards. Now I had to leave, and quickly. I reached for my phone, took one more look at those few words that had changed my life in an instant, and deleted the message without replying to it. Stay out of sight and out of contact.

I dialled a number in the United Kingdom.

'Hello, how can I help?' The female voice was anonymous, bland.

'This is Lawrence, I need to speak with Freddie. It's important.'

'I'll see if I can reach him and have him call you.' And without any pleasantries she hung up.

The minutes dragged by. I ordered another Diet Coke and made sure I was out of earshot of the few customers whiling away their Sunday. My impatience got the better of me and I texted Freddie directly, contravening the normal protocols.

*Pls get back to me. Urgent*, I tapped.

When my phone buzzed on the table three minutes later, I nearly jumped out of my seat.

'This is Freddie. What's happening?' It was reassuring to hear a familiar voice, to have a counsellor.

'Freddie, can you go read the *Time* magazine website, the story on al-Qaeda planning to bomb the New York subway?' I paused, not wishing to sound alarmist but also wanting to convey the urgency of the moment. 'I think we have a problem,' I added.

'Hold on, I'm not at home, give me ten minutes.'

I could hear that he was driving. Probably a relaxed Sunday afternoon with his girlfriend, or returning home after a pub lunch. I felt a flash of envy; Paris had turned solitude into loneliness.

My initial shock was giving way to a sense of clarity. I hailed a taxi and went to my hotel near the Champs-Élysées. I would pack and be ready to leave if told to.

I didn't have to consider my next move for very long.

'Holy shit' were Freddie's first words when I picked up. 'Where the hell did this come from?'

'I have no idea but I'm furious.'

'We need to get you back here quickly. Get the first train from Gare du Nord. We'll meet you at Waterloo.'

I always find that train journeys help contemplation. Perhaps it's the smooth, even motion or the passing tableau of silent countryside that lulls you into reflective mood. On the journey from Paris I had plenty to contemplate. The questions came thick and fast. Would I have to quit espionage? Would the Brits protect me? How long before someone in al-Qaeda put two and two together? What else in the Suskind book could damage me? All I had was the tease of a magazine article.

And what on earth would I do with my life now? There's nothing sadder than a washed-up spy.

I also thought about my family in Saudi Arabia and Bahrain. I might now never be able to see them again.

One question kept resurfacing. Who leaked and why – and just how much?

The train passed into the dark tunnel that would take me under the sea and into England.

Freddie was buried in the sports section of the *Sunday Times* when I stepped down onto Platform 21 at the Waterloo International Terminus. The World Cup was underway in Germany; all of England was transfixed.

'Well, this is all very unfortunate,' he began, indulging his preference for dry understatement.

He could tell I wasn't amused.

Alastair arrived.

'Rest assured, we're going to take care of you,' he said.

'We have no idea how all this emerged,' Freddie continued as we walked to the concourse. 'But it's seriously bad news.

People like you don't exactly walk through our door every day.'

'Where are we going?' I asked. 'What's the plan?'

'We're taking you home, but you're not staying there.'

My minders wanted me to cool my heels somewhere anonymous for a few days. It would not look good if they escorted an agent home only to find out he had been murdered a day or two later. And at that point, there was no knowing whether al-Qaeda had identified me as the mole and had sent someone to kill me. It was very unlikely but not impossible and hardly worth the risk. After all, Abu Muslim knew where I lived; he could have shared that information with anyone.

The journey passed largely in silence. There was little more Freddie or Alastair could tell me and it wasn't the right time to ask about my future. I didn't even know what I wanted.

As internal exiles go, the Randolph Hotel on St Giles' was not entirely disagreeable. A Victorian pile in the heart of Oxford, it was full of fifty-something Americans who were unnecessarily loud at breakfast. The university's students had gone down for their long summer break and the colleges were gearing up for their lucrative summer schools, so the place had a transitory air that suited my mood.

I registered under an assumed name, and there were no questions asked. My account had been 'taken care of'. For the next few days I was one of thousands of commuters trekking into London through England's green and pleasant land. How had a studious boy from Saudi Arabia, deeply immersed in religious history and philosophy, ended up surrounded by bankers and civil servants on the 8:23 A.M. train to London Paddington?

My meetings in the conference rooms of London hotels were sober and ultimately dispiriting. My career in espionage hung in the balance. We read and reread the section on Ali in Suskind's book.[24] We did at least enjoy the passage claiming that the existence of Ali disproved the conventional wisdom that the 'United States does not have any significant human sources – or humint – assets inside al-Qaeda'.

Alastair enjoyed reading aloud that my supposed CIA handlers had contacted me 'through an elaborate set of signals' and that President Bush had been fascinated that I was cooperating with the CIA. He would tease me about cheating on MI6. The account provided to Suskind seemed like a PR campaign for the brilliance of US intelligence, despite the fact it was the British who had recruited, cultivated and run me.

There was an extra detail in the Suskind book that on first reading offered a glimmer of hope. It described Ali as a source from *within Pakistan* (authors' emphasis) 'who was tied tightly into al-Qaeda management'. I had, of course, been in Bahrain at the time of the *mubtakkar* plot, but given the multiple clues to my identity in the Suskind account, my handlers believed the detail did little to mitigate my exposure. I had, after all, spent a great deal of time in Pakistan before 9/11.

For now, my handlers said, there was no question of my going back into the field. They were groping around for alternatives.

'I can't exactly walk into normal life,' I said. 'I have no academic or professional qualifications, unless you count being a jihadi since the age of sixteen.'

'You've always liked books,' Freddie said one day, in a tone of desperation. 'How about getting a job in a bookstore, and we'll make up the difference financially?'

'I don't see myself stacking *Harry Potter* or recommending *Jihad for Dummies*,' I replied with undisguised impatience. 'And I really want to know how this happened. This was information that I provided to you, seriously valuable intelligence. Three years later an American journalist blurts it all out, even says I was working for the CIA. So he's wrong and yet he still ruins my career.'

'Well, we don't have the answers yet,' Alastair said. 'But we suspect the leak came from the White House, from the office of the vice president.'

'Cheney?' I asked incredulously.

'Well, not him necessarily, but someone in his office. That's what we suspect after reading the Suskind book. Most of his information appears to have come from former CIA people and the White House.'

'So let me get this right,' I said. 'I am one of less than a handful of people working inside al-Qaeda for Western governments. I have identified senior leaders, was on the inside of plots in Bahrain, Saudi Arabia, and provided the only intel you have on al-Qaeda's WMD programme. And in my spare time I tracked networks here in England, a job that's even more urgent now.

'And MI6 thought my work so important that you shared it with the CIA, which then took it to the White House, which then gave it to a journalist. Which means you now have one fewer than a handful of agents inside the world's most dangerous terrorist group.'

I was actually quite pleased with my peroration, which was followed by an awkward silence.

'That's not quite the way I'd put it,' Freddie said meekly, not even looking at me.

'Not only that,' I resumed. 'The CIA thought the *mubtakkar* so frightening that they tested it and took a mock-up to the president's desk in the Oval Office. And yet no one seemed to think the guy who supplied the intelligence on where it might be used was worth protecting.'

It was useless. I knew MI6 was not responsible for the leak; there was a bigger play going on. The British liked to show the US they punched above their weight, still brought gold to the table, still knew how to deploy and gather human intelligence better than anyone. In the process, they shared information that was thrown into the roulette wheel of leaks and spin for which the US government was notorious.

It is not clear when exactly the Americans learned my identity. Despite the 'special relationship', British and US intelligence do not, as a general rule, share the identity of key human sources. It is possible the Americans zeroed in on my identity soon after I alerted the British to the *mubtakkar* plot against New York in 2003. But it is more likely that they put the pieces together after the plot against the US Fifth Fleet was thwarted in the summer of 2004. If the Americans had known the British had a double agent inside the cell tasked with making the devices, surely they would not have pressed so hard for quick arrests? After the names of those arrested were published and my repatriation to the UK was reported in the media, the Americans must have twigged (if they had not already) that I was a British spy. I imagine the British likely complained to the Americans that they had compromised an intelligence operation. Perhaps, in doing so, they brought the Americans into the full picture.

Perhaps I should not have been surprised when MI6 officials told me they suspected the leak emanated from Vice President Dick Cheney's office. At the time it was embroiled in a scandal over the leaking of the identity of the covert CIA employee Valerie Plame to an American columnist. Eight months previously, Scooter Libby, Dick Cheney's chief of staff, had been indicted by a federal jury in connection with the leak investigation.*

The price of *this* leak was surely exponentially higher than the Plame case. Besides my life being put in danger, I was still involved in vital work for British intelligence. Not only had I been identifying movers and shakers among the jihadi community in Britain; I also had an inside track on how al-Qaeda was moving money and personnel between Iraq and Afghanistan. Beyond the missions I was already working on, we would lose unknown opportunities to track down terrorists. And there would be plenty of them, in Britain and across Europe, planning and carrying out attacks over the next decade.

In the weeks after my Paris 'moment', my handlers came up with some routine tasks to keep me engaged – going through all the maps, photographs and documents that we had shared over the years, looking for new clues. But I knew my work undercover, in the Gulf and in Britain, had been fatally compromised.

---

* He would later be convicted of obstruction of justice, perjury and making false statements, but would serve no jail time after President George W. Bush commuted his sentence.

MI5 instructed me to spread the word that I was moving overseas and then cut contacts with all the extremist circles in the UK.
The services relocated me to a high-rise apartment near the financial hub of Canary Wharf in London. I woke up every morning
expecting to find that al-Qaeda had denounced me publicly and
called on jihadis everywhere to put me out of circulation. But for
the time being at least there was silence.

In typically British fashion, I was given a good send-off by
current and former MI6 colleagues at Fort Monckton. It was quite
the gathering: I had never seen so many controllers in one place.
The visit ended with a flourish as the laptops and other devices I
had used while serving HM Government were used for target practice on the range.

To complete the erasure of my existence as a spy, I was asked
to dream up a new name, something neutral rather than Arabic. I
suggested Aimen as it could be anything from Pakistani to Irish,
and borrowed half of my grandfather's name, which was Muhideen.
Henceforth, I would be Aimen Dean.

Soon after my ceremonial farewell from British intelligence, I received an unlikely email. It was from George, the
MI5 psychologist. He had not been at Fort Monckton for my
farewell bash, which was a strictly MI6 affair. He asked if we
could meet.

I arrived at an Italian bistro off the Strand on a blustery
evening, the orange-tinted clouds skidding through the sky.

'Goodness, you look just the same,' he said. 'Will you never
age?'

After months of feeling neglected if not rejected, it was comforting to get a warm welcome.

'You have no idea how hard I had to fight to even see you,' he
said. The protocol for British intelligence agencies is to cut contact
to a minimum when agents are being transitioned away from
service.

'I might get into trouble for saying this, but I can't believe the
way you are being treated.'

He looked at me with genuine concern, even anger.

'Their suggestion you work stacking books or in an Oxfam store is an absolute disgrace after all you've done for them. They have to take their share of responsibility for what happened. This is just total bullshit. Just say no to everything they throw at you and leave the rest to me.'

In the weeks and months after my recall to London, I had struggled to come to terms with the transition to 'ordinary life'. I was affronted and deeply wounded by the way I had been 'dropped' – like a striker for whom the goals had dried up – through no fault of my own but, rather, thanks to excessive trust in the American cousins.

I told George that I'd been lonely and disorientated. I could hardly return to the Gulf. I'd probably be jailed in Saudi or murdered in Bahrain, and I was already a known quantity to the Qataris. And in all three places I knew al-Qaeda sympathizers still at large who might have some awkward questions for me.

'I really want to stay here,' I told George. 'It's become my home, but to any prospective employer I'm a blank sheet of paper. My adult life has been rubbed out by al-Qaeda and British intelligence.' For some reason I began to laugh at the absurdity of it all, which appeared to relieve George.

'Anyway, I'm not retreating to some remote hillside like some dissident IRA guy on the run. Obviously, after the publication of the Suskind book, I'm going to keep a low profile. But I'm not going to try to start a new life under a false name I'd never remember and with plastic surgery making me look like Mr Bean.'

I was beginning to enjoy my own gallows humour. The evening revivified me. George was sympathetic, reassuring – and reminded me that, despite everything, I still had plenty to offer. And it was true that to al-Qaeda associates I still seemed to be the 'brother' in deep cover in Europe. Nothing suggested my contacts were yet compromised by revelations in the Suskind book.

As we parted on the Embankment, a brisk breeze blew papery brown leaves in a jig. I shook George's hand.

'If someone in al-Qaeda is able to work out that I am "Ali" and then find me, they have my respect and I'll take my chances,' I said. We shook hands and I walked away towards Temple Underground station.

# MY NINTH LIFE: A GRAVEYARD IN SYRIA

## 2006–2015

For two years I lived in limbo, a vagrant of the spy world. I changed all my contact details and stayed away from jihadi circles in the UK, leaving the impression that I was coming under suspicion and needed to lie low. I spent hours walking besides the Thames, watching the pleasure boats and the dredgers churn through the tea-brown waters. Yet a stay of execution is no more than that. Late in 2008, on one of those November days when it seems impossible that the sun will ever reappear, I received a call from Oliver, a former Controller at MI6. The service needed to talk to me.

I was invited to a quiet café near Trafalgar Square to meet a senior MI6 officer named Rachel, who had supervised my handlers at MI6. I knew it had to be bad news; she didn't leave the office for routine chats. As I walked up Whitehall, mist draped the buildings of government in a hazy grey.

Rachel was accompanied by a junior male MI6 officer who was presumably a note-taker. They were sitting at a corner table looking awkward. I had met Rachel once before and she never failed to make an impression. In her mid-forties, she had intelligent eyes and high cheek bones and reminded me of Vanessa Redgrave. Her patrician tone conveyed authority. The welcome was warm, almost sympathetic, which only confirmed my suspicion that I was not about to hear glad tidings.

'Tea, Aimen?' she asked. I wondered whether the wheels of British foreign policy would ever move without it.

Amid the chink of cups, she readjusted her Hermès scarf, took a briefing note from her handbag and cleared her throat.

'This isn't easy,' she began. 'The Americans have intercepted a message. From Abu Yahya al-Libi.'

Her voice was almost a whisper.

Al-Libi, a Libyan, as his fighting name suggested, was a star inside al-Qaeda, his reputation burnished by a spectacular escape from the US detention facility at Bagram Airbase in Afghanistan three years before.[1]

'Its circulation seems limited,' Rachel continued. 'It's gone to AQ individuals in Saudi, Kuwait and Bahrain. Basically, it says you have betrayed the cause, as it were, and that anyone who encounters you should kill you.'

'As simple as that,' I replied with a hint of irritation.

'But it doesn't order people to hunt you down and kill you,' Rachel added, looking for a silver lining.

'It's a comforting but fine distinction,' I said with a wry smile.

I looked out into the street; a gaggle of schoolchildren on an outing were chatting excitedly. I yearned for their innocent, untroubled life.

For the rest of *my* life I would need to look over my shoulder, and trust to providence that I would not run into the wrong people at the wrong time. As I felt my chest tighten I told myself not to panic. There were steps I could take to reduce the risk.

'Yes, well, clearly we will stay across this,' she continued. 'It does suggest they think you are in the Gulf, which is some comfort. But obviously exercise caution, and I wouldn't think about going home for birthdays or funerals.' The British never could resist a line of understatement.

'I'll obviously need to move again,' I told her, dreading having to return to my apartment in Canary Wharf and pack my life up yet another time.

'Yes, I'm so sorry about that,' she replied.

I feared it would be only a matter of time before the fatwah was spread more widely. With Islamists who had known me still spread out across London, living too long in any one location would be risky.

'How did they work it out?' I asked.

'Someone read the Suskind book, though I'd love to know how they got hold of it in the tribal territories of Pakistan. Not al-Libi, obviously. We are guessing it may have been Adam Gadahn who worked it out.'

Gadahn: the young self-assured Californian I had escorted from Peshawar into Afghanistan exactly ten years earlier. Then barely out of his teens, now he was forging a role as al-Qaeda's mouthpiece, thanks to his perfect English and communications skills.[2]

Not for the first time I felt a stab of anger towards the leaker or leakers who had briefed Ron Suskind. The British still suspected that at least one had been in the office of Vice President Dick Cheney. With two terms nearly completed, many senior officials in the Bush administration were looking forward to lucrative jobs in the private sector or six-figure book deals. I, on the other hand, was on al-Qaeda's list of things to do, thanks to some loose lips in Washington.

The message from al-Libi was delivered to the man who had organized the memorial for my friend Khalid al-Hajj back in 2004 – a Bahraini al-Qaeda operative called Mohammed.* And it was followed by a fatwah issued by someone else who'd been at that meeting: none other than the firebrand cleric Turki Binali. I'd never understood why someone so openly militant and supportive of al-Qaeda had evaded a long jail sentence in Bahrain.

The first thing I did that night was to shave off my beard. When the condensation cleared from the bathroom mirror, the person looking back at me seemed stressed but at least he looked different, maybe even younger.

In the weeks that followed, all my senses were on alert whenever I travelled around London. I deployed my counter-surveillance

---

* During stints in Afghanistan before 9/11, Mohammed had grown close to a number of Libyans in al-Qaeda, including Abu Yahya al-Libi.

training as I walked the streets, sometimes abruptly changing route if I noticed the same person behind me for too long. I carried on using the Underground but avoided the stops and routes I had taken during my Londonistan years. The sense of liberation I had once felt taking public transport was replaced by anxiety. The Tube line south from Waterloo towards Tooting was now out of bounds, as were several lines leading into northern and eastern reaches of the capital. Whenever I was on the Tube I carefully examined the faces around me, watching out for anybody staring my way too intently.

One afternoon, I jumped onto a packed train at High Street Kensington. A heavily bearded Pakistani-looking man boarded the same carriage. I recognized him immediately; he had been one of Babar Ahmad's disciples in the Tooting Circle. I turned away quickly, hoping he hadn't seen me, but when I glanced back he was staring right at me. His momentary puzzlement had turned to anger and he began barging aside passengers to get to me.

I slid out of the train just before the doors closed and hurried down the platform. When I reached the top of the stairs – out of breath – I heard him shouting at me from below. My attempt to lose him had failed. My pulse was racing. At the exit I inserted my travel card into the reader but it spat it out without letting me through. It was like being in a Hitchcock film, my pursuer closing in as I fumbled with my card. I tried again. This time the barrier opened. I surged forward into the arcade and darted into a Boots pharmacy. My training was kicking in; I took cover in the furthest aisle and studied the reflection in the window. I waited there for ten minutes praying he'd not seen me enter the store. It seemed unlikely he'd have a weapon, but there was always the chance he would call up reinforcements.

After ten minutes I moved slowly into the high street until I was sure I'd lost him. My throat was dry. I went into a café and ordered a large Diet Coke to calm myself down. He had looked at me with naked fury. It was clear the fatwah had reached Londonistan.

Not long afterwards, I learned from a contact in Bahrain that it was Yasser Kamal, the cell leader in the Fifth Fleet plot, who had asked Binali for the fatwah against me. Kamal had served just a few months in jail before terror charges against him had been ruled unconstitutional by Bahrain's Supreme Court in 2006.* He was furious to discover (thanks to the Suskind book) that I had been the mole inside the plot and had every intention of liquidating me should the opportunity arise.

If Kamal knew I was the informant, he might get to my brother Moheddin. I had no idea whether they were still in touch. Moheddin had heard the accusations that I was 'Ali' in Suskind's book but refused to believe them. His conspiratorial mindset saw it all as a wicked plot to sow dissension in jihadi ranks.

I wanted to tell Moheddin how and why and when I had abandoned al-Qaeda. In fact, I owed him the explanation. Better to forestall his anger and disappointment with a full confession than allow him to find out another way. That meant going to Bahrain, where Yasser Kamal and others would no doubt like to meet me. It was a risk I had to take.

Not long after my tea party with MI6 in the Strand I flew to Bahrain and booked into a hotel with half-decent security. I called my brother and told him I was on a brief stopover. Could we meet for dinner?

His tone seemed relaxed; I deduced word had not reached him. I proposed a fish restaurant I knew well, a discreet place with private tables. I didn't want flapping ears catching snippets of my confession, nor staring eyes if my brother raised his voice.

---

* The Supreme Court had ruled that Article 157 of the Bahraini penal code under which Kamal and the others were charged was unconstitutional because it criminalized 'thought crimes'. I had mixed feelings about the ruling. On the one hand it was very welcome because it cleared my brother's name. But on the other hand I knew that Kamal had engaged in much more than thought crimes. The premature arrests meant there had not been enough evidence to to catch them red-handed. The ruling was a reflection of the very different standards applied to Sunni and Shia militants in a Kingdom under minority Sunni rule.[3]

I also chose a public place because I hoped it would mute his response.

I arrived early and remained out of sight, ready to move fast should my brother bring along someone else who would like to 'catch up'. Thankfully, he arrived alone and seemed to detect that I was nervous. We talked about family and friends, and then I lowered my voice and recited the lines I had rehearsed.

'There's something you have to know and I don't think it will make you very happy. For several years now I have been an agent for the British government. I lost faith in al-Qaeda. I couldn't stomach the civilian casualties, nor Zarqawi's butchery.'

He stared at me; for a few moments I thought he was going to cry. Instead he looked down as if to gather his thoughts, and then looked at me with a mixture of pity and sympathy.

'I didn't know, but somehow I thought you had left,' he said simply.

I wanted to put the best gloss on my spying.

'Remember that morning in 2004 when we were arrested. I knew they were coming and I got rid of stuff that I feared could have incriminated you.'

He looked both upset and grateful.

'I don't know whether to say thank you or tell you to go away,' he said, almost murmuring. 'But now it makes sense. Harath told me recently that the night before we were arrested you gave him a big bag of stuff and told him to drop it in a dumpster at least three blocks away.'

'That's right,' I said. 'He was a good boy; he was just doing what his uncle said!'

'I felt for sure they'd find some grounds to send me to prison again,' Moheddin said.

'I had to protect you. I don't want to boast, but by 2004 I'd been one side or the other in this treacherous game for years. I could smell the danger. The only reason you can sit at dinner with me now is that I knew what was going on.' I decided to press home the point. 'Imagine – never seeing the boys grow up. Maybe they'd be very different now without their father around.'

He nodded slowly and stared out of the window for a few moments, as if looking for some emotional anchor. But he also wanted to talk about me – to discover for himself where betrayal, self-preservation and conviction intersected.

'Was it also . . .' he began to ask, and hesitated. 'Was it because al-Qaeda didn't know how to use your abilities, your leadership potential? Was it the Egyptians? Did you just get bored?'

He was trying to put the best gloss on my confession, trying to recast my actions as a snub to al-Qaeda for not recognizing my talent. He simply could not bring himself to accept my motivation, my firm belief that I was serving God by turning against al-Qaeda. He still believed the movement's goals were fundamentally sound, even if the likes of Zarqawi had given it a bad name.

I found out from my other brothers in the following months that Moheddin agonized about my decision. He continued to believe that al-Qaeda had simply not understood how to use my talents or keep me busy. He knew better than most that I was quickly bored and given to impulse. He seemed to gloss over or reject the notion that the East Africa bombings and the growing civilian casualties had alienated me from al-Qaeda. I had a 'mistaken' sense of compassion and humanity, in Moheddin's eyes, that had led me to defect to the British.

Moheddin abruptly rejected the fatwah against me, saying it was a political ploy by my enemies. Such was his faith in me – or his immense capacity for denial – that he continued telling me about developments in Gulf jihadi circles.

Al-Qaeda had certainly done a poor job of making the case for the prosecution. Al-Libi's denunciation had a very small circulation and was very sparse; it did not set out a case against me using the evidence of Suskind's book. To some who moved in al-Qaeda's orbit, it seemed I was the victim of an internal power struggle. And Binali was not the most popular figure within al-Qaeda, where he was regarded as an ambitious blowhard.

Even Abu Hafs al-Baluchi had doubts about the fatwah, telling my brother that al-Qaeda had never given me a chance to defend myself. I met him for the final time early in 2009. He had come to Bahrain quite openly and I felt reasonably sure he wouldn't kill me. We took a walk along the shore of the Gulf.

It was a rare blustery day; the normally placid Gulf was choppy, with whitecaps chasing along the shore.

'I've never been so busy,' he said. I privately lamented, not for the first time, that I was no longer on MI6's books. 'I have twenty people helping jihadis from Iraq get to Afghanistan and Pakistan. They are all foreign fighters; there is no place for them in Iraq now these Awakening Councils have turned against the Islamic State.'*

The US surge in Iraq, and powerful Sunni tribes turning against the Islamic State, had disturbed the hornet's nest.

By al-Baluchi's reckoning, his group had helped more than a thousand individuals make the perilous trip across Iran. Some had joined the Taliban in its fight against the US-backed government in Afghanistan. It had taken a million dollars, much of it paid out as bribes in Iran and Pakistan, and an intricate logistical chain to move them.

Many of al-Qaeda's best and brightest – or at least its best survivors – were now all conveniently gathered in one area just as the incoming Obama administration escalated the drone campaign.

Thankfully, al-Baluchi didn't mention recipes for poisons again. Some months earlier he had complained to my brother that the nicotine formula hadn't worked.

'Tell Ali that I send my best wishes – and that the rabbits are still alive,' he had joked.

\*　　　\*　　　\*

* In October 2006, al-Qaeda in Iraq declared itself the Islamic State of Iraq after merging with five other Iraqi insurgent groups. The Awakening Councils were formed in Sunni areas of Iraq, with substantial US support, to turn on the group. For the next four years, the Islamic State of Iraq was under constant pressure, but it survived.[4]

Despite George's support, I had struggled to adapt to life after active service. There was a perverse addiction to the work that made normal life utterly deflating. I was like one of those soldiers who spend months in some remote outpost being fired upon every day or trekking through the jungle behind enemy lines and who later hanker for the danger, hardship and camaraderie of bitter endurance. Occasionally, I would meet former handlers, especially if al-Baluchi had news, but British intelligence liked to keep ex-informants at arm's length.

I also needed to work. I had received a substantial one-off 'pension' when the American leak ended my career, but I was working through it rapidly given the cost of living in London.

In the end, a combination of George, my book-keeping abilities and my knowledge of how al-Qaeda was raising and moving money came to the rescue. A controller at MI6 – one of the most senior officials in the service – had left government to take up a job at a big international bank, which had substantial business in the Middle East. Part of his remit was to analyse political risk in countries where the bank did business (and that was most) and to help it avoid being an unwitting conduit for terrorist cash. He needed help and asked me to become a consultant.

I was almost pathetically grateful for the opportunity. But the deal was nearly unstitched in a moment of absurd theatre. During the due diligence, a woman from MI5's personnel department was gathering information to ensure my suitability for such a role.

At the end of their conversation, one of my handlers added casually, 'Oh, he's diabetic and addicted to Coke.'

Some part of the remark did not register. The woman looked surprised.

'Really? For how long?'

'For as long as we've known him.'

'Did you try to help him kick it?'

'Not really – how he looks after his health is his own affair. It didn't affect his work.'

Only later did the distinction between the Coke in a red can and coke as a white powder become apparent.

My appointment was fortuitous: 'political risk' was about to take on a whole new meaning in the Middle East. In the spring of 2010, it seemed that the Islamic State in Iraq (ISI) was on the ropes. Abu Omar al-Baghdadi, its leader, was killed in a joint Iraqi–US operation, along with another leading member of the group, Abu Ayyub al-Masri.[5]

Most intelligence assessments were that ISI was finished and that al-Qaeda was also on life support, whittled down by the aggressive drone campaign ordered by President Obama and the US Treasury's laser-focused targeting of its finances. Yes, it was still causing trouble in North Africa and Yemen, where its expert bomb-makers were devising imaginative schemes to smuggle bombs aboard Western airliners, but bin Laden was nowhere to be seen. Al-Qaeda was more of a brand than an organization.

Even so, I felt there was a risk of complacency in the corridors of power, especially with the imminent departure of US combat forces from Iraq. My contacts in the region and my understanding of the way the Islamic State in Iraq had evolved suggested it was built to survive against the odds.

My alarm grew late in 2010 when I met Moheddin in Bahrain. 'Abu Hafs al-Baluchi is still the courier,' Moheddin said. We were whispering on the balcony of his apartment while Lebanese pop songs blared from the stereo indoors. Just in case. 'He's carrying messages between Abu Bakr al-Baghdadi and al-Zawahiri.' (Baghdadi had replaced his namesake as the leader of the Islamic State in Iraq.)

At the same time, al-Baluchi was taking a healthy commission from the money flowing between Iraq and Afghanistan to help fund the nascent Baluchi insurgency in Iran.*

---

* That insurgency persisted after the 2010 capture and execution by Iran of Abdul Maliq al-Rigi, the leader of Jundullah. After his death, Abu Hafs al-Baluchi formed another Sunni resistance group, Ansar al-Furqan (Guardians of the Criterion), whose stated aim was 'to topple the Iranian regime and raise

'Baghdadi is trying to persuade Zawahiri that he has a plan to revive the group, but he wants his blessing. It's called "aggressive hibernation".'*

According to al-Baluchi, while suffering, ISI was not exactly on the verge of extinction.

For a start the group was hardly out of money, thanks to bank robberies and extortion rackets that would have made the Cosa Nostra blush. By Baluchi's account, Baghdadi had decided to devote no less than $120 million to buying and building businesses in Sunni parts of Iraq: Baghdad, Mosul, Ramadi, Fallujah, Samarra, Baquba and Tikrit. These businesses had to interact with people – they were cafés, barber shops and grocery stores – and they had to be located near government offices and security facilities such as army bases, prisons and police stations. In this way, they would be able to spy on officials.

The money was spread among dozens of cells. Part of the profits would establish car dealerships and garages to give the group mobility. And part would be spent on buying farms, remote from the surveillance of government agencies.

None of this ambitious plan was committed to paper. Instead, according to al-Baluchi, it resided in Baghdadi's head. This was a man who had learned by heart the Koran and other religious texts; he had a phenomenal memory for detail. It was the first step in a clever plan to gather intelligence for the day that ISI would relaunch the insurgency.

The intelligence came as a shock to my new employers at the bank. The directors shared the consensus view that Iraq had turned a corner and the insurgency was limping towards its demise. The bank was planning substantial investment in what it regarded as a promising market buoyed by recovering oil production. My

---

the word of Allah and lift injustice against the oppressed'. The group appears to have been well resourced, but Iranian authorities announced in 2016 that al-Baluchi (real name: Hesham Azizi) had been killed in a large security sweep the previous year.[6]

* The term in Arabic is *As Sabat Ashetwee*.

contrarian view did not go down well with some managers, but the bank scaled back its commitments to the 'new' Iraq. I later received a personal note from the chairman thanking me for having warned of the perils ahead.

Over the next two years, sources spoke of underground ISI networks in Sunni strongholds frightened by the new Shia hegemony. Sectarian poisons were sinking deeper into Iraq's political fabric. Bombings and assassinations were on the rise, and the government of Nouri al-Maliki was only making matters worse by pursuing a narrowly sectarian agenda.

The foundations that Baghdadi had laid were used to dramatic effect. ISI declared its ambition, renaming itself in April 2013 the 'Islamic State in Iraq and Syria' (ISIS) to take advantage of the latter's collapse into civil war.[7] But it needed to replenish its ranks with hardened fighters and experienced soldiers and bureaucrats; thousands of them were held in maximum security prisons.

The placing of ISI businesses, plus the necessary cash to bribe mid-level (and not so mid-level) officials, was the ace in the hole. On the evening of 21 July 2013, ISIS fighters simultaneously launched raids on the infamous Abu Ghraib prison outside Baghdad and another jail in the capital. Both held senior al-Qaeda members. In one night, ISIS added about a thousand experienced insurgents to its ranks. The raids were precise and devastating. At Abu Ghraib, dozens of mortar shells were fired at prison buildings and then car bombs were detonated to break open entrances, before attackers wearing suicide vests swarmed in.[8]

Transporting, hiding and feeding a growing shadow army of thousands of militants demanded all the preparations that Baghdadi had made. But much of that planning had been done without Western intelligence – or, apparently, the upper echelons of the Iraqi government – hearing a whisper.

Developments in Iraq played out against the background of the Arab Spring, which had fleetingly promised so much. It had been stifled, strangled at birth, by the twin toxins of chaos and then resurgent authoritarianism. Into this vortex stepped the Islamic

State and other jihadi groups, in Syria, Iraq and across much of the Muslim world.

Once again the Arab world seemed incapable of progress. Millions of Muslims sought solace – and answers – in their faith. Political upheaval and conflict, heightened religious awareness and the spread of social media as a propagator all stoked a resurgent passion for Islam. There was also more interest than ever in the Islamic prophecies, among ordinary people and not just jihadis, with one survey suggesting that more than half of Muslims expected to see the arrival of the Mahdi in their lifetime.[9]

Against this background, the emotional and psychological issues of an individual could quickly take a dark turn. I encountered one dramatic example of this while working with a large Belgian construction company involved in building the extension to the Suez Canal. They had contacted me because of my work on 'insider threats' – employees and contractors who might harbour militant Islamist sympathies.

A manager of the company called me to express concern about one of their workers.

'We have an Egyptian engineer,' he said, 'and he seems troubled. He used his computer at work to print out ten pages about prophecies and fighting for the Black Flag.'

I looked at what he'd been researching and called back.

'You need to look a bit deeper into his online activities and what else might be going on in his life,' I told them.

The engineer had recently been divorced. His personal life in turmoil, he had begun communicating with a jihadi group in Sinai, the vast tract of desert adjoining the Canal. They were telling him that they were the instruments of God's will, and he could not resist what had been prophesied in the Koran. The engineer was clearly being turned, with dangerous implications for the company's personnel and its project in Egypt.

The company dispatched him to Cairo but was apprehensive about informing the authorities, fearing he would disappear forever into the bowels of a high-security prison. It offered him counselling and it worked. The mercy shown – and the opportunity for him to reconsider – put an end to his contacts with the terror group then growing in strength and ambition in northern Sinai.*

By 2013, resurgent jihadism was sending tremors worldwide – from northern Nigeria to the remote deserts of Algeria, the teeming cities of Iraq and Bangladesh. The Syrian civil war was an incubator for militancy – already, jihadi groups were beginning to eclipse more moderate opposition. Governments the world over were scrambling to understand and counter newly minted jihadi networks.

During the Iraq insurgency many militant Salafis believed that it was only a matter of time before jihadi armies would emerge in Yemen and Syria. By early 2013, they were thrilled by the course of history. The black flags literally flew in Iraq, Yemen and Syria. Fighting was still raging in parts of Abyan in Yemen's tribal areas, where al-Qaeda in the Arabian Peninsula – the most potent of all the affiliates – had seized territory in the chaotic aftermath of the Arab Spring. In the eyes of many Muslims, this fulfilled the prophecy that 'from the region of Aden and Abyan 12,000 warriors shall rise to fight for God and His messenger.'[10]

Given the draconian rule of the Assad dynasty in Syria, it had seemed unlikely that the country would become a front for jihad anytime soon. Then in March 2011, in the town of Daraa, the regime had brutally lashed out against teenagers who had spray-painted anti-Assad slogans, and soon the streets of Syria's cities echoed to the chant of '*ash-sha'b yourid isqat al-nithaam*', or 'The people demand the fall of the regime'. Protest invited repression which prompted resistance – and soon that resistance had a jihadi colouring. To groups like al-Qaeda and their supporters, this was galvanizing. The Prophet had foretold that Syria would be the

---

* The group with which he was communicating would in November 2014 pledge its allegiance to ISIS. A qualified engineer in its ranks would have been extremely useful.

epicentre of the end-of-days battles. Not only would the Mahdi's armies congregate in Damascus[11] but Jesus Christ would also descend to the city.[12] Moreover, the Prophet had said the most righteous of all the armies would emerge in Syria (the Levant).

*'If you are alive at that time then join the army of the Levant, for it is the good land of good people.'*[13]

Many Muslims around the world saw the descent of Syria into civil war and the descent of the Arab world into chaos as evidence that these epic battles were already underway. The fall of Ben Ali, Mubarak, and perhaps soon Bashar al-Assad made it seem like the era of 'tyrannical rulers' foretold by the Prophet was coming to a close, making possible the establishment of a new Caliphate and the arrival of the Mahdi. This electrified jihadis around the world.

The Syrian conflict was a rallying call for young Arab (and European) Sunni militants who wanted to join the fight against the Assad regime and its Iranian backers. Two of my own family were among the thousands who made the journey to Syria.

The first was my cousin Abdur Rahman. In May 2013, the family received news that he had been killed while fighting for the al-Qaeda-aligned group Jabhat al-Nusra near Damascus.* Abdur Rahman's death was a watershed for my favourite nephew, Ibrahim, one of Moheddin's sons, with whom just years earlier I had been playing hide-and-seek. Very soon after Abdur Rahman's death he too had gone to Syria. He left a last will and testament, writing that 'the Prophet said go to Syria.'

I was furious with my brothers for not dissuading him and had several heated phone conversations with Moheddin and Omar.

---

* Jabhat al-Nusra first emerged in Syria in 2011 after Abu Bakr al-Baghdadi dispatched a Syrian deputy, Abu Mohammed al-Julani, across the border to build up the group's operations there. In 2013 the group split into two factions. One remained loyal to Baghdadi and was absorbed into a new group called the Islamic State in Iraq and Syria (ISIS). The other maintained its allegiance to Ayman al-Zawahiri and continued to call itself Jabhat al-Nusra (it is now known as Hayat Tahrir al-Sham).

Exasperated, at one point Moheddin said: 'It's his choice. Remember – you went.'

I had no answer to that.

Like Abdur Rahman, Ibrahim had at first joined Jabhat al-Nusra. He'd had a narrow escape when its fighters lost out to the Islamic State in the city of Raqqa.[14] ISIS – or Daesh as it would become known in the Arab world – was rapidly becoming a force to be reckoned with in Syria as well as Iraq. A lot of Nusra fighters joined the newly named ISIS after its leader, Abu Bakr al-Baghdadi, had announced in April 2013 he was taking control of al-Nusra, setting the stage for a bitter split between ISIS and al-Qaeda. Ibrahim told me ISIS was seeking to dominate everything.

I tried to stay in touch with Ibrahim through occasional Skype calls. It was not easy. I encouraged him to join a different Islamist group – concerned that his association with al-Nusra would tar him as a terrorist in the eyes of Western (and not a few Arab) governments. He journeyed through Syria's chaos from Raqqa to Idlib and joined a famous commander, Abu Issa al-Sheikh. And he sent me a photograph of himself brandishing an AK-47, a broad and all-too-innocent smile on his face.

Idlib was the magnet for many jihadis, much of it beyond the Syrian regime's control and accessible via the adjoining border with Turkey. They were of dozens of nationalities, including a growing number of Uighurs – Muslims from the Chinese region of Xinjiang, a vast stretch of mineral-rich desert abutting the Himalayas. It was the Uighurs that brought me an unusual and unexpected assignment.

On a torpid Dubai morning in May 2013, I received a call from a well-placed intermediary for major Chinese companies. We had known each other for several years because of my consultancy work. Her job was to make introductions that would later yield lucrative contracts. Once in a while, she would seek out my thoughts on who was up and who was down in the various royal courts of the Gulf.

On this occasion, she had a rather different client: China's Ministry of Public Security. The Ministry was grappling with militancy among the Uighurs. Officially, Xinjiang was an 'Autonomous Region', but that did not preclude heavy-handed action by the security forces. Riots in 2009 involving clashes between Uighurs and ethnic Han Chinese had left dozens dead.

The Chinese authorities were going to great lengths to dilute the ethnic and religious identity of Uighurs. A towering statue of Mao Zedong overlooked the main square of the oasis city of Kashgar, which was closer to Aleppo than it was to Beijing. The authorities discouraged mainstream Islamic practices such as fasting during Ramadan, and frowned upon men growing beards and women wearing headscarves, to dilute Muslim identity.

The response of hundreds of young Uighurs was to leave – crossing mountain frontiers into Pakistan and Afghanistan. They had a ready sponsor, the Turkistan Islamic Party, which actively supported the Taliban, and soon became a regular fixture in Afghan provinces like Kunar.* Despite never being more than a few hundred, their fighting abilities had an outsize impact. They believed passionately in a global *Ummah*.

'My clients,' said the intermediary in a cool efficient tone, 'want to get a sense of Uighur migration to the Syrian conflict, how it's resourced, the travel flows, you know. I thought you might be able to help.'

I had not given much thought to the 'Uighur factor' in international jihad but was intrigued. It beat writing reports on political risk that appeared to get parked on some virtual shelf by the clients that commissioned them. Even so, I was surprised that after several years out of the espionage business it should be the Chinese rather than the British or another Western power that came calling. It demonstrated how Chinese security and commercial interests were fast expanding throughout South Asia and the Middle East.

---

* The Turkistan Islamic Party (TIP) is the biggest Uighur jihadi group. It built up a significant presence in the tribal areas of Pakistan in the years after 9/11 and subsequently established a significant base of operations in Syria, particularly in Idlib province. Its goal is to create an Islamic State in Xinjiang province in western China and surrounding areas.

'I will be in Dubai next week; perhaps we could meet,' she said.

And a week later, passing drivers might have asked why this odd couple – the Arab man in flowing white robes and the immaculately dressed Chinese woman – were walking among the desert scrub of the United Arab Emirates.

She rattled off a synopsis of the mission as seen by her client.

'You're in Turkey a lot,' she said, 'and that is where we would like to focus. We believe that some Uighur militants are getting support from the Uighur and Turkmen communities in Istanbul. We need to know how much, who's involved, who are the leaders. We've heard that one influential figure was once a student of Abdullah Azzam.* Is it a trickle or a stream and does it threaten to become a flood which will one day return to Beijing?'

The Uighur are a Turkic people; tens of thousands fled China in the 1930s and after the Communist revolution. There was another spate of refugees after the violence flared in Xinjiang in 2009. For a long time, the Turkish authorities had an open-door policy, providing Uighurs with residency almost automatically. Recently, the welcome had become more tentative as China made its objections known. Nevertheless, there were already about 400,000 Uighurs in Turkey, and the numbers were growing.

'We have our spies among the Uighur,' my Chinese guest said, 'but they are not the smartest. We need a sense of how close the ideological links are between them and jihadi groups in Syria. What are the Turks doing? Are they just letting this happen? Are they even encouraging it?'

She got high marks for candour; there were no coded hints in the message.

'I'll need a cover story, something watertight,' I said. 'I can't just roam around the suburbs of Istanbul. And I'll need a guide, someone who knows this scene and speaks Turkish.'

'Figure it out and let us know, within a week,' she responded. 'Money won't be an issue.'

---

* Abdullah Azzam was a Palestinian cleric who played a pivotal role in rallying jihadis to fight against Soviet forces in Afghanistan.

Over the next week, I studied hard – researching where the Uighur community was strongest, reaching out to the few Turkish contacts I could trust. I knew this mission would carry risks of a different sort. The government of Turkey would not want anyone investigating whether it supported Uighurs joining certain groups in Syria. Nor would the tightly knit Turkic community want a Gulf Arab sniffing around.

For a short while I entertained the thought of reviving the Kashmiri food business but realized it would look odd trying to sell such refined products in a lower-middle-class suburb of Istanbul. Even so, the idea prompted another. I could be a Saudi importer looking for ethnic foods. Uighur cuisine was popular in Saudi Arabia, especially its rice and kebabs. *Polu* was one speciality – carrots and chicken fried in oil with onion and then added to rice. It sounds simple, but a truly Uighur *polu* is special.

In my guise as a food entrepreneur I would be seeking out the best Uighur ingredients and chefs for export to the Gulf. Uighur chefs were already working in their dozens in Mecca and Medina. I chose to go in Ramadan, which fell in July. It might seem perverse that I picked the month of fasting for a food tour, but the evening meal of *Iftar* would bring everyone together.

Through a friend of a friend I found an intelligent and discreet Turkish speaker based in Europe who might be helpful. The fact that she was not a Turkish citizen was a bonus; it made her less prone to any retribution by the Turkish authorities. It was quite immaterial that she had also been a finalist in an international beauty contest, wearing the sash and tiara down the runway before turning her mind to getting a university degree.

I will call her Dilay.* I can relate that she was taller than me, with luxuriant raven-coloured hair that cascaded well below her shoulders. When we spoke via Skype, I discovered someone who was self-assured, perceptive and fascinated by my field of work. We chatted amiably for half an hour but I knew that our more serious

* A pseudonym.

conversation had to be face-to-face. This was not going to be a straightforward assignment.

A few days later, Dilay landed in Dubai, greeting me with a gleaming smile, taking off her tinted glasses to reveal eyes that were somewhere between almond and caramel.

'Aimen, so nice to meet you,' she said, extending her long fingers to shake my hand with a gossamer touch.

I was awkward and nervous for the first few minutes in her company. I had rarely been solely in the company of a woman. It didn't help that she was several inches taller than me. But her relaxed, almost careless air quickly put me at ease.

'So,' I said when we arrived at one of Dubai's more exclusive eateries, 'this is rather a sensitive research assignment. I can't tell you who the client is, but it will involve us having – shall we say – false credentials.'

She raised an eyebrow and took a sip of sparkling water.

'Sounds intriguing.'

'Basically, we need to discover whether the Uighur community is getting involved in militancy, whether some of them are trying to get into Syria, whether there's a pipeline from China that's going through Turkey. And who are the organizers?'

'Should be easy enough,' she laughed. 'I have colleagues at my university who may be able to give us some background help – at least steer us in the right direction. And my Turkish is still fluent thanks to Mum and Dad.'

'Of course,' I said, 'we will be very careful and deliberate – but I assure you I have done this sort of work before.'

'So I heard,' she said, with another raised eyebrow. 'I don't know that much but our mutual friend had given me an idea that you were "close to the British" and had "worked with some interesting people".'

Those long fingers sketched out inverted commas as she spoke.

'Well, I hardly look like James Bond,' I said, with the driest delivery I could manage, 'but I am a better operator.'

I outlined our 'legend' for the mission, which made her laugh. She was certainly not easily intimidated.

'I had better get a Uighur recipe book,' she said – that charming smile again.

For the next five weeks, Dilay was the consummate researcher, feeding me with details about the areas where Uighurs lived, their mosques and community organizations – and of course their food and restaurants. We chose different family names. I was still apprehensive that her public profile might be a handicap.

We met again at the Istanbul Hilton on a humid afternoon in late June. She wore a hijab with her dark glasses and a long dress favoured by more conservative Turkish women. I almost didn't recognize her as she glided through the lobby.

She had brought valuable intelligence.

'I am told,' she said, as we shared a pot of tea, 'that the man who knows about the flow to Syria is often at one of the restaurants near the main mosque in Zeytinburnu.'

'That's interesting. How do you know?'

'A friend who's an academic knows someone in Turkish intelligence. He says there are jihadi tendencies among the Uighurs, but most of their fire is directed at China.'

Zeytinburnu is a crowded, working-class area on the fringes of Istanbul – and home to 90,000 Uighurs by some estimates. Some Turks called it Little Uighurstan, but there are Iraqis, Uzbeks and Kyrgyz communities there, too. It's truly a Central Asian melting pot.

We went on our first expedition the following afternoon. Dilay was excited and a little nervous, but she camouflaged it expertly. Besides modeling, she had studied drama and had a minor film role. It all helped.

Zeytinburnu certainly did not feel or look Turkish. Old men in Chinese clothes with long wispy beards sat outside cafés, waiting to eat as soon as dusk arrived. Lagman-makers hurled thick wads of noodle in the air prior to chopping them for the saucepan. A pedestrian boulevard was lined with shops selling leather goods; there were enough jackets to supply a division of Hells Angels. Once in a while, we would glimpse the flag of what was known as the East

Turkistan Independence movement, a white crescent and star on a mid-blue background. Cheaply printed Turkic newspapers were on sale at kiosks.

Dilay had difficulty understanding the heavily accented Turkish spoken by the Uighurs. We drifted through the neighbourhood, working on our act as culinary tourists, until we came to the mosque. It occupied the ground floor of a nondescript ochre-coloured building dotted with air-conditioning units. Men were beginning to arrive for evening prayers. A few doors away was the Turkistan restaurant we were looking for. It was closed – awaiting the rush of *Iftar* – but a middle-aged man was sitting outside on a white plastic chair. He told us in halting English and sign language that it would open at 8:00 P.M. And then he switched to near-fluent Arabic and asked what had brought us to Zeytinburnu.

'I'm in commercial research,' I replied. 'We are looking for business opportunities for food importers in Saudi Arabia.'

It was the start of a long conversation that embraced cuisine, culture and the life of the Uighurs. The man introduced himself as Abdul Majeed. He had left China in 1985 because he and his family were marked as troublemakers by the Chinese authorities. He had attended the Islamic university in Islamabad and then moved to Afghanistan for several years when the Taliban were in control, before resuming his northward trek to Kazakhstan.

It seemed we had miraculously stumbled on the very individual the Chinese were most exercised about – the man said to be at the heart of the jihadi pipeline. Dilay's research was paying outsize dividends at our very first meeting.

'While I lived in Pakistan I knew many leaders of jihad, including Abdullah Azzam,' Abdul Majeed said with pride. He had wanted to open a training camp for Uighurs.

'How long have you been in Turkey?' I asked as casually as I could.

'I came here five years ago; I have just received Turkish citizenship. It helps to ingratiate yourself with the ruling party here. I try to make sure the Uighur community are loyal supporters,' he said with a grin.

Not wishing to push my luck, I said nothing about my own jihadi past: stick to the food, I told myself.

We attended the *Maghreb* prayers as Abdul Majeed's guest (Dilay with the women) and then dined at the Turkistan, where we met some of his friends from the mosque. Talk turned inevitably to Syria, then in the third year of its civil war and the stage for an emerging struggle between ISIS and al-Qaeda for the mantle of jihad. We had a long conversation about the 'suffering of nations'.

Before we parted that evening, Abdul Majeed gave me a list of restaurants we should check out. Happily, several were places Dilay had been advised to visit to meet the 'right people'.

'Well, we're done,' I laughed to Dilay while in a taxi back to the hotel. 'Day one, the first guy we meet, and he's the main man. I had told the client there was a less than twenty percent chance that we'd find him.'

But I also felt uneasy: I had developed a genuine rapport with Abdul Majeed and his friends and had begun to understand the Uighurs' suffering. I felt uncomfortable at the prospect of telling the Chinese how Abdul Majeed and company were supporting jihad in Syria.

We spent the best part of two weeks travelling Turkey by plane, train and bus – seeking out Uighur communities to the point where we truly were experts in their cuisine. I could easily have written '101 Great Uighur Eateries in Turkey' were there a market for such a book. But we also sought out the most prominent Uighur figures, including Seyit Tumturk – deputy leader of the World Uighur Congress.

We met Tumturk at his home in the city of Kayseri. The place was an industrial powerhouse on the vast Anatolian plain in central Turkey. But it was also home to mosques dating back to the Seljuk era; parts of it were like stepping back into the Middle Ages. Religiously conservative, it has often been described as a clearing house for Uighurs, who make it their first destination in Turkey.

I went through the food routine with Tumturk, who seemed genuinely gratified that someone should care about Uighur cuisine. He invited me to celebrate *Iftar* at his home, an old and humble place with a large courtyard dripping with grape vines. The muffled sounds of the city drifted through the cool evening air.

Tumturk led evening prayers for a dozen or so men who had come to his house to break the fast. He spoke good Arabic, and I was surprised to hear him pray for the mujahideen's victory in Syria, Afghanistan, Somalia and Iraq.

'And we ask Allah to bestow protection and mercy on Mullah Muhammad Omar, our most noble cleric,' he concluded.

There can't be many prayer services in Kayseri, I thought, that end with a prayer for the welfare of the leader of the Taliban. But Tumturk knew his audience. Among them was a young Uighur man who also spoke good Arabic. He told me he had left China two years previously and had spent half the time since with Jabhat al-Nusra – he had only recently returned from fighting in Syria. The young Uighur had been in the area where my nephew Ibrahim was fighting. I took a chance.

'I guess you never met a young man by the name of Abu Khalil al-Bahraini,' I asked, using my nephew's *kunya*.

He was stunned.

'Yes, I did – near Saraqib, a week ago.'

'That's my nephew,' I told the assembled Uighurs, and even felt pride in doing so. 'My family has a long history with jihad.'

I felt still more conflicted. I knew that my nephew had gone to Syria because he thought the struggle against the Assad regime was a noble cause and because jihad there was an important step towards fulfilling the prophecies. Perhaps some of these Uighurs were similarly motivated.

The young Uighur quickly disabused me of the sympathy welling up inside me.

'Please,' he said, 'look at this.'

He flicked open his phone. There was murky footage of him in a room of bare walls and naked light bulbs. A man, kneeling and with his hands bound, came into view. The young Uighur stepped forward and grabbed the back of his head before drawing a large knife across his throat.

He closed the phone.

'He was a soldier of the criminal Assad regime. We captured him and I executed the pig.'

I am rarely speechless but at that moment could not utter a word. I turned away and said a silent prayer seeking guidance to understand the futility of it all and fervently hoping that my nephew had not descended to such barbarity.

At our second and final meeting with Abdul Majeed in Istanbul we laid out our plan to infuse the Gulf with the best of Uighur food. I then – as subtly as possible – led the conversation towards Syria again. I needed details.

'Of course we are helping Uighur to reach Syria,' he said. 'It is our duty. We have helped about three hundred reach Syria; most are from Turkey but some come from Europe and Canada. We provide guides and money. We have some safe houses.'

'Who do they join?' I asked, trying to sound no more than vaguely interested.

'Mainly Jabhat al-Nusra; a few have gone to the Islamic State. But mainly they want to see the creation of an Islamic Emirate in Syria. They see it as a springboard for creating something similar back home. They want to take the jihad back to Beijing and Shanghai.'

No wonder the Chinese were so anxious.

The mosque where we had prayed was the headquarters for the operation, and Majeed was one of three senior figures who directed it.

I said a reluctant farewell to Dilay in Istanbul.

'What will you do with everything we found out?' she asked at our final dinner.

'I'll write up a report for my client,' I replied a little defensively.

By now she had guessed the client was the Chinese government. We were both equivocal about the mission; we had met some good people driven by a sense of injustice to join the rebels' cause in Syria. Having escaped China, they had rejected an easy life in Istanbul or Kayseri. But some had also taken to bloodletting in Syria with alarming ease.

Over the course of our stay, Dilay had met a lot of Uighur women and warmed to them.

'I just feel we may have done the wrong thing here,' she said suddenly. 'These people really are persecuted in China. But I also know some of them have done terrible things in Syria. Even the wives have execution videos on their phones, and they're proud of them. And if you talk to them about the Chinese, they just want to kill as many as possible.'

I shook my head; there were no answers.

My report to the Chinese included enough detail to impress and intrigue. I had another call from the perfectly dressed go-between who had met me in Dubai. Would I come to Macau for further discussions?

The Venetian hotel in Macau is one of the most flamboyant and opulent in a place where flamboyance is standard practice.

I arrived in a limousine laid on by the Chinese, flanked by two young intelligence officials who looked more like graduate students from a high-tech institute than counter-terrorism agents. They were deferential to the point of obsequiousness. Clearly, they had been told that I was an important guest. In near-perfect English, they welcomed me to the gambling paradise of the Orient and pointed out various landmarks (all of them built within the last decade) on the way to the Venetian.

They handed me a room key and said I should rest ahead of meeting the head of the counter-terrorism agency and other officials. I did not need to be asked twice; it seemed I had been on the move constantly for months. My suite was so huge that I felt I needed a GPS device to get to the bathroom. But as soon as my head rested on the outsize pillow in the outsize bed, jet lag did the rest.

The following day, I was met by two very earnest men in suits without ties.

'I hope you are refreshed, Mr Aimen,' one said. 'Please, we are going to another hotel to talk and enjoy some hotpot.'

The conversation lasted seven hours, accompanied by near-constant note-taking as I expanded on my written report.

I also took it upon myself to advise a more nuanced approached to the Uighur 'problem', suggesting as politely as I could that the exercise of some 'soft power' in Xinjiang might yield better results than cracking heads. One of my interviewers sighed.

'We agree; there are better ways. But the local officials in Xinjiang see only the fist as the way to deal with the Uighurs. They are pig-headed. They also make a lot of money in the process.'

At the end of the marathon briefing, I was asked if I would return to Turkey. I didn't think it was such a good idea. My new friends in Zeytinburnu might ask when the first orders for Uighur delicacies were expected, or even begin to make enquiries about my Saudi sponsors. The Chinese wanted me to obtain copies of identification papers and passports, which seemed a bridge too far.

My Dubai intermediary also thought that any further missions would invite trouble.

'They don't know when it's smart to stop,' she confided to me when we met under the chandeliers of the hotel. We'd taken cover in an alcove from the hordes of gamblers, some excitedly hopeful as they entered the Venezia, others crestfallen as they left. 'You've done enough; don't overexpose yourself,' she said, 'but please be very cordial with the head of counter-terrorism.'

I'd almost forgotten; there was yet another meeting. I was struck by a feeling that my extravagant surroundings were small reward for the intensity of the Chinese demands.

I was taken through a series of heavy wooden double doors, through gambling rooms that were ever more exclusive, with marble tables, solid gold chips and carpets that drowned out the ambient noise. There was a Rolex on every wrist and a young woman at every elbow. So these were the gambling halls of the multimillionaires, I thought, where six figures were lost (and rarely made) in the time it took to sink a cocktail.

We entered the cigar room, inexplicably but expensively decked out in tartan. It was so contrived that I nearly began to laugh; I half expected to see Robert Burns in one of the ruby-red armchairs. The walls were panelled in dark mahogany, and the shelves carried luxuriously bound books in English that I assumed had not been touched, let alone read.

I very nearly didn't see the chief of Chinese counter-terrorism. He was barely 4 feet 9 inches tall, a quiet and self-effacing man. I thought he looked like an ancient peasant from the countryside. But the expensive cigar said otherwise. With crashing insensitivity, my hosts offered me a cigar and a single-malt Scotch. I declined politely and asked for a Diet Coke.

The other officials (my hotpot friends) drew up chairs to help translate the chief's questions. They looked petrified and were clearly in awe of this mandarin. He spoke slowly and softly, pausing to puff on his Cuban cigar.

'We are very grateful for your help. It is of course not easy for us to get our own people inside the Uighur groups,' he began. 'My colleagues say your debrief has been very informative. We see this relationship lasting for many years,' he added, waiting for the translation to sink in. 'It's clear why you were of such value to the British.'

I nodded weakly and thought of the way Dilay and I had stumbled into the Uighur hierarchy in Istanbul. This would not be an auspicious moment to disagree. But I did try out my earlier gambit.

'I hope my work was helpful. But as I told your colleagues, the best approach would be to address some of the Uighurs' grievances at root. I would be more than happy to advise on what I would call soft measures to alleviate the situation in Xinjiang and counter extremism.'

As my words were translated, the diminutive chief's expression hardened. This was not the sort of advice he wanted, even though I had a sense that the translators were adjusting my language from the nervous pauses in their Mandarin. Even so, he seemed determined to keep the encounter cordial.

'Let's see how the relationship may proceed,' he said, jamming the butt of his cigar into an enormous glass ashtray. 'But for now, as a token of our gratitude, please take this.' He handed me an envelope. 'There are many luxury stores here,' he said. 'I hope you will find yourself something agreeable.'

The ways of the Communist Party of the People's Republic, I thought to myself. Inside the envelope was $25,000; a bonus in addition to the $25,000 I had been given before the Turkey trip. It was indeed agreeable, but I couldn't escape a pang of guilt. I had no desire to see news reports that Abdul Majeed or Tumturk had been found dead with a bullet wound to the head.

Outside, I caught up with my initial Chinese contact. She was, as always, immaculately turned out – wearing a lime green silk dress to her ankles.

'How does someone like that become the head of counterterrorism?' I asked, splaying my hands wide.

'Party politics,' came the soothing reply. 'He's one of the old gang; they stick together.'

A few days later, I sent the Chinese an encrypted email profuse with thanks but politely declining the proposal to return to Zeytinburnu. It was just too dangerous, I said, unless I had a budget to buy food and hire chefs, a way to reinforce my 'legend'.

Funding the enemy was a step too far in Beijing's eyes.* But the Uighur pipeline into Syria continued to expand. Within three years, intelligence estimates had some 4,000 Uighurs of fighting age inside Syria – with another 3,000 family members. They were mainly based in Idlib, the stronghold of Jabhat al-Nusra.[16] A few hundred

---

* In the months and years after my mission for Beijing, the Uighur problem only worsened. Not long after my visit to Macau, knife-wielding attackers dressed in black stormed the railway station in Kunming, the provincial capital of Yunnan. At least twenty-nine people were stabbed to death, more than a hundred injured. Authorities described the assault as an 'organized, premeditated, violent terrorist attack'.[15]

had thrown in their lot with ISIS, and later died in their scores defending Mosul.

The aftermath of 9/11 had touched every corner of the world; even China was not immune. The Taliban might have been ejected from Kabul, but their continuing resistance had provided the Uighurs with an escape route. How ironic that the government of Pakistan had gone with its begging bowl to Beijing seeking investment and trade even as its security services continued helping the Taliban on the quiet.

But my dalliance with China's security services would soon be overtaken by personal tragedy.

Below me was Dubai in its extravagant modernity, the buildings piercing the late afternoon sky through a soup of haze. I wasn't looking forward to my visit; pitching clients was one of my least favourite occupations.

It was 5 September 2013. A glowering sun was sinking into the endless desert of Saudi Arabia. An hour earlier I had left Bahrain with a sense of unease that I could not explain. And now I had to face the prospect of glad-handing corporate climbers who knew nothing about the Middle East (beyond the Gulf property market) and cared less.

Sometimes I was annoyed by this bubble of ostentatious wealth in the Emirates. I looked out at the rest of the Arab world – Yemen, Iraq, Libya, above all Syria – and saw the suffering and chaos that the Gulf States had only aggravated with their billions and their 'favoured parties'.

As the plane taxied to its stand, I flipped out my phone. Fifty-six WhatsApp messages? All but two were from a family group created to keep the Durrani clan connected across time zones and lifestyles. I read the first from a cousin in Saudi Arabia.

'Deepest condolences on the martyrdom of Ibrahim.'

I didn't understand and hurried down the chain. Dozens more messages.

'Sadness and pride Ibrahim should have sacrificed his life with such bravery.'

'Too young to be accepted by God . . .'

As my fellow passengers began the usual scramble to the exit, I buried by head in my hands.

Ibrahim had been killed somewhere in Syria, his youthful idealism cut down before his twentieth birthday.

I didn't know where or why or how, just that he was now gone.

I cursed the era of the app. A private phone call, words of warning and preparation, a sympathetic voice would have been more dignified than a stream of messages to decipher, piecing together a tragedy from the discontinuous reaction to it.

I wearily picked myself up and left the plane, avoiding the quizzical glances of the cabin crew. Everyone else was long gone, rushing to their next appointment or a connecting flight. But the life had been kicked out of me. I wandered in a daze through the bustling terminal, oblivious to all but my private grief.

I had spoken with Ibrahim just a few days earlier. The Skype call kept breaking up, but we had persevered. Now every word came back to me. He was happy, full of news from the battlefield, confident in the cause. He had the optimism of a young man who felt he could change the world. I remembered the feeling. I was in a way proud of him for following his beliefs, but my pride was vastly outweighed by alarm at his naivety and the growing savagery of the Syrian conflict.

Years earlier, we had talked about his passion for graphic design and Photoshop, and I had encouraged him to pursue his studies in England, even offering advice on courses and places. Now I only wished bitterly that I had pursued the idea with greater vigour.

I cancelled my meetings for that evening in Dubai. The thought of a bunch of dry MBAs in expensive suits discussing margins and square footage was too awful. I wanted to mourn alone. As I gazed out of the hotel window at Dubai's glittering night skyline, I felt somehow comforted by its anonymity, the cloak of solitude and silence. I watched the lights in anonymous living rooms and offices flicker on and off, and felt gnawing guilt. Had my own experiences encouraged my nephew – even subconsciously – to follow in my footsteps? I had left suburban peace to travel to Bosnia and fight for the mujahideen against the hated Serbs only days after my sixteenth birthday. I had desired martyrdom more than anything else.

Had I said anything to Ibrahim that had driven him to emulate me? Had Moheddin told Ibrahim of my adventures in Afghanistan, of my joining al-Qaeda and meeting Osama bin Laden himself? Among some of my family, that was still something to be celebrated rather than denied.

I recalled a previous chat on the family WhatsApp group. Moheddin had started it – saying that Syria had become the new Bosnia because so many foreign fighters had gone there.

'Problem with Arab Jihadis wherever they go ...' I had responded. 'They do 2 things ... they take a national struggle and make it an ideological one. Then they want to lead instead of allowing locals to.'

Moheddin had joined in.

'So you think they should leave?'

'No, they shouldn't leave but they must not lead. They need to fit in with what Syrians want to do.'

The discussion had become heated. Moheddin said I was accepting colonial boundaries, to which I'd replied that I was thinking more of ethnic and tribal identities.

Now I wished I'd simply said: 'Yes, they should leave – not their business.'

At that moment, my phone rang. I glanced at the number. It was Moheddin calling from Bahrain. I breathed deeply, bracing myself.

He was in tears, of course. I was embarrassed and troubled to hear him so broken and at a loss for words. Within seconds, I felt the tears rolling down my cheeks, too.

Eventually, he told me what had happened. Ibrahim and a few other fighters had been defending a hilltop position near Areha in Idlib. There had been a surprise attack by regime forces, supported by Iranian militia and Hezbollah fighters from Lebanon. Ibrahim and his comrades had been hopelessly outgunned; the attackers had 23mm anti-aircraft guns and had created a dust storm to confuse them. Then they had come up the hill from the other side.

'Ibrahim and his men thought the guys coming up the hill were reinforcements, so they lowered their guard,' my brother said, sighing sadly. 'They were overwhelmed. The enemy was able to close in and killed them.'

The next day, other fighters had retaken the position and retrieved the bodies of Ibrahim and the two fighters killed with him. They'd been buried in a village near Saraqib.

As Moheddin recovered his composure his pain suddenly became pride.

'Ibrahim had the courage of a lion; he deserves his place in paradise and he has made his family proud. No death is more honourable than one waging jihad. And he went because he was answering the call of the Prophet.'

I had thought the same thing in Bosnia, Afghanistan and the Philippines.

As I listened to Moheddin's tribute to his own son, I saw the rhythmic flashing lights of a jet drifting upward from the international airport and at that moment made up my mind. I would go to Ibrahim's graveside in Syria to pay my respects. It was morally the right thing to do. But because some in al-Qaeda knew me as a traitor, it was also a rash and dangerous thing to do.

The following day, I contacted an old friend in Turkey, Orcan, who ran a lucrative smuggling business across the border. We had been in Bosnia together nearly twenty years previously; he also knew Moheddin. Now in his late forties, his relatively youthful features were betrayed by a beard that was almost white.

'My nephew has been killed in Idlib,' I told Orcan over the phone. 'I want to go and pay my respects at his grave.'

There was a moment's silence.

'Are you sure?' he asked, more aware than most of the chequerboard of rival groups that competed in northern Syria. 'Some people there would kill you if they see you.'

He knew that I had long ago given up al-Qaeda.

'I am offering you $1,000 to get me in.'

There was a sigh at the other end of the line.

'You will have to shave your beard off and I need $200 for bribes.'

'I'll keep my moustache and a goatee,' I replied, reflecting on how surreal our conversation was becoming. I had hated being clean-shaven; it had lasted all of six months.

His orders, no doubt intended to dissuade me, continued.

'You will leave your phone, your passport, anything that identifies you, in Antakya,' a Turkish border town where he then lived. 'You will need to avoid al-Nusra and the Khorasani.'

'And the who?' I asked. It was the first time I had heard about the Khorasan group, a cell of al-Qaeda veterans who had moved to Syria in an effort to make it a springboard for attacks on the West.* There were not many of them, but they were in the area I intended to visit, around Idlib. And I had known one or two of them in a previous life. I would not be able to explain myself should we meet.**

I spent a few days kicking my heels in Antakya (modern-day Antioch), a pleasant town in the Turkish province of Hatay framed by steep hills with the broad Orantes river cutting it into two halves. Its old quarter had been preserved and restored in an effort to

---

* In September 2014, in the opening salvo of the air campaign in Syria, the US launched cruise missiles against camps they believed were linked to the Khorasan group after learning of a plot by them to bomb Western aviation.[17]
** Another would soon travel to Syria: Said Arif, the one-time chief of al-Qaeda's London intelligence apparatus who had introduced me to Abu Qatada in London. He arrived in October 2013 and took on a leadership position among al-Qaeda-aligned jihadis. He was killed in a Coalition air strike there in 2015.[18]

encourage tourism. But just as Vienna had become a place of intrigue and espionage after the Second World War, so the rivalries of the Syrian conflict had seeped across the border and into Antakya. There were plenty of men idling in cafés who looked at best dubious.

Orcan collected me in his battered Peugeot and we made our way to Bab el-Hawa, one of the few crossings still functioning, a place where aid trucks queued to get into Idlib province and wounded fighters came the other way in dusty ambulances. Getting across was surprisingly easy; you just had to know the right border officials.

As a regular visitor to northern Syria, Orcan was well known at some of the checkpoints, which was reassuring. But the sands were shifting so quickly that a roadblock could spring up or a village change hands unexpectedly. Orcan was always checking the insignia at roadblocks.

I was nervous and alert but not frightened. What will be will be, I thought; my power to change destiny was nil.

As we drove towards Sarmada, the first place of any consequence inside Syria, Orcan reached under the driver's seat and pulled out a pistol – a Beretta.

'If it all goes wrong,' he said drily, 'use it. At least you'll go down fighting.'

'It's loaded,' he added unnecessarily.

I checked the safety catch and slid it into the glove compartment.

There were a few moments of silence.

'We're at a difficult moment,' he continued. 'Loyalties, territory – they are, shall we say, fluid. If we are stopped, be cheerful, greet the guards at the checkpoints. You are a Palestinian Kuwaiti and you've come here because you've heard your nephew has been killed.'

The Kuwaitis were generous donors to al-Nusra; it made sense.

I knew he was taking a huge risk in escorting me: if we were stopped by the wrong people and they suspected me, his life would be in as much danger as mine.

We jolted over a few more potholes; a pickup truck passed us, loaded with goats that gazed at us as if somehow asking what on earth we were doing here.

'This Islamic State – it's emerging everywhere. And some of Nusra have defected to it; we just don't know which,' Orcan said.

As we might encounter Nusra checkpoints, this was not comforting. ISIS was developing a reputation for extreme brutality. A few weeks earlier, Orcan told me, a commander in the moderate Free Syrian Army had been beheaded in the town of Dana, which we were about to pass through.

With a sigh of relief, we negotiated Dana without incident and drove on into the open countryside.

It was by now mid-September and the weather was glorious: warm, glowing days under azure skies so at odds with the destruction in the towns and villages we passed through. We moved from one safe house to another.

Orcan turned left and right on dusty tracks and minor roads.

'Why are we zigzagging across Idlib?' I asked. 'We don't have that much time.'

'I want to avoid Nusra checkpoints; pass through Ahrar al-Sham territory wherever possible.'

Ahrar al-Sham was an Islamist group with Turkish backing; it didn't have the fearsome reputation of al-Nusra.

Orcan preferred attack as the best method of defence when we came to a checkpoint in the middle of nowhere.

He pulled up and wound down his window, presenting ID to the scruffy youth on duty.

'Where's his ID?' the boy asked, nodding in my direction.

'You don't want to mess with this guy,' Orcan said laughing. 'He's very important.'

The checkpoints we came to were mostly run by Ahrar al-Sham and sympathetic. 'God bless you, brother' was the phrase we heard time and again. In the years to come, the group would have its guts ripped out by ISIS and al-Nusra.

From Dana we drove south to Atarib, another place that might have been a picturesque market town once but was now pulverized by war. We bunked down for the night in a small apartment above a shop. Orcan told me some local Nusra fighters were staying in the same building so I thought it best to keep a low profile.

Shortly after I woke up the next morning, there was a commotion in the building.

I went to the window. A faint whirr in the sky became more distinct, though we could see nothing.

We heard the shouts first. '*Baramil, baramil!*' – barrel bombs.

All across Syria, these crude but powerful bombs dropped from regime helicopters provoked terror among ordinary people, who bore the brunt of their random destruction. The weapon had no purpose but to maim and terrorize civilians; it was good at both.

A detonation shook our building and an immense mass of yellow-grey smoke – the shape of a cauliflower – took over the horizon.

'My God,' said Orcan.

We saw the Nusra fighters leave our building and run towards the nearby smoke.

'It's safer to be outside than in,' Orcan said, beckoning me to follow.

We followed the Nusra fighters. Men covered in sweat and dust were running towards the scene with shovels and picks. A fire truck's brown hose snaked across the road. People were running from neighbouring houses.

Choking dust filled the air. I coughed uncontrollably; my throat felt parched and caked.

'We must help,' Orcan said.

We ran towards what remained of a two-storey house which had been sheared in two by a barrel bomb. A woman – a mother, sister or aunt – was screaming and beating her head. I looked at the mass of pancaked concrete and thought that no one could have survived such an impact.

The shout went up again – '*Baramil!*' Another explosion shook me to the core and seconds later – almost gracefully – another mass of smoke and dust rose over the town.

I had seen death before – on the hillside in Bosnia and in the aftermath of an explosion gone wrong at Darunta. I had seen what explosives, mortars and shells could do to the human frame, rendering a body unrecognizable, shredding it. Nothing prepared me for this scene, in a town of ordinary people: these were not fighters but women and children as well as men.

Despite the horror I could not turn away; somehow I needed to see what had happened. A girl, limp and lifeless, perhaps six or seven years old, was carefully picked from the rubble. I will never forget her tousled black hair made grey by the dust, nor the arms of the man who carried her gingerly from the scene, tears streaming down his face.

Perhaps even more distressing were the anguished cries of children, carried away in unspeakable pain, limbs nearly separated from their bodies. I knew – the men carrying them knew – there was little other than prayer that could be offered for them. These places had no hospitals or clinics; by the time they reached what passed for a hospital in Saraqib they would be gone.

I was consumed with a fury that I had never known before, one that outstripped my anger over the tragedy of Fallujah nearly a decade earlier. It was a raw lust for revenge against the Assad regime. I now understood why these people would go on fighting; they were driven by rage against an almost casual genocide.

Two hours later, we finally left Atarib; there was nothing more to be done. Perhaps a dozen people had been killed – the merest fleck in a war that would count its dead in the hundreds of thousands.

For what seemed like hours, we drove in silence. Several times I felt tears well up as my mind repeated the image of the little girl being lifted from the wreckage. I clenched my fists until the knuckles were white.

'Maybe,' I said at last, 'I will stay here and fight, like my cousin and nephew.'

Orcan turned to me in astonishment. He, too, was on the verge of tears.

'If you stay here, someone will find out your true identity soon enough and the jihadis will kill you. And what does it achieve?' he sighed. 'Nothing.'

Numbed by what we had seen, we arrived in the town of Saraqib in the late afternoon. It was not far from my destination, a field that had become an improvised cemetery near the village of Kafr Nabl. We took refuge in a safe house belonging to a local charity.

Once an important agricultural centre on Syria's wide northern plains, with a population of some 30,000 before the war broke out, Saraqib had suffered extensive damage. The Syrian army had seized it early in 2012, destroying large portions of the town and killing dozens of residents. In turn, Syrian soldiers had been killed in cold blood when rebels retook the town later that year.[19] It now had the air of a ghost town. Walls were daubed with primitive depictions of Assad's helicopters bombing mosques; the water tower had received a direct hit and there was no running water. But there was an air of defiance among those who remained. In just a few neighbourhoods, roads were being swept; market stalls were open; mechanics tried to breathe new life into ancient, battered cars.

I could not tell whether the house where I was sheltering was unfinished or had been damaged, and might have said the same about dozens of others. The furnishings were bare: tattered chairs and tables scavenged from other homes that had been wrecked, threadbare carpets. Supplies of cooking oil, rice and cracked wheat were stacked to the ceiling in preparation for the winter.

The charity's director had come to meet me. So had local Syrian fighters of Ahrar al-Sham, Jund al-Aqsa and al-Nusra – all militant Islamist groups who had a presence in the town. They had not yet started killing each other. The Syrian revolution was still a noble cause, for these young Syrians and for the outside world.

Thin and unkempt with apprentice beards, they had apparently not seen a shower in weeks. They were simple local boys, dressed in mismatched civilian and military clothing with trainers rather than military boots on their feet, but they had aged beyond their years thanks to months of fighting.

I quickly calculated none of the al-Qaeda-aligned Nusra fighters posed an immediate threat. None had been beyond the local area and it seemed highly unlikely they would be aware of the fatwah to kill me. These young men insisted the tide was turning against the army and the hated regime militia known as the *shahiba*. Plenty of soldiers – especially the lower-ranking Sunni – were not going to spill their blood for Assad, they predicted confidently.

The fighters were kind, honest young men for whom the rebellion had yet to lose its meaning. The absolute distrust among different groups that would eventually cripple the insurgency had not yet reared its ugly head. One young man with a wispy beard and thin, angular face expressed the hope that I would join them. If only he knew, I thought.

Another fighter pressed me on why foreign governments seemed so willing to allow Assad's killing machine to continue its work unhindered.

'And now we have to fight Hezbollah, too,' he said. 'Why is it okay for Assad to have foreign fighters from Lebanon, Iraq and Iran, but not for foreign fighters to help us?' I had no answer but heartfelt sympathy.

'I don't understand it either,' I said. 'But I grew up in Kuwait; I can't speak for the West, and I wouldn't want to.'

As night fell, I lay down on a bed-mat among the rice and lentils and pulled a heavy rug over me. I had brought diabetes tablets with me to regulate my blood sugar levels, but I felt dizzy and weak. Perhaps it was the shock of what I had seen. Every sinew seemed to ache from the stress of the journey. The dust of Atarib had permeated my clothes; it smelled of death.

More than once I asked myself whether I really was here in northern Syria. I felt the shape of the Beretta tucked under the bed-mat; I imagined pulling it out quickly. And every minute I saw the girl pulled from the wreckage. I understood warfare well enough to know that I was deeply traumatized.

I slept uneasily, dreaming repetitively that a group of jihadi gunmen had entered the safe house and ordered me to come with them.

As we drove across the plains the next morning, we witnessed widespread and often random destruction. On several occasions we had to stop the car and head for the nearest ditch as barrel bombs were dropped on nearby villages. Idlib province was under daily bombardment; the regime's helicopters and planes were overhead most of the day. But in 2013 they had not yet been joined by Russian airpower. Much worse was to come.

Orcan's frustrations boiled over. He may have been a smuggler, making money off all sides, but he had compassion for the Syrian people.

'You have connections in the West. Tell them what you see here; tell them to come and bomb Assad.'

It was a message I heard constantly. Local aid workers and civilians all had the same refrain: 'Why are we getting no help when Assad massacres everyone?'

The despair was all the greater because the United States had recently backed off bombing Assad's forces despite a gruesome chemical weapons attack on a rebel-held suburb of Damascus. And now the most apocalyptic and brutal of groups, the Islamic State, was taking advantage of the rapidly disappearing space for moderate factions, even trying to devour its own offspring, Jabhat al-Nusra.

'ISIS is taking it to Nusra,' Orcan told me. 'I don't know if they can hold on.'*

From its strongholds near the Iraqi border, ISIS was lashing out at other groups in northern Syria, trying to extend its

---

* In November 2013, al-Qaeda's leader Ayman al-Zawahiri finally made clear his disapproval of ISIS's power grab in Syria. He stated firmly that Jabhat al-Nusra was to be 'an independent branch of al-Qaeda that reports to the general command.' ISIS, of course, took no notice, setting the stage for the bitter rivalry between it and al-Qaeda that followed.[20]

territorial control towards the Turkish border. It would hold a huge swathe of northern Syria before being driven back between 2015 and 2017.

'So we have ISIS and Assad. Thank you, world,' Orcan said.

I soon saw at first hand how a new generation of foreign jihadis were beginning to graft themselves onto the Syrian rebellion, like parasites looking for a host. They combined passionate belief that the world was approaching the end-of-days with deep Salafi-jihadi chauvinism. There was an unremitting hardness about them that was worlds away from my wide-eyed idealism twenty years earlier.

At a makeshift hospital run by the charity in whose house I had sheltered, I met two Libyan fighters. They had been wounded fighting against government forces, but despite their obvious pain their eyes shone with intensity.

One grabbed my wrist insistently.

'We came because the Prophet told us to come,' one of them said. 'This is the land where the Islamic State will be created; this is where Jesus Christ will come.'

And holding his index finger high, he went on:

'*A victorious band of warriors from my followers shall continue to fight for the truth . . .*'

As he spoke I saw his eyes fill with tears not of pain or frustration but euphoria.

'*. . . They will be at the gates of Damascus and its surroundings, and they will be at the gates of Antioch and its surroundings.*'

I had heard the *hadith* constantly in Afghanistan, but there it seemed to be distantly aspirational. Now it was real and close at hand. The Libyan fighters were well aware that the very place we were having this conversation – Idlib province – was close to the ancient Syrian city of Antioch.

The message was repeated wherever I went. Kazakhs, Moroccans, Uighurs – they had all converged on Syria because this was where the *Malahem* would be fought – the epic battles foretold by the prophecies.* The defeat of the Assad regime was incidental to their greater goal.

It was the Islamic State that brought the most apocalyptic and tendentious interpretations of the prophecies to Syria and Iraq. The impression I had of ISIS – reinforced by what I heard during that journey – was that it had discipline and coherence. Al-Qaeda under Ayman al-Zawahiri, by contrast, seemed almost quaint. Zawahiri would pontificate from his mountain hideout while al-Qaeda affiliates in places like Yemen and North Africa went about their very particular wars.

'The trouble is,' I told Orcan, 'you can take ten members of al-Qaeda and ask them what they want, and get ten answers. Take ten members of ISIS, and you will get just one answer.' He shook his head sadly. The moderates were even more helpless. 'The Free Syrian Army have nothing to show, no message to convey, no philosophy. Why don't they say, "We are here to protect and defend you against ISIS and against the regime"?'

I looked out at the olive groves, untended amid the rubble of farm buildings.

'It's like Bosnia, but it's going to last a lot longer,' Orcan said with a heavy sigh. 'It will end only when the last man is left standing.'

I looked back towards the demolished structures.

Like a fever breaking, my emotional impulse to stay and fight had evaporated. It was obvious from what I had seen and heard so far in Syria that al-Qaeda and ISIS were hijacking what had been an honourable uprising. This not only doomed the rebellion to failure because it would lose international legitimacy, but it also meant Syrians would be caught in the crossfire between a brutal regime and merciless jihadi groups. But that was exactly the regime's calculation.

* Al-Qaeda in the Arabian Peninsula named its media arm Al-Malahem Media.

On a bridge over the River Bosna, nearly twenty years earlier, I had been torn between fighting against injustice and the futility and despair of war. Nowhere would hope be so cruelly snuffed out than in Syria.

There was silence for the last part of our journey. As the sun sank towards the horizon and a chill suddenly touched the breeze, we arrived at a desolate piece of scrub on the edge of a village.

'This is it,' I said simply.

I climbed out of our dusty, rattling car. I knew I didn't have long. To drive the back roads of northern Syria at night was a risk too far. There were a few simple gravestones sunk into the hard ground. They had nothing but names, quickly painted because there were so many more to paint, I guessed.

I moved from one to the next; all seemed recently dug. In the distance I could hear the thud of artillery or mortars, and again the distant whirring of a helicopter.

Suddenly, Ibrahim's grave was in front of me. Scrawled in black paint was the name Abu Khalil al-Bahraini – his *kunya*. Concrete had been poured roughly in front of the headstone to protect his burial place.

I imagined his burial: a hurried affair attended by just a few fellow fighters, who no doubt had buried many comrades before Ibrahim and had wondered whether the next prayers would be said for them.

I asked Orcan to take a photograph of the site; in time I would show it to Moheddin. I was gripped by an immense sadness, but also anger and no little guilt. Of course, it was a tragic waste of a young life, but it was also a mere blip on the Syrian battlefield that would change nothing. It was an utterly futile death, as futile as the victims of Atarib; that is what I hated so much.

I recalled Moheddin's pride at his son's sacrifice, that he had been martyred defending his religion. It suddenly struck me how much I disagreed. Young, impressionable men from all over the Arab world – and Muslims from further afield – were being seduced by the call of jihad. They came here as moths to a light. Many were assigned suicidal missions or impossible defences; others had been duped by a perverted interpretation of Islam. And not a few had brought their psychopathic tendencies with them.

Suddenly, a conversation I had had two years previously came back to me. It was with a former British intelligence official. On a bright morning early in 2011, as the Arab Spring seized the world's imagination, we had met for lunch.

'What's going to happen in Syria?' he had asked, two weeks after protests had first erupted against Bashar al-Assad.

I remember feeling deep unease at the time. 'Civil war,' I had told him. 'Perhaps a million dead, and it will last ten years.'

'The worst-case scenario,' he suggested.

'No, the most likely. And I have a feeling that some of my own family will fight and die there.'

I, too, had once felt the thrill of marching to war – with rose-tinted expectations of defending fellow Muslims against Crusader aggressors. I was even younger than Ibrahim when I had set off for Bosnia in a whirl of religious fervour. I had wanted to be part of an Islamic Vanguard far removed from the obsolescent ruling classes of Arabia. Nineteen years earlier, I had stood at the graves of other fighters, burning with the same sense of devotion and purpose that had inspired my nephew. Just like me he had gone to wage jihad to fight injustice.

In time I had become disenchanted with the way the likes of Sheikh al-Muhajir manipulated the sayings of the Prophet for the narrow end of attacking the 'Crusaders' or spreading chaos in Arab states, setting Sunni against Shia and seeking to justify the deaths of innocents as part of a global religious war.

Ibrahim would never know the luxury of such reflection nor the perspective that comes with maturity.

I said a short prayer in the gathering gloom and briefly looked at the names scrawled above other hastily dug graves. A few leaves from a stand of poplars drifted across the graveyard as the breeze picked up with the onset of dusk.

Orcan, standing a few feet away and smoking his twentieth cigarette of the day, was beginning to shift from foot to foot. I could almost feel him checking his watch. I turned and murmured my thanks to him. I did not look back.

# REFLECTIONS

The battles across Syria continued remorselessly after my brief glimpse into the inferno. Orcan told me in 2015 how the atmosphere had been transformed. America's obsession with battling the Islamic State had alienated people who had once hoped the US and its allies would rescue them from Assad. Distrust, despair and militancy swirled in a toxic combination.

'If you come now,' he joked darkly during a phone call in mid-2015, 'there will be an execution party.'

When I survey the Muslim world now, I look back to my time in Bosnia and the Philippines, even my first visit to Afghanistan, as almost innocent expeditions in pursuit of an ideal. I felt the call of jihad when it meant something noble and courageous. I have also seen jihad in its most vicious and totalitarian colours. I have literally fought for it and – as it came to be defined by al-Qaeda and ISIS – against it.

My 'betrayal' of the cause earned me a fatwah that is still in force today. I take some comfort from the fact that most of those who would like to see my demise have themselves been killed, including the man who authored my death sentence, Turki Binali, who was taken out in an air strike in north-eastern Syria in the spring of 2017.*

---

* After I encountered him in 2004, Binali became even more radical. He rounded on his former mentor, Abu Mohammed al-Maqdisi, the hardline

Abu Khabab al-Masri, the doyen of Darunta, fled his laboratory the day before US air strikes obliterated much of the site in October 2001.* US intelligence collected fragmentary information suggesting he had resumed research on chemical weapons and poisons in the tribal territories of Pakistan.[3] Despite a $5 million price on his head, he survived for another seven years before the 'Rewards for Justice' programme and a missile caught up with him. Lamenting his martyrdom, al-Qaeda promised Abu Khabab had 'left behind him a generation who will seek revenge and punishment with God's help'.[4]

One of that generation was Dudley's own psychopath, Abu Muslim. After skipping bail in the UK, he'd fled to Pakistan. There is intelligence suggesting he then traveled to the badlands and met up with none other than Abu Khabab.[5] I had often spoken to him about Abu Khabab and, if he indeed trained with him, perhaps he'd sought to follow in my footsteps. Abu Muslim was arrested in Pakistan in 2007 and deported to the UK, where he served three and a half years in jail. Then in 2012 he joined militants in the tribal areas of Pakistan and then travelled to Syria to join ISIS.

By 2015, using the name Muslim al-Britani, he had become one of the most prolific ISIS fighters on Twitter, sharing images of his bomb-making workshop and posting guidance on electronic components for bombs and the chemicals needed to make poisons. He threatened to blow up MI6's headquarters

---

Salafi cleric who had provided spiritual guidance to Abu Musab al-Zarqawi in his early years. After ISIS declared a Caliphate, Binali became the group's chief theologian, issuing fatwahs justifying its actions.[1]

* A *Guardian* journalist who visited the site a month later found that Abu Khabab's workshop did not suffer a direct hit. He found 'a makeshift laboratory packed with bottles of poisons, including cyanide, bomb instruction manuals and ... antiquated gas masks ... strewn across the room'. In 2008 several unnamed US officials told the *Los Angeles Times* they believed Abu Khabab had a link to the development of the poison gas device al-Qaeda planned to deploy in New York. They, of course, knew this because of my intelligence.[2]

and interviewed online by a British newspaper said: 'All I see for the UK in the horizon are dark black clouds.'*

He also boasted about his prowess in 'producing sophisticated IED's'. An intelligence source told me in 2017 that Abu Muslim was thought to have been involved in ISIS efforts to develop bombs that could be smuggled onto aircraft disguised as laptop batteries. I was told these efforts had been inspired by news coverage of exploding Samsung Galaxy Note 7 mobile phones.** It seemed he'd become quite the inventor. I was told he was also involved in adapting commercial drones to carry bombs or explode on impact, which became an important part of the ISIS arsenal as it came under attack in 2017.

I had clearly underestimated the 'bruva' from the West Midlands. So, apparently, had the British security services. I frequently wondered why, after being released from prison, he'd been allowed in 2012 to leave the country. At time of writing, I have no idea whether he is still alive. I hope not.

So many of the men I once counted as friends and comrades are dead: Khalid al-Hajj, Farouq al-Kuwaiti, the mild-mannered Safwat. My one-time lab partner Hassan Ghul and Adam Gadahn, the American I had escorted to join the group, were among those killed in US drone strikes.***

Many who could not be counted as friends are in jail. Abu Nassim, the Tunisian psychopath I had encountered in Darunta,

---

* Abu Muslim claimed his British passport had been cancelled in 2013, tweeting: 'I just wana thank the Home Secretary Theresa May 4 taking my British Citizenship away.'[6]
** I was also told by intelligence sources that Abu Muslim was regarded as particularly skilled in electronics and circuitry and had provided training in bomb circuitry to ISIS members with some grasp of English, including recruits from Europe and North America. Intelligence about the plan to create laptop bombs led to a ban on laptops in aeroplane cabins on certain Middle East flights to the United States and the UK for several months in 2017. The bans were lifted after enhanced screening measures were put into place.[7]
*** After being released by the CIA, Ghul was killed by a US drone strike in Pakistan's tribal belt in 2012.[8]

travelled to fight in Syria before slipping into Libya, from where he helped plan the March 2015 attack on the Bardo museum in Tunis and the June 2015 attack on a beach in Sousse, killing over fifty holidaymakers from Europe and around the world. After pressure mounted on ISIS in Libya, he was apprehended and extradited to Tunisia where he was convicted in connection with the two attacks.*

Others are still at large, like Dundee native Abu Abdullah al-Scotlandi. He was designated by the United States as running a 'front organization' for al-Qaeda based in Pakistan that financed al-Qaeda and other jihadi groups in Afghanistan.[10] Also at liberty at the time of writing is Yasser Kamal, the great persuader behind the Bahrain plot in 2004 and the man who connected me with Dudley's own Abu Muslim. His life's mission appears to be to liquidate me. While I feel it unlikely that he has the guile to track me down in Europe, I would think twice about a visit to Bahrain, especially since the warning I received in 2016.

The world, and especially the Islamic world, has become a darker place since I set out for Vienna as a naive and bright-eyed sixteen-year-old. The range of opposing and mutually intolerant perspectives has grown exponentially. Common ground and tolerance among Shia and Sunni has evaporated, even in places where sectarian strife used to be rare.

'The spectrum of those who practise the faith is widening to convulsive effect,' the historian Tom Holland wrote in 2015.[11] The Islamic State widened that spectrum still further. As Graeme Wood observed the same year, ISIS drew its fair share of psychopaths and adventure-seekers. But from its perspective its behaviour was 'a sincere, carefully considered commitment to returning civilization to a seventh-century legal environment, and ultimately to bringing about the apocalypse'.**

---

* After 9/11 Fezzani was captured, detained at the US detention facility at the Bagram air force base, and later transferred to Italian custody. His acquittal on terrorism charges in 2012 was one example of prosecutorial inadequacies in Europe. After he was deported to Tunisia he rejoined the jihadi cause.[9]

** It should be stressed, however, that there is no conception of a sudden apocalypse in Islam. The arrival of the Mahdi and the rule of Jesus Christ is

As I write this in the spring of 2018, I have had much time to reflect on how the global jihadi threat is evolving and the steps I believe are necessary for the civilized world to prevail. In my lifetime I have witnessed two intersecting struggles evolve. One is the asymmetrical war between international jihadi groups and the world at large (the West and at times Russia and Arab governments, too). This has manifested itself in attempts to bring down airliners, and attacks in European cities or on hotels frequented by Westerners in remote places like Mali.

Both al-Qaeda and ISIS have exported their ideology to a small, alienated fraction of the Muslim communities of Europe and North America. Young men – impressionable, angry – grasp a distortion of religion to justify acts of violence against the societies where they live but which they have come to loathe.

Some – a few, but enough – have moved from idle boast to terrible deed, driving trucks into vacationing crowds or shooting dead scores of people at a concert. Bomb-makers have hidden in nondescript apartments in Manchester, Brussels and Paris – even Sydney. The age of encrypted communication has aided conspiracies and the transfer of deadly technical skills. This sporadic, attritional conflict consumes acres of media coverage and outsize police resources in Europe. But to me it's an offshoot of a much larger battle – a civil war – among Muslims, locked in an epochal struggle over the meaning of Islam and its place in a rapidly modernizing world.

Two decades ago I listened to muezzin on opposing sides of the front lines in Afghanistan compete in singing out the call for evening prayers. It was a metaphor for my religion: the ascetic medieval fundamentalism of the Taliban against the pro-Western Islamic nationalism of the Northern Alliance.

How has this happened? Some scholars go back centuries, to the Reconquista that ejected Muslim rulers from much of southern

---

foretold to lead to a victorious period for Islam preceding the final Day of Judgment. It is for this glorious 'beginning of the end' phase of history that al-Qaeda and ISIS strive to create the preconditions.[12]

Europe, and the failure of the Turkish siege of Vienna in 1683. Europe's agricultural and industrial revolutions followed, while much of the Islamic world made slower strides towards modernity. The age of colonialism, and superior Western economic power, subdued Muslims in their homelands, from French Morocco to the Dutch East Indies.

'The Muslim,' as Bernard Lewis put it, 'has suffered successive stages of defeat.'[13]

In the age of the modern nation-state, Arab societies have scrabbled for a stable way of governing, from absolute monarchy to military dictatorship and one-party rule, even Marxism. Add the dislocating effects of urbanization, the rapid homogenization of global popular culture, the impact of pan-Arab television networks, the lack of social mobility and opportunity, endemic corruption: the diagnosis of the sickness has many causes.

This frustration is not exclusive to Muslim countries but has aggravated a sense of disequilibrium and humiliation among the millions of Muslims who are not among a tiny and (often) Westernized elite. Some of these Muslims heard those in the pulpits and the madrassas who said that pagan innovations were to blame, and the only recourse was to return to the Holy Book, in other words to fundamentalism.

There were, of course, intellectual underpinnings for this – such as the works of Qutb that I devoured as a teenager. But there were also moments in history that fed the polarization of Muslim opinion and the development of Salafi jihadism, and several of the most significant occurred in a single year: 1979.

## THE WAR WITHIN ISLAM

The convulsions of 1979 changed our religion and our politics forever. I was just months old when the year dawned but have lived with its consequences all my life. Just days before I was born, the Shah of Iran declared martial law in an effort to quell Islamist-led protests. A cleric scorned by the Shah's government as a 'mad Indian poet' moved from his exile in Iraq to a village near Paris to begin agitating for the Shah's overthrow. That cleric was Ayatollah Ruhollah Khomeini.

Within weeks of the new year, the Shah was gone, swept away by the protests of millions that seemed briefly to bring all of Iran – Communists, democrats and Islamists – together. In much of the West, Khomeini was portrayed as a spiritual leader who would usher in some form of Islamic democracy. My oldest brother, Moheddin, and his contemporaries had a very different feeling. Where we lived – in Saudi Arabia's Eastern Province – there was a restive Shia minority that might take heart from events across the Gulf. The mutual mistrust between Sunni and Shia, which had ebbed and flowed across the centuries, acquired a new piquancy.

Just as the Shia ayatollahs in Iran were taking power, so Sunni militancy – in Pakistan, Egypt, even Saudi Arabia – was also beginning to gather strength. My family, like millions in Saudi Arabia and across the Muslim world, was stunned when Sunni militants attacked the Grand Mosque in Mecca in November 1979. As many as 400 armed jihadis infiltrated the Mosque, taking thousands of worshippers hostage. It took Saudi special forces, with the help of tanks, artillery and even French expertise with toxic gas, nearly two weeks to flush out the militants.[14]

The leader of the group, Juheiman al-Oteibi, rejected Saudi Arabia's modernization. He saw the al-Saud dynasty as guilty of corroding the moral values of Saudi society. He and his followers also believed the Mahdi was about to descend to earth to lead Muslims in an apocalyptic battle against the infidel. In the months before they seized the mosque, al-Oteibi and dozens of his followers had night visions that his soon-to-be brother-in-law Mohammed Abdullah was the Mahdi.[15] This not only strengthened their resolve to act but propelled them towards seizing the Great Mosque. According to a well-known *hadith*, near the end-of-days this messianic figure would be given allegiance at the site of the Kaaba* in

---

* Muslims believe the Kaaba was the first site of worship of God on earth and was rebuilt by the Prophet Ibrahim (Abraham) but then fell into being

order to rid the earth of wrongdoing and injustice. It was an early example of the power of prophecy.[16]

Many young Saudis were appalled by the attack and by the merciless reaction of the Saudi army, which in their view had desecrated the holiest place in Islam with its blunt use of force. One of those horrified was a young Osama bin Laden, scion of one of the Kingdom's wealthiest families.

The siege at Mecca reverberated throughout the Muslim world. Ayatollah Khomeini proclaimed that Israel and the United States were behind the plot. That was enough to drive enraged protestors in Pakistan to attack and burn down the US embassy in Islamabad. Pakistan, too, was changing. Its military dictator, General Zia ul Haq, was intent on making it a more Islamist society. Zia had overthrown the democratically elected prime minister, Zulfikar Ali Bhutto, in 1977 and had him hanged in April 1979. Zia ul Haq would direct the infamous ISI – with whom I had some awkward interaction – to support the Afghan mujahideen.*

Not all was confrontation in the Middle East that fateful year. The day I was born, President Jimmy Carter, whose administration would be crippled by events in Iran, finally persuaded Israeli Prime Minister Menachem Begin and Egyptian President Anwar Sadat to put pen to paper after twelve days of secret negotiations at Camp David. It was an historic agreement that would lead to the celebration on the White House lawn of a peace treaty between Arab and Jew. The 1979 Peace Treaty was optimistically cast as the foundation of a broader reconciliation between Israel and its Arab enemies. But it hardened the hearts of the 'rejectionists', most of them radical Islamists, to whom Egypt had surrendered its role as the bastion of Arab resistance. These Islamists were revolted by the secularization of Egyptian society under first Nasser and then Sadat. One of them – a young surgeon recently married – was Ayman al-Zawahiri.

---

used as a site for idol worship until the Prophet Mohammed founded Islam.
* In the decade after 1979 the United States channeled billions of dollars to Pakistan's ISI, who in turn distributed funds to the mujahideen. They were the proxies in America's efforts to bleed the Red Army in Afghanistan.

Peace with Israel would set in train a conspiracy among Islamist radicals including within the Egyptian army that would lead to Sadat's assassination two years after that moment of sunlit optimism in Washington. Zawahiri had only a marginal role in the conspiracy but Sadat's assassination, on 6 October 1981, would thrust him into the limelight as one of the leading intellectuals of Egyptian jihad.

By then Zawahiri had become immersed in the aftermath of a seismic event that closed 1979 as dramatically as the Shah's fall had opened it. On 24 December, Soviet tanks rolled across the border into Afghanistan, the vanguard of an invasion that would set off the horrendous war between the Red Army and the Afghan mujahideen. The invasion would draw thousands of Arabs to the region, including Zawahiri. They provided humanitarian aid; they provided weapons; and they joined that resistance. Jihad was going international.

Other events that year had indirect but just as profound consequences for the Arab world and for the growing polarization that would disable it for decades to come. One was almost overlooked altogether in the West, even among Arabs. It was the purge of the Baath Party in Iraq which made Saddam Hussein an unchallenged dictator, his megalomania given free rein to launch wars against Iran and Kuwait. He also built a ruthless security apparatus, some of whose number would later help build the Islamic State in Iraq into the most potent jihadi group yet seen.

I justify this historical diversion for two reasons. These events demonstrated in many ways the effects of Western (and Soviet) intervention in the Middle East. This chunk of land, and especially the region between Cairo and the Gulf, is at the centre of the world, a crossroads of both maritime and land routes. It is resource-rich, home to two thirds of the world's oil and gas reserves and a sizable fraction of its mineral wealth. It was inevitably going to be a sandbox of competition and conflict. As many of its states have been so lavishly armed, it will remain so and at a higher level of lethality.

The second and more important reason is that much of what is playing out today has its foundations in or was unleashed by those events in 1979: Sunni versus Shia, Persians against Arabs, the battle pitting the conservative monarchies (and in Egypt's case the military) against political Islam, represented by the Muslim Brotherhood and more radical shades.

In a very short period of time, a series of unrelated events can coalesce to change the course of history. Such was the case in 1979 across the Arab and Muslim world. This upheaval has affected millions of Muslim families, including my own. My brother Moheddin was among so many from Saudi Arabia, the Gulf States, Egypt and elsewhere who felt driven by the Soviet invasion of Afghanistan to join jihad against the godless Russians. My cousin and nephew died in Syria opposing the regime of Bashar al-Assad. And I, of course, pledged allegiance to Osama bin Laden.

After a lifetime as a participant in and observer of Islam's civil war, I reject the reductionism of some Western observers. In his famous 1990 essay, Bernard Lewis said that in the 'classical Islamic view, to which many Muslims are beginning to return, the world and all mankind are divided into two: the House of Islam, where the Muslim law and faith prevail, and the rest, known as the House of Unbelief or the House of War, which is the duty of Muslims ultimately to bring to Islam'. This would lead to what Lewis called 'a clash of civilizations – the perhaps irrational but surely historic reaction of an ancient rival against our Judeo-Christian heritage, our secular present and the worldwide expansion of both'.[17]

Sadly, many Muslims would subscribe to this perspective rather than acknowledge the crisis within Islam. They think the conflicts ravaging their lands stem from a Western conspiracy to steal their natural resources. So perfidious is that conspiracy that many Muslims even blame terror attacks in the West, from 9/11 to the November 2015 gun rampage in Paris, on the CIA and Mossad. They interpret these attacks as wicked plots to put Western boots on the ground and drones in the air across the Middle East.

This persecution complex is the outgrowth of a sense of hopelessness among millions who see their lives as bereft of opportunity and their social environments as stacked against them. They think politics is useless and, unable to change the system, they set out to smash it. Many Muslim states are home to a proliferation of non-state actors because the state is held in contempt. It provides few services, is corrupt and frequently oppressive. Jihadism has become the Muslim version of anarchy – on steroids.

Many of the men who became my friends or brothers-in-arms were convinced of the righteousness of their cause, of their duty to wage jihad. Wherever they looked, they saw a civilizational war, or, rather, overlapping wars. The West was the enemy, but so were the corrupt Gulf monarchies, which were merely American puppets. And as the years passed, especially when Abu Musab al-Zarqawi's sectarian loathing was inherited by the Islamic State, a third war began: doctrinaire Sunni militants against messianic Shia fundamentalists.

## THE POWER OF PROPHECY

The Islamic State and al-Qaeda have had plenty of 'personality disorders' among their numbers: sociopaths and psychopaths. But the conviction I saw in the gleaming eyes of Khalid al-Hajj, the young Canadian Muslims who had come to Bosnia, the attendees at Awlaki's Dudley lecture, the wounded fighters in Syria and dozens more derived from intense religious faith and an unshakeable belief that Islamic prophecy would guide the *Ummah* to a purer state.

So many attempts by outsiders to capture the essence of these groups have underplayed their spiritual underpinnings. Western analysts tend to study jihadi movements through the prism of their own assumptions, believing that such groups will weigh risks and benefits and act rationally. Al-Qaeda was quite capable of that as the meticulous planning of the 9/11 attacks showed. But, ultimately, global jihad is guided by very specific interpretations of the Koran and the *hadith*.

In al-Qaeda, the pitch has been simple. One of the group's preachers cites a verse from the Koran or a *hadith* foretelling great battles to come, and poses a straightforward question to his audience: 'Do you think you know better than God? Do you think He would have left us without a blueprint for the future? Do you not see that the long-fore-told epic battles have begun in Yemen, Syria and Iraq?'

If prophecies about our lives in this world were now coming to pass, then the promise of paradise for martyrs in the next world was surely guaranteed.

Both al-Qaeda and ISIS were intent on creating the conditions on earth for the glorious end phase of history foretold by the Prophet Mohammed, in other words on speeding up history through their actions. They would be the Victorious Vanguard and fly the Black Banners, a powerful religious symbol.[18] According to that *hadith* I had heard so many times in Afghanistan, 'If you see the Black Banners coming from Khurasan, join that army, even if you have to crawl over ice; no power will be able to stop them.'*

When Zarqawi's group declared the 'Islamic State of Iraq' months after his death in 2006, its leaders believed its creation was necessary because the Mahdi's arrival was imminent and he would need help in fighting epic battles against the infidel near the end-of-days. And the Mahdi would be anointed in Mecca, according to *hadith* predicting that 'the armies of Iraq and the Levant will come and join him in Mecca.' So overthrowing the House of Saud was a priority for Abu Bakr al-Baghdadi, a theme to which he repeatedly returned.[20]

ISIS's mission was to execute God's strategy as ordained 1,400 years ago. It was (and to many still is) a powerful message: 'The end-of-days is approaching, and if you want to be a true Muslim, on the right side of history, you had better join us soon.'[21] Similarly, the prophecies about the location of 'Five Armies' destined to fight the epic battles explain why al-Qaeda has focused its efforts in Afghanistan, Pakistan, Yemen, Iraq, the Maghreb and especially Syria. Given Syria's prominence in the prophecies, it's little surprise that both al-Qaeda and the Islamic State were galvanized by its upheavals.

---

* One of the extremists captivated by the prophecy was Boston Marathon bomber Tamerlan Tsarnaev. He played a video entitled 'The Emergence of Prophecy: The Black Flags of Khorasan' on his YouTube account before the April 2013 attack.[19]

'We wish to see the armies of Mujahideen setting out from al-Sham [Syria] to liberate al-Quds [mosque in Jerusalem],' Osama bin Laden's son Hamza said. 'Everything in Jihad in al-Sham assumes a heavenly dimension.'[22] Equally, at the beginning of the insurgency in Iraq, Abu Musab al-Zarqawi had said: 'The spark has been lit here in Iraq, and its heat will continue to intensify – by Allah's permission – until it burns the Crusader armies in Dabiq.'[23]

Dabiq is a nondescript village in northern Syria, but it is described in a *hadith* as the venue of an epic end-of-days victory for the armies of Islam against those of Rome (the West), after which they would conquer Constantinople before seizing Rome[24] and witnessing the emergence of the Antichrist and the return of Jesus Christ.[25] ISIS devoted considerable efforts to capturing and holding the village before being expelled by Turkish-backed fighters in 2016.

Months before declaring a Caliphate, Abu Bakr al-Baghdadi goaded America. 'Very soon you will be in the direct confrontation – you will be forced to do so, God permitting,' he said.

The grisly execution of Western hostages was in part an attempt by ISIS to draw an invading force to northern Syria to help fulfil this prophecy. In one of their chilling videos, a fighter standing on a hill above Dabiq later identified as Abu Abdullah al-Britani declared: 'We are waiting for you in Dabiq. Try, try to come and we will kill every single soldier.'[26]

It might seem perverse that ISIS would welcome the formation of a powerful coalition with immense aerial power that would inevitably destroy it. But the sight of aircraft only increased the belief that the longed-for epic battles were materializing.

'Our Prophet (peace be upon him) has informed us of the *Malahem* (epic battles) near the end of time. He gave us good tidings and promised us that we would be victorious in these battles,' stated al-Baghdadi.[27]

For three years, ISIS strived to build its shining city upon a hill, even if it was most people's vision of hell. But it added a coda, using the prophecies to redefine what victory meant. Its chief ideologue, my old nemesis Turki Binali, indicated that according to the prophecies a handful of 'righteous' Caliphs might need to rule after Baghdadi before the Mahdi returned.[28] ISIS brainwashed thousands of children so they would carry the mantle forward.

I have seen the power of prophecy. I have also seen its price. It impelled the Islamic State to throw wave after wave of men into battles they were destined to lose, as at Kobane. ISIS's interpretations of the *hadith* were a recipe for absolute intolerance and alienated every other faction on the ground. But what need of strategic patience if the end of times is approaching and victory is assured?

Even the declaration of a Caliphate was tempting fate – a clarion call to the Islamic State's enemies, al-Qaeda among them. God had promised there would be a Caliphate, ISIS spokesman Abu Muhammad al-Adnani explained.* The time had come for Muslims to wake from their sleep and face the epic battles.[29] But many Muslim scholars said the preconditions for the declaration of a Caliphate were not met. And in declaring the Caliphate, ISIS attached its legitimacy to the holding of territory. When it began to lose that territory it had to explain why.

As the dark grey on maps, denoting areas controlled by ISIS, shrank and disappeared, its leaders mobilized the prophecies again. True followers would fight many battles and endure much suffering, just as Constantinople had only fallen to the Ottomans after dozens of attacks over centuries. Tribulations were necessary to purify the faith of Muslims and make them deserving of ultimate victory.[30]

After rushing to declare war on the entire civilized world, Baghdadi stressed the need to be 'patient in both victory and in defeat'.[31] The will to fight was more crucial than the loss of this city or that province. There was a new fluidity to its 'timetable'. As Will McCants wrote, 'the "great battle" [at Dabiq] will come to pass because God has promised it would; but this isn't that battle because all the other preceding prophecies haven't come to pass.'[32]

---

* He quoted Koran 2:30. 'Indeed, I will make upon the earth a successive authority.'

As the battle for Mosul began, Baghdadi promised that the names of fighters who defended the city would be inscribed in the history of Islam with those of the Prophet's earliest companions. 'This is but a precursor to the victory and conquest that God has promised,' Baghdadi said. And he quoted a prophecy:

> 'God says, "Indeed, they were about to drive you from the land to evict you. And then they will not remain after you, except for a little."'[33]

ISIS followers were fond of reciting one particular *hadith*:

> 'A group of my Ummah will not cease to fight at the gates of Damascus and at the gates of Al-Quds [Jerusalem] and its surroundings. The betrayal or desertion of whoever deserts them will not harm them in the least. They will remain victorious, standing for the truth, until the Final Hour rises.'[34]

In other words, the rest of the world would confront and *nearly* vanquish them, but ultimately they would triumph amid desertion and against all odds. Of course, it's easier to believe God is on your side when you are 'remaining and expanding' rather than being pummelled. But for the leadership and ideologues of the Islamic State the rhythm of seizing and losing territory was like breathing in and out.*

The ideology, postulated by Binali and Abu Abdullah al-Muhajir, the self-satisfied theological brain behind Zarqawi's ultra-violent brawn, will unfortunately live on – even if the Caliphate is a memory.

---

* ISIS spokesman Abu Muhammad al-Adnani said in May 2016: 'Do you think America that defeat is the loss of a city or land? Were we defeated when we lost the cities in Iraq and stayed in the desert without a city or land? And will we be defeated, and you victorious, if you took Mosul or Sirte or Raqqa or all the cities and we returned as we were in the beginning? No, defeat is losing the will and the desire to fight. [. . .] We don't do jihad to protect a land or to liberate or control a land. We do not fight for finite power or position, or the ruins of a mortal world. If our aim was one of these things, then we would not have fought the world together and all peoples in all areas.'[35]

Ranging from ruminations on the merits of beheading, torturing or burning prisoners to thoughts on assassination, siege warfare and the use of biological weapons, Muhajir's legacy is crucial to ISIS and indeed whatever follows it. In essence, it is a way to render practically anything permissible if it can be spun as beneficial to the jihad. ISIS has written itself a blank cheque for the future.

## THE HARE AND THE TORTOISE

ISIS's draconian ideology is inimical to al-Qaeda, whose priority is to entrench itself among guerrilla struggles and uprisings, to attract support and build grassroots allegiances rather than impose its rule through terror. Al-Qaeda has a buffet of aims; there's only one item on the ISIS menu.

Their differences have been fuelled by animosity among leaders, but they are essentially philosophical. ISIS believes all jihadis must obey the Caliph. Al-Qaeda never believed ISIS acquired enough territory or support to found a legitimate Caliphate. ISIS has sweepingly embraced *takfirism* – the excommunication of all Muslims who don't agree with it, while al-Qaeda has applied the doctrine in a limited and specific way. ISIS extended its draconian view of non-Muslims – Yazidis and Christians – to include the Shia. One reason that ISIS destroyed the al-Nuri great mosque in Mosul, from which Abu Bakr al-Baghdadi had declared the Caliphate, was because its demolition was preferable to seeing the Shia-dominated (and therefore in its mind heretical) Iraqi security forces occupy the pulpit and use it as a propaganda coup. Al-Qaeda, by contrast, historically had a more nuanced (though not exactly generous) attitude towards the Shia but it has hardened over time.

While al-Qaeda looks to the guidelines of 'defensive jihad' in its struggle to restore Muslim sovereignty (jihad *al-Tamkeen*), ISIS holds that their Caliph has sovereign power to set the rules in waging this struggle just like early Caliphs did in waging 'offensive jihad'. ISIS seeks to model itself on armies of conquest in the early

Islamic period and holds that the Caliph can sanction almost anything and everything, from taking slaves to confiscating property, as long as it does not contradict the group's view of how these early Islamic armies behaved.*

In my view, and in the view of a good number of Islamic scholars, *hadith* that endorse the stoning of individuals or throwing homosexuals from rooftops are essentially fabrications. Al-Qaeda leaders have frowned on such practices, even if their foot soldiers have committed atrocities.** While some of the differences between al-Qaeda and ISIS might seem esoteric, they are unbridgeable to Salafi-jihadis.

In contrast to al-Qaeda, where celibacy was the norm, the taking of female slaves became an industry within ISIS. After the group swept through northern Iraq in the summer of 2014, it captured thousands of Yazidi women and girls. It was a cynical recruiting tool calculated to appeal to young, sexually frustrated recruits, and justified by interpreting the Koran and *hadith* as legitimizing the rape and sexual enslavement of non-Muslims, especially those regarded as polytheists.

Slavery, especially of non-Muslim women, was very much part of the eighth-century fabric proudly worn by the Islamic State. Al-Adnani before his death in 2016, said: 'We will conquer your Rome, break your crosses, and enslave your women. If we do not

* Al-Qaeda focuses on how early Muslim communities resisted occupation to set the guidelines for how it should fight. Enslaving populations was not a feature of such defensive jihad. Under the concept of defensive jihad, Muslims do not need to receive instructions from a central authority to fight. Al-Qaeda has mirrored this by allowing affiliates a significant amount of flexibility. ISIS, by contrast, has focused on how early Islamic rulers fought 'offensive' jihad for guidelines for how to fight, arguing that because some early Islamic rulers carried out massacres and enslaved resisting enemy populations they can, too. Because all authority rests with the Caliph, ISIS does not have an affiliate system like al-Qaeda.
** According to a report compiled by Amnesty International, during al-Qaeda's occupation of swathes of Yemen's tribal areas between 2011 and 2012, the group inflicted 'a raft of gross and deeply disturbing' punishments including crucifixions, public executions, amputations and floggings.[36]

reach that time, then our children and grandchildren will reach it, and they will sell your sons as slaves at the slave market.'[37]

If al-Qaeda unleashed the inner psychopath among its recruits by dehumanizing non-Muslims, ISIS allowed it to run riot. The group's use of sex slaves was sanctioned by none other than Turki Binali, the Bahraini jihadi who had issued a fatwah against me. A ruling by his ISIS fatwah department said it was 'permissible to have intercourse with the female slave who hasn't reached puberty, if she is fit for intercourse'.* The sexual repression of the al-Qaeda era was, in fact, replaced by a sex-crazed jihad in which the basest of human instincts were given free rein. When Baghdadi repeatedly raped the American hostage Kayla Mueller, he viewed it as an act of worship.[39]

I simply can't imagine that anyone with whom I fought in Bosnia could have subscribed to such a view. Some among us felt that no punishment was cruel enough for the Bosnian-Serb militia. But no one saw rape and slavery, nor burning offenders alive, as pillars of Shariah. While most of us in Bosnia had felt an impulse to liberate and to protect, ISIS wanted only to dominate and terrorize.

The future landscape of jihad is difficult to predict, so intense are the ideological disputes and so fluid the situation on the ground. However, given the many bitter differences between ISIS and al-Qaeda that I have outlined, I feel there is very little chance that al-Qaeda and ISIS will agree to form a jihadi behemoth. The two will continue to compete but neither will deliver a knockout blow. Some – a few – adherents may change sides, but the two groups will continue in parallel, probably never to coalesce. Al-Qaeda may

---

* ISIS's English language Dabiq online magazine claimed that 'one should remember that enslaving the families of the kuffār and taking their women as concubines is a firmly established aspect of the Sharī'ah.' ISIS's sex slavery has been enabled by women in the group. In another article later published by Dabiq, a female Islamic State member stated, 'I and those with me at home prostrated to Allah in gratitude on the day the first slave-girl entered our home.'[38]

gain the upper hand because of a strategy based on cultivating support rather than imposing force.

Al-Qaeda, the tortoise competing with the hare, has shown a grim-faced resilience. It found ungoverned spaces and picked up the scent of injustice – especially in Yemen and in Syria. The chaos and polarization that followed the Arab Spring in 2011 created opportunities that even al-Qaeda leaders would have scarcely believed possible a few years earlier. The emergence of Jabhat al-Nusra in Syria, an al-Qaeda affiliate until a tactical and awkward parting of ways in 2016, gave the group renewed relevance. Al-Nusra and its successive rebrands became the most powerful rebel group in north-western Syria.

Twenty years after al-Qaeda initiated its campaign of global terror, its fortunes are reviving.[40] Many thousands belong to aligned groups in Syria, Yemen, Somalia and the Sahel. Al-Qaeda is continuing to try to rebuild a presence in Afghanistan beneath the wings of a renascent Taliban. In the years after the Arab Spring, the organization's goals shifted from plotting large-scale international terrorist attacks towards building up its presence in the Arab and Muslim world. Ayman al-Zawahiri had signalled the shift in focus when in 2015 he instructed al-Nusra leader Abu Mohammed al-Julani not to use Syria as a base to attack the West.[41]

In their drive to take advantage of the security vacuum, al-Qaeda-aligned groups are being guided by two strategic maxims long held by Zawahiri. The first is the need for the jihadi movement to gain the support of the Arab and Muslim masses (a priority that Abu Musab al-Suri had long stressed). The second is the need to take control of territory to create staging points for future expansion.

We have seen this play out in Yemen. Al-Qaeda in the Arabian Peninsula reached out to Sunni tribes to make common cause against the Shia Houthis and rebranded itself as Ansar al-Shariah to broaden its support base. The same strategy was applied in Syria, where al-Nusra built up a proto-emirate in Idlib province and focused on winning support and allies on the ground, at least until it fell out with head office and embarked on an internecine fight with other rebel groups. In Afghanistan, al-Qaeda has doubled down on its allegiance to the Taliban while trying to establish a home-grown affiliate in the Indian subcontinent.

Al-Qaeda also perversely benefited from the far darker vision of ISIS in three ways. When Salafi clerics came together to call for jihad to be reclaimed, even rescued, from ISIS, they implicitly looked to al-Qaeda's alternative. Secondly, the sudden emergence of ISIS drew the fire of the Western intelligence community; al-Qaeda was 'yesterday's threat'. Thirdly, al-Qaeda's – in relative terms – 'moderate' approach to jihad better positioned it to raise funds from sympathizers in the wealthy Gulf countries. Al-Qaeda survived by holding true to its religious ideology and attacking the behaviour of the ISIS leadership.

In 2015, al-Qaeda began to groom a famous name to attract a new generation to jihad. Osama bin Laden's son Hamza carefully avoided being dragged into a spitting contest with ISIS and instead called for jihadis to unify their ranks. But more than his father, he embraced aggressively anti-Shia rhetoric.[42] A ploy to lure away the remnants of ISIS? Or a recognition of a new and brutally sectarian landscape?

If there is anything that might halt the al-Qaeda revival it is infighting. Staffed by middle-class revolutionaries and led by a pomp-ous Egyptian far less charismatic than bin Laden, it has at times resembled a debating society, with minor differences of opinion fed by clashes of ego evolving into major rifts. Among 'al-Nusra' rebels in Syria a rift hardened between a larger faction, consisting of Syrian, Lebanese and Palestinian fighters, which separated from al-Qaeda, and a smaller faction, made up of Saudis, Jordanians and others, which remained loyal.* Al-Qaeda will fight to the bitter end to main-tain its black banners in Syria, which it views as the epicentre of the epic battles. It will seek to consolidate its rear base in Afghanistan and sustain its far-flung affiliates. While its strategy has been

---

* In a 28 November 2017 audio statement, al-Qaeda leader Ayman al-Zawa-hiri condemned the larger faction for their 'violation of the covenant' and for 'cracking down . . . on those brothers who held to their pledge'.

different in recent years to the one I heard bin Laden pronounce, al-Qaeda may be tempted to renew its campaign of terror attacks in the West. The arrival at 1600 Pennsylvania Avenue in 2017 of a president who has made inflammatory remarks about Muslims, targeted Muslim countries with travel bans and recognized Jerusalem as Israel's capital, fuelled the anti-Americanism that once made attacks against 'the head of the snake' such a unifying cause. President Trump's embrace of the House of Saud added further octane.

'The actions undertaken by the impudent Crusader Trump revealed the true face of America', Zawahiri declared in the spring of 2018. "This is a moment of truth . . . let us fight America everywhere.' Al-Qaeda's affiliate in Yemen retains significant capability to launch attacks against Western aviation and other targets, despite a large increase in air strikes against it in the first year of the Trump administration.[43]

Given Russia's role in Syria in support of the Assad regime, it is equally a target should al-Qaeda decide that an international campaign of terrorism suits its goals. Even China is in al-Qaeda's sights, not least because thousands of Uighur Muslim fighters have trekked to Syria, Iraq and Afghanistan in the past decade.

Sadly, I don't see an end to the Muslims' civil war anytime soon, nor an end to the different strains of jihadism advanced by al-Qaeda and whatever succeeds ISIS. Both groups have resources and years (in al-Qaeda's case decades) of experience working underground. They have developed a talent for seeking out ungoverned spaces. The continuing impossibility of securing and governing Afghanistan and Yemen provide the best opportunities of all.

To the Afghans victory is defined by your patience outlasting that of your enemy. I recall during a trek through the Afghan province of Nuristan twenty years ago coming across a stooped farmer with a face hardened and wrinkled by the elements. He was tending to saplings on a mountain slope, tenderly gathering soil around their roots.

I stopped to talk to him in my broken Dari.

'What are you growing?' I asked.

'Pistachio,' he said, exposing a couple of jagged teeth.

'What month do you get the nuts?'

'In thirty years,' he said. 'They're for my grandchildren.'

As for Yemen, it will take a generation to recover from decades of conflict and environmental collapse. Any form of government worthy of the name is still years away.

Libya, Somalia, Iraq and Syria, the Sahel region and the jungles I once roamed in South East Asia also continue to offer breeding grounds for jihad.

Both al-Qaeda and ISIS will continue to dream of creating their perfect 'Islamic State', even if their paths and ideologies will be distinct. They will also look for new ways to attack the West.

## AN INVENTIVE ENEMY

I worry often about the technology of the *mubtakkar* leaching out to ever more jihadi groups and being developed as a new weapon of terror. Abu Khabab's deputy Abu Bakr al-Masri remains unaccounted for. He always dreamed of travelling to Yemen. If he did, it is possible that he shared expertise developed in Darunta with the al-Qaeda in Yemen explosives expert Ibrahim al-Asiri. Al-Asiri was the brains behind the so-called 'underwear bomb' attempt in the skies above Detroit on Christmas Day 2009 and is widely viewed as the most dangerous bomb-maker to have emerged since 9/11.[44]

The *mubtakkar* blueprints have likely been accessed by thousands of jihadis online. The instructions spread like a virus from one al-Qaeda website to another, making it impossible for security services to permanently remove the content from the web.[45] In 2009, I noticed detailed blueprints for the *mubtakkar* had again been posted online and immediately alerted MI6, but I was told it had been downloaded more than 700 times before the British were able to take down the post. In 2015 it was disclosed that the blueprints had been found in the possession of a terrorist cell arrested in Egypt.*

---

* A file named 'mubtakkar' was recovered from alleged members of the al-Qaeda-aligned Ansar al-Shariah Brigades, a terrorist group accused of

If a small terrorist cell in Egypt was able to access the blue-print, I am sure larger groups have it and are working assiduously to make it more lethal. ISIS, after all, had access to laboratories at Mosul University and some of Saddam's chemical weapons engineers among its number.[47] It experimented with chlorine and sulphur mustard attacks in Syria and Iraq.[48]

One straw in the wind was a plot in Australia, uncovered in 2017, in which two brothers were allegedly planning to build an 'improvised chemical dispersion device' that would release highly toxic hydrogen sulphide. The plotters had allegedly received instruction from an ISIS controller in Syria, who had been put in touch with them by a third brother who was with the group.[49] I fear the technology might be deployed one day.

Communications and propaganda are and will continue to be a critical piece of the battlefield. The wide availability of end-to-end encryption apps allows terrorists to communicate in secret, which has revolutionized their ability to plan, coach and provide information. Many plots and attacks in the West in recent years have involved extremists being remotely instructed from overseas, dramatically increasing terrorist groups' reach.[50] The ISIS terrorist cell which attacked Paris in November 2015 and Brussels in March 2016 was communicating via these apps with their handlers in Syria. In the run up to the Brussels attacks they were able, without being detected, to record long audio briefings for these handlers, discussing attack plans and asking technical questions related to making the TATP explosive they used in the attack.[51]

The imagination and innovation of these terror groups should not be underestimated. Those working in counter-terrorism need to prepare for a range of new threats, from weaponized terrorist drones to poison gas attacks to continued efforts to design bombs that can defeat airline security.

---

plotting to target security services and Christians. The file, as described in Egyptian courtroom proceedings against twenty-three alleged members of the cell, had striking similarities to the file posted by the Bahrain cell.[46]

With the explosion of terror attacks worldwide, jihadism has evolved in my lifetime. I was one of the youngest members of the first generation, which came of age in jihad against the Russians in Afghanistan and among the mountains of Bosnia. The second generation emerged during the Iraq War. And now there is a third generation of often tech-savvy youngsters, who have grown up amidst the carnage and upheavals unleashed since the Arab Spring and the rise of far-right anti-Muslim extremism in the West. Ahmed Hassan, an Iraqi orphan and teenage refugee convicted of attempting to blow up a London Underground train in 2017, was barely two years old at the time of 9/11.[52]

## HOW TO WIN

The scourge of global terror can only be confronted in a multi-dimensional way. Air strikes and drone attacks, training regional armies, putting more police on the streets of Western cities, better intelligence sharing, staunching the flow of money – these are all necessary but obvious steps.

But the social and sectarian issues I have outlined also have to be addressed. As John Brennan said when he was the director of the CIA, 'We have to find a way to address some of these factors and conditions that are abetting and allowing these movements to grow.'[53]

Targeting the appeal of the ideology is paramount.

The US National Security Strategy, published in 2006, recognized the imperative of 'winning the battle of ideas, for it is ideas that can turn the disenchanted into murderers willing to kill innocent victims'.[54] But first we have to understand the idea. In 2014, the *New York Times* published confidential comments about the appeal of ISIS by General Michael K. Nagata, the then US Special Operations commander for the Middle East.[55]

'We have not defeated the idea,' he said. 'We do not even understand the idea.'

For a time ISIS was almost put on a pedestal, a force that could not be overcome. We mythologized the ideology that sustained it.

At the same time we insufficiently probed their means of control, how relatively few men could control cities through a mixture of fear, extortion and favour.

I hope this book has helped trace the evolution of jihadi ideology and I hope it provides at least some guidance for Muslims to get involved in what is a defining struggle for the soul of Islam. Muslims, not Western governments, must win the battle of ideas. We must reject absolutely and vocally the notion that the Islamic State or al-Qaeda are somehow representative of our religion, that beheadings, slavery and crucifixion are valid today because they were seen as legitimate in the Middle Ages. That means challenging and refuting the teaching of the likes of Abu Abdullah al-Muhajir and his book, *The Jurisprudence of Blood*.

After terror attacks in the United Kingdom in 2017, Prime Minister Theresa May said that defeating the ideology that inspired such attacks 'is one of the great challenges of our time, but it cannot be defeated by military intervention alone'. She went on: 'It will only be defeated when we turn people's minds away from this violence and make them understand that our values – pluralistic British values – are superior to anything offered by the preachers and supporters of hate.'[56]

It sounded as if she saw it as a government programme – one that would educate Muslims in the ways of Westminster. Well-intentioned perhaps, but irrelevant to the larger struggle. The most effective counter-narrative at this stage is not to offer Western democracy, which has had a terrible track record in the Arab world, but alternatives grounded within the history and traditions of the Islamic world. The assault must – can only, for the time being – be waged from within Islam.

One step in this direction was a twenty-three-page open letter published in September 2014 repudiating ISIS and Abu Bakr al-Baghdadi. It was signed by many prominent Muslim scholars around the world and it picked apart point by point the group's claims to Islamic legitimacy.[57] Counter-narratives from mainstream clerics are helpful but they may also be a dialogue of the deaf, simply because they come from a moderate perspective. To those seduced by the message of al-Qaeda or ISIS, the messengers will be seen as traitors to Islam, seduced by Western lassitude. The jihadis dismiss many of their critics in the Muslim world as 'dollar scholars'.

As Labib al-Nahhas, a senior and moderate voice within the Syrian Islamist group Ahrar al-Sham, put it: 'The Islamic State's extremist ideology can be defeated only through a home-grown Sunni alternative – with the term "moderate" defined not by CIA handlers but by Syrians themselves.'[58]

Moderate imams – whether in the community or visiting prisons – are not going to impress young men already halfway to jihad. Islamic academics and theologians cannot alone formulate counter-messaging against al-Qaeda and ISIS. They don't understand what makes these groups tick.

To make an impact, to chip away at the certainty which binds such groups, requires us to recruit respected Salafi fundamentalists, men whose ideological outlook is close to that of the terror groups but who eschew their violence. Men who have already travelled that route and then seen a better way can be precious allies. They can help detect and disrupt radicalization; they can help rehabilitate those either tempted by or convicted of conspiracies. But they have to be credible, and their work can only flourish in a society where tolerance and diversity are championed. A rise in hate crimes; a resurgence of the far right on both sides of the Atlantic; a sense that police don't afford equal protection to all; discrimination in the workplace – these are just a few of the factors that will undercut any efforts to counter radicalization. There's a great danger that in Europe, maybe even in the United States, too, Islamist and right-wing extremists will feed off each other in a vicious cycle.

ISIS and al-Qaeda lash out most ferociously against Salafi critics for a reason – because they feel their certainty undermined. 'Quietist' Salafis believe in personal purification rather than involvement in the political sphere, and reject taking up arms. While the jihadis believe they are God's instruments in ushering in a Caliphate near the end-of-days, their Salafi critics believe only God can and will bring about the victory for Islam foretold in the prophecies, making the battle for the soul the only one that matters. Salafis are well versed in the religious texts on which al-Qaeda and ISIS rely, and well placed to undermine their controversial interpretations of the *hadith*.

As purists, Salafis can demonstrate that those who rail against 'revisionism' of the faith and demand a return to a medieval brand of Islam are themselves guilty of the worst revisionism. Of course, Salafis themselves have an uncompromising view of the perfect Islamic society, one that is theocratic and intolerant of dissent. And many have travelled the road from uncompromising Salafism to taking up arms and ultimately to global jihad. It was a journey I took before seeing it as a futile descent into a cycle of violence. But there are some among them who reject the bleak and joyless inter- pretation of Islam being spouted in many shabby prayer halls around Europe.

In too many places Islam has become a religion based on fear of damnation and sin. There are echoes of fundamentalist Christianity in the US and the seventeenth-century Puritans in England. In our religion, our relationship with God is based on three pillars: love of the Lord, hope for forgiveness and fear of damnation. All three must receive equal weight, as historically they have. But in recent decades imams around the world have responded to globalization and the rise of a permissive liberal culture in the West by placing overwhelming emphasis on hellfire and damna- tion. They have created a generation of the guilty. Their sermons warn of the torture and torment waiting in the hereafter for those indulging in alcohol, drugs, sex before marriage and other vices. It is a message of damnation which has driven many young men to martyrdom as a way to atone for their sins.

Certainly, among second- and third-generation immigrants to Europe, many young Muslim men feel marginalized, conflicted, discriminated against and rootless in societies where their parents often tried hard to be accepted. Opportunities are few, unemploy- ment high. They often reject their surroundings and retreat to the edge of society where alcohol, drugs and petty crime are the language of defiance. If and when their crimes lead to jail time, they are all too often vulnerable to siren voices preaching a short cut to redemption.

As Alain Grignard of the Belgian federal police has pointed out, a generation ago European security services were mostly dealing with Islamists who were being radicalized into violence, but they are now mostly dealing with violent young men involved in petty crime and street gangs who are then becoming Islamized.[59] Young Muslims in the West have much greater exposure to such vices than the average teenager in Riyadh or Algiers. And so it follows that their perceived need for redemption is all the greater.*

Take, for example, the case of Abdelhamid Abaaoud, a young Belgian who became a notorious figure within ISIS before returning to Europe and dying in a shootout with police after leading the cell that attacked Paris in November 2015. His sister Yasmina told the *New York Times* that Abaaoud did not attend the mosque before leaving for Syria and ISIS – and wasn't especially interested in religion.[61] But he had gone to prison several times, and it was apparently there that, like so many Western jihadis, he found a radical, violent version of Islam.[62] A significant proportion of ISIS-linked plots in the West have involved extremists with criminal records.[63] It has often been within prisons that young Muslim men have found an anchor and structure that their lives lacked, a path to redemption. That path could easily become a short cut to paradise – as a suicide bomber in Syria or on the streets of Europe. It may be a warped form of religious conviction based on scant knowledge of the Koran, but it is conviction nevertheless. Those who avoid prison often fall prey to silver-tongued preachers who operate outside the mainstream 'community' – men like Khalid

---

* This helps explain why the percentage of the Muslim population that has been mobilized to fight as foreign fighters in Syria and Iraq is significantly higher in Belgium, the UK, France and Germany than in much of the Arab world, including Saudi Arabia.[60]

Zerkani in the Brussels district of Molenbeek. When he was ultimately tried and convicted in 2015, Zerkani was described by the judges as propagating 'extremist ideas among naive, fragile and agitated youth', and as the 'archetype of a seditious mentor'. But by then, his influence had set many young men on the path to jihad, including Abdelhamid Abaaoud.[64]

Many Muslim communities in Europe are now microcosms of the communal tribalism that plagues their home countries. An intolerant, hectoring minority takes the quiet majority hostage, tries to bully and threaten them into submission. Their view is that there are no circumstances in which a Muslim may work with a non-Muslim, that loyalty to a fellow Muslim, whatever his motives and however depraved his behaviour, is paramount.

Allegiance to religion stifles any other form of allegiance, to society or even family. I think back to the youth of Tooting, sneering towards their parents and their communities in their narrow certainties.

Unless we stand up to this, we face the competing totalitarianism of the jihadi extremist and the far right, feeding off each other. We have to reject blind faith and embrace faith with justice. As the medieval scholar Ibn Taymiyyah wrote: 'It is said that God allows the just state to remain even if it is led by unbelievers, but God will not allow the oppressive state to remain even if it is led by Muslims.'[65]

Oppression and intolerance should have no place in contemporary Islam.

I believe we as Muslims need to embrace and celebrate the advances of human creativity, political emancipation and science, rather than reject them as corruptions of the modern world. The Koran, after all, was the first to describe the 'Big Bang' that ushered in the universe.

*'The heavens and the earth were one piece which We tore asunder.'*[66]

I view the Koran as a book of secrets which Muslims will better understand as their lives progress and as the generations pass. The Big Bang meant nothing to my great-great grandfather, but for many Muslims living today the mystery of the verse above has been unlocked by advances in scientific knowledge.

It is not the holy texts that need to be reformed. It is our understanding that needs to evolve. It is not that Islam needs reforming, it is that the message of God should be better understood.

Salafi critiques of jihadism can help improve security in our societies, but that security ultimately depends on the broader Muslim community challenging the message of extremist preachers.

Within the global jihadi movement there are weaknesses and divisions waiting to be exploited. The glue that holds such movements together is a potent combination of certainty and unity. It is also the source of their vulnerability. Undermine their absolute belief that they will end up in heaven, sow seeds of doubt and dissent, exploit and widen ideological discord – and there will be far fewer jihadis ready to become martyrs. Indeed, Abu Bakr al-Baghdadi invited Muslims to challenge him when he said in Mosul in July 2014: 'If you find what I say and do to be true, then assist me. And if you find what I say and do to be false then put me right.'[67]

We should aid those with even a sliver of doubt. We have to undermine the theology peddled by Baghdadi, Adnani and Binali by shouting persuasive and authentic readings of the Koran and *hadith* from the rooftops.

The holy texts themselves offer the most persuasive response. The Koran says there are people who

> 'pervert words from their contexts and they have forgotten a portion of what they were reminded of'.[68]

The Prophet issued a warning to Muslims not to mistake civil war or *fitna* for jihad, because 'every Muslim house will suffer because of it.'

Why must Islam be so severe and unforgiving, as ISIS ideologues like Muhajir insist? God says:

> *'Indulge people with forgiveness and enjoin kindness, And turn away from the ignorant.'*[69]

Nor is forcible conversion to be applauded. Persuasion and tolerance are woven into the fabric of Islam. God says:

> *'Call to the way of your Lord with wisdom and fair exhortation, And debate with them what is best.'*[70]

Nor is there any justification in the Koran or *hadith* for wanton and arbitrary slayings.

> *'And do not slay the soul whom God has made inviolable, except with due cause.'*[71]

Perhaps worst of all is the corruption of the very concept of jihad. In an audio sermon in 2015, Abu Bakr al-Baghdadi said, 'Islam was never for a day the religion of peace. Islam is the religion of war.'[72] But without a legitimate cause or vision, jihad is nothing more than criminality. In one of his speeches, ISIS ideologue Abu Muhammad al-Adnani said: 'God bless Prophet Muhammad who was sent with the sword as a mercy to all worlds.' It was a typical manipulation of the Koran and *hadith*.[73]

The Koran says of the Prophet: 'We did not send you, except as a mercy to all the worlds.' It is unconditional, universal. But the phrase 'sent with the sword' is part of a *hadith* that concerned a certain time and place long ago. Adnani and others in ISIS worked up toxic hybrids of prophecies whose sell-by dates have long passed, and fobbed them off on impressionable, adoring audiences.[74]

In the course of my research in the past decade, I have found that many of the *hadith* commonly used by al-Qaeda and ISIS, including a significant number cited in this book, have dubious lineage – especially those containing prophecies about the emergence of the Mahdi and the Black Banners.* But very little has been done to challenge that illegitimacy.

The initiative by Saudi Arabia's Crown Prince Mohammad Bin Salman in 2017 to establish a *hadith* centre in Medina overseen by senior Islamic scholars from around the world to 'eliminate fake and extremist texts' and curb interpretations put forward by terrorist groups to justify their violence was long overdue. A Saudi clerical official said the centre would strive 'to learn and understand the *hadith* – to liberate people from the darkness of thought, the extremism and misinterpretation of the book of God and the teachings passed down to us through the Prophet'.[75]

Ironically enough, the emergence of groups that would distort Islam was actually foretold. Imam Ali, the son-in-law of the Prophet Mohammed, warned:

> '*If you see the black flags appearing then do not leave your homes. Stay where you are. Do not move an arm or a leg. For a people no-one cares about will appear. They will seek the truth. But they are never given the truth. Their hearts are as hard as iron. They are the founders of the State but they do not honor any covenant or agreement. Their hair is as long as women . . . They are known by the names of their villages and cities.*'[76]

---

* There are tens of thousands of *hadith* in the various collections circulating today. A significant number, including those foretelling the emergence of a holy army of the Black Banners from Khurasan, were first written down during the Abbasid revolution against the Umayyad dynasty just over a century after the death of the Prophet Mohammed. The Abbasids created a new Caliphate ruled from Baghdad rather than Damascus. Perhaps not coincidentally, the revolutionary Abbasid armies emerged from Khurasan and fought under black standards. The third Abbasid ruler went so far as calling himself 'Caliph Mahdi'. This makes it likely a significant number of *hadith* were simply invented by the Abbasid propagandists to provide their cause with

Almost every word matches what the group led by al-Baghdadi came to represent. They were like the *Khawarij* (dissenters) of the seventh century. The *Khawarij* regarded themselves as the only true Muslims and their interpretation of Islam was merciless. They held that the women and children among disbelievers should be enslaved and the men put to death. That's exactly what happened to the Yazidi minority in Iraq. The *Khawarij* emerged during times of upheaval and civil war, when the elite had become unjust. The *Khawarij* saw the earliest years of Islam as the perfect age and everything afterwards as a drift towards disbelief, some of them held that jihad was the sixth pillar of Islam.

The Prophet identified the *Khawarij* as heretics. According to one contemporary account that is widely accepted, he said:

> *'Towards the end of time, a group will emerge, young of age and simple of minds, who will speak the most beautiful words but whose faith does not go deeper than their throats. Wherever you find them you must kill them since those who will kill them will be rewarded on the day of Resurrection.'*[77]

With ISIS and al-Qaeda weaponizing the prophecies, Muslim scholars need to answer. Not to do so would be to surrender on a key field of battle. Tens of millions across the Muslim world have become fascinated with these sacred mysteries.

---

religious legitimacy. Furthermore, the notion that a single man could in the seventh century provide his followers with tens of thousands of sayings and have them all faithfully recorded seems inconceivable. In assessing the reliability of *hadith*, modern scholars will need to look at the credibility of the individuals involved in orally transmitting them all those centuries ago, their political agendas and the viability of their chain of narration. They should also nullify any *hadith* that are contradicted by the Koran, including those relating to punishments such as stoning. The renowned Islamic scholar Muhammad Nasiruddin al-Albani dedicated his life to overhauling how *hadith* are graded for reliability before his death in 1999, but his work is far from complete.

Reclaiming the prophecies will be a challenging task because of the extremists' skill at spinning the sacred texts into a theological web justifying their actions. ISIS and al-Qaeda have distorted the sacred texts of Islam. They have done so by cherry-picking the verses that suit their agenda and wildly extrapolating from others. I saw up close how al-Qaeda's silver-tongued preachers did it and I abandoned their ranks because of it.

Not all see it this way. In March 2015, the influential American magazine *The Atlantic* published a much-quoted cover story, 'What ISIS Really Wants', which extensively featured the viewpoint of the Lebanese-American scholar Bernard Haykel.

'People want to absolve Islam,' he said. 'It's this "Islam is a religion of peace" mantra. As if there is such a thing as "Islam"! It's what Muslims do, and how they interpret their texts . . . and these guys [ISIS] have just as much legitimacy as anyone else,' he added, rejecting the notion the group had distorted the texts of Islam. 'Slavery, crucifixion, and beheadings are not something that freakish [jihadis] are cherry-picking from the medieval tradition.'

Haykel is correct that the sacred texts of Islam, just like the Old Testament, contain verses espousing violence. In many cases, those texts described periods of war and brutal conflict. But I reject as a wildly inaccurate affront the argument that 'these guys' can claim legitimacy.

The vast majority of the world's nearly two billion Muslims are horrified by their crimes. The likes of ISIS have deceived tens of thousands of Muslims and disfigured our religion, but perhaps that was foretold.

*'The Antichrist will appear from a valley between Iraq and the Levant and will cause chaos and mayhem where he goes.'*[78]

Muslim communities have to do a better job of identifying, ostracizing and confronting the preachers of hate. Avoiding them, or muttering about them under our breath, is not enough.

There must also be a still greater effort in the virtual sphere – where the extremist narrative, through videos, online lectures and applications such as Twitter and Telegram, frequently went unchallenged. There needs to be a more systematic response that leverages the know-how of technology companies to stifle the online space for extremism. How is it, for example, that the lectures of al-Qaeda's most famous ideologue, Anwar al-Awlaki, whose siren call I heard in Dudley, could remain available on so many platforms for so long, even after his words proved inspirational in so many terror attacks in the West?

Progress has been made in taking down the accounts of militant groups and their sympathizers. And we have to be realistic: stifling the online appeal of such groups can only achieve so much. Those intent on a stabbing rampage or driving a truck into a crowd don't need guidance on the Internet, even if their online habits stoke their rage.

The delivery of the counter-narrative is as important as its content. The pulpit, scholarly tracts embedded with Koranic verses, have roles to play but are not very effective vehicles. ISIS's appeal among the disaffected young Muslims of European cities was based on slick multilingual videos, with high production values. It recognized, to put it bluntly, that most teenagers in the early twenty-first century have a three-minute attention span.

You only need to look at the numbers on YouTube to know that what's needed is a viral campaign of savvy and punchy two-minute videos undermining the message that has been propagated by ISIS and extremist preachers of all stripes. These must be produced by Muslims and taunt and mock such messaging, showing in graphic form its hypocrisy. Why, for example, was so little done to attack the savagery – and the utter absence of religious justification – when ISIS burned alive a Jordanian pilot in a cage? According to my sources, there was real disquiet within ISIS about both the crime and its propagation online, but too little was done to exacerbate the dissent. Prophecies like the one foretelling the emergence of an evil group flying the black banners could be used in these videos.

Properly done, such a campaign has the potential to sow the seeds of doubt among those joining groups like ISIS. And it can help inoculate others who might be vulnerable to their message. This pool of the vulnerable, the impressionable, has expanded hugely because of the tide of foreign fighters who went to Iraq and Syria between 2014 and 2016, some of whom have returned home true believers still. This cohort of foreign fighters who survived will be the officer class of the terrorist networks of the future.

While the majority of the million plus refugees from Syria and other conflicts that have come into Europe in recent years have tried to assimilate, the large number of dislocated young Sunni men trying to make their way in a new society will be an attractive target for extremist proselytizers. In Iraq, ISIS groomed many thousands of young boys as 'Cubs of the Caliphate', indoctrinating them in ways we are only beginning to understand.

These are all challenges of which we must be aware but not afraid. There are too many Muslims today who would rather bury their heads in the sand than confront the crisis of our faith. There is ultimately a stark choice for every one of us. Side with justice and humanity – regardless of religion, creed or colour. Or never give up a Muslim brother to non-Muslim authorities, no matter what they might be planning or might have done, and defend any and every action undertaken in the name of Islam, however un-Islamic.

Beyond the ideological challenge, and the need to devise an 'exit strategy' for thousands of young men lured to al-Qaeda and ISIS, there needs to be root-and-branch reform in the Middle East. The Arab world is a swamp fed by corruption and the misconduct of elites, a lack of viable institutions, poor governance and ideological and sectarian rivalry. It is also awash with weapons. Swamps invite only mosquitoes and disease. Instead of draining the swamp, the outside world has competed to kill mosquitoes.

So how do you drain the swamp? Better governance – which admittedly may seem like a hopeless quest at times – is a big part of the response. So is economic growth and political stability. And better education is also vital: the best way to ward off disease is inoculation.

I believe it is necessary to establish stronger and more just nation states in the Arab and Muslim world. The prophet Mohammed himself stressed that safety, security and stability are blessings from God. This requires robust governing institutions working for the interests of the people and the rule of law. A healthy form of nationalism and patriotism – or in other words a sense of citizenry – is an antidote to the jihadi vision of a borderless Ummah and the chaos that it has produced.

This does not mean trying to quickly graft democracy onto societies whose institutions are too weak to support it. It means embracing and adapting those forms of government that have offered stability within an Islamic framework. Balancing Islamic tradition and observances with the reality of the modern world is the best medium-term strategy to erode the appeal of ISIS, al-Qaeda and like-minded groups. It will likely take decades, but it has to start somewhere and sometime.

To me that means developing and modernizing one of the few systems of government to provide a measure of stability in the Arab world. Monarchies in the Gulf, Jordan and Morocco have performed better than other forms of government in delivering progress and security to their citizens, even if they do suffer from a 'democratic deficit'. They also have a legitimacy that's often lacking among other forms of government.

For sure, monarchies have their own secret police and less than stellar human rights records. We are not seeking perfection here: we are seeking a form of contemporary government that works for Muslims, and especially Arab Muslims. They are not going to become liberal democrats in our lifetimes – period.

Secondly, we as Muslims have to begin to build some middle ground that allows rapprochement, co-existence at least, between Sunni and Shia. At the time of writing, it seems that the 'rejection-ists', who trade insults and bomb each other's places of worship, are invincible. In Iraq both Shia militias and ISIS have terrorized the population. In Syria, Hezbollah fighters, as well as Shia from Iraq, Syria, Pakistan and Afghanistan recruited into militia trained by Iran, have in their tens of thousands fought Sunni jihadis. In Yemen, Houthis backed by Iran have fought al-Qaeda fighters. In Saudi Arabia, ISIS suicide bombers targeted Shia areas to try to poison relations between the communities.

There is a real risk larger scale sectarian conflict will break out across the Middle East, fuelling even more widespread extremism. Fundamentalist belligerents either side of the Sunni–Shia divide believe they are engaged in an end-of-days battle that will soon see the return of the Mahdi and an ultimate victory for their version of the faith. They view Syria as the epicentre of this struggle. Shia Muslims believe the Mahdi is the twelfth and last imam who will reappear from hiding after hundreds of years near the end of time to right the historical injustice suffered by the Shia.* Like ISIS or al-Qaeda, Hezbollah and the Shia militia of Iraq are willing to fight to the death to bring about the Mahdi's return. As Hezbollah's Deputy Secretary General Naim Qassem put it, 'Our actions but pave the way for Imam al-Mahdi's emergence.'[79]

It would be easy and tempting for governments to back the groups they identify as sectarian and ideological allies. But it will only deepen the fault lines that criss-cross the region.

Modern history shows us that rapprochement need not be in the realms of fantasy. When Mohammad Khatami was president of Iran, he visited Saudi Arabia and signed a security pact with the Kingdom. King Fahd was effusive about Khatami's reformist policies, and between 1997 and 2005 there was a genuine relationship between the two Gulf powers. It was driven in no small part by commerce. The family of former Iranian President Akbar Hashemi Rafsanjani had significant business interests on the other side of the Gulf and Rafsanjani himself visited Saudi Arabia to advance

---

* They believe he is a direct descendant of the Prophet's son-in-law Imam Ali and his son Imam Hussein, whose martyrdom in the Battle of Karbala in AD 680 created the schism between Sunni and Shia Islam and remains the root cause of the sectarian bloodshed in the Middle East.

reconciliation. Then came the hostility of Mahmoud Ahmadinejad, who succeeded Khatami, and the deterioration of the regional situation.

## HOPE

I do not pretend for a moment that the challenges ahead are anything other than immense. Since 1979, the situation of the *Ummah* has deteriorated drastically, buffeted by centrifugal forces. An 'arc of crisis' has spread – like an eclipse – across a vast expanse of territory from the western Sahara to the rainforests and teeming cities of South East Asia. Violence in the name of Islam is one of the great challenges of our times. Entire communities have been wiped out on the killing fields of Syria and Iraq, millions banished from their homes. Skilled bomb-makers have honed their deadly craft in Yemen, operating with impunity in a collapsed state. In the years since I stood at Ibrahim's grave on that late summer evening, the battle has only deepened; it has become more viscerally sectarian.

But I live in hope. A year after I left Idlib, I married, after being introduced by friends to a strong, sympathetic and deeply spiritual woman. She was as modern as the fundamentalists were backward. At the beginning of our first date, I had a strange request for her.

'Would you mind if I explain a few things – about my childhood and youth?'

Three hours later I finished relating my journey from Khobar to Canary Wharf via too many battlefields. Her expression was – rather than one of shock or disappointment (or worse still boredom) – one of utter curiosity.

'So you're really something of a revolutionary,' she said when I was done. And she continued to pepper me with questions.

'Aren't you frightened by all this?' I asked at one point.

She laughed.

'Put it this way: if they come for us I will happily kill them.'

As I arrived home that night, I was euphoric. I knew we

were destined for a future together. Five months later we were married.

And she told the wedding party in Dubai: 'Just so everyone knows, if Aimen tries to make me wear a hijab, I will force him to wear one too.'

I was recently blessed with becoming a father. My wife might be described – not surprisingly – as a lioness, fiercely protective of her family.

My belief in God has never been stronger. The Islam I now follow is an Islam of private contemplation, spiritual reflection and study rather than communal worship. Long gone are the days I considered myself a Salafi. What I think important now is *how you live your life* and *how you treat others*. I believe God has provided guidance in both respects through the Koran, but no believer should call their religion the only pathway to God.

I have seen plenty of goodwill and optimism among Muslims, in the crowded streets of Peshawar among people who have nothing, in the mosques of my hometown where Islam was taught as an uplifting force, among the young fighters of northern Syria who wanted above all to be freed from the repression of a vicious police state.

I think of that quiet field near Saraqib every day, of my dearest nephew hastily laid to rest there, his grave unvisited and untended ever since that September day in 2013 when I stood by it in the gathering gloom.

Like his father and (I hope) his uncle, Ibrahim was motivated not by blind hatred but by a hatred of injustice. In the words of the Koran,

> 'Let not the hatred of a people swerve you away from justice. Be just, for this is closest to righteousness . . .'[80]

If and when Muslims unite under this command, my religion will begin to heal.

# CAST OF CHARACTERS

## FAMILY

| | |
|---|---|
| Moheddin | My eldest brother |
| Omar | Another brother |
| Ibrahim | Moheddin's son. Sadly, he followed in my footsteps. |
| Abdur Rahman | My cousin who also tragically followed in my footsteps |

## KHOBAR

| | |
|---|---|
| Khalid al-Hajj | Childhood friend; second leader of al-Qaeda's Saudi wing |
| Yusuf al-Ayeri | Islamic Awareness Circle instructor; first leader of al-Qaeda's Saudi wing; aka 'Swift Sword' |
| Sayyid Qutb | Egyptian ideological godfather of global jihadi movement |

## BOSNIA

| | |
|---|---|
| Hazam | Palestinian from Milan on my bus trip into Bosnia |
| Marwan | The other Milanese Palestinian on the bus trip into Bosnia |
| Anwar Shaaban | Egyptian leader of the Mujahideen Brigade in Bosnia |
| Abdin | Bosnian jihadi whose female relatives were raped |

| | |
|---|---|
| Omar Abdel Rahman | Egyptian 'blind sheikh' implicated in 1993 World Trade Center bombing |
| Abu Ayoub al-Shamrani | Saudi cleric who instructed me in Bosnia |
| Abu Dujana | Saudi jihadi who witnessed beheadings of Serbs in Bosnia |
| Badr al-Sudairi | Saudi commander in Bosnia. Later in Londonistan; aka Abu Zubayr al-Hayali. |
| Abu Harf al-Libi | Senior Libyan jihadi in Bosnia killed with Anwar Shaaban |
| Ahmed | Friend from Bosnia jihad who helped me in Qatar |

## THE CHECHEN FRONT

| | |
|---|---|
| Ibn al-Khattab | Saudi jihadi commander in Chechnya |
| Fathi | Tunisian dentistry student I met at charity office in Baku |
| Mohammed Omar | Local driver we used in Baku to smuggle supplies to Chechen jihadis |
| Shamil Basayev | Chechen jihadi leader |

## PHILIPPINES

| | |
|---|---|
| Farouk al-Kuwaiti | Kuwaiti jihadi I spent time with in Bosnia, Afghanistan and the Philippines, who became al-Qaeda's senior envoy to South East Asia. Also known as Omar al-Farouq |
| Abdul Nassir Nooh | Jihadi fixer in Manila |
| Ahmed Doli | Senior member of Moro Islamic Liberation Front in Mindanao |

## ABU KHABAB'S DARUNTA FACILITY

| | |
|---|---|
| Abu Khabab al-Masri | Egyptian master bomb-maker and chemist; my jihadi mentor |
| Abu Bakr al-Masri | Abu Khabab's Egyptian deputy |
| Hassan Ghul | Pakistani apprentice of Abu Khabab; later courier for al-Qaeda |
| Abu Nassim | Real name: Moez Fezzani; Tunisian at Darunta later implicated in Bardo and Sousse attacks |

| | |
|---|---|
| Safwat | Egyptian from London who trained with Abu Khabab |
| Abu Musab al-Zarqawi | Founder of al-Qaeda in Iraq, the group which morphed into ISIS |

## AL-QAEDA

| | |
|---|---|
| Osama bin Laden | Founder of al-Qaeda |
| Ayman al-Zawahiri | Egyptian deputy to bin Laden; later al-Qaeda's leader |
| Abu Ubaidah al-Banshiri | Top Egyptian aide to Osama bin Laden before death in 1996 |
| Abu Hafs al-Masri | Egyptian chief of operations for al-Qaeda before 9/11 |
| Khalid Sheikh Mohammed | 9/11 mastermind whom I first met in Bosnia |
| Abu Abdullah al-Muhajir | Real name: Abdulrahman al-Ali; senior al-Qaeda theologian; mentor to Zarqawi |
| Mustafa Abu Yazid | Senior Egyptian al-Qaeda operative |
| Abu Khayr al-Masri | Egyptian al-Qaeda operative who later became deputy leader |
| Abu Hamza al-Ghamdi | Senior Saudi Qaeda operative who recruited me; chief of bin Laden bodyguard |
| Abu Abdullah al-Maki | Saudi al-Qaeda suicide bomber in 1998 attack on US embassy in Nairobi. Also known as Abu Obeydah al-Maki. |
| Abdulaziz al-Juhani | Saudi bodyguard to bin Laden |
| Abd al-Aziz al-Masri | Egyptian al-Qaeda bomb-maker |
| Mariam bin Laden | Sister of Osama bin Laden |
| Abu Yahya al-Libi | Libyan al-Qaeda operative who would issue kill order against me |
| Khalil al-Deek | American Jordanian al-Qaeda operative |
| Adam Gadahn | American al-Qaeda operative and spokesman |
| Abdul Hadi al-Iraqi | Iraqi al-Qaeda commander on the front lines in Afghanistan |
| Saif al-Adel | Senior Egyptian al-Qaeda operative |
| Abdul Aziz al-Omari | Saudi 9/11 'muscle' hijacker I spent time with in Kabul |
| Abdul Rasheed al-Filistini | Palestinian al-Qaeda operative; my partner in Kashmiri food business |

Qasim al-Raymi — Yemeni jihadi I met in Bosnia; later leader of al-Qaeda in Yemen

## OTHER JIHADIS IN AF-PAK

Abu Zubaydah — Peshawar-based Saudi gatekeeper for Arab jihadis in Afghanistan

Abu Said al-Kurdi — Iraqi deputy to Abu Zubaydah; later quarter-master of Chechen jihad

Mohammed Hanif — Afghan doctor who accompanied me on first trip into Afghanistan

Salahadin — American Moroccan instructor at the Abu Rawdah camp in Darunta

Abu Musab al-Suri — Syrian leading jihadi strategist; real name: Mustafa Setmariam Nasar

Ibn Sheikh al-Libi — Libyan head of Khalden camp in Afghanistan

Abu Abdullah al-Scotlandi — Scottish jihadi close to al-Qaeda; real name: James McLintock

Abdul Shukoor Mutmaen — Taliban's Sports Minister

## LONDONISTAN AND THE UK

'Mohammed al-Madani' — Saudi Londonistan figure I met during Bosnian jihad

Babar Ahmad — British jihadi webmaster I met in Bosnia; part of Tooting Circle

Said Arif — Al-Qaeda's intelligence chief in London; later senior figure with group in Syria

Abu Qatada — Palestinian Jordanian cleric who was major figure in Londonistan

Abu Hamza al-Masri — Hook-handed Egyptian radical cleric at Finsbury Park Mosque in London

Omar Bakri Mohammed — 'Tottenham Ayatollah' who founded al-Muhajiroun

Saajid Badat — Member of Tooting Circle recruited into al-Qaeda plane shoe-bomb plot

Abu al-Fidaa — Stuttgart-based jihadi fundraiser

Abu Walid al-Filistini — Palestinian Londonistan cleric who was sidekick to Abu Qatada

# CAST OF CHARACTERS

| Zacarias Moussaoui | So-called 9/11 'twentieth hijacker' |
| 'Abu Hudhaifa al-Britani' | British jihadi who quit the country shortly before 9/11 after being warned to leave |
| Anwar al-Awlaki | American Yemeni jihadi cleric; later senior figure in al-Qaeda's Yemen wing |
| Mohammad Sidique Khan | 7/7 London bombings ringleader |
| Shehzad Tanweer | 7/7 London suicide bomber |
| Germaine Lindsay | 7/7 London suicide bomber |
| Abu Muslim | Dudley 'nicotine plotter'; later became ISIS bomb-maker. Real name: Hamayun Tariq |
| Javed | Abu Muslim's sullen sidekick |
| Ahmed | Abu Muslim's even surlier sidekick |

## THE ARABIAN GULF POST 9/11

| Akhil | Saudi chemistry teacher plotting poison gas plot on New York |
| Bassam Bokhowa | Bahraini IT technician who digitized *mubtakkar* blueprints |
| Nasir bin Hamid al-Fahd | Chief theologian of al-Qaeda's Saudi wing who issued WMD fatwah |
| Abu Hafs al-Baluchi | Courier/smuggler from Iran's Baluchistan region; ex-fan of Bob Marley |
| Turki Binali | Bahraini zealot who issued fatwah to kill me; later architect of ISIS sex slavery |
| Hamza al-Rabia | Al-Qaeda's Egyptian external operations chief before 7/7 bombings |
| Yasser Kamal | Bahraini al-Qaeda member; ringleader of Fifth Fleet plot |
| Omar Kamal | Brother of Yasser; arrested in connection with the Fifth Fleet plot |
| Hamad Kamal | Another brother of Yasser |

## THE LEVANT

| Abu Bakr al-Baghdadi | ISIS leader who declared himself to be Caliph in 2014 |
| Abu Issa al-Sheikh | Jihadi commander in Syria |
| Abu Mohammed al-Maqdisi | Jordanian hardline Salafi cleric who mentored Zarqawi |

## SPIES

| | |
|---|---|
| Ali Mohanidi | Captain in Qatari security services |
| Colonel al-Nuami | Head of Qatari's domestic security service |
| Tom | Senior MI5 counter-terrorism official |
| Harry | MI6 official who first debriefed me |
| Richard | My first MI6 handler; doppelgänger of King Edward VII |
| Nick | My first MI5 handler; *Jurassic Park*'s Sam Neill could play him |
| Alan | My second MI5 handler; fan of Everton FC |
| Aziz | British embassy driver in Pakistan |
| Freddie | My second M16 handler, who took over after 9/11; *Simpsons* fan |
| Kevin | My third MI5 handler, who took over after 9/11 |
| George | Kind MI5 shrink with resemblance to George Clooney |
| Nish | Young MI6 analyst |
| Alastair | My third and final MI5 handler; an Arabist |
| Dilay | Ex-model who helped me report on Uighurs in Turkey |
| Oliver | Former senior official at MI6 |
| Rachel | Senior MI6 supervisor |

## OTHERS

| | |
|---|---|
| Abdul Majeed | Uighur jihadi in Istanbul |
| Seyit Tumturk | Turkey-based deputy leader of World Uighur Congress |
| Orcan | Smuggler who brought me into Syria from Turkey in 2013 |

# ACKNOWLEDGEMENTS

## AIMEN DEAN

The nature of the spy business limits the number of people I can acknowledge by name. I would like to thank the British intelligence officials who mentored me and guided me. You know who you are. During the eight years I worked for MI5 and MI6 I was never asked to take any unnecessary risks and I always felt my handlers had my back. The British intelligence services are deservedly lauded for their professionalism and integrity. Their mostly unheralded work continues to save many lives.

I would like to thank my co-authors Paul Cruickshank and Tim Lister. Over the last three years we spent hundreds of hours working together as they documented and investigated my story. Their deep knowledge and painstaking research were essential to this book.

Both Paul and Tim have reported on al-Qaeda for many years and their expertise was vital in providing context to this story. Just months after 9/11 Tim was filing reports for CNN from Tora Bora as the United States bombed Osama bin Laden's last redoubt in Afghanistan. More recently he has reported from the front lines in the war against ISIS in Syria and Iraq. Paul is CNN's Terrorism Analyst and the Editor-in-Chief of *CTC Sentinel*, the renowned flagship publication of the Combating Terrorism Center at the United States Military Academy at West Point. Paul and Tim's previously co-authored book *Agent Storm*, the 2014 memoir of a

Danish double agent who spied on al-Qaeda in Yemen for the CIA, was named by the *Guardian* as one of the top ten spy books of all time. There could not be two better people to help me tell my story.

Many thanks to Alex Christofi our really excellent editor at Oneworld and their team on both sides of the Atlantic. I also greatly appreciate the efforts of our literary agents Richard Pine at Inkwell Management and Euan Thorneycroft at AM Heath and their teams.

I am so thankful to the millions of Muslims around the world standing up to the extremists who have sought to corrupt our religion. The battle is far from won, but we can prevail.

Lastly I'd like to thank my wife for all her support, intuition, guidance and wisdom. She has filled my life with hope and love.

## PAUL CRUICKSHANK AND TIM LISTER

Thank you, Aimen Dean, for working with us to tell your extraordinary story, and for your kind hospitality and good humour over these past few years. We've learned so much from you. We admire your bravery during your days as a spy and your sangfroid in the years since. Thanks for your forbearance as we stepped into the shoes of your intelligence handlers and went over each of your lives again and again. It was difficult to tell your story in only nine acts. There are very few who have lived a life as full as one of yours.

Huge thanks to Alex Christofi, our amazing editor at Oneworld. Your editorial vision and feedback made the book immeasurably better. Thanks also to the entire transatlantic Oneworld team, including Jon Bentley-Smith, Paul Nash, Kate Bland, Caitriona Row, Thanhmai Bui-Van, Becky Kraemer, Mark Rusher, James Jones and Hayley Warnham.

Thanks to copy-editor Richard Collins and proofreader David Inglesfield. Proper copy-editing and proofing still matters.

## ACKNOWLEDGEMENTS

We are very grateful to Oneworld's visionary founders Juliet Mabey and Novin Doostdar for making this project possible.

We'd also like to thank our literary agent Richard Pine and Eliza Rothstein, Lyndsey Blessing and the whole team at Inkwell Management in New York, as well as Euan Thorneycroft and his team at AM Heath in London. We deeply appreciate your continued efforts on our behalf.

We are grateful to those who provided us with invaluable feedback on the manuscript and those whose scholarship and insights have illuminated our understanding of the threat posed by jihadi terrorism. Special thanks in this regard to Lawrence Wright, Ali Soufan, Richard Walton, Bruce Hoffman, Magnus Ranstorp, Raffaello Pantucci, Anne Stenersen, Sidney Alford, Hamish de Bretton-Gordon and Vince Houghton.

We'd also like to thank Bryan Price, Brian Dodwell, Muhammad al-Ubaydi and Don Rassler at the Combating Terrorism Center at West Point for sharing their deep insights on the evolution of al-Qaeda. Big thanks to our CNN colleagues Christiane Amanpour, Ken Shiffman, Matt Scheibner and Kimberly Arp Babbit. Special thanks as always to Nic and Penny Robertson for their counsel and support.

Most importantly we'd like to acknowledge the patience, feedback and support of our families as we plunged into another real-life spy story. In Paul's case, his parents and his wife and their wonderful family on both sides of the Atlantic. And in Tim's, three generations: father Michael, wife Helena and children Archie, Sam, Verity and Rafaella.

# NOTES

## MY FIRST LIFE: THE UNLIT CANDLE

1. This book also cites *hadith* from Tirmidhi, Abu Dawood, Ibn Majah, Ahmed, Tabbarani, Ibn Majah, Tabbarani, Said bin Mansour, Ibn Hajar and Albani.
2. Vahid Brown, 'Foreign Fighters in Historical Perspective: The Case of Afghanistan', in Brian Fishman eds, 'Bombers, Bank Accounts, and Bleedout: Al-Qa-ida's Road in and Out of Iraq', Combating Terrorism Center at West Point, 2008, p. 25.
3. Thomas Hegghammer, *Jihad in Saudi Arabia: Violence and Pan-Islamism since 1979* (Cambridge University Press, 2010), p. 25.
4. Sayyid Qutb, *In the Shade of the Koran*. For an English translation of this section see Roxanne L. Euben and Muhammad Qasim Zaman (eds), *Princeton Readings in Islamist Thought: Texts and Contexts from al-Banna to Bin Laden* (Princeton University Press, 2009), p. 147.
5. John Calvert, *Sayyid Qutb and the Origins of Radical Islamism* (Oxford University Press, 2009), p. 260.
6. Ayman al-Zawahiri, 'Knights Under the Prophet's Banner' (2001); Peter Bergen, *The Longest War: The Enduring Conflict Between America and al-Qaeda* (Free Press, 2011), p. 23; For a succinct account of how Qutb's ideas influenced the jihadi movement see Trevor Stanley, 'The Evolution of Al-Qaeda: Osama bin Laden and Abu Musab al-Zarqawi', *The Review*, April 2005.
7. Abu Dawood: 3462.
8. Sheikh al-Hawali said in a 1991 sermon: 'What is happening in the [Arabian] Gulf is part of a larger Western design to dominate the whole Arab and Muslim world.' Peter Bergen, *Holy War Inc: Inside the Secret World of Osama bin Laden* (Free Press, 2002), p. 81.

9. Biography of Ibn Taymiyyah, Sunnahonline.com.

10. Tirmidhi: 2701.

11. Tirmidhi: 1663.

12. David S. Hilzenrath and John Mintz, 'More Assets on Hold in Anti-Terror Effort', *Washington Post*, 13 October 2001; 'The World Almanac of Islamism 2014', American Foreign Policy Council (2014), p. 516; Evan Kohlmann, 'The Afghan-Bosnian Mujahideen Network in Europe', Paper Presented at CATs, Swedish National Defence College, May 2006, p. 13.

13. Mark Urban, 'Bosnia: Cradle of modern jihadism?' BBC News, 2 July 2015.

14. What is left of al-Sadiq camp can be seen in this BBC *Newsnight* report (time code 9.00): https://www.youtube.com/watch?v=M6QIopgwuIU.

15. Sayyid Qutb, *Milestones* (1964), p. 63.

16. Ibid., p. 62.

17. 'The Abolition of the Caliphate', *The Economist*, 8 March 1924.

18. For an enlightening commentary on Qutb, see Paul Berman, 'The philosopher of Islamic terror', *New York Times*, 23 March 2003.

19. For more detail on the battles, see Evan Kohlmann, *Al-Qaida's Jihad in Europe: The Afghan Bosnian Network* (Berg, 2004), pp. 125–47; Kohlmann (2004), op. cit., p. 129.

20. For more details on the Battle of Vozuća, see the transcripts in the Rasim Delic case, International Criminal Tribunal for the Former Yugoslavia, 24–25 September 2007. http://www.icty.org/x/cases/delic/trans/en/070924IT.htm; http://www.icty.org/x/cases/delic/trans/en/070925IT.htm; and the judgement http://www.icty.org/x/cases/delic/tjug/en/080915.pdf.

21. Tom Downey, 'The Insurgent's Tale: A Veteran Foot Soldier Reveals His Role in Jihad', *Rolling Stone*, 5 December 2005.

22. Mitrović, 'Crimes on Ozren had all elements of a genocide', SRNA, 27 August 2015.

23. Some of the images contained in videos circulated by the group can be seen in this local media report: http://arhiv.slobodnadalmacija.hr/20010927/temedana.htm.

24. Case information Sheet, Indictment and Judgement: Trial of of Rasim Delic, Communications Service of the International Criminal Tribunal for the former Yugoslavia. http://www.icty.org/x/cases/mucic/cis/en/cis_mucic_al_en.pdf; http://www.icty.org/x/cases/delic/ind/en/del-ind060714e.pdf; http://www.icty.org/x/cases/delic/tjug/en/080915.pdf.

25. One *hadith* states that near the end of time: 'You will fight in Arabia, and God will grant you victory, then against Persia, and God will grant you

victory, and then against the Romans [Europeans], and God will grant you victory, and then against the Anti-Christ, and God will grant you victory' (Muslim: 2900). Another states Rome will be conquered after Istanbul. (Ahmed: 6468).

26. A translation of al-Ayeri's biography posted in the first two issues of *Sawt al-Jihad* magazine can be found at https://uleemaulhaqq.wordpress. com/2009/04/29/shaykh-yusuf-al-uyayris-biography.

27. See 9/11 Commission Report (2004), pp. 145–8; Yosri Fouda and Nick Fielding, *Masterminds of Terror: The Truth Behind the Most Devastating Terrorist Attack the World Has Ever Seen* (Arcade, 2003).

28. On the numbers see Urban, op. cit., and his BBC Newsnight report.

29. The term was used by President George H. W. Bush in an address to Congress on 11 September 1990.

30. For an account of the death of Shaaban, see Kohlmann (2004), op. cit., pp. 168–70.

31. On 20 October 1995, a suicide bomber in a car attacked a police office in the Croatian town of Rijeka, injuring several. Years later, after I started working for British intelligence, I learned from the Saudi jihadi Abu Zubayr al-Hayali that Shaaban had ordered the attack because of alleged Croatian complicity in the CIA-organized rendition of the leader of the Gama al-Islamiya, Abu Talal al-Qasimi (aka Tala't Fouad) from Croatia to Egypt. US intelligence also believed Shaaban was behind the Rijeka bombing. See 'Black Hole: The Fate of Islamists Rendered to Egypt', Human Rights Watch, 9 May 2005; Kohlmann (2006), op. cit., p. 16.

32. US intelligence also developed information on this. See Kohlmann (2006), op. cit., p. 16.

33. Jamie McIntyre, 'U.S. vows terrorist bomb won't affect Saudi relationship', CNN, 13 November 1995.

34. Bin Mansour: 2197.

35. Qutb (1964), op. cit., p. 63.

## MY SECOND LIFE: JALALABAD AND THE JUNGLE

1. 'Treasury Designates Al Haramain Islamic Foundation', United States Department of the Treasury, 19 June 2008.

2. See Lawrence Wright, *The Looming Tower* (Alfred A. Knopf, 2006), pp. 215–16.

3. The Russian security services later accused Haramain of wiring $1 million to Chechen rebels in 1999 and arranging to buy 500 heavy weapons for

them from the Taliban. Russia pressured Azerbaijan to close the Haramain operation in Baku in 2001. See Marc Ginsberg, 'A Field Guide to Jihadi Dagestan and Chechnya', *Huffington Post*, 22 April 2013. And Sharon LaFraniere, 'How Jihad Made Its Way to Chechnya', *Washington Post*, 26 April 2003.

4. See Andrew Higgins and Alan Cullison, 'Terrorist Odyssey: Saga of Dr. Zawahiri Sheds Light On the Roots of al-Qaeda Terror', *Wall Street Journal*, 2 July 2002; in the 1990s EIJ and al-Qaeda operated an NGO in Baku as a source and conduit for funds and to support Chechen rebels. 9/11 Commission Report pp. 58, 69–70, 471; The Trial Testimony of Fadl, United States vs bin Laden, 6 February, 2001, pp. 301–3.

5. Ibid.

6. 'If the Chechens and other Caucasian mujahideen reach the shores of the oil-rich Caspian Sea the only thing that will separate them from Afghanistan will be the neutral state of Turkmenistan,' Zawahiri wrote later. 'This will form a mujahid Islamic belt to the south of Russia that will be connected in the east to Pakistan.' Wright, *The Looming Tower*, p. 249.

7. Zawahiri has written little about his time in Azerbaijan and Russia.

8. 9/11 Commission Report, p. 148

9. For more, see Bergen (2006), op. cit., pp. 94, 106.

10. For more, see Scott Shane, 'Abu Zubaydah, Tortured Guantánamo Detainee Makes Case for His Release', *New York Times*, 23 August 2016.

11. This is what he told me. Other accounts state he arrived in Afghanistan in 1987.

12. 'FBI 100 – First Strike: Global Terror in America', FBI, 26 February 2008; FBI Transcript of Interview of Abdul Basit Mahmoud Karim (Ramzi Yousef), 14 February 1995, p. 2, cited in Kohlmann (2004), p. 72.

13. For more details on the bomb, see Jan Hoffman, 'Trade Center Defendants Encouraged', *New York Times*, 16 April 1997.

14. See Peter Bergen and Paul Cruickshank, 'Revisiting the Early Al-Qaeda: An Updated Account of its Formative Years', *Studies in Conflict & Terrorism* 35:1 (2012), pp. 1–36.

15. 9/11 Commission Report, pp. 109–10.

16. Bergen and Cruickshank, op. cit.; Bergen (2006), op. cit., ch. 3–4.

17. Ibid.

18. James Gordon Meek, "Black Hawk Down" Anniversary: Al Qaeda's Hidden Hand', ABC News, 4 October 2013.

19. United States v. Usama bin Laden: Indictment, United States District Court, Southern District of New York, 4 November 1998, p. 20.

20. Bergen and Cruickshank, op. cit.; Bergen (2006), op. cit., p. 67.
21. A further 372 were wounded in the attack. Bruce Riedel, 'Captured: Mastermind behind the 1996 Khobar Towers attack', Brookings Institution, 26 August 2015.
22. Tirmidhi: 2269.
23. David Kirkpatrick, 'Saudi Said to Arrest Suspect In 1996 Khobar Towers Bombing', *New York Times*, 26 August 2015.
24. An English translation of the declaration can be read in the primary source section of the website of the 9/11 Memorial Museum.
25. 'If you see the black banners approaching from Khurasan, then join them for the Mahdi will be among them' (Ahmed: 21796); 'An Army shall rise from the East that will pave the way for the Mahdi's rule' (Ibn Majah: 4086).
26. Michael M. Phillips, 'Launching the Missile That Made History', *Wall Street Journal*, 1 October 2011.
27. For an excellent account of the rise of the Taliban, see Ahmed Rashid, *Taliban: Militant Islam, Oil and Fundamentalism in Central Asia* (Yale University Press, 2000).
28. See Rashid, op. cit., ch. 3
29. See testimony of Vahid Mojdeh in Bergen (2006), op. cit., pp. 162–4.
30. His cousin, Abu Muaz al-Kuwaiti, had been a senior commander in the Mujahideen Brigade.
31. Romesh Ratnesar, 'Confessions Of An Al-Qaeda Terrorist', *Time*, 23 September 2002; 'Terrorism in Southeast Asia', Congressional Research Service Report for Congress, 7 February 2005; 'Profile: Omar al-Farouq', BBC News, 26 September 2006.
32. Hernel Tocmo, 'Maute patriarch an ex-MILF member, says military official', ABS-CBN News, 7 June 2017.
33. '9/11 Commission Report', pp. 147–8.

# MY THIRD LIFE: THE PLEDGE

1. Ibn Assakir: 538. Some theologians have questioned the authenticity of this *hadith*. But al-Ghamdi told me that events had proven its authenticity. It was an early example to me of the theological elasticity used by hardline jihadis.
2. The prophecy of the five armies comes from a compilation of *hadith*: There will come a time when three armies of Islam shall simultaneously rise, one in Syria, one in Yemen and one in Iraq' (Abu Dawood: 2165; Ahmed 16748). 'There will come a time when armies will rise simultaneously, one

in the Levant, one in the Yemen, one in the East and one in the West [i.e. the Maghreb]' (Albani: 3090). Al-Qaeda leaders believed the East referred to the armies foretold to march from Khurasan (Afghanistan) around the time of the emergence of the Mahdi to liberate Jerusalem (Ahmed: 21796). Al-Qaeda emphasizes liberating Jerusalem because of this prophetic *hadith*: 'If you the caliphate take Jerusalem as its capital then know that the upheavals, wars and great change are at hand and the Day of Judgment is closer than my hand on your head' (Abu Dawood: 2535).

3. Ahmed: 21796. See also Ibn Majah: 4086: 'An Army shall rise from the East that will pave the way for the Mahdi's rule.'

4. Ahmed: 11110.

5. Tabbarani: 638. Much later I discovered that this *hadith*, as well as a significant number of others quoted by al-Qaeda ideologues on the prophecies, have a weak claim to authenticity.

6. Al-Qaeda's self-serving interpretation of the prophecy was that the fight against 'the Jews' would help bring about the arrival of the Mahdi. The more common view among Salafi Muslims is the one supplied by the fifteenth-century scholar Imam Ibn Hajar. In his *hadith* commentary 'Fateh al-Barri', Hajar wrote that the *hadith* refers to a battle *after* the arrival of the Mahdi against the Antichrist and his Jewish army near the end of time. This interpretation did not suit al-Qaeda's purposes because it implied believers should wait for divine intervention rather than taking matters into their own hands.

7. For a useful commentary on this, see William McCants, *The ISIS Apocalypse: The History, Strategy and Doomsday Vision of the Islamic State* (St. Martin's Press, 2015), pp. 22–7.

8. It revealed that bin Laden, whose father hailed from Yemen, came to believe before his death he might be the 'Qahtani' – a Yemeni figure foretold to pave the way for the Mahdi. Bin Laden wrote that before 9/11 an al-Qaeda operative told him he had dreamed this. A few al-Qaeda recruits I encountered in Afghanistan thought bin Laden was the actual Mahdi. The *hadith* about the Qahtani is obscure and considered by most Muslim scholars to be of weak authenticity. Bin Laden's Abbottabad diary can be viewed at www.cia.gov/library/abbottabad-compound/index.html. Also, see 'Abbottabad documents: Bin Laden paves the way for the emergence of the Mahdi', al-Arabiya, 15 November 2017.

9. One *hadith* foretold 'Constantinople shall be conquered, blessed be that arm and blessed by its leader' (Ahmed 18977).

10. McCants (2015), op. cit., pp. 116–17; Ayman al-Zawahiri, 'The Islamic Spring Series' (episode 3), As Sahab, 21 September 2015.

11. At this time al-Muhajir was al-Qaeda's second most senior theologian after Abu Hafs al-Mauretani.

12. Al-Muhajir claimed this had been foretold by Koran: 17:4–7.

13. Bin Mansour: 2197.

14. Bergen, 'The Osama bin Laden I know' (2006), op. cit., p. 173.

15. 9/11 Commission Report, pp. 111–12.

16. Ben Farmer, '9/11: HQ where bin Laden plotted atrocities', *Daily Telegraph*, 5 September 2011.

17. Exhibit 941, 'Substitution for the Testimony of Khalid Sheikh Mohammed', United States vs Moussaoui, p. 4; 9/11 Commission Report, p. 235.

18. See Bergen and Cruickshank, op. cit.

19. Andrea Galli, 'Arrestato il tunisino Fezzani, leader di Isis reclutatore in Italia', *Corriere della Sera*, 14 November 2016.

20. Cesare Giuzzi, 'Isis, caccia alla rete di Milano: "Rischio terroristi tra i profughi"', *Corriere della Sera*, 14 August 2016; Cesare Giuzzi, 'Libia, "Arrestato Abu Nassim" Era reclutatore di jihadisti in Italia', *Corriere della Sera*, 18 August 2016.

21. https://www.cdc.gov/botulism/general.html.

22. 'The Commission on the Intelligence Capabilities of the United States Regarding Weapons of Mass Destruction', Report to the President of the United States, 31 March 2005, p. 269.

23. A book published by a French terrorism researcher in 2002 contained an extract of a letter addressed to Abu Khabab listing certain types of waste from a nuclear reactor which could be weaponised to contaminate an area. However nothing he ever said to me suggested he had any real interest in developing 'dirty bombs'. See Roland Jacquard, *L'Archive Secretès d'al Qaida* (Jean Picollec, 2002), p. 291.

24. Scott Stewart, 'The Biggest Threat Dirty Bombs Pose is Panic', *Forbes*, 11 September 2014.

25. George Tenet, who was CIA director between 1997 and 2004 later wrote that al-Qaeda operatives acting under the supervision of Ayman al-Zawahiri had at some point in the 1999–2001 period set up a small anthrax lab in Kandahar and that efforts to isolate anthrax had proceeded in parallel with planning for 9/11, according to intelligence that reached the CIA after the attacks. I was never told about these efforts during my time in al-Qaeda in Afghanistan between 1997 and 2001. I am deeply sceptical it ever came close to weaponizing anthrax. Tenet claimed the arrest of two operatives involved in the programme and other actions in the months after 9/11 had 'neutralized the anthrax threat, at least temporarily'. See George Tenet, *At the Center of the Storm: The CIA at America's Time of Crisis* (HarperCollins, 2007), pp. 278–9.

26. George Tenet later discussed in his memoir the CIA's attempts after 9/11 to learn more about any nuclear threat al-Qaeda posed. He wrote: 'One senior al-Qa'ida operative told us that Mohammed Abdel-al-Aziz al-Masri, who had been detained in Iran, managed al-Qa'ida's nuclear program and had conducted experiments with explosives to test the effects of producing a nuclear yield.' Based on what Abu Khabab and al-Ghamdi told me about al-Qaeda's plan to spread disinformation, I do not believe these experiments were of any consequence. Just weeks before 9/11, Osama bin Laden met at least one retired Pakistani nuclear scientist and discussed the idea of developing a nuclear device. The group had made a failed attempt in the early 1990s to purchase uranium. But the US government in 2002 judged there was 'no credible information that al-Qa'ida had obtained fissile material or acquired a nuclear weapon'. See Tenet (2007), op. cit., pp. 261–8, 275; 'The Commission on the Intelligence Capabilities of the United States Regarding Weapons of Mass Destruction', Report to the President of the United States, 31 March 2005, p. 272; Peter Bergen, 'Reevaluating Al-Qa'ida's Weapons of Mass Destruction Capabilities', *CTC Sentinel* 3:9 (2010).

27. We discussed sarin gas. Aum Shinrikyo had used it in March 1995 in an attack on the Tokyo subway which killed twelve, but Abu Khabab thought producing the gas was well beyond the capabilities of our facility. The Japanese death cult also launched several failed attempts in the spring and summer of 1995 to kill Tokyo subway commuters with hydrogen cyanide gas, but I only became aware of these attempts years later. See also 'Chronology of Aum Shinrikyo's CBW Activities', Monterey Institute of International Studies, 2001.

28. See Markus Binder and Michael Moodie, 'Jihadists and Chemical Weapons', in Gary Ackerman and Jeremy Tamsett (eds), *Jihadists and Weapons of Mass Destruction* (CRC Press, 2009), p. 133.

29. Text of the 'World Islamic Front's Statement Urging Jihad Against Jews and Crusaders', Al-Quds al-Arabi, 23 February 1998.

30. https://fas.org/irp/world/para/docs/980223-fatwa.htm.

31. In May 1998 bin Laden and al-Zawahiri held a press conference for a select group of Pakistani journalists at the al-Faruq camp south of Khost to talk up their 'Worldwide Islamic Front for Jihad Against the Jews and the Crusaders'. Abu Hafs al-Masri and Abu Hamza al-Ghamdi were also in attendance. I was at the camp at the time but was told to stay away from the journalists. For more on the press conference see Bergen (2006), op. cit., pp. 202–4.

32. Ahmed: 3079.
33. Bergen and Cruickshank, op. cit.; Bergen (2006), op. cit., pp. 108–9.
34. For more on al-Ayeri, see Hegghammer (2010), pp. 118–29, and Hegghammer, 'Islamist violence and regime stability in Saudi Arabia', *International Affairs* 84:4 (2008), pp. 701–15; Jarrett M. Brachman, *Global Jihadism: Theory and Practice* (Routledge, 2009), pp. 79–81, 143; Roel Meijer, 'Yusuf al-Uyayri and the making of a revolutionary Salafi praxis', *Die Welt des Islams* 47:3–4 (2007), pp. 422–59.
35. There are several verses in the Koran which explicitly forbid suicide. For example: 'And do not kill yourselves. Surely, Allah is Most Merciful to you' (Koran: 4:29); 'Do not kill yourselves with your own hands, but do good, for God loves those who do good' (Koran: 2:195). The Prophet also said: 'Whoever kills himself on purpose ... will be in the Fire' (Bukhari: 5778).

## MY FOURTH LIFE: ESCAPE FROM AL-QAEDA

1. Anne Stenersen, *Al Qaida in Afghanistan* (Cambridge University Press, 2017), pp. 149–54. Ali Soufan, *The Black Banners: The Inside Story of 9/11 and the War Against Al-Qaeda* (W. W. Norton, 2011), pp. 78–80 and 93–4. See also the November 1998 conclusions by the FBI: http://www.pbs.org/wgbh/pages/frontline/shows/binladen/bombings/summary.html; 9/11 Commission Report, p. 155. For an account of the Africa Embassy bombings see Tod Hoffman, *Al Qaeda Declares War, The African Embassy Bombings and America's Search for Justice* (ForeEdge, 2014), pp. 10–16.
2. See Zubair Qamar, 'Al-Tatarrus; Al-Qaeda's Manipulation of the "Law on Using Human Shields"', zubairqamar.com, 14 November 2013; 'Ali Gomaa defends Ibn Taymmiyah', Almesryoon, 1 March 2015. As reported by the Saudi newspaper *Asharq al-Awsat*, Ibn Taymiyyah's al-Tatarrus fatwa can be found in 'Comprehensive Essays and Fatwas of Ibn Taymiyyah', Vol. 28, pp. 537–546. Mishari al-Zaidi, 'The Concept of al-Tatarrus from Ibn Taymiyyah and the Mongols to Casablanca and Riyadh', 8 August 2003.
3. Abu Musab al-Suri's real name is Mustafa Setmariam Nasar. For more on his life and impact, see Brynjar Lia, *Architect of Global Jihad: The Life of Al-Qaeda Strategist Abu Mus'ab Al-Suri* (Oxford University Press, 2009); Paul Cruickshank and Mohanad Hage Ali, 'Abu Musab Al Suri: Architect of the New Al-Qaeda', *Studies in Conflict & Terrorism* 30:1 (2007), pp. 1–14.
4. Bergen (2006), op. cit., p. 184.

5. In response al-Suri wrote to al-Qaeda's high command on 19 July 1998: '[Bin Laden's] latest troublemaking with the Taliban and the Leader of the Faithful [Mullah Omar] jeopardises the Arabs, and the Arab presence today in all of Afghanistan, for no good reason. It provides a ripe opportunity for all adversaries, including America [. . .] to serve the Arabs a blow that could end up causing their most faithful allies to kick them out . . . I think our brother [bin Laden] has caught the disease of screens, flashes, fans, and applause.' When some in the Taliban were angered by al-Qaeda's East Africa bombings the following month, bin Laden responded by pledging allegiance to Mullah Omar. See Lia, op. cit., pp. 284–5; Alan Cullison, 'Inside Al-Qaeda's Hard Drive', *The Atlantic*, September 2004; and Vahid Brown, 'The Façade of Allegiance: Bin Ladin's Dubious Pledge to Mullah Omar', *CTC Sentinel* 3:1 (2010).

6. See Stenersen (2017), op. cit., p. 78.

7. 'United States and Saudi Arabia Designate Terrorist Fundraising and Support Networks', United States Treasury Department Press Release, March 31, 2016.

8. Bergen (2006), op. cit., p. 143; Nic Robertson and Paul Cruickshank, 'Jihadist Death Threatened Libya Peace Deal', CNN, 28 November 2009; Profile of Ibn Sheikh al-Libi, The Rendition Project.

9. For more on al-Banshiri, see his profile by the Combating Terrorism Center at West Point.

10. Raffi Khatchadourian, 'Azzam the American: The making of an Al Qaeda homegrown', *New Yorker*, 22 January 2007.

11. Coalition intelligence sources who examined the footage believed it might have been filmed at Darunta. But having reviewed the footage, I believe it was very likely filmed at al-Qaeda's headquarters at Tarnak Farms near Kandahar. Although the audio quality is poor a voice which I'm fairly sure belongs to al-Qaeda bombmaker Abd al-Aziz al-Masri can be heard on the recording. These experiments were likely based on the research being done in Darunta. Abu Khabab told me that Abd al-Aziz sent at least two trainees to Abu Khabab's lab in Darunta around early 1999 to learn how to make poison gas and other chemicals. See 'Disturbing scenes of death show capability with chemical gas', CNN, 19 August 2002.

12. 'Here Are The Four Main Poison Gases Used In World War I', *Business Insider*, 21 May 2014.

13. 'The Commission on the Intelligence Capabilities of the United States Regarding Weapons of Mass Destruction', Report to the President of the

United States, 31 March 2005, p. 270. For more on phosgene, see https://emergency.cdc.gov/agent/phosgene/basics/facts.asp.

14. Much later I learned the French logged the call I had made from Abu Zubaydah's phone.

15. In October 1998 Abu Hamza, the firebrand preacher at Finsbury Park mosque, had released a public statement warning Westerners to 'stay out of Yemen'. Transcript of 17 April 2014 trial proceedings USA vs Mustafa Kamel Mustafa, US District Court, Southern District of New York, p. 26.

## MY FIFTH LIFE: UNDERCOVER

1. 'Britons Convicted of Yemen Bomb Plot', BBC News, 9 August 1999; 'Abu Hamza's Car Scam Sons Jailed', BBC News, 28 May 2009; James Gillespie and Richard Kerbaj, 'Abu Hamza fathers criminal brood', *Sunday Times*, 30 September 2012.

2. Rory Caroll, 'Yemen Trial to Start this Week', *Guardian*, 24 January 1999.

3. 'Yemen Executes Islamic Kidnapper', BBC, 17 October 1999.

4. The indictment: USA vs Mustafa Kemel Mustafa, US District Court, Southern District of New York, 6 February 2006; Transcript of 17 April 2014 trial proceedings USA vs Mustafa Kemel Mustafa, US District Court, Southern District of New York; 'Radical Cleric Jailed for Life by US Court', BBC News, 9 January 2015; David Barrett, 'Abu Hamza trial: The terrifying Yemen hostage-taking behind conviction of London preacher', *Daily Telegraph*, 19 May 2014; 'Abu Hamza was "mouthpiece" for 1998 Yemen kidnappings group', BBC News, 13 May 2014; Document 103, USA vs Mustafa Kamel Mustafa, United States Court of Appeals for the Second Circuit, Docket No. 15–211, 11 January 2018, pp. 7–11; Jonathan Schanzer, 'Yemen's War on Terror', Orbis, Volume 48, Issue 3, Summer 2004, pp. 517–531.

5. Philip Johnston, 'Phone Tap Prevented Abu Hamza Trial in Britain', *Daily Telegraph*, 29 May 2004.

6. For more, see Robert Verkaik, 'The trials of Babar Ahmad: from jihad in Bosnia to a US prison via Met brutality', *Observer*, 19 March 2016.

7. 'Conversation with Terror', *Time*, 11 January 1999.

8. In the December 1998 *Time* magazine interview with journalist Rahimullah Yusufzai, bin Laden added. 'And if I seek to acquire these weapons, I am carrying out a duty. It would be a sin for Muslims not to try to possess the weapons that would prevent the infidels from inflicting harm on Muslims.'

9. For more, see Thomas Joscelyn, 'Another al-Qaeda veteran reportedly killed while leading Jund al-Aqsa in Syria', *Long War Journal*, 27 May 2015.

10. See Peter Nesser, 'Abu Qatada and Palestine', *Welt des Islams* 53 (2013).

11. Duncan Gardham, 'Nightclub Bouncer who became cleric of hate', *Daily Telegraph*, 8 February 2006; Ben Farmer, 'The Finsbury Park Mosque: radical hotbed transformed to model of community relations', *Daily Telegraph*, 19 June 2017.

12. 'Abu Hamza Profile', BBC News, 9 January 2015. For more on Abu Hamza al-Masri's journey to jihad, see Duncan Gardham, 'Nightclub bouncer who became the cleric of hate', *Daily Telegraph*, 8 February 2006.

13. Philip Johnston, 'Phone Tap Prevented Abu Hamza Trial in Britain', *Daily Telegraph*, 29 May 2004; 'Abu Hamza arrested', BBC News, 15 March 1999.

14. Philip Sherwell, 'Abu Hamza "secretly worked for MI5" to "keep streets of London safe"', *Daily Telegraph*, 7 May 2014; United States vs Mustafa Kamel Mustafa, United States Court of Appeals for the Second Circuit, Document 95-2, 12 December 2017, pp. 7, 97–8.

15. 'Don't Mess with Mary Quin', *CBS 60 Minutes*, 2 October 2016.

16. Paul Cruickshank and Nic Robertson, 'London ringleader Khuram Butt was intensely investigated', CNN, 6 June 2017; Dominic Kennedy, 'Radical al-Muhajiroun group is behind most UK terror plots', *The Times*, 21 March 2015.

17. Ben Quinn and Matthew Weaver, 'After Guantánamo: what became of the Britons freed from the US camp?', *Guardian*, 22 February 2017.

18. For more on al-Hayali's arrest, see Andrew Buncombe, 'Terror suspect in Morocco holds key to al-Qa'ida', *Independent*, 19 June 2002, and for the reaction to his return home: https://www.youtube.com/watch?v=D-XPP0Kpo20.

19. Dominic Casciani, 'Babar Ahmad: The godfather of Internet jihad?', BBC News, 17 July 2014.

20. Verkaik, op. cit.

21. Qutb (1964), op. cit., p. 75.

22. See Kevin Jackson, 'Al-Qaeda's Top Scholar', Jihadica, 25 September 2014.

23. See Judith Miller and Jeff Gerth, 'Al-Qaeda; Honey Trade Said to Provide Funds and Cover to bin Laden', *New York Times*, 11 October 2001.

24. Paul Cruickshank, 'Transatlantic Shoebomber knew Bin Laden', CNN, 20 April 2012; 'Operative details al-Qaeda plans to hit planes in wake of 9/11', CNN, 25 April 2012; Badat deposition in the trial of Adis Medunjanin, United States District Court for the Eastern District of New York, 29 March

2012; Mark Honigsbaum and Vikram Dodd, 'From Gloucester to Afghanistan: the making of a shoe bomber', *Guardian*, 5 March 2005.

25. The three precursor chemicals of TATP are public knowledge. See 'Marketing and Use of Explosive Precursors', European Commission Press Release, 20 September 2010.

26. For more on terrorists being trained to make TATP, see Paul Cruickshank, 'Learning Terror: The Evolving Threat of Overseas Training to the West', in Magnus Ranstorp and Magnus Normark (eds), *Understanding Terrorism Innovation and Learning* (Routledge, 2015), ch. 7.

27. 'Israeli-Palestinian Fatalities Since 2000 – Key Trends, United Nations Office for the Coordination of Humanitarian Affairs', August 2007.

28. Philippe Naughton, 'TATP is suicide bombers' weapon of choice, *The Times* (London), 15 July 2005; Ben Doherty, 'Manchester bomb used same explosive as Paris and Brussels attacks, says US lawmaker', *Guardian*, 25 May 2017.

29. For more on al-Qaeda's front-line fighting in Afghanistan, see Stenersen (2017), op. cit., ch. 7.

30. See Mitchell D. Silber, *The Al-Qaeda Factor: Plots Against the West* (Pennsylvania University Press, 2012), pp. 95–106, 289; 'US Holds Senior al-Qaeda Figure', BBC News, 27 April 2007; Carol Rosenberg, 'Alleged al-Qaida commander reveals new name in Guantánamo court', *Miami Herald*, 17 May 2016. Also, see 'Office of the US Military Commissions Charging Sheet for Abd al-Hadi al-Iraqi', 10 February 2014.

## MY SIXTH LIFE: JIHAD FOR A NEW MILLENNIUM

1. For an exhaustive and well-researched account of the attacks, see: John B. Dunlop, *The Moscow Bombings of September 1999: Examinations of Russian Terrorist Attacks at the Onset of Vladimir Putin's Rule* (Ibidem, 2012).

2. Michael Wines, '2d Deadly Apartment Blast Hits Moscow', *New York Times*, 13 September 1999; 'Who is behind the bombing?' BBC News, 16 September 1999.

3. 'Russia "reclaims" Dagestan villages', BBC News, 26 August 1999; Steve Harrigan, 'Rebels say they're out of Dagestan; Russia says war continues', CNN, 23 August 1999; Helen Womack, 'Rebels stage new invasion of Dagestan', *Independent*, 5 September 1999. For a profile of Basayev, see Liz Fuller, 'Chechnya: Shamil Basayev's Life of War and Terror', Radio Free Europe, 10 July 2006.

4. 'Russia's bombs: Who is to blame?', BBC News, 30 September 1999.

5. Amy Knight, 'Finally, We Know About the Moscow Bombings', New *York Review of Books*, 12 November 2012; Maura Reynolds, 'Fears of Bombing Turn to Doubts for Some in Russia', *LA Times*, 15 January 2000; David Holley, 'Russians wonder: Bomb plot or drill?' *LA Times*, 4 March 2007; Dunlop, op. cit., p. 182; David Satter, *Darkness at Dawn: The Rise of the Criminal Russian State*, (Yale University Press, 2004), p. 28.

6. Gregory Feifer, 'Russia: Three Years Later, Moscow Apartment Bombings Remain Unsolved', Radio Free Europe/Radio Liberty, 6 September 2002; 'Russia Bombs Airport in Grozny,' Radio Free Europe/Radio Liberty, 23 September 1999; Satter, op. cit., p. 28.

7. For an excellent account of the situation in Russia at that time, see Sergei Kovalev, 'Putin's War', *New York Review of Books*, 10 February 2000.

8. John Sweeney, 'The Fifth Bomb: Did Putin's Secret Police Bomb Moscow in a Deadly Black Operation', Cryptome, 24 November 2000; Kovalev, op. cit; Neil MacFarquhar, 'Vladimir Putin's Quotes: A Collection for the Discerning Russian Official', *New York Times*, 29 December 2015.

9. 'Russian Sends Ground Troops Into Chechnya, Raising Fears', Associated Press, 1 October 1999.

10. See Michael Specter, 'Russians' Killing of 100 Civilians In a Chechen Town Stirs Outrage', *New York Times*, 8 May 1995; and 'Case Study: Russian Federation, Chechnya, Operation Samashki', International Committee of the Red Cross; 'The situation of human rights in the Republic of Chechnya of the Russian Federation Report of the Secretary-General', United Nations Commission on Human Rights, 26 March 1996.

11. For a few of the murky details, see Sweeney, op. cit.

12. Kovalev, op. cit.

13. http://www.alamy.com/stock-photo-russian-president-vladimir-putin-left-and-tony-blair-right-in-the-22905095.html.

14. 'Scars remain amid Chechen revival', BBC News, 3 March 2007.

15. Nick Paton Walsh, 'Moscow flat bombers get life for killing 246', *Guardian*, 13 January 2004; David Satter, 'The Unsolved Mystery Behind the Act of Terror That Brought Putin to Power', *National Review*, 17 August 2016. For an excellent review of the events leading up to the bombings, see Richard Sakwa (ed.), *Chechnya: From Past to Future* (Anthem Press, 2005).

16. See Stenersen (2017), op. cit., p. 96, 101.

17. See Mary Anne Weaver, 'The Short, Violent Life of Abu Musab al-Zarqawi', *The Atlantic*, July/August 2006.

18. Joby Warrick, *Black Flags: The Rise of ISIS* (Doubleday, 2015), pp. 50–1.

19. Weaver, op. cit.; Ali Soufan, *Anatomy of Terror: From the Death of bin Laden to the Rise of the Islamic State* (W.W. Norton, 2017), p. 117.

20. Warrick, op. cit., pp. 54–6; Weaver, op. cit.

21. Warrick, op. cit., pp. 47, 60–61, 65.

22. Ahmed: 19156.

23. 'HUJI chief still at large', *The News* (Pakistan), 23 September 2008.

24. Warrick, op. cit., pp. 64–5.

25. Tenet, op. cit., p. 125.

26. Warrick, op. cit., pp. 63–4; Soufan (2011), op. cit., pp. 132–141.

27. 'Khalil al-Deek: al-Qaeda's Digital Pioneer', SITE Intelligence Group, February 2009; Judith Miller, 'Dissecting a Terror Plot From Boston to Amman', *New York Times*, 15 January 2001; 9/11 Commission Report, pp. 174–8; Ali Soufan, *The Black Banners: The Inside Story of 9/11 and the War Against al-Qaeda* (W.W. Norton, 2011), pp. 132–6, 140–5.

28. There are conflicting accounts on whether al-Zarqawi was granted an audience with bin Laden. For more, see Brian Fishman, 'Revising the History of Al-Qai'da's Original Meeting with Abu Musab al-Zarqawi', Combating Terrorism Center, 25 October 2016; Warrick, op. cit., p. 66; Saif al-Adel, 'Jihadist Biography of Abu Musab al-Zarqawi' (first circulated in 2005 and reposted on a jihadi forum in 2009); Fuad Husayn, *Al-Zarqawi: The Second Generation of al-Qaeda*, serialized in *al-Quds al-Arabi* in 2005.

29. Abu Qatada also became a source of support for Zarqawi's fledgling group. See testimony of Shadi Abdalla in Bergen (2006), op. cit., p. 358.

30. For more on al-Muhajir's influence, see Maysara al-Gharib, 'The Hidden History: al-Zarqawi As I Knew Him', posted on jihadi websites, September 2007; Charlie Winter and Abdullah K. al-Saud, 'The Obscure Theologian Who Shaped ISIS', *The Atlantic*, 4 December 2016. And Ziad al-Zaatari, 'Takfiri Literature Makes Headway in Lebanon', Alakhbar English, 11 September 2012; Hassan Abu Haniyeh, 'Daesh's Organisational Structure', Al Jazeera Centre for Studies, 4 December 2014.

31. After the fall of the Taliban, Zarqawi moved to a camp in Khurmal in northern Iraq staffed by some of the veterans of the research efforts into unconventional weapons at Herat. At the Khurmal lab there was evidence group experimented with poison gases, such as hydrogen cyanide, and poisons. In November 2004, coalition forces discovered a Zarqawi-affiliated laboratory in Fallujah. Their analysis of the recovered materials revealed his associates 'may have had the capability to employ an improvised chemical device of simple design [releasing] cyanogen chloride, hydrogen cyanide . . . called a "Mobtaker"'.

    In 2004 Jordanian authorities announced they had thwarted a Zarqawi directed plot to set off a poison gas cloud in Amman involving a Herat-trained operative. Between 2006 and 2007, Islamic State [of Iraq] fighters carried out a series of chlorine bomb attacks in the country. In 2017, ISIS allegedly provided two brothers in Sydney with instructions on how to build a poison gas device. Their plot was thwarted in July of that year.

For more on ISIS and chemical weapons, see Chris Quillen, 'The Islamic State's Evolving Chemical Arsenal', *Studies in Conflict & Terrorism* (2016), pp. 1019–30; 'Fallujah Update: Insurgent Chemical/Explosives Weapons Laboratory', Combined Press Information Center, Multinational Force Iraq, 26 November 2004; Tenet, op. cit., pp. 277–8; Columb Strack, 'The Evolution of the Islamic State's Chemical Weapons Efforts', *CTC Sentinel* 10:9 (2017); Andrew Zammit, 'New Developments in the Islamic State's External Operations: The 2017 Sydney Plane Plot', *CTC Sentinel* 10:9 (2017).

32. It would become known as the al-Guhraba camp. Lia, op. cit., pp. 250–64.

33. Brian Fishman, 'Revising the History of Al-Qai'da's Original Meeting with Abu Musab al-Zarqawi', *CTC Sentinel* 9:10 (2016).

34. For more on al-Suri's al-Ghuraba classes, see Cruickshank and Hage Ali (2007), op. cit.; Lia, op. cit., pp. 250–59.

35. Lia, op. cit., p. 107.

36. Ibid., pp. 156, 260.

37. For a translation of key extracts, see Lia, pp. 307–11 and 431. For more on al-Suri and WMD, see Paul Cruickshank and Mohanad Hage Ali, 'Jihadist of Mass Destruction', *Washington Post*, 11 June 2006.

38. Cruickshank and Hage Ali (2007), op. cit., pp. 1–14; Lia, op. cit., p. 314.

39. 'Fight them in God's Way. This is not imposed on you except in relation to yourself. And rouse the believers.' Koran 4:84

40. Ahmed: 18406.

41. Khomeini once said: 'We place this revolution in the hands of the Mahdi. If God pleases, let this revolution be the first step toward the appearance of the One Whom God Has Preserved, and let it pave the way for his arrival.' Hosam Matar, 'The Mahdi and Iran's Foreign Policy', Al-Akhbar, 11 January 2013.

42. In March 1999, Andrew Krepinevich, a defence policy analyst, testified before Congress that it would be difficult to transform the US military 'in the absence of a strong external shock to the United States – a latter-day "Pearl Harbor" of sorts'. In September 2000, after Abu Hafs made the reference, the Project for a New American Century released a report which stated transformation would likely take a long time 'absent some catastrophic and catalysing event – like a new Pearl Harbor.' See 'Rebuilding America's Defenses: Strategy, Forces and Resources For a

New Century', The Project for the New American Century, September 2000; Anthony Summers and Robbyn Swan, *The Eleventh Day: The Full Story of 9/11* (Ballantine Books, 2012), pp. 115, 483.

43. Khalid Sheikh Mohammed told US interrogators that in either March or April 1999 bin Laden backed his plan to fly hijacked aircraft into targets in the United States. The 9/11 Commission stated bin Laden at Abu Hafs al-Masri's urging, gave the green-light for KSM's 9/11 operation sometime in late 1998 or early 1999. Exhibit 941 'Substitution for the Testimony of Khalid Sheikh Mohammed', United States vs Moussaoui, p. 4; 9/11 Commission Report, p. 149.

44. 9/11 Commission Report, p. 232.

45. Ibid.

46. Ibid., pp. 1–7.

47. Ibid., p. 166.

48. 'IOC allow Taliban observers at Sydney', Reuters, 19 August 2000.

49. Quoted in multiple reports, including Rob Gloster, 'IOC withdraws invitation to Taliban', Associated Press, 25 August 2000.

# MY SEVENTH LIFE: SOMETHING BIG

1. According to the 9/11 Commission, Mohamed Atta, the lead 9/11 hijacker, flew to Spain on 8 July 2001 for a meeting with plot coordinator Ramzi Binalshibh. The latter said he had told Atta that 'bin Laden wanted the attacks carried out as soon as possible' because he 'was worried about having so many operatives in the United States'. Atta replied he required about five to six weeks before he could provide an attack date. According to Binalshibh, Atta called him in mid-August to indicate that 11 September had been selected. Binalshibh warned two Hamburg associates that they should leave for Afghanistan without delay if they wanted to get there before it became more difficult. It was a similar message to the one Abu Hafs told me to deliver to the four jihadis in Britain. See 9/11 Commission Report, pp. 244, 249.

2. See Jackson, op. cit.

3. Stenersen (2017), op. cit., p. 146.

4. See the account of Abu Walid al-Masri (Mustafa Hamid) in Bergen (2006), op. cit., pp. 341–4; Anne Stenersen, *Al-Qaeda's Quest for Weapons of Mass Destruction: The History Behind the Hype* (VDM, 2008), pp. 29–30.

5. Documents on a computer used by Ayman al-Zawahiri and Abu Hafs al-Masri indicated al-Qaeda leaders had earmarked $2,000 to $4,000 as 'start-up costs' for WMD development in what became known as the

Zabadi project. According to the Wall Street Journal: 'In a letter dated May 23 [1999] and written under one of Zawahiri's aliases, the author reports discussing some "very useful ideas" during a visit to Abu Khabab ... In a letter dated May 26 and stored in the computer under the same alias as earlier correspondence, the author says he was "very enthusiastic" about the Zabadi project ...'

From what can be deduced from the *Wall Street Journal* disclosures, the correspondence on the project dried up after June 1999. That month a memo addressed to 'Abu Hafs' indicated that a dedicated laboratory still needed to be built. I never heard Abu Khabab talk about a project called Zabadi. Nor would he have been impressed by such a modest sum. Internal al-Qaeda letters held by the Combating Terrorism Center at West Point depict Abu Khabab as a mercenary, angering senior jihadis at times for pocketing cash he was supposed to dedicate to research.

For more on the cooperation between Abu Khabab and Zawahiri, see Allan Cullison and Andrew Higgins, 'Computer in Kabul holds chilling memos: PC apparently used by al-Qaeda leaders reveals details of four years of terrorism', *Wall Street Journal*, 31 December 2001; Alan Cullison, 'Inside al-Qaeda's Hard Drive', *The Atlantic*, September 2004; Stenersen (2008), op. cit., pp. 35–6; Souad Mekhenet and Greg Miller, 'He's the son of Osama bin Laden's bomb-maker. Then ISIS wanted him as one of their own', *Washington Post*, 5 August 2016.

6. 9/11 Commission Report, pp. 257 and 534 (note 16).

7. 9/11 Commission Report: pp. 256–63; George Tenet, At the Center of the Storm: The CIA at America's Time of Crisis (HarperCollins, 2007), p. 149–152.

8. 9/11 Commission Report, p. 339, pp. 261–2.

9. See Exhibit 941, 'Substitution for the Testimony of Khalid Sheikh Mohammed', United States vs Moussaoui, pp. 21, 28–31, 51.

10. 'Moussaoui Statement of Facts, United States vs Zacarias Moussaoui', United States District Court for the Eastern District of Virginia; Tenet, op. cit., pp. 201–2.

11. 'Osama claims he has nukes: If US uses N-arms it will get same response', *Dawn*, 10 November 2001.

12. But understandably, intelligence agencies continued to be concerned that al-Qaeda might develop a nuclear capability. In 2007, after retiring as director of the CIA, George Tenet wrote: 'From the end of 2002 to the spring of 2003, we received a stream of reliable reporting that the senior al-Qa'ida leadership in Saudi Arabia was negotiating for the purchase of three Russian nuclear devices.' He added that there had been shifting accounts on the

question of WMD by al-Qaeda operatives in detention and that 'our inability to determine the fate of the Russian devices presented great concern not only for me but for the White House.' Tenet, op. cit., pp. 272–7. I believe the 'shifting accounts' were part of a misinformation campaign by al-Qaeda to keep the Americans guessing and embroil the CIA in a wild goose chase. I had learned from Abu Khabab and Abu Hamza al-Ghamdi before 9/11 that al-Qaeda had decided to plant a rumour it had obtained several nuclear warheads.

This was not the only example of alarmism. Weeks before the Iraq War, British officials told the BBC that al-Qaeda had gained the expertise and possibly the materials to build a radiological device, after sourcing radioactive isotopes and doing development work in a laboratory in the Afghan city of Herat. The BBC was told the intelligence was partly based on information received from British spies who had infiltrated al-Qaeda. I am sceptical the British had other agents inside al-Qaeda, but it cannot be ruled out. The information I provided British intelligence between 1998 and 2001 was almost the opposite of these claims. I never heard anything from Abu Khabab or others about al-Qaeda making progress in creating a radiological device. The timing of the leak should also raise eyebrows. See Frank Gardner, 'Al-Qaeda "was making dirty bomb"', BBC News, 31 January 2003.

13. Saif al-Adel, 'Jihadist Biography of the Slaughtering Leader Abu Mus'ab al-Zarqawi' (2005).
14. 'UK to deport Abu Qatada to Jordan', Al Jazeera, 12 August 2005.
15. Ron Suskind, *The One Percent Doctrine: Deep Inside America's Pursuit of Its Enemies Since 9/11* (Simon & Schuster, 2006), p. 146.
16. For more on on al-Qaeda's preparations to attack Saudi Arabia, see Hegghammer (2008), op. cit., pp. 709–10; Brachman, op. cit., pp. 140–41.
17. 'Abu Qatada Timeline', BBC News, 10 May 2013.
18. 'American killed in Saudi explosion', BBC News, 7 October 2001.
19. Binder and Moodie, op. cit., p. 133.
20. For more details on the composition and effects of these poison gases, see: https://www.cdc.gov/niosh/ershdb/emergencyresponsecard_29750039.html, https://www.cdc.gov/niosh/ershdb/emergencyresponsecard_29750038.html.
21. Brachman, op. cit., p. 141, and Hegghammer (2010), pp. 122 and 170–185.
22. By late 2002 al-Ayeri – or Saif al-Battar as he then styled himself – had emerged as one of the most prominent jihadi ideologues. He stressed in his books and on al-Qaeda web forums the need for eternal jihad against the West to stop it extinguishing the soul of Islam. A tract he published after 9/11, *Constants on the Path to Jihad*, was later popularized among English-speaking jihadis by the American Yemeni preacher Anwar

al-Awlaki. In another treatise, 'The Future of Iraq and the Arabian Peninsula After the Fall of Baghdad', he presciently argued that the US invasion of Iraq would result in a quagmire for the United States and stoke jihadism in Iraq and throughout the Middle East. Hegghammer (2010), op. cit., p. 173; J.M. Berger, 'The Enduring Appeal of Al-'Awlaqi's "Constants on the Path of Jihad"', *CTC Sentinel* 4:10 (2011).

23. Ron Suskind, *The One Percent Doctrine* (2006), pp. 195–8. Suskind's book contains a detailed account of the *mubtakkar* plot against New York. There are several differences between what Suskind was told by his sources and my own recollections.

24. Paul Cruickshank and Tim Lister interviews with senior former US counterterrorism officials, 2015–2017. (Subsequently cited as Cruickshank & Lister US CT interviews.)

25. Ibid.

26. Suskind, op. cit., pp. 195–8.

27. See George Tenet, *At the Center of the Storm: The CIA During America's Time of Crisis* (HarperCollins, 2007), pp. 273–4. The poison gas plot against the New York subway was also confirmed by other officials. Robert S. Mueller, III, Director Federal Bureau of Investigation, The City Club of Cleveland, Cleveland, Ohio, 23 June 2006; 'Senator: NYC subway plot by al-Qaida was real', Associated Press, 21 June 2006.

28. Ray Kelly, *Vigilance: My Life Serving America and Protecting Its Empire City* (Hachette Books, 2015), p. 213.

29. Tenet, op. cit., pp. 273–4.

30. Suskind, op. cit., pp. 219–20.

31. Kelly, op. cit., p. 213. Bokhowa's arrest and the discovery of the *mubtakkar* blueprints on his computer is also referenced in Suskind, op. cit., pp. 192–5.

32. 'Bahrain breaks up terror cell', Arab News, 16 February 2003; 'Bahrain smashes "terrorist cell"', BBC News, 15 February 2003.

33. Ibid.

34. Suskind, op. cit., p. 195.

35. Suskind, op. cit., pp. 197–8; Kelly, op. cit., p. 213; Cruickshank and Lister US CT interviews.

36. Sammy Salama and Edith Bursac, 'Jihadist Capabilities and the Diffusion of Knowledge', in Ackerman and Tamsett (eds.), op. cit., pp. 112–3.

37. 'A successful subway attack would cause widespread panic, shut down the system for many days, overload health care facilities, and leave a legacy of fear and anxiety among the American public'. Salama (2006), op. cit., p. 4.

38. Tenet, op. cit., p. 273.

39. In a report submitted to the United Nations in April 2003, the

United States stated: 'We judge that there is a high probability that al-Qaeda will attempt an attack using a CBRN [chemical, biological, radiological or nuclear] weapon within the next two years.' Transcript: *Anderson Cooper 360°* – 'Does al-Qaeda have chemical weapons?', CNN, 10 June 2003.

40. The fatwah, 'A Treatise on the Legal Status of Using Weapons of Mass Destruction Against Infidels', was dated March 2003 according to jihadi websites and probably took at least several weeks to prepare. It was published online in May 2003. The fatwah can be viewed at: www.ilmway.com/site/maqdis/MS_860 and is discussed in Ackerman and Tamsett (eds), op. cit., pp. 29, 74, and 103; Stenersen (2008), op. cit., p. 32; Tenet, op. cit., p. 274.

41. Fahd selectively quoted from *hadith* to try to circumvent Koran chapter 2 verse 205 ('And when he goes away, he strives throughout the land to cause corruption therein and destroy crops and animals. And God does not like corruption'), which some jihadis believed prohibited biological and nuclear attacks.

42. Tenet, op. cit., pp. 273–6; Al-Battar media via Twitter, 24 August 2015.

43. Salama (July–August 2006), op. cit., pp. 2–5; Salama and Bursac, op. cit., pp. 110–12; Stenersen (2008), op. cit., pp. 61–2, 79.

44. Dexter Filkins provides a brilliant account of the operation in 'Aftereffects: Presidential Theft; Bank Official Says Hussein's Son Took $1 Billion in Cash', *New York Times*, 6 May 2003.

45. Warrick, op. cit., pp. 69–71.

46. For more on Zarqawi's insurgency see Ibid., pp. 101–223.

47. See the Suicide Attack Database (1974 to 2016) of the Chicago Project on Security & Threats at the University of Chicago. Also Katherine R. Seifert and Clark McCauley, 'Suicide Bombers in Iraq, 2003–2010: Disaggregating Targets Can Reveal Insurgent Motives and Priorities', *Terrorism and Political Violence* 26:5 (2014).

48. In 2005 Zarqawi stated: 'I met with Shaykh Abu Abdullah al-Muhajir [in Afghanistan]. A conversation ensued between us on the ruling of martyrdom seeking operations. The Shaykh was of the view that they are permissible. I read his valuable research on the issue and listened to many of his recordings. Eventually, God opened my heart to his position so that not only did I come to see them as permissible, but as desirable, too.' See Abdullah al-Saud, 'The Spiritual Teacher and His Truants: The Influence and Relevance of Abu Mohammad al-Maqdisi', *Studies in Conflict & Terrorism* (June 2017).

49. Al-Zaatari, op. cit.; Winter and al-Saud, op. cit.; 'Abu Mus'ab al-Zarqawi under influence: one mentor?', Alleyesonjihadism (blog), 15 May 2012; Al-Gharib, op. cit.; Jim Muir, '"Islamic State": Raqqa's loss seals rapid rise and fall', BBC News, 17 October 2017; al-Saud, op. cit.

50. Michael Weiss and Hassan Hassan, *ISIS: Inside the Army of Terror* (Simon & Schuster, 2016; updated edition), p. 30; Loretta Napoleoni, *Insurgent Iraq: Al Zarqawi and the New Generation* (Seven Stories Press, 2005), p. 157.

51. For more on how couriers were tracked in the hunt for bin Laden, see Mark Bowden, *The Finish: The Killing of Osama bin Laden* (Atlantic Monthly Press, 2012), pp. 116–8, 247–8.

52. For an account of the attacks, see Owen Bowcott and David Pallister, 'The message is: you're not safe here', *Guardian*, 14 May 2003.

53. Hegghammer (2010), op. cit., p. 203–4; Brachman, op. cit., p. 143.

54. Hegghammer (2010), op. cit., pp. 204–10.

55. Ibid., p. 205; Brachman, p. 148.

56. For more on al-Qaeda's terrorist campaign in Saudi Arabia, see Hegghammer (2008), op. cit., pp. 701–15.

57. McCants (2015), op. cit., p. 115.

58. Koran 4:75.

59. See Lawrence Wright, 'The Terror Web', *New Yorker*, 2 August 2004. It would take MI6 months to corroborate my information about al-Rabia.

60. Iran and al-Qaeda share an enmity towards the United States and the House of Saud, but there were limits to Iran's tolerance of al-Qaeda on its soil. In 2003, Iran detained several senior al-Qaeda operatives including Saif al-Adel, Abu Mohammed al-Masri, Abu Khayr al-Masri. They were housed for years inside a military compound in the Tehran area along with members of bin Laden's family, including his son Hamza. By 2015 it was reported they had been all released. Notwithstanding the high profile detentions, Iran continued to allow al-Qaeda operatives to use the country as a transit point for operatives and funds and, according to the US government, still does to this day. For more on al-Qaeda and Iran, see Assaf Moghadam, 'Marriage of Convenience: The Evolution of Iran and al-Qa'ida's Tactical Cooperation', *CTC Sentinel* 10:4 (2017).

61. Abu Dawood: 2165; Ahmed 16748.

62. At the time Rabia reported to al-Qaeda's 'number three', Abu Faraj al-Libi. The latter, who had been in touch with bin Laden in the years after 9/11, was captured in Pakistan in May 2005. When al-Libi was interrogated by the CIA, he claimed not to know a courier whose existence had been confirmed by four other detainees, including Hassan Ghul. His strenuous denial led the CIA for the first time to believe this mystery courier was possibly a key messenger for Osama bin Laden. Tracking down the courier eventually led the CIA to bin Laden's Abbottabad hideout. See Bowden, op. cit., pp. 119–22; Craig Whitlock and Kamran Khan,

'Blast in Pakistan Kills Al-Qaeda Commander', *Washington Post*, 4 December 2005; 'Detainee Biographies', Office of the Director of National Intelligence, September 2006. https://fas.org/irp/news/2006/09/detainee-bios.pdf.

63. Suskind, op. cit., pp. 318–21.

64. 'Bahrain releases six "militants"', BBC News, 23 June 2004.

65. Ron Suskind, op. cit., pp. 323–4.

66. Craig Whitlock and Kamran Khan, 'Blast in Pakistan Kills Al-Qaeda Commander', *Washington Post*, 4 December 2005.

67. Suskind, op. cit., p. 318.

68. See 'Bahrain Plot Alleged', *Gulf Daily News*, 15 July 2004; Shereen Busheri and Mazen Mahdi, 'Six Bahrainis Rearrested', *Bahrain Tribune*, 15 July 2004; Kanwal Tariq Hameed, 'Terrorism Charges Rejected', *Gulf Daily News*, 27 June 2006; 'Bahrain: The Next Target For Islamist Militancy?', Jamestown Foundation, Terrorism Focus, 6 August 2014.

69. US embassy traffic on the case, released years later by WikiLeaks, can be seen here: https://wikileaks.org/plusd/cables/04MANAMA1708_a.html, https://wikileaks.org/plusd/cables/04MANAMA1665_a.html.

70. 'Bahraini Militant Back in Custody after Court Escape', AFP, 14 September 2004; Mohammad Almezel, 'Man accused of terror plot released in related case', *Gulf News*, 13 January 2005; Hameed, op. cit. https://wikileaks.org/plusd/cables/04MANAMA1671_a.html.

71. https://wikileaks.org/plusd/cables/04MANAMA1671_a.html.

# MY EIGHTH LIFE: NICOTINE

1. For more on this meeting, see Steve Swann, 'A Truly Dangerous Meeting of Minds', BBC News, 3 April 2015; for more on Awlaki's lecture series that winter in the UK, see Scott Shane, *Objective Troy: A Terrorist, a President, and the Rise of the Drone* (Crown, 2015), pp. 146–50.

2. Steve Swann, 'A Truly Dangerous Meeting of Minds', BBC News, 3 April 2015.

3. Rory McCarthy, 'Sad, bloody end to Bigley saga', *Guardian*, 9 October 2004.

4. Edward Wong, 'British Hostage is Beheaded in Baghdad', *New York Times*, 8 October 2004. Damien McElroy, Sean Rayment and Aqeel Hussein, 'Bigley made last desperate dash for freedom before being taken to his doom', *Daily Telegraph*, 10 October 2004.

5. This is what I learned. Part of the story was reported by *Times* journalists

Hala Jaber and Ali Rifat, 'Bigley beheaded after MI6 rescue backfired', *The Times*, 10 October 2004. According to their account, Zarqawi's group had claimed two of Bigley's captors had accepted a large sum of money to help him flee. See also McCarthy (2004), op. cit., and Jason Burke, Gaby Hinsliff, and James Robinson, 'Hostage in last-ditch escape bid', *Observer*, 10 October 2004.

6. Osama bin Laden would later publish a paper called 'The Practical Steps to Liberate Palestine' in which he argued that backing jihadis in Iraq provided a rare opportunity to make a move against Jordan which in turn would be the ideal springboard to liberate Palestine. A key goal of both bin Laden and Zarqawi was to liberate Jerusalem because, according to the prophecies, it would be the seat of the Caliphate near the end-of-days. See Osama bin Laden, 'Practical Steps to Liberate Palestine', As Sahab Media, March 2009.

7. 'Al-Zarqawi group claims allegiance to bin Laden', CNN, 17 October 2004.

8. Paul Wood, 'Iraq's hardest fight: The US battle for Falluja 2004', BBC News, 10 November 2014. See also Ralph Nader, 'The Destruction of Mosques in Fallujah: An Open Letter to George Bush', 9 December 2004.

9. Koran 5:32.

10. Anne Stenersen, *Al-Qaeda's Quest for Weapons of Mass Destruction: The History Behind the Hype* (VDM, 2008), pp. 48–50; 'Killer jailed over poison plot', BBC News, 13 April 2005; 'Ricin: Killer with no antidote', *Manchester Evening News*, 20 June 2005; 'The Deadly Recipes', BBC News, 13 April 2005.

11. Nic Robertson, Paul Cruickshank and Tim Lister, 'Documents give new details on al-Qaeda's London bombings', CNN, 30 April 2012; Duncan Gardham, '7/7 inquest: Mohammad Sidique Khan on MI5's radar before 9/11', *Daily Telegraph*, 6 May 2011; 'FACTBOX-What MI5 knew about the London bombers', Reuters, 30 April 2007.

12. 'One year on, a London bomber issues a threat from the dead', *Guardian*, 7 July 2006.

13. Hekmat Karzai, 'Afghanistan and the Logic of Suicide Terrorism', RSIS Commentary, 27 March 2006. .

14. Anne Stenersen, 'Al-Qaeda's Foot Soldiers: A Study of the Biographies of Foreign Fighters Killed in Afghanistan and Pakistan Between 2002 and 2006', *Studies in Conflict & Terrorism* 34 (2011), pp. 184.

15. Martin Bright and Gaby Hinsliff, 'Chaos as First Terror Orders are Used', *Observer*, 12 March 2005.

16. Shiv Malik, 'Briton claiming to be former Taliban bomb expert "joins Isis"', *Guardian*, 20 November 2014.

17. Zawahiri's letter to al-Zarqawi was obtained by the United States during counter-terrorism operations in Iraq and can be viewed here:https://ctc.usma.edu/harmony-program/zawahiris-letter-to-zarqawi-original-language-2/.

18. John F. Burns and Kirk Semple, 'US Finds Iraq Insurgency Has Funds to Sustain Itself', *New York Times*, 26 November 2006.

19. Nazila Fathi, 'Iran Executes Sunni Rebel Leader', *New York Times*, 20 June 2010.

20. Benjamin Runkle, *Wanted Dead or Alive: Manhunts from Geronimo to Bin Laden* (Palgrave Macmillan, 2011), p. 200.

21. Among many accounts of Zarqawi's demise, see Dwight Jon Zimmerman, 'JSOC and the Hunt for Abu Musab al-Zarqawi: The End Game', Defence Media Network, 26 May 2013. http://www.defensemedianetwork.com/stories/jsoc-and-the-hunt-for-abu-musab-al-zarqawi-the-end-game/.

22. William Maclean, 'Al-Qaeda ideologue in Syrian detention – lawyers', Reuters, 10 June 2009.

23. Ron Suskind, *The One Percent Doctrine: Deep Inside America's Pursuit of Its Enemies Since 9/11* (Simon & Schuster, 2006).

24. Ibid., pp. 216–20.

## MY NINTH LIFE: A GRAVEYARD IN SYRIA

1. Michael Moss and Souad Mekhennet, 'Rising Leader for the Next Phase of Al-Qaeda's War', *New York Times*, 4 April 2008.

2. On Gadahn's 'career' in al-Qaeda, see Joseph Serna and Shelby Grad, 'Adam Gadahn: Al-Qaeda terrorist, California native and grandson of a Jew', *Los Angeles Times*, 23 April 2015.

3. Almezel, op. cit.; Hameed, op. cit.

4. For more on the founding of the Islamic State of Iraq see Kenneth Katzman, 'Al Qaeda in Iraq: Assessment and Outside Links', Congressional Research Service Report for Congress, 15 August 2008.

5. Bill Roggio, 'US and Iraqi forces kill Al Masri and Baghdadi, al Qaeda in Iraq's top two leaders', *Long War Journal*, 19 April 2010.

6. 'Leader of Sunni militant organization in Iran killed: Intelligence Minister', Reuters, 25 August 2016; 'Head of Ansar al-Furqan terrorist group killed in Iran', Press TV, 22 April 2015.

7. Hania Mourtada and Rick Gladstone, 'Iraq's Branch of Al-Qaeda Merges with Syria Jihadis', *New York Times*, 9 April 2013; Anthony Cordesman, 'Violence in Iraq: The Growing Risk of Serious Civil Conflict', Center for Strategic and International Studies, 9 September 2013.

8. Mushreq Abbas, 'Al-Qaeda Militants Raid Iraq's Abu Ghraib, Taji Prisons', Al-Monitor, 25 July 2013.

9. According to a 2011–2 survey of Muslims in various parts of the world: 'In most countries surveyed in the Middle East and North Africa, South Asia and Southeast Asia, half or more Muslims believe they will live to see the return of the Mahdi'. See 'The World's Muslims: Unity and Diversity', Pew Research Center, 9 August 2012, p. 65.

10. Ahmed: 3079.

11. 'A band of warriors of my followers shall fight for the truth at the gates of Damascus and its surroundings and at the gates of Jerusalem and its surroundings, until the day of Judgment' (Ibn Hajar: 4309). Another prophecy previses that Muslim fighters will gather in Ghouta near Damascus in the epic battles. McCants (2015), op. cit., p. 100.

12. 'The Antichrist will appear from a valley between Iraq and the Levant and will cause chaos and mayhem where he goes [. . .] then when he is assured of his power, Jesus Son of Mary will descend at the White Minaret on the east side of Damascus, his hands resting on the wings of two angels, every follower of the Antichrist will die of Jesus' scent. Then Jesus will track the Antichrist at Lod [a town in modern day Israel] and kill him there' (Muslim: 2937).

13. Abu Dawood: 2165; Ahmed: 16748.

14. By mid-2013 ISIS was firmly in charge of Raqqa. That remained the case until its liberation in October 2017. Sarah Birke, 'How al-Qaeda Changed the Syrian War', *New York Review of Books*, 27 December 2013.

15. Hannah Beech, 'Deadly Terrorist Attack in Southwestern China Blamed on Separatist Muslim Uighurs', *Time*, 1 March 2014.

16. Ben Blanchard, 'Syria says up to 5,000 Chinese Uighurs fighting in militant groups', Reuters, 8 May 2017.

17. Joan Lowy, 'US official says Khorasan Group threat to aviation', Associated Press, 26 September 2014.

18. For more on Said Arif, see Thomas Joscelyn, 'Another al-Qaeda veteran reportedly killed while leading Jund al Aqsa in Syria', *Long War Journal*, 27 May 2015. See also: https://www.un.org/press/en/2014/sc11521.doc.htm.

19. James Foley, 'Syria: Inside the latest assault on Saraqeb', Global Post, 28 March 2012; 'Fresh violence after Syria accepts UN peace plan', Associated

Press, 29 March 2012; Dominic Evans, 'Syria army quits base on strategic Aleppo road', Reuters, 2 November 2012.

20. 'Al-Qaeda chief disbands main jihadist faction in Syria: Al-Jazeera', Agence France Presse, 8 November 2013.

# REFLECTIONS

1. For more on Binali, see Carl Bunzel, 'The Caliphate's Scholar In Arms', Jihadica, 9 July 2014; 'Coalition forces killed Turki-al-Bin' ali', CENTCOM Media Release, 20 June 2017.

2. Rory McCarthy, 'Inside Bin Laden's chemical bunker', *Guardian*, 17 November 2001. Judith Miller, 'Pentagon Says Bombs Destroy Terror Camps', *New York Times*, 10 October 2001. Josh Meyer, 'Al-Qaeda is said to focus again on WMD', *Los Angeles Times*, 3 February 2008. A senior US intelligence source confirmed Abu Khabab's link to the development of the device to my co-authors. Cruickshank and Tim Lister US CT interviews, op. cit.

3. Josh Meyer, 'Al-Qaeda is said to focus again on WMD', *Los Angeles Times*, 3 February 2008.

4. 'Al-Qaeda: Weapon Expert Among Dead Heroes', CNN, 3 August 2008.

5. Information from intelligence source, 2016–2017.

6. Malik (2014), op. cit.; John Hall and Tom Wyke, 'Inside a Brit's ISIS Bombmaking Factory', *Daily Mail*, 22 April 2015.

7. Evan Perez, Jodi Enda and Barbara Starr, 'New terrorist laptop bombs may evade airport security, intel sources say', CNN, 1 April 2017; David Sanger and Eric Schmitt, 'US Cyberweapons, Used Against Iran and North Korea, are a Disappointment against ISIS', *New York Times*, 12 June 2017; Micah Maidenberg, 'Laptop Ban On Planes is Lifted, US Officials Confirm', *New York Times*, 20 July 2017.

8. After Hassan Ghul's capture in 2004 helped reveal bin Laden's courier network, Ghul had been transferred from CIA custody to Pakistan in 2006, where he was released and rejoined the al-Qaeda fold rising to become its military operations chief. Greg Miller, Julie Tate and Barton Gellman, 'Documents reveal NSA's extensive involvement in targeted killing program', *Washington Post*, 16 October 2013.

9. Andrea Galli, 'Arrestato il tunisino Fezzani, leader di Isis reclutatore in Italia', *Corriere della Sera*, 14 November 2016; 'IS commander wanted by Italy arrested in Sudan: lawmaker', AFP, 14 November 2016; 'Bardo museum attack suspect extradited to Tunisia', AFP, 23 December 2016;

'Tunisia beach attack: "Mastermind" named', BBC News, 7 January 2017; 'Top ISIS recruiter in Italy Fezzani arrested', ANSA, 14 November 2016; 'Tunisia: 30 anni a terrorista Fezzani', Ansa, 24 February 2018. See also: https://www.therenditionproject.org.uk/prisoners/tunisi.html; https://wikileaks.org/gitmo/pdf/ts/us9ts-000168dp.pdf.

10. 'United States and Saudi Arabia Designate Terrorist Fundraising and Support Networks', United States Treasury Department Press Release, 31 March 2016.

11. Tom Holland, 'We must not deny the religious roots of Islamic State', *New Statesman*, 17 March 2015.

12. Graeme Wood, 'What ISIS Wants', *The Atlantic*, March 2015.

13. Bernard Lewis, 'The Roots of Muslim Rage', *Atlantic Monthly*, September 1990.

14. For an excellent account see Yaroslav Trofimov, *The Siege of Mecca: The Unforgotten Uprising* (Allen Lane, 2007).

15. Al-Oteibi's brother in law was Mohammed Abdullah al-Qahtani, which was consistent with the prophecies. According to one *hadith*: 'There will come a time when God will send a man from my descent. His name just like mine, and his father's name is just like my father's name . . .' (Abu Dawood: 2230). The Prophet Mohammed's father's name was Abdullah. Trofimov, op. cit., pp. 37–8 and 46–52.

16. One *hadith* foretelling the return of the Mahdi states: 'There will come a time when a civil war erupts when a king dies and a man will leave Medina towards Mecca. People will follow him and in Mecca he will be forced to accept the people's allegiance to him between the Kaaba and the Station of Ibrahim . . .' (Abu Dawood: 4285).

17. Lewis, op. cit.

18. Abu Bakr al-Baghdadi has cited *hadith* on the Victorious Vanguard. 'There will not cease to exist a group from my nation fighting upon the truth, manifest until the Day of Judgment. Then, Jesus son of Mary will descend', he said in a May 2015 audio speech, referring to Ahmed: 21286.

19. 'The Road to Boston', Report by the Majority Staff of the Homeland Security Committee, March 2014, p. 15.

20. McCants (2015), op. cit., pp. 32, 39–41.

21. ISIS spokesman Abu Muhammad al-Adnani stated this explicitly in a speech circulated online in 2011. 'We will remain God willing until the Day of Resurrection, and the last people of us will fight the Antichrist. Please hurry up, as we still hope you to repent to God. [. . .] Do hasten before regret is due, as the battlefield outcome is determined, and there are but a few days left.' Abu Muhammad

al-Adnani, 'The State of Islam will Remain Safe', al-Furqan Media, 7 August 2011. Not long after Abu Bakr al-Baghdadi echoed these remarks. 'Come . . . for the Great Battles are about to transpire.' McCants (2015), op. cit., p. 100.

22. Hamza bin Laden, 'The Cause of al-Shām is the Cause of Islam', As Sahab Media, 14 September 2017.

23. His words are quoted on the masthead of the first issue of ISIS's online magazine, Dabiq, issued in July 2014.

24. According to a *hadith*, when asked by disciples which city would fall first – Rome or Constantinople – the Prophet answered Constantinople (Ahmed: 6468).

25. 'The Last Hour would not come until the Romans would land at al-Amaq or in Dabiq. An army consisting of the best of the people of the earth at that time will come from Medina. [. . .] They will then fight and [the surviving third of the army] would be the conquerors of Constantinople. And as they would be busy in distributing the spoils of war and hanging their swords by the olive trees, Satan would cry: the Antichrist has taken your place among your family [. . .] then Jesus son of Mary would descend' (Muslim: 2897).

26. In November 2014, another ISIS executioner, Mohammed Emwazi, appeared in Dabiq with the severed head of an American hostage, saying, 'Here we are, burying the first American Crusader in Dabiq, eagerly waiting for the remainder of your armies to arrive.' 'Dabiq: Why is the Syrian town so important for IS', BBC News, 4 October 2016.

In a message released after the group's attack in Paris in 2015, Baghdadi mocked the West for not sending in ground troops. 'They know what awaits them in Dabiq [in] terms of defeat, death, and destruction. They know that it is the final war and after it, God permitting, we will invade them and they will not invade us, and Islam will dominate the world anew until the Day of Judgment.' Abu Bakr al-Baghdadi, 'So Wait, We Too are Waiting with You', 26 December 2015. See also Abu Bakr al-Baghdadi, 'And Allah Knows But You Do Not Know', 19 January 2014; McCants, op. cit., p. 104.

27. Abu Bakr al-Baghdadi, 'March Forth Whether Light or Heavy', 14 May 2015.

28. 'Therefore, the caliphate is a prophetic promise foretold [by the Prophet]. The just caliphs are twelve in number . . . five of them appeared in the early period . . . The last of the [righteous Caliphs] will pave the way for the Mahdi,' Binali wrote, shortly before Baghdadi declared a Caliphate; A translation of Binali's April 2014 treatise can be found in McCants (2015), op. cit., pp. 179–81. A link to the Arabic version can

be found in Cole Bunzel, 'The Caliphate's Scholar-in-Arms', Jihadica, 9 July 2014.

29. Adnani, 'This is the Promise of Allah', 29 June 2014.

30. Abu Bakr al-Baghdadi, 'This is what Allah and His Messenger had Promised Us', 2 November 2016.

31. Ibid.

32. William McCants, 'Apocalypse Delayed', Brookings Institution, 17 October 2016.

33. Baghdadi, 2 November 2016, op. cit. He was quoting from Koran 17:76.

34. Ibn Hajar: 4309.

35. Adnani, 'And Those Who Were to Live Might Live after a Clear Evidence', 21 May 2016.

36. Mohammed Jamjoum, 'Amnesty details "horrific abuses" in southern Yemen', CNN, 4 December 2012.

37. Adnani, audio statement, 'Indeed Your Lord is Ever Watchful', released 21 September 2014.

38. Cole Bunzel, 'Caliphate in Disarray: Theological Turmoil in the Islamic State', Jihadica, 3 October 2017; Rukmini Callimachi, 'ISIS Enshrines a Theology of Rape', *New York Times*, 13 August 2015; 'Islamic State (ISIS) Releases Pamphlet On Female Slaves', MEMRI, 3 December 2014; Dabiq, Issue 4, October 2014; 'Slave-Girls or Prostitutes', Dabiq, Issue 9, May 2015.

39. Atika Shubert, Bharati Naik and Bryony Jones, 'Convert or die: ISIS chief's former slave says he beat her, raped US hostage', CNN, 11 September 2015; Rukmini Callimachi, 'ISIS Enshrines a Theology of Rape', *New York Times*, 13 August 2015; James Gordon Meek, 'ISIS Leader Abu Bakr al-Baghdadi Sexually Abused American Hostage Kayla Mueller, Officials Say', ABC News, 14 August 2015.

40. Yara Bayoumy, 'How Saudi Arabia's War in Yemen has made al-Qaeda Stronger and Richer', Reuters, 8 April 2016; Michael Horton, 'Fighting the Long War: The Evolution of Al Qa`ida In the Arabian Peninsula', *CTC Sentinel* 10:1 (2017); Bruce Hoffman, 'The resurgence of Al-Qaeda', The interpreter, Lowy Institute, 13 March 2018.

41. James Novogrod, 'Al-Qaeda in Syria: Our Focus is Assad, Not West', NBC News, 27 May 2015; Thomas Joscelyn, 'Analysis: Al Nusrah Front "committed" to Ayman al Zawahiri's "orders"', Long War Journal, 29 May 2015; Charles Lister, 'The Dawn of Mass Jihad: Success in Syria Fuels al-Qa`ida's Evolution', *CTC Sentinel* 9:9 (2016).

42. Ali Soufan, 'Hamza bin Ladin: From Steadfast Son to Al-Qa`ida's Leader in Waiting', *CTC Sentinel* 10:8 (2017).

43. Eric Schmitt and Saeed al-Batati, 'The U.S. Has Pummeled Al Qaeda in Yemen. But the Threat Is Barely Dented', *New York Times*, 30 December 2017; Ayman al-Zawahiri, 'America is the First Enemy of the Muslims', As-Sahab, 20 March 2018.

44. For more on al-Asiri's plots, see Paul Cruickshank, Nic Robertson and Tim Lister, 'Al-Qaeda's Biggest Threat', CNN, 16 February 2012.

45. Sammy Salama, 'Special Report: Manual for producing chemical weapon to be used in New York subway plot available on al-Qaeda websites since late 2005', *WMD Insights* Issue 7, July–August 2006, pp. 2–5.

46. Mohammed Mousa, 'Al-Mubtakkar: A Chemical weapon to target institutions was among the evidence against Ansar al-Sharia', *Al Wafd*, 21 October 2015. goo.gl/oofUVJ; 'A deadly chemical weapon among the evidence against "Ansar al-Sharia Brigade"', *Albawaba News*, 21 October 2015. http://www.albawabhnews.com/1562303; Nermin Suleiman, 'Within the evidence against Ansar al-Sharia: Chemical weapon to threaten discotheques and cinemas', *Dotmsr*, 21 October 2015. goo.gl/KtRQNs.

47. Columb Strack, 'The Evolution of the Islamic State's Chemical Weapons Efforts', *CTC Sentinel* 10:9 (2017); Gareth Browne, 'Isis tests deadly terror chemicals on live victims', *The Times*, 20 May 2017.

48. Eric Schmitt, 'ISIS Used Chemical Arms at Least 52 Times in Syria and Iraq, Report Says', *New York Times*, 21 November 2016.

49. Paul Maley, 'From Syria to Sydney: how the airport terror plot unfolded', *The Australian*, 5 August 2017; Australian Police National Media Press Conference, 4 August 2017; Andrew Zammit, 'New Developments in the Islamic State's External Operations: the 2017 Sydney Plane Plot', *CTC Sentinel* 10:9 (2017).

50. See Rukmini Callimachi, 'Not "Lone Wolves" After All: How ISIS Guides World's Terror Plots From Afar', *New York Times*, 5 February 2017; Seamus Hughes and Alexander Meleagrou-Hitchens, 'The Threat to the United States from the Islamic State's Virtual Entrepreneurs', *CTC Sentinel* 10:3 (2017).

51. Paul Cruickshank, 'Discarded laptop yields revelations on network behind Paris, Brussels attacks', CNN, 25 January 2017; Scott Bronstein, Nicole Gaouette, Laura Koran and Clarissa Ward, 'ISIS planned for more operatives, targets during Paris attacks', CNN, 5 September 2016.

52. Ian Cobain, Kevin Rawlinson, Vikram Dodd and Damien Gayle, 'Iraqi teenager appears in court accused of Parsons Green bombing', *Guardian*, 22 September 2017; 'Parsons Green Tube bombing: Teenager Ahmed Hassan jailed for life', BBC News, 23 March 2018.

53. Eric Schmitt, 'In Battle to Defang ISIS, U.S. targets its Psychology', *New York Times*, 28 December 2014.

54. George W. Bush, 'The National Security Strategy of the United States of America', the White House, March 2006, p. 9.

55. Schmitt, op. cit.

56. 'TEXT-UK Prime Minister May's statement following London attack', Reuters, 4 June 2017.

57. Lauren Markoe, 'Muslim Scholars Release Open Letter To Islamic State Meticulously Blasting Its Ideology', Religion News Service, 24 September 2014. 'Open Letter to Dr Ibrahim Awwad al-Badri, alias "Abu Bakr al-Baghdadi," and to the Fighters and Followers of the Self-Declared "Islamic State"', 19 September 2014. The full letter can be viewed here: http://www.lettertobaghdadi.com/14/english-v14.pdf.

58. Labib al-Nahhas, 'The deadly consequences of mislabelling Syria's revolutionaries', *Washington Post*, 10 July 2015.

59. Paul Cruickshank, 'A View from the CT Foxhole: An Interview with Alain Grignard', *CTC Sentinel* 8:8 (2015).

60. Efraim Benmelech and Esteban F. Klor, 'What Explains the Flow of Foreign Fighters to ISIS?' NBER Working Paper No. 22190, April 2016, Table 5, p. 20.

61. Andrew Higgins, 'Belgium Confronts the Jihadist Danger Within', *New York Times*, 24 January 2015.

62. Guy Van Vlierden, 'Profile: Paris Attack Ringleader Abdelhamid Abaaoud', *CTC Sentinel* 8:11 (2015).

63. Simon Cottee, 'Reborn Into Terrorism: Why are so many ISIS recruits ex-cons and converts?', *Atlantic Monthly*, 25 January 2016.

64. Andrew Higgins and Kimiko de Freytas-Tamura, 'A Brussels Mentor Who Taught Gangster Islam to the Young and Angry', *New York Times*, 11 April 2016. https://www.counterextremism.com/extremists/khalid-zerkani; Pieter Van Ostaeyen, 'Belgian Radical Networks and the Road to the Brussels Attacks', *CTC Sentinel* 9:6 (2016).

65. Ibn Taymiyyah, 'Al-Amr bil Ma`ruf'.

66. Koran 21:30.

67. Abu Bakr al-Baghdadi, Sermon at the al-Nuri mosque in Mosul, video posted by ISIS, 5 July 2014.

68. Koran 5:13.

69. Koran 7:199.

70. Koran 16: 125.

71. Koran 17:33.

72. Abu Bakr al-Baghdadi, 'March Forth Whether Light or Heavy', 14 May 2015.

73. Abu Muhammad al-Adnani, 'Say, Die in Your Rage', 26 January 2015.

74. Koran 22:107; Open letter to al-Baghdadi, op.cit., p. 2.

75. Naser al-Wasimi, 'New Saudi Body to Discredit Terrorist Use of Islamic Teachings', *The National*, 19 October 2017.
76. This was quoted in 'An Open Letter to al-Baghdadi', op. cit., p. 17.
77. Bukhari: 4770. *Khawarij* derives from the Arabic word *kharaja* – 'to go out' or 'to leave' the main body of Muslims.
78. Muslim: 2937.
79. Naim Qassem, *Hizbullah: The Story from Within* (Saqi Books, Kindle Edition, 2012) ch. 7 (last page).
80. Koran 5:8.

# INDEX

References to footnotes are indicated by fn.